CW01513039

1

Death on the River Avon

Copyright

appropriate acknowledgements in any future additions.

First published in the United Kingdom in 2022 by Dan Rafferty and Ken Davies.

Dedication

This book is dedicated in memory of my late sister-in-law Ann Rafferty, beloved wife of my brother Terry and a wonderful mother and grandmother.

Prologue

Marion Busby, an eighteen-year-old university student at Bath Spa university, was busy putting on her winter coat and scarf. Christmas would arrive in ten days' time and next week she would go home to her parents in Swansea to celebrate it with them. Being an only child, she knew that her parents would want her home to help dress the Christmas tree. Then her mum would take her into Cardiff to finish off doing the Christmas shopping.

Most of her friends at the Uni had already left for the Christmas holidays. However, Marion had delayed her departure by pretending to her parents that she had vital course work to catch up on and needed access to the library at the university. That was a lie! She could hardly tell her parents that the real reason for delaying her return home, was that she had a date tonight. After all, they were strict Welsh Methodists and any mention of a boyfriend would have led to an almighty row!

It was 10.45pm on this cold winter night when Marion stuck her head into the communal kitchen of the university apartment and said good night to Brenda, another student that had also delayed her return home, for the Christmas holidays. Marion told her friend she would be back around two or three in the morning. She then let herself out of the block which was situated in the accommodation area on the campus. She took the short walk to the bus stop, wrapping her scarf more tightly around her neck trying to repel the cold wind. There were only four other students on the bus, which was hardly surprising as most had already returned home for the holidays. The fact that it was also a bitterly cold night had deterred many people from venturing out.

She took her seat and texted Andy, the handsome young personal trainer that she had met on Tinder, a popular dating App in the UK. She hadn't met Andy in person yet, but they had chatted a lot online. His facial pictures showed a gorgeous young guy with adorable puppy eyes and sexy lips. Although still a virgin, she was quite happy to let Andy sort that out! Of course, she would have to keep Andy a secret otherwise her parents would invoke the equivalent to the Spanish inquisition! Her text to Andy said, "On the bus honey. See you outside Lambrettas in about 20 mins xxx" A few minutes later, Andy replied, "Hi baby, sorry I'm running late at the gym – last client was 20 mins late. Don't worry, my dad is going to meet you coming off the bus and will let you into my flat. I will be as quick as I can. Xxx" Marion's initial instinct was to text him back and say that she could wait in Lambrettas, which is a pub attached to a hotel next door. But Andy had already arranged for his dad to meet her. She thought that Andy was being sweet and sending his dad to meet her and take her to the flat on this cold winter night was very thoughtful. So, she texted Andy again. "Oh, that's sweet of you. Will he know who I am?" A few seconds later came the reply. "Yes, dad knows all about you. Xxx"

Marion sat back in her seat and put her phone in her handbag. She was very petite and only five feet tall. She had long blond hair and blue eyes. She was thinking about how caring Andy was by sending his father to meet her just because he was running late and didn't want her to get cold. She couldn't wait get her hands on his fabulous body. She was smiling as she thought that she wanted this date to last forever. In a way it would but not in the manner that she was hoping for!

Chapter One

The City of Bath in Somerset, South West of England, is a beautiful city steeped in history, particularly that of the Romans. Indeed, no matter where you look in Bath, there are many monuments and reminders of the time when the Romans occupied the city. There is even the two-thousand-year-old, Roman Baths, which attracts almost six million visitors and tourists to the city, each year.

Bath is not a large city and so it is extremely easy for an able-bodied person to walk its length and breadth, in the course of a couple of hours. There are several distinctive features other than the Roman Baths which attracts many tourists. There is also the perfectly proportioned Bath Abbey, which is situated close to the River Avon, a very fast-flowing river which itself is a distinguishing feature. The most spectacular aspect of the river is the famous Pulteney Weir, where millions of gallons of water flow every day. There is also the magnificent and much filmed, Royal Crescent with its spectacular view over the world heritage city with its honey-coloured Georgian architecture.

For lovers of culture, there is the Theatre Royal, which has been described as the most beautiful theatre in England, whilst for the academically minded, Bath boasts two universities, (Bath and Bath Spa) which together boost the indigenous population of only 90,000 Bathonian's by a staggering term-time influx of 23,000 students, many of whom will experience their first taste of freedom away from the supervision and guidance of their parents or guardians. One such student was Linda Carson, who at the age of eighteen, was part of Bath Spa's intake of new students, the previous September. Tragically, her days in this beautiful city would be cut very short, just like Marion Busby, some six months earlier.

Overall, Bath is a beautiful and vibrant city in which to live and work and it's not surprising that it attracts so many visitors and tourists who play a particularly important part in supporting the city's revenue. In addition to the local citizens, the visitors and tourists need the protection of the police and it is the responsibility of the Avon and Somerset Constabulary to provide that protection. The main police station is situated on Manvers Street, an ugly 1960's building but well placed to cater to the demands of the populace. The police station is just a few minutes' walk from both the train and bus stations and is remarkably close to the Abbey. This is where Detective Chief Inspector Dan Skelton and his team work.

Dan Skelton was born in a small town, east of Glasgow forty years previously. He went to school in Scotland and decided in his early teens that he wanted to be a detective. A very bright boy with a huge zest for life, he also decided that whilst Scotland is a beautiful country, it is damn too cold a place to live. He decided that he wanted to live in London but before doing that, a university degree was going to be a fundamental requirement if he was going to make a successful career whether in the police or elsewhere. And so, he chose to study criminology at Bath Spa University. It was during his three years studying for his degree, that he fell in love with the city and was determined, that after graduation, he would one day return as a police detective. Skelton graduated with a 2.1 degree in criminology and, like many of his contemporaries, decided that a gap year was not for him. He wanted to get into the police immediately and get his foot on the ladder of advancement. He drew the line under advancing any further when he became a detective chief inspector. Whilst this gave him a high level of authority, it allowed him to continue to investigate major crimes without too much administrative paperwork.

Initially, Skelton joined the London Metropolitan Police as a graduate recruit and he immediately impressed his superior officers with his bright intelligence and aptitude for hard work. He swiftly rose in the ranks and by the time he was thirty-five he was a detective inspector having served in numerous branches of the service, including the flying squad as well as the murder squad. Skelton had a passion for detective work and he soon realised that if he sought further promotion, then this would lead to more administrative work, rather than fighting crime. That was not something that he wanted. Skelton wanted to fight crime, not shuffle papers.

He made it known to his superiors that he would not be applying for further promotion and this decision was reluctantly accepted by his own boss, Detective Superintendent Alan Warwick. Skelton and Warwick, on being introduced, very quickly formed a warm relationship, partly fuelled by the fact that both were keen horse racing fans. Skelton was hugely impressed by Warwick's encyclopaedic knowledge of the sport, and with both living close to Sandown Park Racecourse in Surrey, it was not long before they were going to the races together.

Skelton was not a tall man at five feet ten, but he possessed an athletic body and was in great shape, there not being an ounce of fat on him. Skelton could easily have made a career in modelling, as not only did he have a fine body but was also very handsome. One thing that set him apart from the officers of his rank was his sexuality. Skelton realised at the age of fourteen that he was gay and was incredibly lucky to accept his sexuality without question, unlike many youngsters who struggle to determine their identity. On joining the police force he kept his sexuality secret as he knew that being openly gay could hinder his prospects of promotion, which was a very sad situation in those days. It was not just the police force that discriminated against gays, historically, it was rife in all manner of professions and occupations. Skelton hated the fact that he could not tell his colleagues that he had a partner, instead he had to effectively lie that he just shared a house with another man. Another thing which Skelton absolutely hated was racism and heaven help anyone making a racist remark in his company. Thankfully, today, laws have been passed to make it a crime to be either homophobic or racist, and Skelton would go out of his way to prosecute any offenders he came across. Depending on the circumstances he would either use the majesty of the law or his fists, which he did, on a few occasions.

It was only when he had become a detective chief inspector and was satisfied that he wanted no further promotion, that he came out of the closet. It was a complete shock to his colleagues and superiors as none had an inkling that he was gay. They knew that he shared a house with a guy called Ken, but had no idea that Ken was his partner. Skelton was delighted that his outing was so warmly accepted and he realised that even the police had generally accepted that it had many gays, both male and female in the force. By and large, most police officers treat gay people with the respect that they deserve, but there are the odd exceptions which Skelton often concluded was the fact that the offender was himself probably a closet gay and most likely married and leading a loveless life. Over the years, Skelton would become a mentor to numerous guys struggling to come to terms with their sexuality, both young guys and middle-aged, single and married. This led him to meeting several female officers who felt able to confide in him that they too, were gay. In a relatively brief period of time, few police officers in the metropolitan police force felt that they had to hide their sexuality. This had a positive impact not only for the police service, but also for the gay community.

Chapter Two

Whilst Skelton enjoyed working in London and living in Surrey, his heart definitely lay in Bath and it was his key objective to move back to that beautiful city whilst he was still a relatively young man. His partner, Ken, also loved the city and he was just as keen to move there at the first opportunity.

On a training course which Skelton had to attend, organised by the Home Office, he met and formed a close friendship with Detective Inspector Patrick Rees of Avon & Somerset Constabulary. Rees was based in Bristol, but lived in Bath, but he preferred working in Bristol as it was a much bigger city and there was far more crime to deal with, especially drug related. Skelton was by this stage openly gay, but most of his friends, were "straight" a term which Skelton found a little insulting as he was just as "straight" as the next person. Skelton preferred the term "non-gay" to describe his friends who did not happen to be gay.

Rees and his wife Julia soon became close friends with Skeleton and his partner Ken. They would regularly attend Bath races together, or an evening at the theatre. Skelton set out his stall for his desire to move back to Bath and Rees promised to help him achieve that goal when a suitable vacancy occurred.

Sitting in his office in Charring Cross Road Police Station, in the heart of London, one Friday afternoon, Skelton's phone rang. The caller screen showed that his friend Patrick was calling. "Patrick, how the devil are you today?" enquired Skelton. "Hi Dan, I'm very well thanks and how's you?" "I'm great thanks, just looking forward to the weekend. We are off to Sandown Park Races tomorrow and we are meeting up with Alan and Marion Warwick for a spot of lunch beforehand." "Oh, that's great, the weather forecast is good, so you should have a great time," said Rees. "What about you Patrick?" "I'm actually working unfortunately Dan, but someone has to keep the streets safe." "Well, I shall certainly rest contented at the races knowing that you are keeping the people of Bristol safe and well!"

"Actually Dan, I've got some interesting news for you. A vacancy has come up in CID based in Bath, are you interested?" Skelton leapt to his feet and shouted down the phone, "Your bloody right I'm interested!"

And so, after formal interviews, Avon & Somerset Constabulary offered Skelton the position of detective chief inspector, based in Manvers Street in the heart of Bath and Skelton was an incredibly happy man. Rees had indicated that the interviews

were a mere formality and so Skelton lost no time
in putting his house on the market and preparing
for the move to Bath. Remarkably, his house sold
the day after and he and Ken found a house in
Coombe Down, a beautiful suburb on the southern
slopes of Bath. The sellers were South African and
were desperate to return home to Cape Town for
personal reasons. So, within six weeks, Skelton
and Ken had left Surrey and moved into their four-
bed detached house in Coombe Down. It had a
huge garden totalling almost an acre in size. This
would be ideal for their three black Labradors,
Brenty-Boy, Josh and Archie. There were also
some fabulous walks nearby where the dogs
would get all the exercise they needed. The
garden was neat and tidy, but Dan & Ken would
create a wonderful garden as they had done at
their previous house.

On his first day, he got to meet the men and
woman whom he would be working with. His
overall boss was Chief Superintendent Mike
Sawyers. Sawyers was quite a rotund character
aged fifty and a passionate lawn bowls player. A
true Somerset man, he was both respected and
admired by his officers for his tough but fair way in
dealing with them. As with most non-criminals

that Skelton encountered, he and Sawyers got on like a house on fire from their very first introduction. Patrick Rees decided to work out of Manvers Street on Skelton's first day, both to welcome Skelton and to introduce him to his new colleagues.

The one person that Skelton was particularly keen to meet was his detective sergeant. Skelton had had some good detective sergeants and some that were not so good. He was a firm believer that the partnership between the DCI and the DS was very much like a married couple or partnership. Both had to have the utmost faith and understanding in each other to make the partnership, the success that it needed to be.

Sawyers and Rees led Skelton to the office that would be his for the duration of his time in Bath and this was next to the detective's open plan office which housed the CID team. Second in charge of this team was Detective Sergeant Bill Alexander. Sawyers made the introduction. "Bill this is your new boss, DCI Dan Skelton". A big beaming smile appeared on Alexander's face which Skelton immediately reciprocated, and both men held out their hands for the handshake. "Welcome aboard sir", said Alexander in the broadest Glasgow accent that Skelton had heard in years. Skelton looked Alexander up and down and guessed him to be about forty. Alexander was a heavy-set man and clearly enjoyed his food. Skelton firmly shook Alexander's hand and said, "Well apart from being cops, we have a lot more in common Bill, I was born just outside of Glasgow". Alexander looked slightly startled and replied, "But that's not a Glasgow accent sir, it's awfully refined" tapping his nose and smiling broadly. Sawyers immediately cut in, "Bill no one will ever accuse you of being refined that's for sure" which caused all four men to laugh. "Aye fair enough sir, I know my place in the pecking order".

Chapter Three

It took Skelton just a week to get settled in and
familiarise himself with the layout of the station.
Manvers Street station was a bit of a muddle, with
the various departments spread over four floors
plus a basement which held the custody suite. In
addition to the various police departments and
offices, there was also a canteen/kitchen which
was well utilised by the officers and support staff,
providing hot food throughout the day. Skelton
had noticed that his DS very much supported the
canteen where, in the morning, he could be found
tucking into a full English breakfast and at lunch, a
three-course affair irrespective of the huge calorie
intake. Alexander was already of ample girth and
the fact that his only exercise appeared to be the

short walk from his desk to the canteen and back again was clearly insufficient. Skelton resolved that as of now, Alexander's food intake would be severely reduced and his daily exercise increased.

Skelton was able to walk to his office every morning, sometimes after having first walked the dogs. Bath is a very hilly city and where Skelton lived, he was on top of a hill. So, walking into the city was a sheer delight for him, it was literally downhill all the way and Skelton loved the fantastic views of the city on his stroll into work. He liked to be in his office by 8am and check his emails and the latest crime reports from the night shift. At 8.30am he would wander into the canteen and grab a bacon roll. In his office he kept a kettle and a small fridge where he could keep low-fat milk. Skelton was very particular about his tea and he adored Twining's English Breakfast. On returning from the canteen one morning, he encountered Alexander in his office. "Morning sir, I see you have a bacon roll about your person." Skelton smiled and said, "Good morning Bill. You are very observant this morning. I do happen to have a bacon roll about my person and I have just walked over a mile to burn off the calories so that I have no regrets about eating it. You on the other hand have driven to the station and for most of the day, you are going to be sitting on your arse except for the exercise you get by walking to and from the canteen. This needs to stop Bill as you will be a heart attack waiting to happen." Alexander looked crest fallen. "Sir, nobody has ever said that to me before and I feel mightily hurt. We can't all have great physiques you know. Some of us just have a tendency not to burn the calories off." Skelton shook his head and looked Alexander in the eye, "Bill I'm saying this as a friend, not as your boss, which I could quite easily do. We need you to get some exercise, so starting today no more canteen for you. As of today, you will join me for lunch as often as work allows. We will have a pub lunch every day that we can." Bill's face brightened up, "Oh, you beauty, a pub lunch and a couple of pints every day, I knew we were going to get along really well sir." "Not quite Bill, we will walk to the pub, you will not have any alcohol. You will drink soda water and eat sparingly and healthily. End of discussion."

Skelton strolled into the CID office after he had finished his bacon roll and saw Detective Constable Peter Lowik hunched over his computer screen. "Good morning Peter, what's new today then?" Lowik looked up from the screen and smiled at Skelton, "Morning sir" he drawled in his Aussie accent. Lowik was from Brisbane in Australia where he had been a cop. At 24 he married his wife, Cara; they had spent part of their honeymoon in the UK visiting relatives of Cara's in Scotland and England. They had visited Bath to see Cara's uncle and were so impressed with the city, that they had hardly stopped talking about it when they returned home. They both quickly realised that if they could possibly live there, they would.

Lowik had longed to be a police officer and he and Cara made the decision to immigrate to England. Lowik joined the Avon and Somerset Constabulary, working as a constable in various towns in the southwest, before finally getting a posting to Bath. After five years in the force, he had made it into the CID. He had only been a detective constable for three months when Skelton joined Bath. Lowik had made an immediate impression on Skelton by his sheer hard work and enthusiasm for the job. Lowik was no clock watcher and would happily spend hours of his own time pursuing a lead.

Responding to Skelton's question, Lowik said "Bit of a bloody mystery going on here sir. In the last two months we have had reports of people finding cash and valuable jewellery going missing from their homes. So far, we have had eight complaints and when we have visited their homes there's been no evidence of a break-in. The victim's range in age from their thirties up to an eighty-year-old lady. Now if there had just been two or three complaints and the victims had all been elderly, you might put it down to the fact that they may have been confused. But the latest complainant is in his early thirties and he swears blind that £200 which had been in his bed side cabinet has been taken. He also is certain that he could smell aftershave in his bedroom which was not his or his partners."

Skelton rubbed his chin and sat on Lowik's desk. "Sounds like someone has obtained a key to the properties. Anything on that?" Lowik shook his head, "Nothing that checks out sir. I'm struggling to make sense of it." "When did the thefts occur Peter" Lowik stood up and stretched his six-foot frame. "Apart from the latest incident which occurred yesterday afternoon, the other complainers are not sure exactly when the thefts took place. It could have been days or even weeks after the items were taken before they realised that they had been robbed" Skelton thought for a moment and then asked Lowik. "You said that the latest theft occurred yesterday and that the complainant said he was certain that someone had been in his bedroom?" Lowik paraded around the room and looked at Skelton. "Yes sir, a Mr Cunningham who lives with his boyfriend up in Coombe Down, had the day off work yesterday.

They were both going to go to Bath races in the afternoon. Mr Cunningham had withdrawn £200 from his bank the previous evening and placed it in his bedside drawer. He and his partner went out yesterday morning to do some shopping and when they got back, Mr Cunningham went to get the cash. He said he noticed the strange aftershave smell as soon as he entered the bedroom. When he opened the drawer, the cash was gone."

"Have you been to the house Peter?" Lowik sat back down on his chair and looked up at Skelton who was still perched on the edge of his desk. "No sir, I was tied up yesterday. Uniform went around and took a statement. No obvious signs of forced entry. The couple had only been out for an hour and so the theft occurred between ten and eleven yesterday morning."

Skelton stood up and thought for a minute. "Okay Peter, this sounds like a serial offender who has somehow found a method of entering and leaving the properties without leaving any evidence of his presence, except for yesterday when he left the scent of his aftershave. The most likely scenario is, that somehow, he has managed to get the victim's door keys or at least he has made copies of them. There must be a link, Peter. So, I want you to contact all the victims and make an appointment for you and me to go and see them in their homes. Let's see if we can find a commonality between these victims which should hopefully lead us to the perpetrator." Lowik got back on his feet and looked at Skelton and almost blurted out his surprise at Skelton taking over the lead detective role in the case. "Oh sir, I didn't mean to hand the case over, it's just that I only started to take it seriously when Mr Cunningham positively stated that someone had been in his bedroom." Skelton smiled at Lowik, "Peter I am not taking the case away from you. I am just going to give you the benefit of my experience. DS Alexander would usually work with me, but this is your case and I am intrigued by it. So, you and I will be the team who will try and solve it, okay?" "Yes of course sir, it will be a privilege to work with you."

Chapter Four

Skelton spent the rest of the morning reading witness statements in relation to an armed robbery, on which his predecessor was due to give evidence in the forthcoming trial. Unfortunately, DCI Smith's evidence would never be given, due to the fact, that he had died. Therefore, a vacancy in the Bath CID had occurred. Apparently, according to Bill Alexander, Smith was very reluctant to visit the doctor. It had been obvious to Alexander that Smith had been ill for months and this was reflected in his work. Once a formidable detective, Smith had begun taking shortcuts and was struggling to fulfil his duties. Eventually Chief Superintendent Sawyers, who had noticed the decline in his DCI, ordered Smith to see the duty police surgeon. This led to his immediate referral to the Royal United Hospital (RUH), where an MRI scan confirmed that he had pancreatic cancer which had spread to the lungs and kidneys. A month later he was dead.

At 12.45pm, Skelton got up from his chair and made his way into the CID office where Alexander was just finishing a phone call. "Right Bill let's go have some proper lunch. I'm in a generous mood today so it's on me." Alexander immediately got to his feet and thrust out his right hand, "Well as a fellow Scot how could I refuse your invitation?" The men shook hands and Skelton said "Follow me Bill, I'm going to take you to a pub that was my local when I was at university here some years ago. I haven't checked it out since I came back to Bath and I may just adopt it as my local again." Alexander thought for a second as to which pub Skelton was referring to. There are many pubs in Bath, some good, others not so good and one or two that Alexander would not enter unless it was to arrest one or more of its occupants.

"So where are we headed sir?" Skelton looked at Alexander and gave him a big smile. "It's a fair walk Bill, but the exercise will do you the world of good." The pub that they were headed for, was the Ale House situated on "Bog Island". Bog Island is so named as it used to have Victorian public toilets which were in an underground basement. Situated only about 500 meters from the police station, the toilets had been sold by the local authority to a company that converted them into a night club. The venture had not been a success and the premises had lain empty for years. The local authority in its wisdom had deprived the local population and literally millions of visitors of an essential facility. Bog Island is the principal drop-off and boarding venue for tourist's coaches. There are no toilet facilities anywhere near Bog Island except the local pubs and hotels. Consequently, the Ale House and the other surrounding pubs and hotels have a daily barrage of visitors wishing to use the toilets. These visitors had not realised that there were no toilet facilities close to their coaches and with only minutes to spare before their coaches were due to depart, had in desperation sought relief in the local hostelries. The visitors had no time to buy a drink in the pubs, with time at a premium, before the coach departed. Therefore, by default, the pubs and hotels had replaced the public toilets and it is they who must foot the bill for the additional water that the toilets use through non-paying customers. Despite a campaign by the local newspaper, the "Bath Chronicle" to have the toilets re-opened, the council refused to do so. Interestingly, the council allows a Christmas market every year, where hundreds of wooden huts are erected by the council and they charge exorbitant rents for stallholders to hire them. This generates substantial income for the council and it is only during the Christmas market that temporary toilets are installed at Bog Island.

Skelton tried to understand the logic that only Christmas shoppers in Bath should be looked after by the council but failed to do so. Nor, did it seem, could most of the residents and visitors to Bath.

On leaving the police station, Skelton and Alexander only needed to turn right and walk a few hundred meters and this would have brought them to Bog Island and the Ale House. But Skelton turned left, leaving Alexander to silently speculate where they were headed. As they walked along Manvers Street, this turned into Pierpont Street, which led to the train station. They crossed the road to the train station and veered left under a railway arch. Alexander realised that they must be heading to Widecombe, a small village just a few minutes' walk away. As they walked through the station's taxi rank, and over the pedestrian bridge over the river Avon, they needed to cross the road which would take them into Widecombe. However much to Alexander's surprise, Skelton turned right, walking in this direction would lead them to the bus station and Alexander thought this a strange route to take, because if they had turned right at the train station, they were virtually next door to the bus station. "I thought you knew your way around Bath Dan", exclaimed Alexander using Skelton's Christian name for the first time. It was an agreed format that outside of the police station

Christian or first names would be used. Skelton would insist that this format applied to all officers irrespective of rank. In a public environment, it would be too easy for the police officers to alert possible suspects that the police were present if they deferred to rank. "Yes Bill, I know my way around Bath very well, all I am doing is ensuring that we both get a bit of a walk before lunch, but it's more for your benefit than mine." Both men exchanged smiles and walked on, in the warm sunshine of the early May Day.

At the bus station, which is primarily used for local services, Skelton steered them left this time walking away from the city centre and towards the coach station, used as a parking area for tourist coaches. When they got to the coach station, they turned right which took them past Bath Arts College, and up to Kings Meade Square. By now Alexander had no idea as to which pub they were heading to. At Kings Meade Square he knew of at least a dozen pubs within a minute or so of walking and all of them perfectly acceptable to him. Skelton led him across the square and onto Westgate Street, which would lead them towards the Abbey, which in turn would bring them out to Bog Island. "Hells bells Dan we are heading back towards the cop shop." Skelton was checking a message on his iPhone but looked at Alexander and said, "not quite Bill but close enough for us to get back to it after we finish lunch."

When they got to the Ale House, Skelton put his arm on Alexander's shoulder and said, "well Bill you will be delighted to know that we have reached our destination and you can enjoy a pint of soda water and lime, whilst I will have to make do with a pint of Fosters!" Alexander stood in the doorway of the pub and gave Skelton a sardonic smile, "Well that's awfully decent of you, are you sure you don't want me to just sip a cup of tea?" "No Bill, let's push the boat out, you can have whatever you want to eat, provided it's a salad!" With Alexander raising his eyes to the sky, the two men entered the Ale House.

Chapter Five

The Ale House is the only pub in Bath which has resident magicians and the pub is also known as the "sleight of hand." The pub has three bars, the smallest of which is the one on the ground floor. Having only six tables, the bar can quickly fill-up. This bar, during the day, is the only one open with the others opening in the evening. Food is served all day long, except during the rugby season when Bath Rugby are playing at home. The sheer number of rugby supporters who squeeze into the bar makes it impossible to serve food except for pies which are a speciality on match days.

As the officers entered the bar, they were surprised to find that there were only a handful of customers sitting at the tables. But this was to prove to be the calm before the storm as ten minutes later, a crowd of tourists walked in and every available space was taken. However, in the few minutes whilst the pub was relatively quiet, Skelton had a chat with the barman who turned out to be the pub landlord Paul, who was also the man behind the concept of having a theme pub where magicians would display their skills. Skelton would soon learn that Paul was indeed the master of the sleight of hand.

Alexander had not been in the pub for about five years and Skelton had only made a brief scouting expedition to it when buying his house a couple of months earlier. Skelton had used the pub when at the university but Paul and his wife, Sarah, would only have been children in those days. Paul greeted them with a smile and given the fact, that they were both dressed in suits, guessed that they were either local businessmen, or were visiting the city for work. Paul introduced himself and both Skelton and Alexander shook his hand and gave him their names. Skelton reasoned that if this was going to be a regular haunt for them, then he should let Paul know exactly who they were.

As Paul poured the drinks, Skelton leaned across the bar and quietly whispered "just to let you know Paul, I'm Detective Chief Inspector Dan Skelton and this is Detective Sergeant Bill Alexander. We work across the road and I have only recently joined Bath police having previously worked in the Met police. But I know Bath very well as I went to university here and I'm delighted to be back.We are hoping to make this a regular place to come to for lunch and we would appreciate it if you just treated us like your regulars and not make it obvious that we are coppers." Paul smiled "Of course not, as far as we are concerned you are just a couple of work colleagues enjoying a drink. We won't advertise it, trust me." This was exactly the response that Skelton had been hoping for and as far as he was concerned, the Ale House would once again become his local pub.

Chapter Six

Lowik and Skelton got into the unmarked police car. As usual, Skelton preferred not to drive as he believed he could spot suspicious activity more easily without having to concentrate on driving. Lowik had set up several appointments with the victims that had reported cash and valuables taken without any obvious sign of an intruder on the premises. That is except for the gay couple who had noticed a strange aftershave in their bedroom. It was a beautiful early May morning and the sun was shining down as Lowik parked the car. They were in Bloomfield Avenue, a leafy street of large detached and semi-detached houses, many occupied by elderly residents.

Mrs Jones had reported the theft of £400 which she kept under her pillow. Lowik had mentioned that the lady was eighty-two years old and recently bereaved and Skelton wondered if she had perhaps mislaid the money rather than it having been stolen. He quickly dismissed this notion when Mrs Jones opened the door. She was a small wiry lady with grey hair, but her eyes sparkled with intelligence and as soon as she spoke Skelton realised that she was not suffering from any signs of dementia. "Mrs Jones, I am Detective Chief Inspector Skelton, and this is my colleague, Detective Constable Lowik." Both officers held out their warrant cards for Mrs Jones to inspect. "May we come in Mrs Jones and have a little chat about the money you reported missing?"

Mrs Jones led the detectives to the sitting room. "Would you gentlemen like some tea or coffee?" Skelton had a busy day ahead of him, but it would have been churlish not to accept the old lady's offer, after all they may be the only visitors she would have that day or that week for that matter. As Mrs Jones poured the tea, Skelton gently asked her about the missing money. "So, Mrs Jones, when did you realise the money was missing?" Mrs Jones sat down in the large armchair and looked intently at the detectives. "Well, it would have happened sometime during the day that I had withdrawn some money from the bank. You see, I had gone to the bank that day and had withdrawn £300. I like to pay most things with cash or cheque, so I tend to keep a fair amount of cash under my pillow. That's not something that my late husband would have approved of! He used to do virtually everything for me but since he passed away, I've found that keeping some cash at home very useful and saves me from having to go into town, which means getting a taxi or relying on friends. When I put the £300 with the other cash, I counted it all up and it was exactly £400." Skelton nodded for Mrs Jones to continue. "When I go to bed at night, I always just look under my pillow to make sure that the money is where it should be. When I looked that night, the money was nowhere to be found. I might be eighty-two Mr Skelton, but I've still got all my marbles you know." Skelton could tell that he was dealing with a reliable, if elderly, witness. He needed to discover if she had noticed anything amiss that day.

"Mrs Jones, I understand that your husband died recently, is that correct?" Mrs Jones gave a small sigh and then smiled "Yes Fred died on the sixth of January this year. It was a blessing really. You see he had cancer. It started in his lungs and then it spread to his liver. He only lived for four months after the diagnoses. But I'm blessed really, we had sixty wonderful years together, so I mustn't complain." Skelton gave her a comforting smile and said, "I'm so sorry for your loss Mrs Jones, please accept our condolences." Mrs Jones shook her head and simply said "Thank you."

"Mrs Jones, our colleagues from the uniform branch visited you the day you reported the money missing. They reported that there was no evidence of a break-in. So, I must conclude that either it was an opportunist theft whereby you may have left a door or window unlocked or someone got access to a key. Do you have any thoughts on that?" Mrs Jones shook her head, "No I am so careful about security, and I always check the doors and windows before I go out. As for a spare key, my husband was a policeman you know. He always said we must never leave a spare key hidden in the garden as thieves know where to look. So, the spare key is with my friends Mary and Jim who live just across the road. They have had the key for nearly thirty years and we've never had a problem with things going missing."

"Okay Mrs Jones after you withdrew the cash, what did you do?" Mrs Jones gave the question some thought and replied. "I did a little bit of shopping and then I got a taxi from outside the

Abbey. When I got home, I put the shopping away and then I went upstairs to the bedroom. I took the £300 out of my purse and placed it with the £100 that was still there. It was Monday and we always have lunch with Mary and Jim on a Monday. We alternate with me and my husband going across to them one week and they come to us the following week. Even after my husband died, we still carried on. Bless them, they are such good friends you know!" Anyway, that day, it was my turn to visit them so as usual, at 12.45 I walked across the road and we had lunch together. At 3 o'clock I left and came home. I always have a little knap in the chair as Jim tends to be a little heavy handed with the sherry." Mrs Jones gave a little chuckle.

Skelton thought for a second. "Do you drive Mrs Jones? Mrs Jones laughed out loud. "Oh no I don't drive; Fred would never have allowed it. You see he was the man of the house and a gentleman. He would drive me everywhere. Now that he's gone, I am reliant on friends and taxis. Skelton was racking his brain for an answer. Had the thief managed to sneak in while Mrs Jones was taking a nap, or had he known of Mrs Jones's likely movements on a Monday? Skelton suspected it was the latter scenario. "Do you by any chance have CCTV Mrs Jones?" Mrs Jones thought for a moment trying to remember what CCTV was. Then the penny dropped. "Oh no we don't have any cameras, but my husband did install security lights both at the front and at the back of the house."

"You said that your husband died in January, Mrs Jones. What happened to his car?" Well, my husband loved his car. He would wash and polish it once a week. When he had the cancer diagnosed, he knew that his driving days were over, so he sold it. Well actually he just took it back to the garage where he bought it. The manager knew that my husband was a really careful owner and the car was serviced regularly." Skelton stood up and walked to the window absorbing this information. "Mrs Jones what kind of car did your husband own and which garage did he use?" Mrs Jones gave a little chuckle. "I'm sorry Mr Skelton but I can't actually tell you the exact model, but it was a BMW. It was only two years old when he sold it. He bought it from the BMW dealer up at Peasedown St John." This is a small village about five miles from the centre of Bath. "The manager looked after my husband really well. He always laid on a courtesy car. In fact, Fred got to know most of the staff well. He insisted that he got to meet the mechanic who was going to be working on the car and always gave them a tip when he collected the car after it had been serviced."

Back in the car, Skelton put on his seat belt and looked across at Lowik as he started the engine. "Well Peter you've interviewed the other victims. Did any of them have a BMW that was serviced at Peasedown St John?" Lowik fidgeted in his seat and checked his rear-view mirror as he signalled to pull out." I'm sorry sir I never asked them about their cars." Skelton rubbed his chin. "Okay here's what you do. Phone them up and find out if they have a car, what make and where it's serviced. We are on our way to see the gay couple now and if I was a betting man, I'd wager that they have a BMW."

Lowik turned off Entry Hill onto Entry Hill Drive and parked the car outside the house of the gay couple. There was a single garage and a driveway. On the driveway was parked a two door Mercedes convertible. As they were getting out of the car, Lowik called across to Skelton "Looks like you were wrong about the BMW sir!" Skelton just tapped his nose and gave a friendly smile. The house was owned by Tom Brown and his civil partner David Lloyd. Brown was a chartered surveyor and Lloyd owned a pharmacy just outside of Bristol, a relatively short drive away unless you hit rush hour traffic.

Skelton rang the doorbell whilst Lowik checked his mobile phone for messages. Brown opened the door and Skelton immediately recognised the face. Brown looked at him quizzically, trying to determine where he had seen Skelton's face before. "Mr Brown? I am Detective Chief Inspector Dan Skelton, and this is my colleague Detective Constable Peter Lowik". Skelton held out his hand and Brown shook it as he did in turn with Lowik. Still standing just inside the door, Brown looked again at Skelton and said, "Have we met before?" Skelton had a photographic memory for faces, but it sometimes took him a while to remember where he had seen the face before. It was not unusual for him to wake up in the middle of the night having just remembered a name to put to a face. Skelton smiled broadly. "We haven't spoken but I saw you in Mandolin's last weekend. I think you were with your partner." Mandolins was the only gay bar in Bath and Skelton had gone there with his partner Ken on Saturday night. He had noticed the young couple dancing and had smiled at them when they were passing them to get to the bar. "Good lord, yes, I remember seeing you now, you were standing at the bar with your boyfriend. I had no idea that you were a policeman. It's not every day you meet a gay police officer that's for sure. Come on in and meet David he's just pouring some ice-

cold beers. Would you gentlemen care for one?"
Lowik looked at Skelton for guidance and Skelton
smiled and winked. "Yes, please said Skelton, it's a
pretty warm day."

After being introduced to Lloyd they all sat down
in the conservatory. They were all now on first
names, so it made for a more relaxed
environment. Skelton led the questioning. "Right, I
understand that on the day the money went
missing, you had been out shopping and that you
had come back to the house prior to going to the
races. Is that correct?" Brown looked at his
partner and indicated that he would answer the
questions. "Yes, that's right, we had gone up to
Sainsbury's in the car to get some shopping. It was
a lovely day, so we took David's car and we were
able to put the roof down. We had been out about
an hour as we stopped off for a coffee on the way
back. David was putting the shopping away and I
went upstairs to shower. As soon as I went into
our bedroom, I could smell the aftershave. It's not
something either of us would use. It's an old
fashioned type that my dad or even grandad
would use. I instinctively knew that someone had
been in our bedroom and I got a bit worked-up. I
ran down the stairs calling for David. I said David,
someone's been in the house." This was the cue
for David to take up the story. "Yes, Tom was in a

bit of a panic, so I put my arm around him and asked him what he was on about. He said he could smell strange aftershave in our bedroom. So, I grabbed the biggest knife we have and the two of us went from room to room to see if we could find an intruder. But there was no sign of anyone and no evidence that anything had been disturbed. We went back to our bedroom and Tom asked me if I could smell the aftershave. Without a doubt, just next to Tom's side of the bed there was a strange foreign scent. Tom opened the top drawer of his bedside cabinet and the money that he was going to use as his betting fund was gone."

Skelton stood up and walked to the nearest window and then turned to face the three men. "I understand there was no forced entry and you both told the uniformed officers that you were certain that the house was locked when you went out?" Tom stretched his legs and looked directly at Skelton. "Yes, the doors were all locked, but we had left a couple of windows upstairs open. A kid with a ladder might just squeeze through the space but I doubt it." Skelton paced forward and asked "Tom you said that you went shopping in David's car. I take it you have a car also, but we only saw one on your driveway." Tom brought his feet together and scratched his ear. "Yes, I keep my car in the garage. David always leaves before me in the morning and gets home after me. That way, I can park my Beamer in the garage. Skelton gave another wide smile whilst Lowik looked down at his shoes. "So, you have a BMW Tom? Which garage do you use?" Tom took another sip of beer and said "I use the dealer out at Peasdown St John. They give a great service and the staff are very friendly. I had the car serviced the day before the money went missing. It was a bloody expensive service and I queried the bill. The mechanic who did the work was quite upset that I had queried the bill and took the trouble to explain exactly what parts needed replacing. But after he had taken the trouble to explain what he had needed to do, I got relaxed about the whole thing. We ended up discussing horse racing!"

Skelton absorbed this snippet of information and walked closer to the little group sitting around the table sipping beer. "Tom, do you have your car keys handy?" Tom stood up and said, "let me get them, they are in the kitchen." Tom returned with the car keys and handed them to Skelton. There were three keys on the bunch as well as the fob for locking and unlocking the car. Skelton guessed correctly that the one key was for the car, one for the garage door and the larger key was the front door key. "Tom when you take your car in for a service do you remove your house key?" Tom gave a slightly nervous cough, "No can't say I do. Why?" Skelton sat back down and looked closely at Tom and David whilst Lowik, who had been following the conversation with great interest, had already concluded that someone at the garage was either making copies of house keys or simply using the actual key when they knew the owner would not be at home. Lowik needed to find out if the other victims had any connection to the BMW garage.

Chapter Seven

Skelton had walked to the station as usual that morning. It was another lovely sunny day and as he enjoyed a peaceful stroll from Coombe Down, which was all downhill through the trendy area known as Bear Flat and past Alexandra Park, he reflected on what a very pleasant commute he now enjoyed. It was all so much different from when he lived in Surrey and had to take a packed train into central London. How he had hated the daily grind of having to stand in an overcrowded carriage with his nose invariably lodged under a fellow passenger's arm pit. It was through that experience of having to smell fellow unwashed passenger's sweat that when he applied his aftershave in the morning, he always splashed some on the back of his left hand. This ensured that in the event of encountering a smelly commuter, he simply raised his hand below his nose so that all he smelt was the fragrance of his own aftershave.

He went to his office and checked his emails and crime reports. Having done that, he had made his way down to the custody suite where he found Sergeant Dave Roddis. Dave Roddis was by his own admission, fat. Skelton had taken an instant liking to Roddis the first time he met him. A few days after arriving in Bath, he and Alexander had executed an arrest warrant on a suspected drug dealer. The suspect had proven to be quite a handful and had done nothing but shout and scream about his human rights in the police car all the way back to the station. As Skelton and Alexander led the handcuffed prisoner to the custody suite, they were greeted by a smiling Dave Roddis "Good morning, Bill and what have you brought us in this morning? And who is this, gentlemen with you?" Nodding to Skelton. Alexander looked across the desk to where Roddis was standing, still smiling in anticipation of being introduced to the stranger. "Oh, Dave have you not met the new DCI? This is Dan Skelton, sir meet

Dave Roddis the best custody sergeant I've ever worked with." Skelton reached across the desk with his right hand outstretched and shook hands with Roddis. "Good morning Dave, delighted to meet you. Bill has told me a few things about you, all of course complimentary!" Roddis looked at Alexander and winked "What lengths you will go to get a pint out of me Bill." All three officers laughed.

It was at this point that the prisoner decided to kick-off again. Clearly bored with the introductions being announced and very much missing his intended morning kip in bed! He shouted at the uniformed sergeant now standing with his arms crossed against his chest. "Hoy, I know my fucking rights, I want a lawyer and I want a cooked breakfast. And you're wasting your fucking time if you think you are going to get anything out of me in the interview. I know my rights and I'm going to sue you bastards for everything you've got." All three officers had encountered such situations many times. In the good old days, Alexander would have given the guy a backhander right across the kisser, but modern custody suites had CCTV cameras everywhere. Skelton had had enough of this character and was just about to tell the prisoner what he thought of his demands, when Roddis intervened.

Roddis put his hands on his head and started to cry like a baby. "Oh god you think you've got problems?" he sobbed. "I'll swap places with you any day of the week mate. He put his head on the desk and continued to sob. Do you know what it's like being married to my wife? I've done 30 years hard labour son with no chance of parole." He placed his hands under his chin and looked up at the prisoner, the tears rolling down his cheeks. Skelton wondered if Roddis was suffering a nervous breakdown, but he caught Alexander's bemused smile and realised that Roddis was a first-rate actor. This was his way of dealing with prisoners with a perceived grievance. The prisoner was taken completely by surprise and Skelton could see that he really thought that the custody sergeant needed some sympathy. The prisoner shuffled forward a little. "Oh, mate I'm sorry. Look I didn't mean to upset you honest." The prisoner looked at Skelton and Alexander, "Its ok I'm going to pass on the cooked breakfast, just take me to a cell, okay?" At that, Roddis raised his head and took out a large white handkerchief and blew his nose loudly. Looking directly at Alexander he said "Number seven please Bill" indicating the prisoner's cell number.

Chapter Eight

As Skelton had walked towards the custody
sergeant's desk this morning, he saw Roddis
amiably chatting to Constable Dave Lake an old
fashioned copper who had over thirty years in the
police service. He knew every criminal in and
around Bath and was a constant source of
intelligence reports that he shared with his fellow
uniformed officers, as well as the CID. Stood
beside Lake was a tall young officer who Skelton
did not recognise. As Skelton approached them,
Roddis gave him a cheery smile and said "Well if

it's not the DCI. And good morning to you sir."
Skelton returned the smile, "Good morning to you
Dave oh and to you too Dave" nodding his head
towards Dave Lake. At this point, the young officer
turned around to face Skelton who guessed that
the lad was about nineteen years old. He was a
very handsome fresh-faced youth with beautiful
brown intelligent eyes. Skelton gave him a friendly
smile and addressing Lake said, "Well who is this
you've snatched from the cradle Dave?"

Dave Lake stood gently aside and said "Sir this is
probationary Constable Luke Meehan and he is
enjoying his first day in our beautiful city. Luke
meet Detective Chief Inspector Skelton." Skelton
advanced forward, his arm outstretched to shake
hands with the recruit. As they shook hands,
Skelton said "Hello Luke and a warm welcome to
Bath. I hope Dave here is looking after you well?"
Young Meehan gave Skelton a firm handshake and
with a boyish smile replied. "Yes sir, everyone has
been so kind to me this morning but I'm still a bit
nervous." The accent was either Somerset or
Wiltshire, but Skelton could not be sure which.
"So, Luke, you're from around these parts then?"
Meehan gave another boyish smile and said, "Yes
sir I'm from Corsham but I spent my first
probationary year working in Bristol before being
transferred to Bath." Corsham was a town in

Wiltshire about six miles from Bath. Skelton rested his arm on the chest high desk or bar as it was properly called. "Well Luke, I'm sure you will be a major asset to us here in Bath. Just listen carefully to what the two Dave's tell you as they have a fantastic insight into everything that goes on in Bath. If you ever need any advice or help my door is always open, even when it's closed if you follow what I mean?" Meehan looked directly into Skelton's eyes and said "Thank you sir. I can't wait to get to out on the streets of Bath, it's my favourite city and everyone is being so helpful."

Skelton bid all three a good day and went to the canteen for a bacon roll. After he was out of earshot, Lake said to Meehan "You would never guess the DCI was gay, would you?" Meehan laughed and shook his head. "Look Dave I'm not falling for that old trick. It's my first day and I expect to get my leg pulled. And you guys want to make sure I put my foot in it on day one. Like I go and say to the DCI, oh so you're gay then, and he smacks me in the teeth. Yes, career over on day one, no I don't think so. If the DCI is gay, then I'm gay right? Good try guys, I might be a rookie but I'm not stupid." Roddis leaned across the bar with both hands on his chin. "Look Luke, seriously the governor is gay. Believe me this is not a stich-up, he lives with his boyfriend in Coombe Down. He used to work in the Met but joined us a few weeks ago. He is openly gay, but you would never suspect it that's for sure. But if you don't believe us, I'm sure he will tell you himself. And in any case, you are the best looking guy in the station now and you can bet he will want to get to know you." Meehan looked at each in turn and just shook his shoulders, "Yea whatever."

Chapter Nine

It was another warm sunny May Day in Bath. Skelton and Alexander had just returned to the station after visiting a witness to a serious assault that had occurred the previous night. It was just after three o'clock and Skelton was sitting at his desk when DC Ross Turnbull knocked on the door and walked in holding a sheet of paper. Alexander was seated across from Skelton, and they had been discussing the information that the witness had given regarding the suspect in the case. "Sorry to interrupt you chaps but we've just had a missing person report and I don't like the look of it." Skelton had come to appreciate that Turnbull was a shrewd detective and if this missing person report was giving him cause for concern, then it needed immediate looking into. "What have you got Ross" asked Skelton as he sat back in his chair cupping both hands behind his neck. Turnbull rested his backside on the edge of the desk and stared at the sheet of paper he was holding in his right hand. "A young girl from Bath Spa University left her accommodation last night just after ten o'clock. Her name is Linda Carson. She told her roommate that she was meeting a friend in town for a drink and would be back around two in the morning. But she never came home and the roommate, a nineteen-year-old girl called Megan Morgan from Swansea, has tried calling her mobile phone without any success. She's appealed for help in finding her flatmate on Facebook, but no one seems to have seen her last night. The girls had been drinking a bottle of wine before Linda left to meet her friend. My concern is that she might have fallen into the river and drowned."

This was a real possibility as it had happened at least eight times in the last few years. The victims had all been young university male students. Usually Freshers, the guys had gone out drinking with their new friends from the Uni. Being young and unused to drinking, they would end up going to a night club after drinking in the bars that offer cheap drinks to students on certain nights of the week. Invariably the guys would become separated from their drinking companions and would try and make their way back to their accommodation. Being late at night and dark and having consumed too much drink, these were the ingredients for a tragedy.

The Bath City section, of the River Avon, is very fast-flowing and deep. It has treacherous undercurrents and anyone unfortunate enough to fall into it, is unlikely to survive unless immediate help is on hand to rescue them. Falling into the river in the early hours of the morning, when few people are around to notice the event, will unfortunately lead to almost, certain death. The river is notoriously unpredictable, and a body might not surface for weeks before it becomes untangled from the mass of underwater hazards such as trees, branches and other obstructions. It is a common misconception that the public assumes that when someone drowns, the body will quickly surface and be found. Regrettably, that is not the case. When a person drowns, they ingest a great deal of water which causes the body to sink. The body will remain submerged until such time as the body starts to decompose and the stomach contents become gaseous. This causes the body to rise. Decomposition is variable depending upon the water temperature and other variables. It can therefore be days or even weeks before the body rises to the surface. Even then it may not be easy to spot if it becomes entangled in weeds by the riverbank.

Such has been the extent of young male students being drowned in the city section of the Avon that the local coroner stated that if it were a human being, it would be classified as a serial killer. So serious had the problem become, that both universities had launched publicity campaigns, using the slogan, "Don't let the River, be your last drink!"

"Well I understand your concern Ross and if this was a male student, I would have said that there is a distinct possibility they have ended up in the river. But this is a female student and as far as I know, we haven't had any females fall victim to the Avon. Certainly not when I was at the Uni, and I've seen nothing since then. Alexander stood up and pushed his chair back. "Sorry sir but you're wrong there. We had a young female student drown back in December last year. Unfortunately, it was another case where she had gone out drinking and she never made it back to the campus. Luckily the body surfaced about a week later. The post-mortem confirmed she was three times over the drink driving limit. She must have tried taking a short cut back to her accommodation. In the dark and being heavily intoxicated, she must have fallen in and that was it. Death was due to drowning."

Skelton rocked back and forth in his chair. "We went to Thailand last December for three weeks. In the whole time that we were there, I purposely did not access the TV nor read a newspaper, so I guess this all happened when we were away. Okay, given the fact that the roommate has had no contact with her since last night, I am concerned. Of course, there could be a simple explanation. The battery in her phone may be dead and she's not been able to recharge it. Maybe she got completely pissed and is now suffering from a massive hangover and hopefully will turn up later today with nothing more serious than a sore head." Skelton thought for a second, "Right let's think the worse. Ross, get uniform to conduct a search along the riverbank. If she came into town for this drink, she is unlikely to have strayed far from the city centre. Start the search at Widcombe and extend it along the riverbank as far as Twerton. Get on to Fire and Rescue and ask them to launch their inflatable and cover the same route. They will be able to access those bits of the river that you can't properly see from the riverbank. Have you got her roommate's contact details there?" Turnbull handed over the piece of paper, "Yes sir it's all here."

"Right, Bill, let's go and pay a visit to the roommate and see what we can learn from her. Let's just hope that by the time we get there, young Linda is popping some paracetamol in a bid to cure her hangover."

Chapter Ten

Linda Carson had been chatting online with a boy from Bath. It was a dating website which she had downloaded onto her phone. The boy said that his name was Tommy, and that he was nineteen years old and worked as a delivery driver. The photographs that he had sent her on Snapchat showed a muscular young man with short blonde hair and he was incredibly handsome. Linda did not have a boyfriend, in fact she was still a virgin but now that she was attending university, she was determined to lose her virginity and young Tommy looked the ideal candidate for the job!

Linda was studying to become a school teacher and she was attending Bath Spa University, which Skelton had attended. Of the two universities, Bath University, teaches traditional degree courses such as engineering, Maths and Physics with the curriculum for these degrees being governed by the central examination bodies at both Oxford and Cambridge. It also boasts an American style sports village which has turned out some excellent Olympic athletes. Whilst Bath Spa is more of a technical college, offering degrees in vocational subjects, which are compiled by the university. On certain courses, there are only ten to twelve hours of lectures per week, with the university still charging its students colossal fees of around £9,000 a year, plus a similar amount for accommodation. With careful selection, some of these degrees might eventually lead to enhanced salaries in later life, such as was the case with Skelton who had studied criminology. However, most of the students would end up with a degree that many employers would regard as meaningless and not a good grounding in the real world. The students would simply end up with debts of more than £30,000/£50,000, dependent on the course and accommodation charges. For a significant number of these graduates, their highly costly degrees would not qualify them for jobs that paid significantly more than which a school leaver, without a degree, would also qualify.

Linda Carson arrived at the Bath Spa campus last September. The campus is situated several miles outside the city and most students rely on the very frequent bus service which runs from the campus into the city every few minutes. She shared an accommodation block with seven other students and enjoyed her own modern bedroom with en-suite bathroom. She shared a kitchen and a common room with her fellow students most of whom were either studying computing or, like herself, teaching. Strangely, for a modern campus, the WIFI was seriously unreliable. There were long periods during the day and night when the WIFI was simply not available, which was a constant frustration for all concerned. This was particularly annoying for the young male students who found it difficult to view their favourite porn sites.

Linda had made varying degrees of friendship with her roommates. However, she and a girl called Megan had hit it off big time from the moment they had introduced themselves to each other. In just two weeks, they had become firm friends, sharing many a secret with each other which they would never share with the other students.

Linda and Megan were sitting in Megan's room and they had just opened a bottle of Pinot Gregio white wine. It was a little after nine in the evening and they had just finished their meal which for the second night in a row was Pasta, surely a common denominator for most students today! The girls were sitting across a small coffee table and as Megan poured the wine, she looked across to Linda and said, "So you're meeting this hunk Tommy tonight then?" Linda gave a slightly nervous giggle as she held out her glass for Megan to pour the wine. "Yes, that's right I'm meeting him at ten thirty and we are going for a drink and then we will go on to a night club. It's our first date, so I will get the bus back about two as I've got a lecture in the morning at nine." Megan gave her a quizzical look and smiled broadly as she finished pouring the wine. "Yeh, right, you are meeting this drop-dead gorgeous Tommy tonight and you're not going to let him shag you?" Linda let out a girly squeal and blushed. "Oh, come on

Megan, this is the first time I will have met him. You don't think he's getting inside my knickers that quick do you? You girls in Swansea might let a lad shag you on the first date but we girls from Basingstoke are far more refined than that!" Both girls laughed out loud and gulped down their wine.

Linda had not shown Megan the photographs that Tommy had sent her on Snapchat. She simply had mentioned that she had been chatting to a guy called Tommy online without specifically mentioning the name of the website. She had however described the boy Tommy as being a six-foot tall hunk who worked out in the gym every day. Linda did not want to give too much information away until she had met Tommy in the flesh and verified that he was as good looking as the photographs he had sent her. After all, she knew for a fact that on the internet, it was easy to send photographs of another person and claim that they were pictures of oneself.

As they finished off the bottle of wine, Linda looked at her watch and saw that it was nine fifty. She calculated that it would take a little more than five minutes to walk to the bus stop. The bus takes about twenty minutes to reach North Parade which is right in the centre of the city adjacent to the Bath Rugby Club Recreation Ground, known as the Rec. Tommy had said that he would meet her as she got off the bus which stopped outside Lambrettas which was both a bar with an adjacent hotel. She liked the idea that they would be meeting in public and that they would just be having a drink. If she did not like him, she could easily make an excuse and leave.

There were only about a dozen passengers on the bus and Linda felt quite nervous about meeting Tommy. She had had a few dates back home, but nothing had come of them. Linda was a very petite girl, being only just over five foot tall and very slim. She had a pretty face and a fantastic smile which showed her fabulous white teeth which she carefully looked after, brushing them at least three times a day. As the bus was pulling to a stop outside Lambrettas, Linda peered out of the window to see if she could see Tommy but to her dismay, there was no one at the bus stop. She looked at her watch, it was just after ten twenty. Tommy had responded to her text that she had sent him, saying that she was on the bus. He confirmed that he would meet her coming off the bus. She guessed that he was on his way. As she was getting off the bus, she thanked the driver and stepped on to the pavement. She had not realised that the CCTV on the bus had recorded her every movement and would be helpful to the police when they came to investigate her disappearance.

At this point, Linda's phone pinged as a text arrived. Like all young people to whom mobile phones and texting are a way of life, she immediately broke off from the dialogue with the driver and read the text. It was from Tommy, saying that he was sorry for the delay and had hoped that she had met his dad. Linda looked away from her phone and her eyes focused on an old guy who was approaching her. The man smiled, and Linda smiled back. The man switched off the phone in his pocket. It was he who had just texted Linda, pretending to be Tommy, who had sent his dad to meet her.

As the bus moved away and turned left on to Manvers Street, Linda wondered how long it would be before Tommy showed up. The man who had been standing by the railings approached her. And she guessed that it was Tommy's father. The man was smiling and seemed like a decent sort, certainly he did not seem aggressive or in any way scary. She guessed the man was in his mid-fifties. He was about five feet eight and clearly well-built, but he had a definite beer belly. "Excuse me are you Linda by any chance?" he asked. A little hesitantly she said, "Yes, my name is Linda, I guess you must be Tommy's father?" The man gave her another smile. "Yes, don't worry, I'm Tommy's dad. Tommy wanted to meet you himself, but his brother called him a few minutes ago from the RUH. He needs a lift home as he broke his arm this afternoon and as I don't drive Tommy has had to go. He is very sorry, but he won't be more than half an hour. So, I am here to be your guardian angel, so to speak." Again, giving Linda a wide smile.

Linda was slightly taken aback by this news, but she was not in any way alarmed, after all the man seemed very friendly and how else would he have known her name? Linda returned the man's smile. "Gosh I am sorry to hear that your other son has broken his arm, is he okay?" The man nodded his head and clasped his hands on his belly. "Yes, James is fine. He's a tree surgeon and he fell off a tree today, the silly bugger. So, Tommy has had to go fetch him home. I bet James gets a mouthful from Tommy when he sees him for going and ruining, your date!" Linda smiled again and relaxed a little. This seemed to be a nice family who looked after each other and the fact that Tommy had gone to help his brother when he needed him could only be good news. It was also thoughtful, that Tommy had sent his father to give her the news, rather than send her a text message which could easily have been an excuse for not turning up, was even more comforting. "Oh, don't worry I can wait here for Tommy to get back. I will be fine." The man shook his head and said "If you think I am leaving you on your own standing outside a pub you must be mad.

Look, Tommy Lives just there" pointing to a door to the left of Lambrettas. "I've got a key, so we can go in and have a drink and Tommy will be along shortly." The man gently touched Linda's right arm and with his other hand produced the door key. "Come on Linda, follow me." The man led the way and Linda followed, not realising that this was the last few steps she would ever take again. Linda was about to die but not quickly, no the man had plans for them both but only he would enjoy Linda's last living hours.

Chapter Eleven

Skelton and Alexander were in an unmarked police car, with Alexander driving. They were headed for the Bath Spa University campus, which was about a twenty-minute drive. It was just after four o'clock and it was a sunny afternoon. As they descended the steep hill towards the Globe, a pub which Skelton had meant to visit since his return to Bath but had not yet had the opportunity to do so, he turned to Alexander. "So, Bill what do you reckon? Has young Linda just got drunk and is nursing a bad hangover or what?" Alexander shrugged his shoulders and sighed. "Your guess is as good as mine. We need to learn a bit more about Linda before we can make that call. For me, I have a completely open mind but I am just dreading that she turns up at the bottom of the Avon! I've seen enough young people come out of it dead and no matter how many times you see it, the experience is always the fucking same!

At the roundabout next to the Globe, Alexander took the first exit and after about one hundred meters, turned left onto the entrance to the campus. A long, narrow driveway led to the main building and further along were the modern residential blocks. It was clear to Skelton that the university campus had at some point in the past been a country estate and most probably a shooting estate. The deep valley that they were now driving through would have been perfect for driving pheasants from the hills above over the waiting guns below. Skelton noted the signpost. "Newton St Loe, Gardens" As they drove past the main reception area, Skelton noticed the waiting bus about to depart into Bath. They needed to find "Lime Block" where Linda shared with Megan. It was located at the far end of the site, on the left.

Skelton had called Megan before leaving the station. Megan confirmed that Linda had not been in contact and had missed two lectures that day. This was worrying news as according to Megan, Linda was very conscientious and had never missed a lecture before. It also worried Skelton, that Linda was not responding to phone calls or text messages. Nor had the Facebook appeal brought any response. Something was clearly wrong, yet there was no evidence to confirm that any harm had come to her. It was still quite possible that she would turn up at some point having either lost her phone or the battery had simply run out.

The detectives got out of the car and walked across the carpark to Lime Block. Skelton pressed the buzzer and the door was almost immediately opened by a young girl with red hair. She clearly looked distressed and Skelton knew instantly that it must be Megan. "Hello, are you Megan?" he asked gently. "The girl had been crying with sheer worry that her friend had not come home and was not responding to all the calls and text messages she had sent. "Yes, I'm Megan, please come on in" she said in her distinctive Welsh accent. Skelton introduced himself and Alexander. Megan nodded her head "Yes, we spoke on the phone. This way please" All three walked into the communal kitchen area, which was covered in dirty dishes. This was clearly student's accommodation thought Skelton. Megan led the officers to her room and she invited them to take the only two seats while she sat on her bed.

Skelton settled himself into the chair but realised he was never going to get comfortable in the cheap piece of furniture. He took out his notebook and placed it on the table in front of him. He noticed the two empty wine glasses and the empty wine bottle. Megan was clearly not a tidy

70

person as was further evidenced by the discarded clothing which littered the floor. "Right Megan, tell us about last night. Just take your time and try to remember everything that you can and what exactly Linda's plans were for the evening" Megan took a deep breath and closed her eyes for a few seconds. When she opened them again, she stared down at the floor and began to speak softly. Both Skelton and Alexander had to listen intently to catch what she was saying in her strong Welsh accent.

"Well, I've known Linda since last September and we've become great friends. She is so bubbly and is always making me laugh. Last night after we had finished our course work, you see we are doing the same course for teachers." Skelton noted this and nodded his head for Megan to continue. "Well, we had some pasta. I made it and when we had eaten, we sat there at the table and had a bottle of wine. Linda had been texting a boy that she was going to meet at half past ten in town." This information was vital to finding Linda and Skelton wanted to know as much about this boy as was possible. "Oh, and who is this boy? Is he a boyfriend or just a friend Megan?" Skelton asked. Megan rubbed her hands and was clearly uncomfortable with what she was about to say. Skelton needed to reassure her that she was not in any trouble. "It's alright Megan, you are not in any way in trouble with us. We just need to know exactly where Linda went last night and who she met. Hopefully, with that information, we can find her and bring her back for the pair of you to enjoy another bottle of wine together." He gave her a big reassuring smile which seemed to help Megan relax a little.

Megan got off the bed and began to walk around the small bedroom. She had her hands on her hips which caused her white skirt to rise slightly. Skelton glanced at Alexander and gave a slight grimace to indicate that the witness seemed genuine and Alexander acknowledged this with a simple nod of his head. "Well, all I know is that his name is Tommy. Linda was meeting him last night for the first time. They had been chatting on a dating website, but Linda never mentioned which one." Skelton managed to hide his concern as this was not looking good based on his experience when working for the Met. Megan turned to face them again. "His name is Tommy and I think he drives a van for a living. Linda said he works out in the gym every day and so he is quite the beef-cake. He sent Linda some photos on Snapchat, but she never showed them to me. She left here to catch the bus into town and he was going to meet her at the bus stop just outside Lambrettas." Now

Skelton had something to work on. First, there would be CCTV on the bus and there are CCTV cameras everywhere in Bath, so wherever she went it would be recorded as would the face of Tommy. Skelton knew that if he obtained an image of Tommy, all that needed to be done was to share the image on Facebook and someone would identify him. Hopefully this would lead him to finding Linda and with a bit of luck all would be well. However, Skelton's gut instinct was telling him that Tommy might have raped her or, even worse, killed her. Skelton made the decision right then. A missing person enquiry does not get a lot of resources, mainly since the missing person usually turns up safe and well. No, this was a suspicious disappearance and needed his and the resources of the Avon and Somerset Constabularies' maximum effort to discover what had happened to Linda.

"Does Linda have a boyfriend Megan?" Alexander asked. Megan sat back down on the bed. She looked directly at both the officers and replied. "No Linda doesn't have a boyfriend. She told me she went out with a couple of boys when she was still at school but nothing serious." Skelton stood up and looked down at Megan and then asked, "Megan, is Linda still a virgin do you know?"

73

Megan gave a slight cough and quietly said "Yes Linda told me she had never slept with anyone."

"Megan, can we see Linda's room please?" enquired Skelton. "Yes of course, follow me." Linda's bed was made up. Dirty clothes lay on a chair and on the floor. There was a photograph on the table of a man, a woman and a young girl. Skelton picked it up and asked Megan "Is this Linda and her mum and dad?" Megan looked at the photograph, "Yes" she said, "It was taken the day before they drove her to the uni. They had gone out for a pub lunch and this was taken to mark the event." Skelton stared closely at the face of Linda. She was a beautiful young girl and looked vulnerable. "Okay Megan, I need to borrow this photograph so that we can get Linda's face on social media etcetera." Megan nodded her head, "Yes of course you can take it, but I've already posted her picture on Facebook, but nobody seems to know where she is." Skelton closed his eyes as he considered this news. This was not looking good!

Skelton had a good look around the room for any clues as to where Linda may have been going with Tommy. He found nothing. There was a laptop sitting on a desk. "Is that Linda's?" Megan looked up. "Yes, that's Linda's. She uses it for uni-work

and for Facebook and maybe a few other apps."
"We need to take this with us Megan, maybe we can locate Linda and Tommy on here. We have experts back at the station who might be able to give us an early indication as to where Linda and Tommy are."

Chapter Twelve

Back at the police station, Skelton was informed that the search of the river was still underway but so far, no trace of Linda had been found. Skelton marched into the CID room and found his entire team had come in for the briefing he was about to give. He already had the face pictures of Linda in his hand. Young Lowik was a whizz kid on computers and he had very quickly worked his miracle on the photograph of Linda with her parents. Now, there was just a photograph of Linda on her own and Lowik had blown it up in size.

"Right folks, here is what we know about Linda Carson." Skelton scanned the room watching the faces of the men and woman under his command. He went on "Linda is 18 years old and last September she arrived as a fresher at Bath Spa University where she is studying to be a teacher. She appears to have been a model student and until today had never missed a lecture. According to her flat mate, Megan Morgan, Linda does not have a boyfriend and, unusually for a student, is still a virgin." Some of the officers could not help but smile. Skelton continued "Megan has told us that after having dinner last night, they shared a bottle of wine and that around ten o'clock, Linda took the bus into town to meet a lad named Tommy. She had never met him before and apparently contact had been made through a dating website, the name of which is not presently known. Tommy was supposed to be meeting her when she got off the bus just outside Lambrettas." Facing DC Turnbull, he asked "Any luck with the bus company Ross?" Turnbull held up his hand which was holding a CD. "I just got back with it now sir. I viewed it at the bus company office and it clearly shows eleven passengers getting on the bus at the campus. All are girls, and all got off at Lambrettas. Unfortunately, it does not show anyone waiting at the bus stop to meet her. I saw Peter working on Linda's photo and she definitely got off the bus at 22.19 hours."

Skelton absorbed this information. "Right, we need to secure CCTV from that immediate area to see if Tommy shows up and which direction they move in. On the basis that they would most likely have headed to a bar or night club, I want you all to divide yourselves up between the most likely bars and clubs that they may have gone to. Bill and I will take North Parade which is where she got off the bus. I also want the city's number plate recognition system to check the registration numbers of all vehicles that passed through the city last night between 22 hundred hours and midnight just in case Tommy was driving a vehicle"

Looking directly at DC Jim Broadbent, "Anything on her phone yet Jim?" Broadbent sat up straight in his chair and cleared his throat. "Not very much sir. Her phone company has confirmed that she used her phone to send a text message to another mobile number at 22.02 last night. The location she was at when she sent the text was Bath Spa Uni. She then travelled, to a point in North Parade, where she received a text message from the number that she had texted earlier. Then at 22.35 her phone was switched off. It has not been reactivated since and the phone number she sent the text message to is a pre-paid. In other words, we will have considerable difficulty in tracing the person that Linda contacted. The phone company is sending me a copy of all the numbers that she communicated with for the last month."

Janet Griffin stood up and said, "Sir, I did a study paper in Bristol on the traceability of cell phones.

The phone of choice by drug dealers and other such criminals, who wish to remain invisible, are the early Nokia phones which are still cheaply available, as part of a pre-paid package where you can get the SIM card and phone for about ten quid. No questions are asked as to the identity of the buyer. These phones don't have the intrusive features associated with the later smart phones such as GPS, WIFI and email. The only way to trace these earlier models is by triangulation using phone masts. The phone companies will do this for us if we make a special request to track a known number. However, it will not provide us with an exact location, just an area of about 100 square meters, from where the phone was used.

In other words, these early phones are basically untraceable and if Tommy was using one of these, then our chances of tracing his phone are very remote to say the least."

All the officers thought about this new information. DC Janet Griffin was thirty-five years old and married to a fellow police officer serving in Bristol. Small in stature, she was incredibly feisty and would leave no stone unturned in any investigation. She was a great asset to the team and Skelton had already noted her down for a possible promotion once she had got her sergeant's ticket. Griffin spoke again. "It sounds to me that she turned her phone off shortly after meeting this lad Tommy. On the other hand, what if it was Tommy who turned it off? He would know that with the phone switched off, we would have no way of establishing exactly where Linda had gone. Given the fact that the person she texted from the bus had a phone, which is virtually untraceable, I get the distinct feeling that this is not a straight forward missing person enquiry." Turning to Broadbent she asked, "Jim have you traced where the phone Linda texted was located last night?" Broadbent shifted slightly in his chair. "It's a different network provider and not as efficient as Linda's. But they have promised to get back to me as soon as possible."

Skelton was becoming increasingly anxious as these revealing facts emerged. This was definitely no longer a missing person enquiry. Someone had abducted Linda; he was certain of that.

Chapter Thirteen

After the team conference broke up, all the officers divided up to which licenced premises they would attend to retrieve CCTV evidence. Skelton and Alexander left the station at 18.30 and turned right. It was a very short walk to North Parade and as they turned right, they first passed the vegetarian restaurant on the corner then passed the night club called Poo Na Na's. Skelton always thought it was quite a mouthful to say, especially if one was drunk!

Next, they came to Lambrettas and Skelton was certain this would hold the key to cracking the case. Skelton had not been in the bar for years, but as he walked in, he could see that little had changed with the décor, except that the pool table had been taken out. Alexander followed Skelton to the bar and was surprised when Skelton turned to him and said, "What are you having Bill?" The young fresh-faced barman said, "Good evening what can I get you?" Skelton looked at the selection of lagers that were on tap and his eyes lit up when he saw the Fosters. "A Pint of Fosters for me" and Alexander said, "make that two please." As the barman poured the drinks, Skelton asked him "Were you on duty last night?" The barman smiled and said "yes, I certainly was. It was a typical Monday night I had about a dozen customers last night, so time dragged on forever. I was glad to close at eleven and go to bed." Skelton paid for the Fosters and as the barman handed him his change, he pulled Linda's photograph from his jacket pocket. "Did by any chance this girl come in last night?" The barman looked closely at the photo. "Nope she definitely did not come in here last night. In fact, I've never seen her in here." Skelton had been hoping that after meeting Tommy, the pair would have come in for a drink and they would have Tommy on CCTV. Skelton was staring up at the camera while the barman responded. Skelton wanted to know about the mysterious Tommy. "Did you have any customers in last night between 10 and 11?" The barman scratched his head for a second. "No, the last customers, a couple of regulars, left about half past nine. I was on my own until I locked up." Skelton thanked the young man and he and Alexander found a vacant table and sat down.

Alexander spoke first. "The CCTV recorders are in the Hotel's reception which is just through that door" pointing to the door beside them. "I had to deal with an assault in here a while back when they still had the pool table. That CCTV camera caught it all on film and the assailant pleaded guilty. He had no defence." Skelton stared up at the camera. "Right Bill lets knock this back and visit reception. It will be interesting to see what the outside cameras show us. We are bound to see Linda getting off the bus and this guy Tommy meeting her. We just need to get his picture posted on Facebook and we will know who he is damn soon. When we know his name, it should lead us to finding out exactly where Linda ended up with him!"

Upon entering the reception office, the manager looked up and recognised Alexander. With a big smile, he got up from his chair and said, "Hello Bill, how are you?" The manager stretched out his hand and Alexander shook it. "I'm good thanks. How about you?" "Oh, if I complained no one would listen, would they?" All three men laughed. Alexander then introduced Skelton to John the manager, but Alexander could not remember his surname, so they stuck to first names. After shaking hands, Skelton asked to see the outside CCTV footage from the previous night. The detective's hearts sank as soon as they looked at it. The cameras only covered the immediate ground in front of the entrances to both Lambretta's bar and the separate hotel entrance, where the smokers tended to congregate. Unless Tommy had stood in the areas immediately outside both entrances, he would not have been picked up by the cameras.

The officers carefully reviewed the film for the relevant times. This merely revealed a couple of guests entering the hotel, neither of which was Linda. Bugger, thought Skelton, they would have to widen the search. The mostly likely candidate for success was Poo Na Na's provided Linda and Tommy went that way.

Skelton & Alexander left Lambrettas and turned left towards Poo Na Na's. Passing through the entrance Skelton looked up and saw the CCTV camera and he hoped that this would give them their first sighting of Linda after she left the bus and more importantly, a clear picture of Tommy. The barman was re-stocking the bar when he heard the officer's footsteps. Turning around to face them, the young heavy-set lad quickly said "Sorry we are not open yet" clearly hoping the two intruders would leave. Skelton and Alexander both pulled out their warrant cards, so that the barman could see that they were police officers. Skelton then produced Linda's photograph and asked the barman if he had been working the previous night. The barman rested both arms on the bar. "Yes, I was working last night but it was pretty dead. Monday nights are never particularly busy unless it's Fresher's week." Skelton turned the photo for the barman to see. "Did this girl come in last night?" The barman took the photo and closely studied it for several seconds. "No, I don't recognise her at all. She's a good looking girl though. Is she in some sort of trouble?" Alexander spoke "She's not in trouble with the police but she went missing last night after getting off the bus outside Lambrettas. We need to view your outside CCTV for last night to see if she came past here." The barman was already coming around to the other side of the bar. "It's in the office, if you come with me, I will show you."

The barman was very helpful and clearly very proficient with a computer, unlike Skelton. They closely looked at the film starting at 22.00 and going right through to 3am. There was no evidence that Linda had walked past the night club. The camera filmed the street outside to monitor customers waiting to be let in. There had not been a lot of customers the previous night and there was not very much foot-traffic, either. Alexander looked to Skelton and said, "They must have gone the other way or crossed the road so that's why we aren't seeing them on this." Skelton was becoming frustrated by the lack of progress to date and was just hoping that his other detectives were having better luck. Skelton took the CD from the barman and added it to the other two that he had taken from Lambrettas.

As they emerged back on the street, Skelton received a text saying that the search of the river had concluded with nothing having been found. That was a slight relief to the enquiry as at least no dead body had yet turned up. They were now heading to a restaurant a few doors to the other side of Lambrettas called Sotto Sotto. They emerged forty minutes later with a fourth CCTV CD. Once again, the outside camera gave excellent viewing of pedestrians and passing vehicles. The only problem was that Linda had not come that way either. Skelton and Alexander walked back in silence to the station. The whole team were now back in the CID office. Each officer, in turn, announced that no one in all the bars and clubs could remember seeing Linda last night and the dozens of CCTV viewings showed that she had not entered any of the establishments.

Skelton sat on Turnbull's desk. He cleared his throat and put up his right hand for silence. "Right, we now know that after she got off the bus one of three things must have happened. She may have been picked up in a car and we need to trace the drivers of every car that drove up or down North Parade last night. The CCTV that Bill and I collected tonight gives us some of that information for traffic travelling along North Parade. There are CCTV cameras at the other end of North Parade which cover the Magistrate's court. We need to recover those in the morning and trace those drivers also. The cameras will tell us if she crossed the road when she got off the bus and walked in that direction. If she emerges on those with Tommy, we can hopefully make better progress. The last possibility is that she went into one of those flats to the left of the hotel. I think there are three separate entrances. Each doorway leads to two flats on three floors. So, we need to go banging on just eighteen flats. I looked as we came back to the station to see if I could see any cameras but there was nothing. If we go around now, we can check with the residents if they saw Linda last night. The thing is, there is a real possibility that she is being held there against her will. So make sure you get entry to the flats and do it in pairs. I want every flat carefully searched. Bill get us six uniform to come with us. Let's go now." Alexander stood up and as he was doing so said, "Hang on a minute sir, those flats probably have cellars as well. We need to search them too." Skelton put his hands in his pockets and said "Yes, I was wondering who would be the first to spot that! He gave Alexander a playful punch on the arm and both men smiled.

Chapter Fourteen

Tommy's father opened the door to the ground floor flat which was only meters from where Linda had got off the bus. As he opened the door he turned around and smiled. "I forgot to tell you my name out there. I am John and don't worry, Tommy should be along in a few minutes." Linda returned the smile and she noticed that the flat consisted of a sitting room, a kitchen and although the other door was closed, she assumed it was Tommy's bedroom. The door to the bathroom was open. Having consumed half a bottle of wine, Linda needed to use the toilet right away. "Can I use the bathroom, please John?" John was closing the door "Yes of course, go away in. I will pour us a glass of white wine for us to enjoy whilst we wait for Tommy to get back."

Linda placed her handbag on the coffee table and went into the bathroom, switching the light on before closing the door, and bolting it locked. John went straight to the handbag and could see the mobile phone sitting in a pouch. He picked it up and switched the phone off and put it in his trouser pocket. He could feel the Viagra which he had taken about twenty minutes earlier, was already working its magic. In the kitchen he already had the wine glasses ready. He could see the pill in the glass that he had prepared for Linda. The drug would work very quickly, and Linda would soon be his. Opening the refrigerator door, he picked out the bottle of white wine and unscrewed the cap. He poured two generous measures and put the bottle back in its place and closed the door. Picking up a spoon, he gently stirred the girl's drink making sure that the pill had fully dissolved. He walked back into the sitting room and held out the glasses as he heard Linda unbolt the door.

Whilst in the bathroom, she had been thinking that Tommy must have a well-paid job if he could afford such a lovely apartment right in the heart of the city. Leaving the bathroom, she walked into the sitting room to see John holding two glasses of wine. "Here you go Linda and good news. Tommy just texted to say that he is parking the van and will be here in about ten minutes".

Linda took the proffered glass of wine and smiling she said "That's great, I can't wait to meet him. Cheers." They clinked glasses, and both took a mouthful of wine. "Sit down on the sofa Linda, Tommy can sit next to you when he gets in. I will sit on the chair." Linda did as she was told. The sofa had a cover over it, probably to hide wear and tear she thought. John, having sat down, smiled across at her again. "Tommy tells me you are studying to be a teacher, is that right?" Linda suddenly felt quite hot and clammy. "Yes, that's right. I only started last September but I am really enjoying it. Do you mind if I take my coat off, I am feeling quite warm, it must be the wine?" John knew full well that it was not actually the wine that was causing her to feel warm but the drug he had put into it. "Yes, by all means take off your coat, let me hang it up for you." Both Linda and John stood up and John walked across to take the coat. He hung it on the door and Linda sat back down.

John sat down and lifted his glass, "Cheers again Linda, I hope you and Tommy make a great couple." Linda raised her glass and took some more wine. A few seconds later the room began to spin. She had to close her eyes to try and stop the spinning and her last conscious thoughts were that she had drunk too much wine. Suddenly she slumped back on the sofa and slid onto the armrest completely unconscious. John looked at her, and the erection in his pants got even harder. John took another sip of wine, stood up, opened the bedroom door and switched on the light. The lights had to be switched on most of the time, day and night as the windows were covered with heavy wooden shutters to help keep out the noise from the traffic and from drunken students boarding the late-night buses back to the university campus.

The King-size bed was covered with a white sheet. There were also white sheets covering the entire floor. The man walked back to the sofa and gently lifted the little girl who hardly weighed six stones. He carefully carried her into the bedroom and placed her on the bed. He then stripped her naked and removed his own clothes. The man then selected a condom and pulled it on his rather large penis. The Viagra plus the sight of the young girl's naked flesh made him extremely horny. Now the fun would begin.

After his first penetration of her, he noticed the slight trickle of blood between her legs. As he thought she had been a virgin and numerous more times that night he ravished her and thrusted his manhood inside her until he was drained. The poor girl was unconscious throughout this ordeal, completely unaware of what this evil monster was doing to her. After his last exertion inside her, he got off and noticed the blood and other bodily fluids that had leaked from the girl on to the bed sheet. The plastic sheets below would prevent the fluids from seeping into the mattress. He looked at the discarded condoms which he had used to defile her and counted seven. One more, than he had used on the first girl to meet the same fate as Linda.

The man got off the bed and went to the bathroom and relieved himself. He walked back to the bedroom and checked that the girl was still breathing. She was. He opened the polythene bag containing the new boilersuit that he had bought a few weeks earlier. He put on the boilersuit and very carefully, he washed the prone girl with a sponge and then very delicately he dried her with a white towel. He took great care to dry her private areas. He could see that she had started to swell there from the trauma that he had inflicted on her.

Next, he dressed her, making sure that he put the knickers back on the correct way around. When he had finished, the girl looked as though she had simply fallen asleep. There was nothing about her appearance to suggest otherwise. It was now 4.30am and it would be getting light outside in about an hour. He was entering the most dangerous part of the operation, but he was a cunning rascal as he often acknowledged to himself, in his own private wicked thoughts. He was relishing the challenge ahead of him.

He took Linda's coat off the door and walked back to the bedroom, where he carefully slipped it back on and made sure he buttoned it up correctly. He was now satisfied that she was good to go. Now he needed to deal with the clothes he had been wearing when he met the girl. He picked them up from the floor where he had dropped them and took them into the kitchen, where the washing machine was located. He put his clothes in the machine. He added the towel which he had used to dry the girl. Next, he put in the washing

93

powder, selected the programme and pressed the start switch. The machine started to fill with water and the man gave a satisfied nod. He had set the washing machine on the boil wash, which would destroy any DNA evidence.

He lifted the girl off the bed and placed her on the sheet on the floor. He carefully wrapped her in the sheet making sure that her mouth and nose were not covered, as it was vital that she was still breathing when she went into the water. From under the bed, he pulled a large sheet of strong cardboard. The beauty of this, was that it was folded and being almost two meters long and a meter wide, it would ensure that the girl could not be seen, and the thick cardboard would give her body protection, whilst being transported.

The man unfolded the cardboard and laid it next to the girl. He then gently laid the still prone body on the cardboard and folded the other half over her body. Next, he took the soiled sheets off the bed and folded them carefully. These he placed on top of the cardboard. He closely inspected the room and noticed the girl's handbag. Picking it up, he slid it inside the cardboard. He then stripped the plastic sheet from the bed which had prevented any bodily fluids from reaching the mattress.

The man carefully gathered all the contaminated sheets from the bed and floor and folded them in a neat pile next to the girl. He took out a small metal tin box from a drawer and placed the used condoms inside it. He laid the box on top of the pile of sheets.

Satisfied that he had removed any possible DNA from Linda, he took off the boilersuit and added it to the pile of sheets. He went into the bathroom and took a long hot shower, thereby removing any of Linda's DNA from his body. When he had dried himself with a towel, he took a bottle of bleach and emptied half the contents over the shower plinth and down the drain, thereby ensuring any possible surviving DNA was destroyed. He did the same with the sink, in case Linda had washed her hands. He removed the hand towel and placed it on top of the sheets. He then took the wine glasses into the kitchen and very carefully washed them and left them to dry on the draining board. He opened the refrigerator door and took out the bottle that contained the pills that he had added to the girl's drink. He placed these on top of the soiled sheets.

Back in the bedroom, he took out his work clothes from the wardrobe and quickly dressed. He stared in the mirror and satisfied with his appearance took out the high visibility vest and put it on. On the back of the vest were the words "Keeping Bath Tidy." Rather than making him highly visible, he knew that no one would pay him the slightest bit of attention as he and his battery powered cart made their way through Bath that morning. He was just the man who emptied the bins and picked up litter. A Mister Nobody, and he would not even attract a modicum of interest and more importantly, suspicion. He and the girl would be almost invisible to the eyes of the early morning commuters. Finally, he picked up his baseball cap and put it on. With its long peak, his face was very difficult to see.

The man had only brought the rubbish cart home once before and left it by the entrance to the flat. He secured it to the iron railings with a padlock and chain. None of the other residents had complained as they all seemed to live such busy lives. Like many flat dwellers in our cities, they barely spoke to one another. And besides any resident entering or leaving the building would just assume that its operator had left it there temporarily.

Unlocking the door, he looked out into the hallway, but nobody was about. He wedged the door open and went to the front door of the building and looked through the spy glass. Nobody outside either, he opened the door and wedged it open too. He walked down the step and opened the wire mesh gate on the rubbish cart. Glancing left and right all he could see were a couple of early morning delivery vans with their drivers scurrying in haste, to make their deliveries and be on their way, as soon as possible.

 The man bent down and easily lifted the brown cardboard package and effortlessly carried it out and placed it gently in the cart. He returned to the flat and removed the loose cover from the sofa. It might contain the girl's DNA. He took it outside and put it in the cart that now contained the body of Linda. However, she was still very much alive but unconscious. He then retrieved the soiled sheets, the bottle containing the remains of the drug and the tin containing the used condoms. These items were all carefully placed in the rubbish cart. He closed the mesh grill on the cart, to prevent anything from falling out, and went back inside. He gave the flat a final inspection, turned off the lights and closed and locked both doors.

Chapter Fifteen

The man walked in front of his cart as the small electric motor hummed. It was gone 4.45am and it was slowly getting light. It was a lovely fresh morning. The weather forecast predicted a high of 21 degrees and for mid-May that was a very acceptable temperature. He turned left on leaving the flat and first left again on to Manvers Street. He stopped occasionally to pick up litter which he placed in the black bag on the back of the cart. As he proceeded along the street, he passed the police station and saw that the car park contained several police cars. No doubt the night shift would be handing over to the day shift at 6am. The litter man was nervous, but he was not showing it. He stopped in front of the police station and picked up an empty beer bottle and placed it in the black bag. He made his way along the street, until he came to the Royal Hotel which is situated opposite the railway station. He crossed the road and veered right which would take him past the bus station. Apart from a few cars with early morning workers inside, he never saw a soul. As he arrived at the bus entrance to the station, he followed the road around to the left which brought him onto the Lower Bristol Road. Turning left again took him onto Poultney Street. He made his way along, occasionally picking up a piece of litter. Not one passing motorist paid him the slightest bit of attention. His camouflage was perfect! The route he was now taking, was bringing him past the rear of the bus station and it would lead him past the rear entrance of the train station, which could only be accessed by a narrow pedestrian bridge. This is called Churchill Bridge and it crossed the River Avon. This section of the Avon is the most dangerous, having been deeply dredged and channelled during massive flood defence works in the 1960's.

A couple of minutes later he turned left onto an uneven track that led down to the river. This was undeveloped piece of land, forming an ancient public right- of- way access to the river. Owing to this right-of-way, it was impossible for developers to build on this site. It was not quite light, so he had to be careful where he walked in case he stumbled and fell. Soon, he was under the foot bridge that crossed the river from the train station. He had hardly seen a soul except for the couple of van drivers that had been making deliveries as he was about to leave the flat. This suited him perfectly. He stopped the cart next to a small landing stage and opened the wire mesh gate. He took off the bed sheets and put them aside. Then he lifted the cardboard containing the girl and gently placed it on the ground. He looked around but saw nobody. He gingerly unfolded the cardboard and put his ear near the girl's mouth and listened. She was still breathing. Bending down, he carefully unwrapped her from the sheet, but not completely. He needed the sheet to protect him from coming into contact, with Linda's clothes. He took a cloth from his pocket and wiped the girl's handbag removing his fingerprints. He threw the handbag in the fast-flowing current and it quickly floated away, no doubt sinking, when the water penetrated the inside or perhaps it would be caught up in vegetation along the riverbank.

The girl now looked exactly as she had done lying on his bed. She was unconscious and once she entered the water, she would drown very quickly. He once again picked her up with the sheet and carried her to the edge of the river. He turned her upright, as if she was about to walk into the river and let her fall, face down. The river immediately claimed her. She was carried away by the fast-flowing current and very quickly she sank from sight. Being unconscious when entering the water, she was unable to make any attempt to save herself. Mercifully, she died very quickly from drowning. The litter man carefully replaced the cardboard and sheets back in the cart and started to retrace his steps.

There was very little traffic on the road and besides it was unlikely that a tired early morning driver would pay any attention to a litter man at that time of the morning. He needed to cross the road to the car park opposite. There was a cross-over for people with wheelchairs at this point, so it was easy to run the electric cart down this and across the road into the entrance to the tiny car park which could only take about a dozen cars.

He veered to the right, keeping close to the row of garages and at the end of the row he stopped. He noticed that he had not triggered any security lights as he had made his way to the garage. He carefully looked around the area and up towards the windows of the flats on Widcombe Parade. Apart from a bathroom light showing to his far right, the entire building was in darkness. The only light showing came from an external light above the rear exit of the pub. He carefully took out his key, unlocked the door and opened it upwards. He then manoeuvred the electric cart inside and closed the door. In the pitch darkness, he had to feel along the wall for the light switch, and on finding it, switched on the two fluorescent tubes.

There were no windows in the garage, so no light could escape except from a tiny gap at the bottom of the door. On the left hand side, he had made a flat work top on which now rested his laptop computer for which he had paid cash. He had been able to access the pub's WIFI, so that cost him nothing. He did not subscribe to any broadband service, so any police enquiries would lead to nothing. There was also a phone charger, but the Nokia phone that he had used to text the girl with, would never be used again. He would destroy it and buy another which of course would be unregistered.

He had inherited a plastic chair from the owner of the garage, and this he used when using his laptop. The only other item in the garage was a CO2 fire extinguisher which was mounted on the right hand side wall.

 Under the worktop opposite, the litter man had stacked some items of bed clothing which were neatly folded and took up little room. Next to these, lay some of his clothes which again were neatly folded and stacked. These had all been used when he had lured Marion Busby to his flat, where he had drugged her and raped her. She too had gone into the river and the police had concluded her death to have been an accidental drowning!

The litter man opened the metal gate on the cart and carefully removed the cardboard and placed it on the blank worktop. Next came the bed sheets that he had removed from his bed as well as the sheets he had spread across the floor of his bedroom. These he carefully folded and made them into a separate pile to the ones already under the worktop. He then removed the tin containing the used condoms and placed it in a drawer that already contained a similar tin. He folded the plastic sheet and stowed it neatly under the worktop. Lastly, he took the cover from the sofa and stacked it neatly away.

Now, he took the boilersuit which he had put on when he had started cleaning up the apartment.

This he also neatly folded and placed it on top of the plastic sheet. Anyone entering the garage would regard it as nothing more than an everyday garage. Perfect!

Chapter Sixteen

The police officers converged in the incident room. From now on this would be the nerve centre of the investigation. It was equipped with computer terminals that would cross reference via the main frame every piece of information input by the detectives. Skelton had been informed that a plea for help in finding Linda would be broadcast on the BBC Points West news at 10.30pm, as well as going out on the other local channel slightly later. He was still very concerned that appeals on Facebook by friends and family had produced no sightings or leads. It was now almost 8pm and the officers were about to go and knock up the residents of the three buildings, housing the flats. There was a mixture of detectives and uniformed officers to help with the search. Skelton went over to where Alexander was standing and placed his hand on his shoulder. "Bill, why don't you hold the fort for a bit? I'd like you to check out all the convicted or suspected sex offenders on our books. Get Dave Lake to help you, he knows every

offender in Bath and most of Somerset."
Alexander nodded his head and said, "Yes of
course sir, consider it done." Skelton took his hand
from Alexander's shoulder and then said "Another
thing to do is to check the voter's roll for those
flats and see who is living there. Run the names
through all our systems, we might get lucky and
find a suspect there. Depending on what we
discover when we carry out our door-to-door
enquiries soon, if nothing comes up, we can all go
home and start again in the morning."

As the officers were filling out of the station,
Skelton noticed the young rookie, Meehan. "Hello
Luke, how are you getting on then?" Meehan
smiled and said "It's been quite a busy day sir. I
helped search the riverbank in case the girl had
gone into the river. It was quite time consuming
and tiring, but we found nothing." They had now
almost reached North Parade. Skelton walked
abreast of Meehan and said "Yes, we are not
hopeful on this one and if we find nothing here,
we all go home and get some sleep. Luke, I've left
the DS back at the nick, why don't you shadow me
when we do the house-to-house or in this case
flat-to-flat enquiries?" Meehan gave Skelton a big
smile and said "That would be marvellous sir. I'll
try not to mess up." Skelton gave Meehan a

playful punch on the arm and said, "You will be fine, I'm sure."

The officers had sorted themselves into three groups, they would knock on the doors of all the flats and interview the occupants and search for the missing girl. It would be unlikely for all the residents to be home, so it might require more than one visit that evening. Skelton led the team to the building nearest the hotel and he pressed the intercom buzzers on several flats before he got a response. One resident had simply released the automatic door lock without even asking who wanted in.

"Right fan out and pick a flat, Meehan and I will take this door to the right. Get to it and be thorough." Skelton banged on the ground floor flat, and a minute later the door was opened by a heavy-set man in his fifties. He was about 5"10 tall, with a bit of a beer belly. His grey hair was thinning on top but he had bright blue eyes. He had an intelligent face and Skelton guessed he was semi-professional. The man was in a short sleeve shirt, wearing blue jeans and trainers. The sight of Meehan's uniform indicated that this was not a social call.

Skelton held out his warrant card for the man to see. "I am Detective Chief Inspector Skelton, and this is Constable Meehan." Meehan flushed slightly that he had got his name mentioned. "I am sorry to disturb you sir, but a girl went missing last night after getting off the bus outside Lambrettas. We are very concerned for her safety. May we come in and have a word with you?" The man looked at the officers sternly and said "Yes, you had better come in, I will help in any way I can." He opened the door further and motioned for them to come in. Edwards had not been expecting the police to have called so early after the girl had been reported missing. After all, they hadn't even bothered to call round when the last girl disappeared!

Skelton scanned the room. It was very clean and tidy. There was a sofa that looked new, it did not have a cover on it. There were two armchairs which matched the sofa and a coffee table. He looked through to the kitchen. It too was clean and tidy. There was a clothes pulley on the kitchen ceiling and some laundry hung upon it. He noticed that the windows had heavy wooden shutters which were likely to shield all day light, from coming in. The bathroom door was open, but the bedroom door was closed. There was a television mounted on the wall and a well-stocked bookcase. The man invited the officers to take a seat and they sat down on the sofa.

Skelton had removed his notebook from his pocket and was holding it ready to record the information he needed from the gentleman. "If you don't mind sir, we will go through a few formalities first please?" The man nodded his head and said, "Sure, fire ahead." "What is your full name and address please?" The man sensed that it would be best to be compliant rather than ask questions. He walked over to the nearest armchair and sat down heavily. "My name is Norman Edwards, and this is flat 2, 46 North Parade." Skelton noted this and then asked "How old are you and what's your date of birth? The man thought and decided there was no harm in saying. "I am fifty-two and my date of birth is the first of March 1964." Skelton then asked, "And what do you do for a living Mr Edwards?" Edwards stretched out and said "I work for the council, nothing very exciting. I work for street cleaning on the clerical side of things. Like admin, ordering supplies, and stuff like that." So, Skelton was wrong on the man's occupation. Skelton glanced at the bookcase again and wondered if the man had for some reason changed jobs. Lots of people give up good jobs owing to stress which Skelton's partner could well testify to. He would refrain from questioning him further about his job for now.

"And were you at home last night around 10.20?" Edwards replied straight away. "Yes, I did my usual thing, I got back from work about ten past six and had a wash. Then I took a curry out the freezer and stuck it in the microwave. I had the curry and washed-up then I sat and watched the telly. After the local news was finished, I went to bed." Skelton noted this and then asked, "Did you happen to look out the window around 10.20pm or did you hear anything unusual?" "No, I never look out the bloody window, those damn wooden shutters are a nightmare to open and close. And I don't recall hearing anything unusual last night. Although some nights it's bloody hard to sleep when the students are waiting outside for the bus home. They get pissed so easy these days and laugh and shout their heads off. I think that's why someone installed those shutters, to help keep the noise out."

Skelton looked directly into Edward's eyes and said, "We are very concerned for the missing girl. We need to discover what has happened to her. That's why we are checking all the flats in this and the neighbouring buildings. Are you sure you know nothing about her disappearance?" Skelton waited for the reaction and wanted to gauge the man's body language. The man stood up abruptly, with his arms folded across his chest and said, "What

109

fucking right have you got marching in here accusing me of harming this bloody missing student?" Skelton squared up to Edwards. "Sit down Mr Edwards, now." There was no mistaking Skelton's command. It was clear, firm and extremely authoritative. Edwards sat back down. "Mr Edwards, I did not allege that you harmed the missing girl, nor did I mention that she is a student. How come you know that she is a student?" Edwards had lost some of the appearance of being self-righteous! Now he was on the back foot and Skelton sensed it.

Edwards crossed his legs and leaned forward in his chair. "Well, you said she was young, so I just assumed she must be a student that's all. I mean that bus stop outside is used by thousands of students, so I put two and two together." Skelton walked across the room, looking closer at the bookcase and the books that it held. "Mr Edwards, have you ever been in trouble with the police? And before you answer that, I will check that for myself" Edwards thought for a second before replying. "I once did get into a fight years ago. I got done for GBH and got fined with a suspended sentence. Since then, nothing." Skelton again recorded this information. "Are you married Mr Edwards, or have a partner living here?" Edwards shifted uneasily in the chair before saying. "I was married but it didn't last. Me and the wife couldn't get on, so we divorced. There were no kids, so we made a clean break."

"Alright Mr Edwards, one last thing. Do you mind if we have a look around the flat before we go?" Skelton saw the glimmer of relief on the man's face that he and Meehan would soon be out of his hair. "No, I don't mind at all, go right ahead and look wherever you want."

Skelton and Meehan had a good look around, but Skelton sensed that if she had been here, she no longer was. His problem for the present was that he had no grounds for arresting Edwards and carrying out a forensic search of the property. As they were leaving the flat, Skelton turned around to Edwards and said, "You don't appear to own a computer sir, is that right?" Edwards was a little startled by the question but looked straight into Skelton's eyes and said "Yes that's right I don't own a computer, you see I'm not into them. I get enough emails at work and I like my privacy, so I don't do that Facebook shit." Skelton himself did not subscribe to Facebook and he could well understand Edwards's frustration with emails, as he spent hours every day answering them.

"You do have a mobile phone, I take it?" asked Skelton. The man produced his mobile from his trouser pocket. It was a basic Nokia. It could make and receive phone calls and send and receive texts. It could not receive or send emails, nor could it connect to WIFI. Skelton tried to disguise his disappointment. If Edwards did not have a computer nor a phone that could connect to the internet, he could not possibly be Tommy. "What's your number in case we need to be in touch again?" Edwards gave Skelton his number and Skelton noted bitterly that it was not the number that Linda had texted. Skelton pulled out his own phone and tapped in the number that Edwards had just given. The phone in Edwards' hand began ringing. It was definitely his number! "One last question Mr Edwards, do you own a motor vehicle?" Edwards shook his head, "No I don't have a car, I don't really need one, living and working in the city. I can walk to the supermarkets to get my shopping plus the bus service is good if I need to go anywhere and the train station is only a five-minute walk. Besides, parking in Bath is a nightmare!

Back at the incident room, it soon became clear that the flat-to-flat enquiries had revealed not a single clue. All the residents, except for a girl who was away on holiday had been questioned and no one had seen Linda or Tommy. They had heard nothing unusual at the relevant time and searches of the flats and basements hadn't turned up anything. Even the flat of the girl on holiday had been searched, as a neighbour had a spare key.

Now the team sat back and watched the appeal for help on the news. The photograph of Linda filled the television screen. They used a photograph of Linda as she was leaving the bus. The quality was good, and it clearly showed the clothes that she had been wearing. The news announcer explained that Linda had taken the bus from campus and had arranged to meet Tommy for a drink. She was seen getting off the bus at Lambrettas. The camera then switched to Superintendent Paul Williams, who was in uniform. The announcer said, "Superintendent Williams how can the public help you to find Linda?" Williams cleared his throat. "We are very concerned for Linda's welfare and it's vital that the public help us to find her. Since she got off the bus at around 10.20pm last night there have been no sightings of her on CCTV. She has not answered her phone which was switched off soon after she left the bus. According to her flatmate she was meeting a young man called Tommy. I would urge Tommy to get in touch with us immediately on the number appearing on the screen now. If Linda can hear this appeal, I would beg her to contact us right away or if she prefers, her mum or dad.

Linda, you have done nothing wrong and you are not in any trouble, but your parents and little sister are desperately worried about you. I would also ask the public if they have seen Linda at any time after she got off the bus to call us now. My officers are waiting to answer your calls."

Almost immediately, the phones started to ring, and Skelton hovered over the desks of his officers as they took the calls. After about half an hour the calls dried up. It was a mixed bag of results. Some of the girls who had been on the bus with Linda called to say just that. None of them remembered seeing anyone at the bus stop except for a man who was aged about fifty or sixty who had been standing just outside the hotel. None of the girls could give a better description and they all said that the man appeared to be waiting for his wife to come out. Skelton would delegate an officer in the morning to visit the girls to see if they could give a better description of the man. Skelton recalled that when he reviewed the CCTV from the hotel, there were a few guests entering and leaving. It was probably one of them, but the footage would be checked again to ensure that those guests entered or left when the girls were getting off the bus. There were the usual crank calls from nutters claiming they were holding Linda or had murdered her. These calls were soon acted upon and proved to be a waste of valuable police time.

Suddenly, Bob Laws entered the room carrying a laptop. It was Linda's and Skelton had passed it over for forensic examination. Laws was one of the computer experts and in little less than four hours, he had dissected the laptop searching for clues. "Sir, I've been right through this." He had Skelton's full attention. "She uses it for her course work, for sending and receiving emails and Face Book. She has a few other apps but nothing of any interest. She is not registered to any dating apps whatsoever on here. I've also been checking all her recent emails including those that she had deleted. There is no mention of this boyfriend called Tommy nor for that matter any other romantic attachment. It's mostly emails to her mum and dad, her sister and friends, telling them how much she is enjoying university."

Skelton clasped his hands behind his neck and gave a huge sigh. "For fuck's sake Bob, I was hoping that the laptop would provide the solution to this mystery, but it tells us nothing. If she didn't communicate with Tommy on her laptop, does that mean that the dating site she was using, along with Snapchat was on her phone?" Laws was standing motionless, one hand in his trouser pocket, the other clutching the laptop. "I'm afraid it does, sir. Without her phone to work on, there's nothing else I can do. I'm really sorry sir but unless we find her phone, there's no way of tracing Tommy or anyone else she chatted with on the dating site."

Skelton sent the day shift home as there was nothing more they could do. The night shift would be left to follow up any potential leads. It had been a long day and Skelton was tired. He arranged for a patrol car to take him home. He called Ken to say he would be home in ten minutes and Ken knew that the first thing his partner would appreciate was one of his Gin and Tonics. Ken was the master of making the quintessentially English drink and Skelton would rarely buy a G&T as few people could mix them to Ken's amazing standard.

Chapter Seventeen

As the kettle was boiling, Skelton was standing in his kitchen watching the morning news on the

BBC. They were showing a repeat of Superintendent Williams' plea for help from the public that had gone out the previous night. Skelton was not optimistic that it would lead to Tommy coming forward or Linda phoning in to say that she had got drunk and was fine. As he poured boiling water over the tea bag in his mug, his thoughts returned to the conversation that he and Meehan had with Edwards. He recalled the defensive body language that Edwards had displayed, which suggested that either he was innocent of any involvement in Linda's disappearance, or that he was trying to hide his guilt. Unless a pressing need surfaced this morning for him to pursue, he would be looking more closely into Edwards, particularly his education and employment history. He would also check on his criminal record in case he had convictions for more than just grievous bodily harm.

Once he was dressed in one of his many magnificently tailored suits, which invariably attracted a great deal of admiration from both men and woman, Skelton left the house and began his morning walk to work. Skelton adored walking and used it both to keep fit and to think. However, there was one place where Skelton did his best thinking and that was under a hot shower. There had been many occasions when he had hit a brick wall in an investigation and he had simply got into the shower and thought things through. He did not quite understand why a hot shower helped him think, but he knew it worked. At this stage of the investigation into Linda's disappearance, he had so few clues to go on, that he simply showered that morning to get clean!

It was another sunny morning and had it not been for the fact that he was worried about the fate of young Linda, he would have been smiling. But Skelton knew that at some stage this would become a murder investigation and that the specially trained family liaison officers were going to have to break the news to her family. As he walked towards the bus station, he had to cross the footbridge over the river Avon. Halfway across, he stopped and peered into the river. Although it was May and the weather was warm and sunny, April had been horrible. It had rained continually most days and so the river was still virtually full. As he stared into the water, he thought "My God, if I fell into that now, I would have no chance." The water was racing past him and bits and pieces of trees and other debris flew past, as the current carried them away at a terrifying speed. Skelton shook his head and walked on.

Skelton went straight to the incident room for an up-date but did not expect much as no one had contacted him to indicate any progress. As expected, the news was as it had been the previous night, no interesting leads. He then went to his office and checked his emails and replied to those that warranted immediate attention. None of them were beneficial in terms of finding Linda. Having finished e-mailing, he went into the CID office. Only Alexander was there, the others were either in the incident room or out on enquiries.

"Morning Bill, how's it going?" Alexander was studying his computer screen and had not noticed the DCI come into the room. Looking up, he saw the DCI giving him a quizzical look. "Morning sir, I've got fuck all to go on! This case is a nightmare not just for that wee girl's family and friends but for us an all. She has just vanished into thin air. I was actually just about to check for any reports of flying saucers the other night." Alexander leaned heavily back in the chair, hands clasped behind his neck and let out a great big sigh. Skelton realised that if Alexander was showing signs of dismay this could have a negative impact on the team's moral. He Skelton, as team leader, needed to motivate his troops.

"Come on Bill, we need to be positive here. It's only day two of the enquiry and nothing has been found to indicate that any serious harm has come to her. We've all had missing person experiences when someone has vanished, and we have thought the worst only for that person to turn up, days, weeks or even months later unharmed." Skelton realised that he was saying this not just for Alexander's benefit but for his own as well. Alexander was keeping the same position in the chair and was looking intently as the DCI went on "Bill, you and I investigate crime and we are both pretty good at that. Now, there is no proof that a crime has been committed. We have several different scenarios that might occur. Linda turns up safe and well, which would be the best result for all concerned. She might have somehow, bearing in mind that she had consumed half a bottle of wine, fallen into the river and drowned. This as you know as well as me, is the most likely scenario but so far, we don't have a body. Or perhaps she got into a car after getting off the bus. Maybe this guy Tommy is holding her or has killed her. Whichever is the outcome Bill, we need to be focused and professional. If we start letting our shoulders drop, moral is fucked."

Alexander stood up, "Aye your right sir, there are a lot of lines of enquiry for us to make so we best get on with them. How about a bacon roll and a nice cup of tea?" Skelton held his hand up and made a high five with Alexander. Both men smiled. "Now you're talking Bill, lead the way."

The two men were sitting in Skelton's office eating their bacon rolls and drinking tea. Alexander had two rolls whilst Skelton had just the one but supplemented that with a KitKat. "Bill, I want us to concentrate on a few specific lines today. We need to go down to the Magistrate's Court and check out their CCTV in case Linda crossed the road and turned right. It's possible that the camera at Soto Soto was obscured when she and maybe Tommy walked past, by a vehicle. Something like a van or a lorry, and anyone on the opposite side of the street would be invisible. From Soto Soto there are no other CCTV cameras until you get to the court. Bath cricket club entrance is opposite the Court, but I think their CCTV only covers the car park itself and the club house. On the off chance that later she crossed the road back to the same side as she got off the bus, then as far as I can tell, the next possible place that there are any CCTV cameras is just after she would turn right into Poultney Road. The first building there is the Co-operative undertakers and I'm not sure that they would have any CCTV. However, you can never be sure that a crackhead might not try and break-into an undertaker. I will call in there and

check it out. That leaves the Royal Oak. While you check the CCTV at the Court, I will do the Oak." Alexander shook his head. "How come you get the pub and I get the Court?" "Simple Bill, I outrank you but since it's you, when you're wrapped up at the Court, come and join me in the Oak." Alexander's face lit up.

"After we have done that, I want us to consider a character called Norman Edwards who lives in a flat right by the bus stop. Alexander looked at Skelton, "I checked him out last night whilst you were doing the flat to flats. I checked the voter's register to see who lived in those flats and then I ran the names through the PNC." PNC is short for the Police National Computer which holds the criminal records for anyone convicted of a crime in the UK. It also holds intelligence information on criminals or those suspected of criminal activity. Alexander continued. "Edwards has one conviction for GBH seven years ago, apart from that, he is not on our radar for anything." Skelton lifted his finger and tapped his nose "Maybe he's a stealth bomber Bill, and our radar has never seen him!"

Whilst Skelton and Alexander were concentrating on the CCTV coverage of North Parade, other officers were concentrating on Bog Island and Manvers Street. The girl would have to appear on someone's CCTV footage. She could not have vanished that was for sure!

Jim Broadbent knocked on the door and entered Skelton's office. Alexander and Skelton looked up as Broadbent walked in carrying a sheet of A4 paper. "Sir, the phone company just sent me details of that phone that Linda texted when she got on the bus. The last signal that the phone made came from somewhere between the Abbey and Northbridge Gardens. It was switched off at 10.15pm that night and has not been switched on again since then." Alexander said what Broadbent and Skelton were both thinking. "Shit! Whoever has that phone knows that if he switches it on, we will know where to find him. My hunch is that the bastard won't be switching it on again. He's probably chucked it in the river already."

Chapter Eighteen

It was 11am when Skelton and Alexander stepped out the door of the station into the bright sunlight. It was already about 19 degrees and it was going to be a warm day. Just as they left the station, the sound of the police helicopter made them look up. Fitted with thermal imaging cameras, the helicopter was searching the river and its banks for Linda's body. This was the first opportunity to use the helicopter to help with the search, as it had been grounded with a technical fault. If Linda's body was floating in the river, the helicopter had a good chance of finding her. However, if the body was trapped underwater, it would not be detectable by the helicopter's cameras. Sometimes the River Avon gave up a body minutes after it had gone in, when someone had witnessed the victim go in and was able to retrieve them. On the other hand, sometimes it was in no rush to give up its prey. Skelton knew full well that it might be days or weeks before Linda's body was retrieved and the longer it took, the more her body would decompose. If she had been killed, any forensic evidence, left by her killer, was likely to be lost.

It was hard to hear with the noise coming from the helicopter, so Skelton and Alexander walked down North Parade in silence. It was only when they reached the Magistrate's Court that Alexander said, "Right sir, I will go and see what I can find on CCTV and meet you in the Oak" "Yes, see you later Bill." Skelton crossed the road and stood at the

124

entrance to the cricket club. A man in a high visibility vest was directing traffic into the car park. Skelton produced his warrant card. "Excuse me but does your CCTV cover this footpath or the road?" The man looked at the warrant card and said, "No the cameras only cover the car park and the club house. Sorry."

Skelton continued down the road and turned right walking under the railway bridge. On his right, he could see the Co-operative Funeral Home and a grey Private Ambulance was just turning into the car park. Skelton had noticed that just about every time he passed the place, the grey van was either driving in or was parked on the loading bay, where another cadaver was being unloaded. It was clearly a busy funeral home and as he drew level with the double gates, he could see a hearse being loaded with a coffin. He walked on and climbed the stairs to the office. He could not see any cameras on the entrance and there were none on the carpark gates either.

He opened the door and went in. A middle-aged lady with white hair sat at a desk and was busy typing away on her computer. She looked up as she heard the door open and saw Skelton closing the door. "Good morning sir, how may I help you?" Skelton approached the desk and withdrew his warrant card. "Good morning to you, I am Detective Chief Inspector Skelton and I'm investigating the disappearance of a young girl on Monday night." The woman stood up and said, "Oh the girl that got off the bus?" Skelton nodded his head, "Yes that's the one. You see there has been no trace of her on any of the CCTV cameras that we have managed to check so far, and I was wondering if she might have come this way rather than gone into town. That's why I have come to ask if you have any cameras here?"

The lady pointed a finger to a point behind Skelton's head. "Well yes, we have a camera there in case someone breaks in. We also have one that covers the loading bay, the carpark and the garage but nothing at the front. It was what Skelton had expected. Having thanked the lady for her help, he left the office and turned right where he could see the Royal Oak about fifty meters away.

Most pubs in Bath open at 11am but there are one or two exceptions to this. This is primarily due to their location. Some pubs just don't get enough custom at lunchtime during the week to make it economically viable to open. So those pubs tended to only open at lunchtime during the weekend including Fridays. Skelton approached the pub and saw that it was closed. He peered through the window, the lights were off, and he could not see anyone. He did, however, hear some hammering coming from somewhere inside. He found a doorbell and pressed it. It produced a heavy ringing which he could easily hear outside.

A few minutes later a man appeared at the door. He made no attempt to open it, but simply shouted through the glass "We are closed." Skelton shouted back. "It's the police" and stuck his warrant card up to the glass so that the man could see it. The man started unlocking the door and Skelton stood back and pocketed his warrant card. Upon unlocking the door, the man stood aside as Skelton entered the bar. As soon as he was inside, the bar man closed the door and locked it. "Sorry we don't open at lunchtime on a Wednesday, it's only the weekend that we do lunchtimes." The man was in his early thirties, about five feet five, and sported a full beard. He was clearly doing some work as he was dressed in old jeans and a tee shirt that had been worn for painting.

"I'm sorry to disturb you sir, but I am Detective Chief Inspector Skelton and I am investigating the missing student from the university." The man looked at him and said "I saw that on the TV this morning. Have you not found her yet?" The man began walking around to the other side of the bar and Skelton waited until the man was facing him again. "No, we haven't found any trace of her so far, despite our best efforts. I was hoping you might be able to help us?" The man gave him a blank look. "Why do you think I could help you?" Skelton rested his arm on the bar and looked at the man. "I take it you are the landlord here?" The man nodded his head and picked up a cloth and started wiping the bar. "Yes, I'm Harry Blake, but I don't understand how I can help you."

Skelton shifted his weight. He pulled out Linda's photo and showed it to the landlord. "Did this girl come into the bar on Monday night?" The man looked straight into Skelton's face and said "Only if she broke in. We don't open on Monday nights." Skelton gave an inward sigh. He ran a hand through his hair and asked, "Do you have CCTV out the front?" The landlord continued cleaning the bar. He looked up again and said "We have CCTV running twenty-four hours covering the inside and the entrance and pavement. I take it you want to see it?"

Skelton and the landlord reviewed the CCTV covering Monday night from between 10pm and midnight. There were not a lot of people out on Monday night, that was for sure. An old man walking his dog. A middle-aged couple holding hands. Three male students who looked drunk and a postal worker heading for the nightshift. Skelton was hoping that Alexander was faring better at the Court. When they finished looking at the film, the Landlord said, "Sorry I can't be more helpful." Skelton gave him a wry smile and his phone indicated a new text message. It was from Alexander and it was short and to the point. "Not a bloody thing."

As the pub was closed, there was no point in Alexander joining him. So, he thanked the Landlord and left. As he walked towards the court he could see Alexander's bulk heading his way. As they met, Alexander gave him a quizzical look and said, "I thought we were meeting in the Oak?" Skelton took Alexander's arm and turned him around. "The Oak is shut Bill, let's go to the Ale House. We both deserve a pint and something to eat." Alexander shook his head "Jesus H Christ how can she have vanished like that?" Skelton had been pondering the same question over and over in his mind. "Tell you what, Paul at the Ale House is a magician maybe he knows how to make someone disappear." Both men smiled and walked up North Parade and as they came to the bridge over the River Avon, Skelton leaned over the parapet and looked down into the river. He thought to himself for a minute and then he put his arm over Alexander's shoulders. "Come on Bill, I think we both could use that pint"

They entered the Ale House just after one. There was only one table free. "Bill, you go and nab that table. What do you want to eat?" Alexander thought for a minute. It was not an extensive menu but what they did serve was good and reasonably priced. "Fish and chips for me." Paul the landlord was just finishing pouring drinks for two Japanese tourists. "Hi Dan, you alright?" Smiling at Skelton as he said so. Skelton returned the smile. "I've had better mornings Paul but that's life." Skelton liked Paul and his wife Sarah and their baby boy, Joshua. They and for that matter, the bar staff made him very welcome. Sean, a young and loud Aussie, was brilliant when the bar was busy. The minute he saw Skelton entering the bar, he would grab a Fosters glass and begin pouring Skelton's favourite lager.

Skelton ordered two pints and fish and chips for the two of them. As he set the glasses on the table, Alexander looked at the date on his watch. "It's not my birthday for another week!" It had become the custom at lunch for Skelton to have a Fosters and for Alexander to make do with a pint of soda water and lime. Skelton sat down against the wall so that he could see what was happening in the bar. "Well Bill, I figured you could do with a beer after such a shitty morning!" The detectives never discussed their work in the pub save to say whether it had been a good morning or otherwise. "We have a briefing at 14.30 when we get back, let's see what that brings.

Chapter Nineteen

They left the Ale House and walked across Bog Island and turned right onto Manvers Street and immediately saw the television van parked in the car park of the police station. The police now had the media on their side, as it was being realised that a young girl who had been missing for two days was unlikely to be found safe and well. Given the history of so many students falling into the river and drowning, the media wanted to be around when Linda was eventually found. The story of her disappearance on Monday night was now the headline story on the local TV and radio stations. The shocking fact that so many young healthy students had fallen into the river in recent years whilst out socialising and drowned, was bad news. Bad news always made headlines and the media wanted to know why Linda had not yet been found, and what were the police doing to find her?

In the incident room, Superintendent Williams was talking on his phone as Skelton and Alexander walked in. Williams saw them immediately and indicated to Skelton that he wanted a word. Williams finished the call and approached Skelton. "Let's have a quiet word in my office." Once in Williams's office, Skelton closed the door, neither man sat down.

Williams stood against the wall, hands in his pockets. He looked tired and drained. At 54 he was only a few years away from retiring and the years of stress in the job were taking their toll. His hair was white as was his moustache and his cheeks had a deep red glow, from the copious amounts of red wine that he had been consuming for years. But his piercing blue eyes still showed his intelligence and his ability to tackle most of the things he encountered in such a demanding role. "I don't get this at all. Since I've been in Bath, we have pulled eight students out of that bloody river plus of course numerous other corpses. With those poor students, we had them on CCTV at various locations in the city. We had them in bars, in night clubs, at the train and bus stations. We even had some of them on our own CCTV outside the station. Now we have this young lass, who is recorded by a camera on the bus that she took, getting off at Lambrettas and after that nothing. Not a single camera that we've checked so far shows her and not one confirmed sighting has been reported by the public. Facebook which in the past has produced some excellent leads has so far not coughed up a single clue. What's your take on this Dan?"

Skelton gathered his thoughts and said "She was somehow lifted as soon as she got off the bus. We are checking the number plates of every vehicle that drove down or up North Parade before and after she got off. Every driver will be interviewed. We are checking with every known sex offender and where they were, when she got off the bus. Many have ankle tags, so it will be relatively straightforward to eliminate most of them as suspects. But my money is on the likelihood that this guy Tommy had planned to abduct her, rape her and kill her. The fact that no one has seen her after getting off the bus leaves me to suspect that she ended up in one of the flats next to Lambrettas. As you know sir, we searched them last night, but she wasn't there. So, either she has been well hidden, or she has somehow been moved."

Williams ran his fingers through his moustache as he absorbed Skelton's thoughts on the case. "What's your plan?" he asked Skelton. "At the moment sir, there is only one resident in a flat right next to the bus stop that's of interest to me.

His name is Norman Edwards and he works for the council in street cleaning. Something to do with administration. But when we were in his flat, I noticed a bookshelf laden with books on chemistry, maths and physics which is not what your average council clerk reads. I think that in the past he was in a profession and either gave it up or was forced out. I am going to be looking into his past straight after this afternoon's briefing." Williams touched Skelton on the shoulder, "Okay Dan, keep me informed. Off you go."

Chapter Twenty

Skelton was sat at his desk with Alexander occupying one of the two chairs opposite. They were both drinking tea. "Right Bill, I want us to concentrate on this Norman Edwards. He tells me he works for the council as an administrator of some description. We need to get onto the council and find out all that we can about him but discreetly of course." Alexander put down his mug of tea and said "That's easy, my sister-in-law works for the council. She just happens to be in human resources and her office is just across the road" Alexander said smugly. Skelton's face lit up as he said "Right, lead the way Bill."

The detectives left the station and walked across the road, where the council had an office. At the reception desk, Alexander was greeted by one of the receptionists. The woman was in her early forties and rather plump. Sitting all day long at a reception desk, was not helping her to lose weight. She seemed like a very pleasant and friendly lady judging by the way she was treating Alexander. "Bill, how are you?" she asked, smiling broadly. "I'm fine thanks Cathy, how's you and the old man?" Cathy wiggled in her chair and said "We're just the same as ever. Have you come to see Jean?" "Yes, could you ask her to pop down, if you don't mind?"

A few minutes later Jean Scott was hugging Alexander and giving her brother-in-law a kiss. "Great to see you Bill and who is this handsome young man that you have brought with you?" Jean was quite a tall lady and obviously very friendly. She was smiling at Skelton waiting for the introduction. "Jean this is my new boss, DCI Dan Skelton." Skelton held out his hand and said, "Hello Jean, I'm delighted to meet you." They shook hands and Scott looked at Alexander and said, "I take it this is not a social call, Bill?" Alexander shook his head and said, "No Jean, can we have a word in your office?"

Jean Scott was head of Human Resources for the council and knew most of its employees but some better than others. They were seated around her desk. "Would you like some tea?" she asked. Skelton was keen to get on with the matter in hand and so declined the offer for both himself and Alexander. Skelton had told Alexander on the way over that he should conduct the meeting, as he was more likely to get more information out of his sister-in-law than him.

"Jean, we are making some enquiries of a delicate nature and we don't want to alert the subject that we are interested in him. So, can you keep this meeting a secret? Particularly, now that we have the television and press camped across the road." Scott shuffled in her chair and looked at her visitors earnestly and said in a conspiratal whisper. "Is this about the missing girl?" Alexander leaned forward in his chair and in a low voice said "Off the record Jean, aye it is, but please don't mention it to anyone. Understand?" Scott raised her eyebrows and shot her brother-in-law a look which clearly implied that the secret was safe with her.

A few minutes later, Scott had the personnel file of Norman James Edwards. Scott quickly read through the file and said "He's only worked for us for just eighteen months. He is employed as an administration clerk in street cleaning, and according to his supervisor's report, he's very diligent and needs little if any supervision. His time keeping is first class and he's not had one day off sick since he started." Skelton was making notes. Scott confirmed his date of birth and address.

"Jean, where did he work before he joined the council?" asked Alexander. "Let me see. Here it is. He had been unemployed for over a year before he came to us. And before that he was a school teacher." Skelton had been right. Now he was thinking to himself what on earth was a school teacher doing helping with cleaning the streets? "What sort of a school teacher?" asked Alexander. Scott was looking at the pages and said "He was a science teacher for fourteen years at a school in Brighton. I'm just looking at the interview notes." The detectives let her continue reading and then she said. "It says that he resigned from the school due to stress. After he resigned, he went travelling abroad and when he came back, he moved to Bath as he was born here. He went on the dole for a while and then applied for the job he's now got."

Skelton asked "Jean, did you get a reference from the school he worked for?" Scott looked up and said "Yes, we did, it's here. Let me read it to you. It's from St Mary's and it is signed by the headmaster a Mr John Matthews. It says that Edwards had been a science teacher at the school for fourteen years and he was the principal science teacher for the last four years. The reason for leaving is shown as stress. There are no adverse comments."

Having got Scott to photocopy the reference from St Marys, the detectives thanked her and left. Now they were sitting in Skelton's office. "Well Bill, so far Edwards' story checks out. Maybe he was stressed-out being a teacher, I know a lot do chuck it in. But the thing is this, how come he just happens to live a few meters away from where Linda vanished?" Alexander coughed and said "It could just be a coincidence, I mean he's only got the one conviction and that was for assaulting a man. He's never come to our attention except for that assault."

Skelton stood up and walked to the window and looked out. The TV crew were filming, and Skelton recognised the reporter speaking into the microphone. "I don't buy into coincidences Bill, for me there is always a reason for something. Linda gets off that bus and vanishes. Not one CCTV camera has picked her up after she gets off the bus, which is frankly bazaar. Edwards just happens to live almost next door to the bus stop. When I interviewed him at his flat last night, I got a gut instinct about him which troubled me. What concerned me most, was that he apparently has no access to the internet except for his work

140

computer. Clearly, someone of Edwards' intelligence would be very unlikely not to have access to the internet. Since we haven't any other likely suspects for now I want you to call the headmaster of St Marys and make us an appointment for tomorrow. You and I are having a run down to Brighton."

Chapter Twenty-One

The secretary showed them into the headmaster's study. Mr Mathews was standing in front of his large Edwardian writing desk. The room seemed more like a library than a study as it was packed from floor to ceiling with books. After the introductions, Mathews sat down in the captain's chair which perfectly matched the handsome desk. Behind the desk was a huge window from which Skelton could see the school playing fields. A man on a sit-on tractor was cutting the grass. Skelton and Alexander sat in the chairs which were considerably shorter than the headmasters, no doubt to give the impression to young schoolboys, of the headmaster's importance.

They had been chatting for a few minutes when the secretary brought in tea and biscuits. The headmaster played mother and poured the tea and milk. When they all had their teacups and saucers before them and a plate of biscuits each, Mathews said "So how can I help you gentlemen?" Skelton would take charge of this interview. "I'm sorry sir, if my Sergeant was a little vague on the phone about the purpose of our visit. But it is highly confidential, and I would like your assurance that you will not discuss this with your staff?" Mathews placed his hands on his desk and replied. "I can assure you Inspector, that whatever it is you and the Sergeant have come to discuss,

142

will not be revealed to a sole. On that, you have my word."

Skelton sipped his tea but did not touch the biscuits, unlike Alexander who was devouring them with relish. "Mr Mathews, you used to employ a Norman Edwards as a science teacher, is that correct?" Mathews shot back in his chair and wrapped his arms around his chest. Beads of sweat were forming on his forehead. Skelton sensed the headmaster's discomfort at the mention of Edward's name. Mathews had withdrawn a handkerchief from his trouser pocket and was mopping his brow with it. Before answering the question, he took a sip of tea.

"Yes, Norman Edwards worked for me for about fourteen years and for the last four years, he was the principal science teacher. He was a first class teacher but very reserved. Why are you asking about him now, he left ages ago?" Skelton ignored the question. "Did you sack him or was he asked to resign sir?" Mathews reached for his teacup and Skelton noticed that his hand was visibly shaking, as he lifted the cup to his mouth. "Well I asked him to resign, I had to after what I discovered." Skelton leaned forward and asked, "And what exactly was it that you discovered?"

Mathews' discomfort was plain to see for these experienced detectives. "Well, this a mixed school. We teach both boys and girls and have a wonderful reputation. Many of our students go on to university and graduate in many disciplines. We have doctors, lawyers, scientists and engineers who attended this school. In fact, my own GP was taught here. Mr Edwards was a fine teacher but there were reports, of how shall I put it, improper touching by him of some of our female students. I mean these are young ladies we are talking about, seventeen and eighteen-year-olds. No girl made a formal complaint, not to me anyway."

Skelton was making notes. "Please go on Mr Mathews." Mathews poured himself some more tea and milk but ignored his guests. "Well, I had a quiet word with him about it, but he denied that he had ever behaved inappropriately with any of the girls. I just had the opinion of some of the other teachers that his behaviour had been inappropriate, you see. I must be conscious of jealousy, Inspector. Edwards was really his own man, he never had any real friends amongst the staff. Then one evening I was working in here. I was preparing for a meeting of the school governors. Everyone had gone home including the cleaners. It was about eight-thirty when I had finished working. I walked out that door and

144

through the assembly hall. I had taken a class that afternoon to cover for a teacher who had gone home ill. The classroom was next to Mr Edwards and I had left my phone in the desk. I only noticed that my phone was missing, as I was finishing work and wanted to phone my wife."

Mathews cleared his throat and closed his eyes, clearly having difficulty with what was coming next. Skelton said, "Please go on Mr Mathews." "Well it was still light enough for me to see so I didn't switch the lights on. As I was passing Edwards' room, I could hear a groaning sort of noise. So, I quietly opened the door just enough to see in. Edwards was sat at his desk and he was looking at his laptop. It was obvious that he was watching pornography. He was masturbating. I was disgusted. I shouted at him. He was horrified that I had discovered him doing what he had been doing. I think we were both equally embarrassed by the situation we found ourselves in. Well to cut a long story short, I seized the computer as it belonged to the school and took it home."

Skelton let Mathews compose himself for a few seconds and then asked, "I take it you reviewed whatever it was that Edwards had been watching?" Mathews placed both his hands on the desk and looked at the officers. "Oh yes, I reviewed it alright. That same night after my wife had gone to bed, I took the laptop out of my bag. It was easy enough to find it. In fact, there were four or five similar videos on the laptop. I never knew you could find such disgusting images online. I don't know if the girls had been paid for what was being done to them or if they were real videos of actual crimes. Whatever, Edwards should never have been looking at them."

"Mr Mathews, I know this is embarrassing for you and I promise not to take up much more of your time. But we need to know what was happening to the girls in the videos. Can you tell us please?" Mathews sat back in his chair and closed his eyes for a few seconds as if he was visualising again what he had seen. He opened his eyes and looked directly at Skelton. "The girls were unconscious. It looked like they had either taken drugs or had been given them. In each of the videos, a different man was having sex with a young girl who I reckon was aged about maybe seventeen or eighteen."

Skelton now had enough information to warrant the arrest of Edwards. "Tell me Mr Mathews what did you do with Edwards?" Mathews leaned forward, his arms resting on the desk. "The next day I had him in here and I told him he could either resign or I would sack him. I told him that his days in teaching were over and that if he applied for a job at another school, I would tell the school what he had been up to. I didn't want to ruin the man, so I told him that if he sought alternative employment, where no young girls were involved, I'd give him a good reference. More than a year or so later, I got a letter from Bath and North East Somerset Council, saying that he had applied for a job in the street cleaning department and so I gave him a reference."

The detectives had what they had come for. Something to justify arresting Edwards and carrying out a forensic search of his flat. Skelton was just about to stand up and thank Mathews for his time when Mathews suddenly jumped to his feet. "Bloody hell, I've just realised what this is all about. A young girl went missing in Bath the other night and you think Edwards is responsible, don't you?" Skelton and Alexander rose to their feet. "Mr Mathews, we have no evidence that Edwards is in anyway responsible for the girl's disappearance. For now, Mr Edwards is just someone who is of interest to us and I'd appreciate it if you kept our conversation to yourself" Skelton emphasised the last word. Mathews bowed his head and looked up. "Yes of course Inspector, this is very embarrassing for me. Rest assured I will consider it privileged information and I will very much keep it to myself."

Chapter Twenty-Two

It was almost 4 o'clock when Alexander drove into the station car park. Skelton had spent a good deal of time on the phone as Alexander drove them back from Brighton. Linda's body had still not been found. She went missing on Monday night and it was now Thursday afternoon but at least Skelton now had a suspect to work on. The officers got out the car and both stretched themselves after the drive back. It was another warm day and the sun warmed their backs, as they walked through the car park to the officer's entrance which was to the left of the public entrance. Alexander swiped his card and pulled the door open. Skelton said, "I'm just going to the loo Bill and then I will pop in and up-date the boss on our little outing to Brighton."

Skelton approached Superintendent William's door and could see through the office window that he was sitting at his desk, on the phone. Skelton knocked on the door and entered. Williams smiled and motioned for him to take a seat. Williams finished the call. "Did you bring me back a stick of rock from Brighton Dan?" Skelton loved rock himself. Whenever he went to a seaside resort, such as Brighton, he would always buy a few sticks of rock. Rock is a sort of candy which is hard to chew but tastes delicious. Skelton had made Alexander stop the car, so that he could buy some. He had three sticks of rock in his jacket pocket. He pulled a stick out and placed it on Williams' desk. "There you go sir, have that on me." Both men smiled. "Thanks Dan, my grandson will love that!"

"Right, down to business Dan. How was your trip to sunny Brighton?" When Skelton finished briefing Williams on the trip, he left and went to his own office. He had decided to arrest Edwards at his place of work. The main reason for this was that he wanted to search his desk and locker for anything which could link him to Linda. He and Alexander would be the arresting officers, but he would also take Lowik and Turnbull along and they would be responsible for the search.

They went in two cars, Skelton and Alexander in the first, followed by Lowik and Turnbull in the second. They drove into the council depot and parked the cars. As they got out of the cars, a man in a white hard hat came out of an office and asked, "Can I help you?" Skelton smiled at the man and said "We are the police. Is Norman Edwards around?" The man was a bit surprised to find four police officers at his depot. The man looked at his watch and said "No he finishes at five, he will have gone home now. What do you want with him?" Skelton walked up close to the man, who he reckoned was about sixty and of a short and stocky build. Skelton looked down on the man and said "I am not at liberty to say why we want to speak to Mr Edwards, but can you show us his locker and desk? And who are you by the way?" The man took off his hard hat and said, "I'm

Martin Smith and I am the foreman here. Norman shares an office with me. He's in charge of admin and keeps all our records and deals with health and safety matters. He does have a locker though which I can show you. Come this way."

The four officers followed Smith through the door of the building, which was a large workshop. Several trucks and a van were parked up and it looked to Skelton that this must be where they maintained them. The workshop was quiet, and it seemed that only Smith was here at present. Smith led them through the workshop and into a small office where there were two basic desks and four chairs. On each desk sat a computer. Smith pointed to a desk by a window and said Norman sits there and that's his computer, but I can tell you now, he's very restricted on what websites he can view due to the strict controls imposed by the council. Unless the website has been authorised you can't access it."

Skelton was not surprised at this information, and he thought it unlikely that given the fact he shared an office, he would leave anything incriminating on the computer. Skelton turned to Lowik "Have a look and see what you can find on there, Peter and check the drawers while you are it." Turning back to Smith, "Can we have a look at his locker please?" Smith said "Aye just follow me. He led them back through the door and to the other end of the workshop, through another door. When they entered, they could see the green lockers mounted on the wall. Smith walked up to a locker and said, "This is Norman's locker, do you want me to open it?" Each locker had a small bronze padlock, all identical to each other. Skelton walked up beside Smith and said, "If you can open it, that would be great."

Smith pulled a bunch of keys from his jacket pocket. It took him four tries before he found the right key to fit the lock. He removed the padlock and pulled the door open. Skelton moved closer and looked inside and groaned inwardly. He had been hoping to find a laptop, tablet or an iPhone. Instead, all he found was a jacket, a pair of pliers and a bag of fruit. He checked the jacket pockets. In the right hand pocket was a Mars bar and in the left hand pocket, a ball of string. Skelton turned to Smith and asked, "Is this the only place he keeps his things in?" Smith had replaced the hard hat on his head which reached up to Skelton's chin. "Yes, this is the only place he keeps his stuff."

They went back to where they had left Lowik with the computer. Turnbull asked, "Any luck with that Peter?" Lowik looked up at them and said "Nope

152

not a thing on here that shouldn't be here. It's clean as a whistle and the only things in the drawers are books and forms."

Chapter Twenty-Three

The four officers left the workshop and went outside to their cars. The raid on Edwards' workplace had been very disappointing. They had all been hoping that Edwards kept some sort of device, such as a laptop or iPhone at work, with which he had communicated with Linda. It was beginning to look like Edwards was in the clear and Skelton was having second thoughts as to whether he had enough reason to even arrest him. A clever lawyer might even bring a civil lawsuit for wrongful arrest.

As they got to the cars, Skelton made his decision. "Ross and Peter, you go back to the office. Bill and I will go to Edwards' flat and see if he's there. If he is, we will arrest him and bring him in for questioning. If we do manage to bring him in, I want Crime Scene Investigation (CSI) to go through his flat to see if there is any evidence that Linda has been in there." Skelton and Alexander got into the car and they drove to Edwards' flat. Alexander parked the car outside and both officers got out.

They walked up to the front door and Skelton pushed the buzzer to Edwards' flat. A minute or so later, the front door opened, and Edwards was staring at them. "Oh, it's you again, what do want this time?" Edwards did not seem in the least bit perplexed by the sight of the police standing on his front doorstep. Skelton was thinking to himself. "Either this guy is totally innocent of any involvement in Linda's disappearance, or he's very confident that's he's covered his tracks really well." Skelton and Alexander climbed the step so that they were standing next to Edwards. "Let's go inside for a minute Mr Edwards" said Skelton as he gently pushed Edwards' shoulder.

When they were inside the flat, Alexander closed the door. They could have arrested Edwards on the doorstep, but Skelton wanted to see the inside of the flat again. The TV was on and the six o'clock news was showing. "Can you turn that off please?" asked Alexander. Edwards picked up the remote control from the armrest of his chair and switched the TV off. Skelton could smell something cooking in the kitchen and it smelled delicious. He went and looked and found the wrapper of an M&S roast beef dinner. The food was cooking in the oven. Skelton switched the oven off and walked back to the sitting room where Edwards had taken a seat, whilst Alexander kept watch over him.

Edwards looked up as Skelton came back, and said "What's this all about then?" Again, Skelton sensed that the man did not seem in the least bit concerned that two detectives were standing in his sitting room. Usually, a guilty person will show signs of discomfort or will often yawn as if they are bored by the whole encounter. Edwards was showing no such signs and once again, Skelton wondered if he was barking up the wrong tree. Yet he could not ignore the fact that Edwards lived so close to where Linda was last seen, literally only a matter of meters away. No, Skelton had no option but to arrest him and hope that the CSI unit would come up with some evidence that Linda had been in the flat and had been killed there. Skelton walked over to Edwards and said, "Stand up." Edwards stood up and Skelton said, "Norman Edwards I am arresting you on suspicion of murder." He proceeded to tell him about his legal rights. When Skelton had finished speaking, Edwards looked him in the face and said "I want a lawyer, this is utter shite and you know it. I've done nothing wrong and when you search the flat you won't find a single piece of evidence against me. And mark my words inspector, I will have my lawyer sue you bastards for wrongful arrest and you and your mate here will be back writing parking tickets or whatever the fuck it is you do, just too upset Joe public."

Skelton and Alexander had heard it all before, but Edwards was very convincing. The one thing that bothered Skelton, and indeed all police officers, was the number of reality television programmes that showed real-life crimes. These inevitably showed how the perpetrator of a crime, usually murder, had been identified through forensic science. Someone contemplating murder could learn an awful lot from such programmes and might be able to leave the crime scene, with little or no DNA evidence being transferred to or from the victim. It is very difficult to remove all traces of DNA from the victim. Likewise, the killer invariably takes away DNA from the victim. Skelton's problem was more compounded by the fact that he didn't even have a victim yet! This was going to be a tough investigation.

"Mr Edwards, what's your lawyer's name? You can call him as soon as we have processed you at the police station." For the first time, Edwards seemed a little less sure of himself as he replied, "I haven't got a lawyer, but I know my rights."

Chapter Twenty-Four

As they drove Edwards back to the station, they passed the TV van that was clearly broadcasting live as the reporter was speaking to the camera. Skelton looked at his watch, it was just after 18.30 and he guessed it would be the local BBC news programme called "Points West". He recognised the reporter but could not recall his name. Alexander waited for the electric gate to open and then drove into the area, which led to the custody suite. The electric gate was closing as Skelton opened the rear door of the car and motioned for Edwards to get out.

Alexander swiped his card in the electronic reader and the door to the custody suite opened. He went in and Edwards followed with Skelton bringing up the rear. Skelton closed the door behind him. All three stood in front of the bar and sergeant Roddis got up and approached from the other side of the bar. "Good evening gentlemen, and what do we have here then?" Skelton rested an arm on the bar and said "Sergeant Roddis, this is Norman Edwards and we have arrested him on suspicion of murder" Roddis sat down at the computer and began typing. Skelton touched Alexander on the shoulder and said, "You process him and come and get me when you are ready" Alexander said, "Very good sir." Skelton walked off.

The CSI team were already assembled in the incident room. Skelton walked in and the officer in charge, Bob Richards stood up. "Right Bob, here are the keys to the flat" and Richards took them from Skelton. "I want you and your team to go over the flat in meticulous detail and see if you can find any evidence that young Linda has been there. I don't need to mention what you are looking for; you all know exactly what to do. However, as you know, we have no sightings of Linda after she got off the bus. We do know from her flatmate that she had arranged to meet a boy called Tommy. I don't think Tommy exists. I think Edwards is Tommy but I've no idea how he persuaded her to go with him to the flat. He somehow communicated with her probably on a phone, but it may have been by way of a computer or iPad. So far, we have found no evidence to suggest that Edwards owns either. I want you to search the flat with a view to finding either a computer, or iPad, or a phone. Finding these devices is paramount to the investigation because that should prove that Edwards was in communication with Linda and he persuaded her to meet him outside Lambrettas. Hopefully you will also find Linda's DNA, in the flat, which could lead us to charging Edwards with her murder. Get to work Bob and bring me some good news, as I can certainly use it."

Skelton walked to his office and sat down at his desk. He began to prepare himself for the interview with Edwards. He wondered whether Edwards would co-operate with him, or on the advice of the lawyer, that he was entitled to consult, might simply opt for a "no comment" response to his questions. He glanced at his watch, it was already 19.10 and he and Alexander had only stopped for a McDonalds on the way back from Brighton. Skelton was feeling hungry. He looked up at the sound of the knock at his door, to see Alexander coming in.

Alexander sat heavily down and said "Right he's been processed sir. We searched him and all he had on him was an old Nokia phone, a wallet containing thirty pounds and some chewing gum. He's had his picture taken, his fingerprints as well as a swab from his mouth for DNA. But if you want my opinion sir, unless CSI find some real evidence in his flat, that the wee girl was in it, then we are fucked!"

Skelton knew if the search of the flat yielded no evidence that Linda had been there, then Edwards would be released, pending further enquiries. Skelton stood up and walked to the window and looked out. The TV van was still parked up, its occupants patiently waiting for news. "Has he contacted a lawyer yet Bill?" Alexander sat back in the chair as Skelton turned to face him, said "Yes, we gave him a list of the names of the duty lawyers and he picked a guy called John Hazard. And believe me, he is a fucking hazard! He always advises his clients to do a "no comment" in interviews, so I don't think we will get anything new out of him tonight."

Skelton had had better days, but he could only deal the hand that he had been given. He was hoping that maybe some of Paul, the magician's magic could help that hand. "Is Hazzard here yet?" Alexander rose from his chair. "No, he's driving back from Bristol and my guess is that it will be eight before he gets here. Then he will need whatever time he wants with his client. So, I don't think we can begin the interview much before nine, sir." Skelton grabbed Alexander by the arm. "Right then, lets you and I go to the Ale House for dinner, I'm starving!"

The door of the Ale House was wedged open, as it was a warm evening. There were about ten smokers sitting outside, doing their best to get lung cancer. Skelton could not abide smoking and was extremely thankful that the government had banned it from restaurants and bars. As they entered the bar, Skelton was surprised to see a new barman standing behind the bar. Turning to Alexander, he asked "What are you having to eat Bill?" Alexander took a menu off the bar and said, "Pie and chips for me." The new barman was just finishing serving a young lady. He looked at Skelton and gave him a smile and asked, "What can I get you sir?" Skelton returned the smile and said "A pint of Fosters please and a pint of soda water and Lime. I haven't seen you behind the bar before, you must be new." The barman replied "Yes, it's my first shift tonight. I used to work here when I was doing my degree, but I live in China now, but I have had to come back to get another qualification so that I can work in China." Skelton thought for a second and made a mental note to get to know the new barman as he seemed an interesting person and could easily become a good friend. Skelton said, "Well my name is Dan, and this is my colleague, Bill." Skelton held out his hand and the barman said, "HI Dan my name is Adam." They shook hands. Adam was about 6" tall, slim and very handsome. He had piercing blue eyes with neatly cut brown hair.

Once they had finished eating, Skelton checked his watch. It was 8.45pm. "Right Bill lets pop across to the flat and see how Richards and his team are getting on. They said goodbye to Adam and left the bar. It was cooling down as they walked across Bog Island towards the flat where two CSI vans were parked outside. The main door was wedged open but the door to Edwards' flat was closed. Blue police tape hung across the main door. Skelton knocked on the door to the flat and it was opened by Richards.

"Any joy so far, Bob?" Richards pulled down his face mask and sighed. "Well so far, we haven't found any electronic devices with which he could access the internet. There is no trace of any blood and to be honest sir, I don't think we are going to find anything. The place is spotless. We even checked the vacuum cleaner and it's been emptied. Either he happens to be a man who is extremely house proud or he is very much acquainted with DNA and has done a superb job in removing every trace of the girl having been here. That of course depends on whether or not the girl was ever actually here sir!" Skelton ran his right hand through his hair and said "Okay Bob, keep going and let me know if you find anything. We are just heading back to interview him now. Catch you later."

Chapter Twenty-Five

Edwards was in his cell when the officers got back to the station. His lawyer was sitting in an interview room finishing off writing a statement. Skelton knocked on the interview room door and entered along with Alexander. Skelton had never met Mr Hazard, but Alexander had met him many times before both at the station and in Court. Hazard knew his stuff and Alexander doubted that they would extract much out of Edwards, with Hazard present. Alexander did the introduction, "Mr Hazard this is Detective Chief Inspector Skelton" Hazard stood up and shook hands with Skelton.

The three men sat down in the interview room. Skelton looked at Hazard and took stock of the man. He estimated that the man was around sixty. His hair was grey, and he was wearing glasses. His dark suit was heavily creased as if he had gone to sleep wearing it. "Mr Hazard, before we commence the interview with your client, is there anything you would like to say?" asked Skelton. Hazard opened his note pad and handed Skelton a sheet of paper. "Inspector, I have advised my client to give a "no comment" response to your questions except to confirm his name and address, his date of birth and where he works. I understand that you interviewed him last night at his flat. That sheet of paper confirms what he told you last night. He has never met the missing girl. She never came to his flat and on the evening, she went missing, he was at home where he cooked himself a meal and watched TV before retiring to bed. My client did not kill the girl and has no idea what has happened to her. I must insist that you release my client so that he can go home. If you fail to do so, I am instructed by my client to launch an action against you for wrongful arrest and we will seek heavy damages against this police force."

Skelton looked at the sheet of paper. It was handwritten and signed by Edwards and dated. It merely recorded what Hazard had just said. Skelton cleared his throat and said, "Mr Hazard, a detailed forensic search of your client's flat is taking place now. It will probably not be completed until tomorrow morning. Mr Edwards will be held until the search is completed.

Depending on the result of the search, your client may be charged with an offence or offences and we will keep him in custody. Should the results of the search be inconclusive, I will release your client pending further enquiries. In the event of your client being charged, the jury will be informed of your client's refusal to answer our questions and they may draw their own conclusions, as to why he refused." Hazard closed his notepad. "Inspector, you are within your rights to hold my client whilst his flat is searched, but I can assure you that my client is very confident that you will find no evidence that the missing girl was ever there."

Skelton and Alexander conducted the interview with Edwards whilst Hazard sat by his side. It was a complete waste of time. Other than to confirm his name and address, date of birth and place of work, Edwards simply replied to all the other questions which Skelton asked, "No comment."

They finished the search of the flat just after two in the morning. Skelton had sent Alexander home when the interview had finished. Hazard also went home whilst Skelton caught up with his emails. Richards knocked on the door and entered Skelton's office. "Bob, did you find anything?" Richards gave him a weary shrug of the shoulders and sat down. "Sir, either he's done a great job of cleaning up, or she was never there. We have found absolutely nothing to suggest that the girl was in that flat." Skelton let this latest set-back sink in for a few seconds and then he said "Shit!" Richards coughed and said, "My lads got Linda's DNA from her hairbrush and what hairs we got from Edward's flat and clothing will be compared to Linda's DNA. But we have no positive indication of either blood or seman in the flat or on Edwards' clothes. We still have work to do at the lab on his other clothing and until that's completed sometime tomorrow, I can't for definite say if she was or was not in that flat."

Richards sat down. "Sir, this guy has got no WIFI access and no laptop or other device with which he could have contacted the missing girl with. There is not a single item in that flat that's in anyway incriminating. There are no signs of any drugs with which he could have used to render her unconscious, should he have somehow manged to get her there. If you ask me sir, I don't think this guy had anything to do with this girl's disappearance!" Skelton stood up and ran his hands through his hair. "Okay Bob, I hear what you say but I think Edwards is a clever bastard and with a degree in chemistry, he will be aware of how to destroy any DNA evidence. Somehow, he's managed to remove whatever DNA evidence was there. Let's just hope that he's only temporally removed it but not destroyed it. Then we will nail the bastard!"

Chapter Twenty-Six

The next morning, Skelton got up at six as usual, but he was feeling tired having not gone to bed until three. Before leaving the house, he had arranged to meet his partner Ken in the Ale House after work. They would have a couple of drinks and then go for a curry. Now as he was walking down the Wellsway towards the area known as Bear Flat, which was about halfway between his house and the city centre, he was racking his brain on his next move with the investigation into Linda's disappearance. She had still not been found despite her vanishing on Monday night and it was now Friday morning. If she had not gone to Edwards' flat, then she must have got into a car.

Edwards did not own a car, they had checked. Then a thought occurred, did Edwards have access to a council van or lorry? He would check that out with the Foreman Smith. He was not going to ask Edwards, as he could easily deny it.

They had already traced most of the owners of the vehicles that had travelled along North Parade at the relevant times, before and after she had got off the bus. The vehicles had been detected by both CCTV and by ANPR (automated number plate recognition) So far, of those interviewed, all had a legitimate reason for having been on North Parade and none had criminal convictions of a sexual nature. Superintendent Williams continued to give press and television interviews, but the public had so far failed to provide any clues as to what happened to Linda once she had alighted from the bus. Skelton was convinced that she was dead and the only hope to identify her killer, would be if he had left some DNA on her body. The thing that worried Skelton most of all was that the longer it took to find her, the body would be decomposing, and vital evidence could be lost. If she was in the river, as Skelton believed that she was, then the water would probably have already destroyed all forensic evidence that the killer might have left.

Skelton went straight to the incident room and was updated on the investigation. Linda had still not been found and there were only a handful of drivers still to be traced. He was going to have to release Edwards unless Richards and his team came up with some evidence to show that Linda had been in his flat. He simply had no evidence to justify his continued detention. He knew that unless he released him when the lab tests were concluded, the lawyer Hazard would threaten a legal challenge. Skelton wanted to avoid that. He left the incident room and found Alexander in the canteen sitting on his own drinking tea and reading the paper. "Good morning Bill, and how are you this morning?" Skelton sat down opposite Alexander and watched the sergeant put down his mug of tea. "I'm fine sir but I guess you did not get much sleep last night." Skelton rubbed his right hand over his face trying to wipe the tiredness away that he was feeling. "I will be okay. But this investigation is not going as well as I'd hoped."

Skelton placed both hands on the table and gazed down at Alexander. "Bob Richards and his team searched Edward's flat and found no evidence of foul play or that she had even been there. They still have some tasks to complete but the results should be in this afternoon. They are comparing some DNA from Linda's hairbrush with the sample you took from Edwards. Our only hope is for a positive match at the very least, establish that Linda had been in that flat with Edwards, otherwise we are going to have to release him without charge."

Alexander stood up and approached Skelton. "Look I know sir how important it is to establish the connection and I fully agree that our only possible suspect now is Edwards. But supposing we are wrong, and Edwards is in the clear! Do you think we've maybe missed something and that we have been focusing too much on Edwards whilst the real culprit is sitting back and laughing at us? If the lab results come back clean, then the press are going to have a field day. We no longer have a suspect and Linda remains missing with not one sighting of her and no body. I've never known a case like this in all my years on the force".

Skelton had been listening intently to Alexander and agreed with his conclusions although very reluctantly. "Bill, I know that if those lab results come back negative then we are very much up a creek without a fucking paddle between us!" Skelton opened the door of the canteen and looked back at Alexander. "I'm going to brief the boss". He stepped out the door and headed towards the superintendent's office.

Superintendent Williams was coming out of his office when he saw Skelton approaching, he turned and held the door open for Skelton and when Skelton entered, he closed the door. Both men sat down at Williams' desk. They both looked tired. "So, Dan, we drew a blank on the search of Edwards' flat, is that correct?" Skelton settled back in the chair and rubbed his eyes. "Yes sir, either Linda never went there or if she did, Edwards has somehow managed to remove all traces of her. We are waiting for some lab results to come in and we expect those to arrive this afternoon. If those are negative, that will leave Edwards, apparently in the clear. In which case I will have to release him pending further enquiries. I don't have another suspect, nor any sightings of Linda either on CCTV, or by members of the public. We are continuing to search the river daily but with all that rain last month, the river is full. It might be that we won't recover her body until the river falls a few feet and that could be a week or two. At least the weather forecast is for more dry weather to continue, so that will help. We are also continuing to search away from the river as well as our ongoing door-to-door enquiries.

Even if the lab results come back negative, my money is still on Edwards, either as her abductor and more likely, her murderer as well. His flat has been thoroughly searched so he's not hidden her body there. He has no car and all vehicles that had been on Northbridge Parade on the night she got off the bus, have been accounted for and eliminated from our enquiries. He could not have carried her that's for sure and even if he had done, we would have picked him up on the multiple CCTV cameras around the city."

Williams stood up and walked across to the window and looked out. The TV van was still parked below. He turned and faced Skelton who was seated. "Well Dan, all we can do is hope that a body turns up soon. That might just give us some clues as to what happened to her. Have you considered the possibility that she might have accidentally fallen into the river?" Skelton stood up and joined Williams at the window. He could feel the heat from the glass as the sun was well up. "I have kept an open mind sir, but I don't think that it's a realistic possibility. Remember, she has not shown up on any CCTV in the whole of the city. The only window of opportunity for her to get into the river was when the bus drove off. She could have crossed the road and climbed the parapet of the bridge and jumped into the river or she could have been pushed. I don't think either of these two scenarios took place. Several vehicles passed by after she got off the bus. A girl climbing

the bridge parapet would not have gone un-
noticed nor would a person be throwing her over
it. No, I am one hundred per cent certain,
someone managed to somehow abduct her and
kill her. So far, I don't have a bloody clue how they
did it, or how they managed to move her body. If, I
can work that out, then it will be drinks all round,
that's for sure!"

Chapter Twenty-Seven

Skelton's day was not going well! He had Alexander drive him to the council depot. He found Smith, the foreman, in the workshop. Skelton informed Smith that Edwards was in custody, which went to explain why Edwards had not turned up for work. Smith confirmed that Edwards had no access to a van or lorry and that Edwards did not own a car. It was Edwards's job to merely attend to all administrative matters. That did not qualify him for a council vehicle. So far as Alexander and Skelton were concerned, their case against Edwards was falling apart, unless the lab could provide definite proof that Linda had been in his flat.

On getting back to the station Skelton received a phone call from his partner Ken. It was not good news or bad news, just disappointing. Ken had to leave on urgent business and would be away for a few days. So, their meeting in the Ale House and subsequent curry, would not be taking place. Skelton did not like dining out on his own in the evening. He decided that he would probably just have a drink in the Ale House after work and take a Marks & Spencer curry home and microwave it. He would also have to go home and feed the dogs and take them for their evening walk. That was something he was looking forward to.

The call from the lab came in just after 4pm. Richards confirmed that there was no DNA evidence to suggest that Linda had ever been with Edwards either at his flat or elsewhere. Skelton broke the news to Alexander as soon as he came off the phone to the lab. Both men sat across Skelton's desk rubbing their heads in their hands. It was Skelton who broke the silence. "Right Bill we are going to have to release him now, we have got absolutely no reason for detaining him any longer and if we did Hazard would have our guts for garters. I'm bloody sure he's our man but how the hell he managed to grab her and then dispose of her body is a complete mystery!" The team had taken the usual calls from the cranks claiming to have murdered her or suggesting where the body could be found. These calls had all been checked out and had been proven to be false.

Skelton and Alexander went to the custody suite and completed the formalities for releasing Edwards pending further enquiries. As Alexander was leading him to the exit to the station, he placed his hand on Edwards' arm and pulled him close. "I don't know how the fuck you did it, but we will work it out, and when we do, you will be back in here double quick!" Edwards' confidence was returning to him, after all the cops had just confirmed that they were baffled by the case. Edwards looked at Alexander and in a confident voice said, "You know sergeant, that's never going to happen. You have got nothing on me. Have a nice weekend, I certainly will!"

At 18.00 Skelton decided to call it a day. He picked up his iPad on which he had downloaded the Times newspaper and walked out of his office and out of the station. He casually strolled towards Bog Island and saw a crowd, sitting outside the Ale House drinking and smoking. The door was open, and the bar was empty, save for a couple of men standing at the bar, enjoying their drinks. Adam was behind the bar, and on seeing Skelton, he smiled and picked up a Fosters glass and started pouring a much-needed pint for him. "Hello Dan, are you on your own tonight?" Skelton smiled at Adam and said, "Yes a change of plan, so I am just going to read the paper and have a couple of pints." Adam smiled and said, "You look as though you need them." Skelton nodded his head and picked up his drink and took it to a table.

After a couple of beers, Skelton got up and said goodbye to Adam and headed home to feed and walk the boys, as he always referred to his dogs.

Chapter Twenty- Eight

The next morning, Saturday, Skelton got up at 7am and let the boys into the garden to do their business. He made a mug of tea and got dressed. He got the boys' leads and all three sat excitedly waiting to go on their morning walk. Brenty-Boy was the oldest dog at 8 and was the best dog that Skelton had ever known in his life. He was a very large black Labrador and when Skelton had picked him up as a puppy, he instinctively knew that this was a very special dog, unlike any he had owned before. They immediately bonded, as did Ken with the new puppy, but Brenty-Boy would only ever have one master and that was Skelton. He proved to be so incredibly easy to train and Skelton totally adored him.

Brenty-Boy's first ever trick, occurred just a few days after Skelton had been training him on how to walk to heel on a lead without pulling, something which Skelton believed that all dogs should be trained in. Having instructed Brenty-Boy to sit, Skelton gently put the lead on the floor whilst it was still attached to Brenty-Boy's neck. To Skelton's utter amazement, Brenty-Boy picked up the lead in his mouth and started parading around the garden showing off his new skill. From that day on, Brenty-Boy hardly ever had to be held on his lead, he would simply walk perfectly to heel whilst carrying his lead proudly in his mouth.

Next in line at the age of 6 was Josh whose father is Brenty-Boy. Although he looked very similar to his dad, his mother was a brown German Pointer, but Brenty-Boy's genes were clearly the predominate ones, as he looked like a one hundred per cent jet black Labrador. Josh did however have one unusual feature in that if out on a walk and he scented game, he would instantly freeze and point with his right front leg. The first time that Skelton witnessed this, he could not help but laugh at the sight of a black Labrador pointing!

The baby of the family was Archie aged just 2, he was slightly smaller than the other two dogs. For what he lacked in size he made up for in intelligence. Whenever Dan or Ken were doing some form of housework or gardening, Archie was always on hand closely inspecting everything that they were doing. He appointed himself, as an inspector of quality control, ensuring that the job in hand was being carried out to his satisfaction.

After taking the boys out for a walk, Skelton showered and shaved and had a light breakfast and another mug of tea. It was now five days since Linda had gone missing and still her body had not been found. Technically, Skelton had the day off but there was no way that he could stop thinking about what had become of her. Suddenly, Skelton recalled that Bill Alexander had said that another female student had drowned in the river last Christmas, a fact that had previously escaped Skelton. He had only been aware of the deaths of several male students who had tragically lost their lives after a night out.

Skelton took out his phone and called Alexander, who answered on the third ring. "Morning sir, how's it going?" Alexander was also having the weekend off unless of course a major development occurred in the investigation. In which case the whole team would be back on duty. "Good morning to you Bill. What are you doing at this moment in time, may I ask?" Alexander cleared his throat and Skelton could hear traffic in the background. "Actually, I'm with the wife shopping when I could be sitting in the garden with a good book and a few tinnies" was the muffled response that came back. Skelton opened the kitchen door and the boys followed him out into the garden. It was another bright sunny day and the temperature was a comforting 18 degrees. "Bill, I'm sure you are going to hate me for this, you, being a lover of shopping and all that, but I'd like to meet up at the station to go over something with you. Is that possible?" Alexander thought for a second, and asked, "How long will it take?" Skelton looked at his watch, it was 11.30 and he did not want to ruin Alexander's day off if he could help it. "Bill if you could meet me at the nick at 12, I don't think it will take much more than half an hour. After that, if you have no plans, I'd be delighted to take you and Mrs Alexander for a meal and a drink. What do you say to that?"

Skelton could hear that Alexander was discussing matters with his wife and after a minute or so Alexander spoke into the phone. "Dan the wife has arranged to meet her sisters for lunch and you know what women are like, I'd probably be superfluous to requirements, so we could have lunch by ourselves and then I can meet up with the wife afterwards." Skelton smiled to himself and said, "Bill could you go a curry?" Alexander laughed "God you know how to make my day Dan.

First you get me off shopping duty and then you take me out for a curry. I will see you at 12."

Skelton walked into town and as he approached the pedestrian bridge by the bus station, he started looking at the river. It did not seem to be flowing as fast as it had been earlier in the week and the level of water had gone down slightly. He stopped halfway across and stared into the black murky water beneath him and thought to himself, that anyone going into that river, no matter how young and fit they were, would almost certainly drown. He walked on and headed for the police station on Manvers Street. As he reached the car park at the front of the station, he saw Bill Alexander crossing the road carrying two large M&S shopping bags. They greeted each other and went into the station.

They went to Skelton's office and when they were both seated Skelton leaned across his desk and said, "Bill I'm sorry to bring you in on your day off but something is troubling me." Alexander leaned closer and asked, "What's on your mind Dan?" Skelton pointed his finger at Alexander and said "The other day, you mentioned that a young girl had drowned in the river last Christmas? Tell me about it Bill." Alexander leaned back and began searching his memory for the details.

"Well, it was a week or so before Christmas just at the time when that terrible flu virus was going around. Half the station was affected by it. The RUH was at bursting point with patients and both the Fire and Ambulance services were at breaking point. We received a missing person report that a young girl student had gone out for the night and had not turned up at her digs the next day. Her name was Marion Busby and I think she was 18 or 19. A fellow student in her dormitory had tried calling and texting her but had received no reply. The flat mate, I think she was called Annie, was not that particularly concerned about her that next day and assumed she had either lost her mobile phone, or the battery had run out. That evening she came down with the flu and took to her bed for three days and nights. In her delirious state, she had forgotten all about Marion. They didn't share a room you see, they lived on campus at Bath Spa Uni and only shared kitchen facilities. And anyway, a lot of students had gone home for Christmas."

Skelton listened intently and raised his arm for Alexander to continue. "Well with us having so many officers off sick, the missing person received little attention other than to check that the girl had not been admitted to the RUH, and as no further reports of the girl being missing had been received, it must have been assumed that she had turned up safe and well. It was about five days after she had gone missing that her mother contacted the Uni saying that she was unable to contact her daughter. The Uni sent a staff member to her room, to find that she was not there, and it was only when they spoke to the house mate that they realised that she was still missing."

Skelton had been listening intently to the story and said, "So it was a combination of unusual circumstances that lead us to do little in an attempt to locate the girl?" Alexander stood up and walked to the window and said, "Yes very much so, it was just one of those unfortunate set of circumstances that sometimes show up and prevented us from doing more to find the girl. But as it turned out, she had simply gone out for the night, had too much to drink and fell into the river trying to get back to campus."

Skelton sat back in his chair and let the information sink in. "What happened next Bill?" Bill rested his backside on the windowsill and continued. "The next day her body was found in the river at Twerton. It was recovered and taken to the mortuary for a post-mortem. Of course, we treated the death as unexplained, and consequently the forensic boys did their stuff and they were satisfied that the poor girl had fallen into the river and drowned. Again, the mortuary was having trouble processing so many bodies due to the flu epidemic which had produced dozens more bodies than usual. The mortuary staff had also succumbed to the flu, so they were having to deal with a whole lot of extra bodies whilst being short staffed. The principal pathologist had come down with it as well. Me and your predecessor the DCI went to the mortuary and persuaded the more junior pathologist to perform the PM. There were no suspicious circumstances, you see, and we were desperate to get the girl's body processed and returned to the family. The coroner gave his permission for the post-mortem to be performed by Dr Thomson. The pathologist said she was three times over the drink driving limit and had drowned. There was no evidence of any physical assault and we concluded that it was just another tragic case, of a student falling into the river, after a good night out."

Skelton stood up, his head bowed deep in thought and then looked straight at Alexander. "Bill did you discover who she had been out drinking with and where she went into the river?" Alexander stood up straight. "As I said, we were incredibly short staffed at the time and to make matters worse it was a couple of days before Christmas. All the students had gone home and so we drew a blank on finding anyone who was with her. We had no reason to suspect foul play, so we prepared a report for the Coroner and I guess he will hold an inquest sometime soon."

Skelton could feel goose pimples on the back of his neck. Something was not right. It would be easy to criticise the investigation with the benefit of hindsight, but he could well understand that some short cuts had to be taken given the circumstances surrounding the case. "Do you know if the pathologist ordered toxicology tests on the blood and urine for drugs?" Alexander thought for a second, "Well if he did, they must have been negative as we closed the investigation as an accidental drowning. He never contacted us again and like I said, we were very short staffed, so I don't think we had any time to chase the pathologist. And to make matters worse, the DCI came down with the flu which left me holding the fort on my own!"

Skelton paced the floor deep in thought and Alexander watched him closely trying to understand the significance of his boss's interest in the case. "Right Bill, I want you to pull me the file on Marion's investigation, including the post-mortem report and the report for the Coroner. I want to take it home and read it comprehensively. There is just a chance that Marion and Linda's disappearance are linked. When you have done that, let's go and have that curry."

Chapter Twenty- Nine

The weekend had passed without Linda's body being discovered. Skelton had spent the weekend reading the papers from the files which Alexander had given him. There was no doubt in his mind that corners had been cut in the investigation, particularly at the post- mortem examination. Upon reading the post-mortem report, he noted that the pathologist had had the blood analysed for alcohol but had failed to undertake any tests for drugs. He was also surprised and highly concerned that the deceased had undergone violent sexual intercourse, prior to her death. Not only vaginal but anal as well. Whilst the pathologist had found no bruising around the throat or arms, there was bruising around the vagina.

The Pathologist had taken swabs from both the vagina and anus but found no traces of sperm in either location, indicating that her sexual partner had worn a condom. Another major concern for Skelton was the fact that the police had from the outset treated the case as simply another drowning, not suspicious but unexplained. The girl's handbag had never been found nor had her phone.

On Sunday evening, Skelton had called Alexander and said he wanted to meet with him on Monday morning at 7.30am.

At 7.30am Monday morning Skelton and Alexander sat around Skelton's desk each with a mug of tea before them. Skelton explained to Alexander his concerns about the investigation into Marion's death and the subsequent post-mortem. Skelton was at pains to emphasise to Alexander that he was not in any way being critical of him or of his own predecessor given the circumstances they had been operating under. Skelton instructed Alexander to go over to the mortuary straight away and find out what samples, if any, they had retained from the post-mortem particularly blood and urine.

It was now a whole seven days since Linda had disappeared and yet no trace of her had been found. Appeals for information were still routinely being broadcast on TV and radio, as well as widespread coverage in the national and local press. Her friends and family made countless Facebook appeals but there had been few worthwhile leads to follow. The broad consensus on the team, was that Linda had been abducted and was most likely dead given the time that had elapsed since she went missing.

At 8am Skelton knocked on Superintendent Williams' door and entered the room. Williams was sat at his desk in his uniform, busy signing various forms and asked Skelton to take a seat whilst he finished. After a few minutes, he rose and picked up the signed papers and took them out to his secretary before returning to his seat. He looked across to Skelton, "Tea or Coffee Dan?" Skelton shook his head, "No thanks sir, I'm fine to go."

"Right Dan bring me up to speed on the missing girl?" Skelton cleared his throat and began what he knew was going to be a pretty tough conversation. "Well as you know sir, no trace of Linda has been found despite very thorough searches and appeals for information. We had to let our only suspect, to date, go free as we have nothing whatsoever by way of forensics to prove that Linda had been with him or in his flat. What concerns me most is the fact that Edwards does not possess a computer, iPad or smart phone which could have been used to arrange a meeting with Linda. I simply don't buy the notion that a well-educated man would not have access to such devices. I therefore want to put him under surveillance to see if we can discover if he is using an internet café or some other setting such as a library where he can access these devices. He could have access to the internet possibly at a location such as a rented garage or lockup." Williams sprung out of his chair, pushed it back and gave Skelton a glowering look.

"Dan, this is not a murder enquiry, at least it's not until we find a body and murder is determined! The cost of surveillance is sky high, and I've already thrown an awful lot of resources at this enquiry from what is an incredibly tight budget. I am spending serious money on this investigation and to now be asked to sanction overtime on surveillance on a suspect on whom you haven't a shred of evidence is just not acceptable. Until or if this becomes a murder enquiry, I am not prepared to sanction your request. I'm sorry but if you saw the budget I must work with, you would understand. So please don't take this personally."

Skelton had expected such a reaction from his boss. Surveillance would have to wait.

"Of course, sir, I understand that budgetary restraints are having a huge impact on the whole force. I will do my best with the officers I have available to keep on top of the enquiry. Sir, I need to bring you up to date on what I regard to be another investigation that is closely related to Linda's disappearance." Williams sat in silence whilst Skelton went through his concerns on the investigation into the disappearance of Marion, and her body being recovered from the river. Williams had so far not interrupted, which Skelton thought might be a good sign. He was wrong!

Skelton had just got to the point of informing Williams that he had dispatched Alexander to the mortuary to find out what samples had been retained from the post-mortem. Still Williams remained quiet and obviously interested. Now the time had come for Skelton to show his hand.

"Now sir, we may have a problem with any samples that were kept from Marion's body during the PM." Williams was getting a little restless and asked, "Oh how so?" "Well sir at the time, the mortuary was very short staffed as we all were. The senior pathologist was off with the flu and a junior pathologist was asked to conduct the PM. Given the conditions and stress that they must have been working under, it's possible that any blood and urine samples were not kept, as this appeared to be a tragic drowning and not suspicious. If in fact there are no blood or urine samples available, we might have a problem."

Williams had been patiently following what Skelton had been saying but he was at a loss as to where it was all leading. "Dan, I'm not sure what you are getting at. Can you enlighten me please?"

Skelton placed his hands on the desk in front of him and continued. "Sir, I think Marion may have been murdered." Williams had suddenly turned much redder than usual. "How the hell do you come to that conclusion?" Skelton removed his hands from the desk and sat straight up. "Well sir, the pathologist failed to test for any drugs in her system. There is a possibility that Marion had been drugged and then raped. The killer kept her alive and when he was finished, simply pushed her into the water and she drowned. We conducted a less than thorough investigation and the killer may have got away with it. Now I think he has killed Linda." Williams stood up and looked down on Skelton, "Are you saying to me, we have a possible serial killer on our hands?" Skelton stood and looked directly into Williams eyes. "Well technically sir, he would have to have killed at least three to make him a serial killer. I think we may be dealing with a double murderer now and if I am correct, he could go on to become a serial killer unless we stop him. If we don't have any luck with the blood sample from the mortuary, then I need you to get authorisation from the Chief Constable for what we may have to do next."

Williams was taken aback by what he had just heard. "Please Dan, sit down" Both men sat down, and Williams said, "Just what is it you are

195

proposing Dan?" Skelton leaned forward, once again resting his hands on the desk. "If the mortuary failed to keep the blood and urine samples from Marion, then we may have to exhume her body in the hope that we can test for evidence of drugs. That could indicate that she was drugged, raped and her body put in the river, to make it look accidental."

Skelton watched Williams keenly trying to work out what the other man was thinking. Suddenly Williams leapt from his seat, bringing his fist down hard on the desk. "Are you bloody mad? You want me to get permission to exhume a dead body which, this force concluded was an accidental drowning. Something, which was confirmed by the pathologist. Do you have any idea what this would do to the reputation of the force? The press would have a field day. We haven't even found Linda's body to carry out tests on her to see if she had been drugged. I'm sorry but, there is no way that I am authorising an exhumation, it could just be a wild goose chase which would not only be bad for the reputation of the force, but the costs would be enormous. You are just going to pin your hopes that Alexander can locate those samples. Now I'm sure you have plenty to do, so I will not detain you any longer. Good day Chief Inspector."

Chapter Thirty

After being dismissed by Williams, Skelton went back to his office and began clearing a stack of emails. He heard a tap on the door and in walked Peter Lowik. "Sir, do you have a minute?" Skelton waved Lowik to take a seat. "Yes of course Peter, what can I do for you?" Lowik looked slightly embarrassed and began hesitatingly, "I know you have plenty going on at the moment sir but it's about the case where people have reported valuables missing despite there being no signs of a break-in." Skelton smiled and said, "Any progress on that yet?" Lowik now looked a bit more confident. "Yes sir. As you suggested, I went and interviewed all the victims. And you were right there a connection. They all own BMW's and all the cars are serviced at the same garage sir. It's the dealer up at Peasedown St John."

Skelton leaned back in his chair and said, "Well done Peter. You and I will give that garage a visit just as soon as I can fit in the time." Lowik stood up and said, "Just say when you want to go sir, and I will drive us up there."

Skelton picked up his phone and called Mike Jones, the Coroner. He carefully explained his concerns regarding the lack of toxicology tests on the blood and urine samples taken from Marion Busby. He went on to explain that Bill Alexander was on his way to the mortuary to see if the samples could be found. Jones reluctantly agreed that it would be prudent to have the analysis undertaken if the samples were found but that the results could be embarrassing to both himself and to the police!

It was lunch time and Skelton had still had no word from Alexander. He was feeling hungry having had an earlier start than usual and had made do with just a bacon roll all morning. He checked his watch, it was 12.40pm. He got up and went through to the detective's room. There were a few officers working away at their workstations others on the phone. He saw Ross Turnbull look up and said to him, "Ross I'm just popping out for a bite to eat. I've got my mobile and radio if you need to contact me." Turnbull gave him a thumbs up and said, "Enjoy your lunch sir."

On leaving the station, he crossed the road and turned right heading in the direction of Bog Island and the Ale House. He had his iPad with him on which he had downloaded the Times newspaper which he planned to read in the absence of Alexander. As he approached the Ale House, he remembered that he needed to get some cash and decided to take a walk to his own bank. It was another warm day and he felt that the twenty-minute round trip walk would help to clear his head. He turned left at the entrance to the Ale House and glanced through the window, to see that young Adam was behind the bar. That pleased him as he always enjoyed his conversations with Adam. He also enjoyed looking at him, as he was a handsome young man.

As he turned into York Street, he had to negotiate his way past the sea of visitors that were engrossed in taking pictures of the Abbey. Some days, it could be very frustrating getting around the city, because of the vast number of tourists milling around. Suddenly, his eyes caught sight of a young man of obvious foreign appearance. Skelton guessed that the lad was about 18 or 19. He was about 5.7" tall, very slim and had a pock marked face. He was wearing dark jeans, a white t-shirt and a cheap black leather jacket, Skelton reckoned he was from an eastern European country. One thing was for sure and that was that the guy was up to no good. Skelton scanned the crowds for the guy's accomplice and it only took him seconds to spot him. The guy's mate was slightly older, maybe

20 and a few pounds heavier. He was similarly dressed almost like they were wearing uniforms. The older guy was a bit shorter maybe 5.5" and his face was also pock marked. His head was shaven, which made him appear a little more frightening than his mate.

Skelton had seen these types of guys in London. They were pick pockets. They usually worked in teams of between six and eight. The guy who stole the purse or wallet was known as the dipper. Once he had taken the purse or wallet, he would slip it to his accomplice sometimes known as the banker. They usually picked expensive shopping streets such as Regent Street or Oxford Street, where scores of wealthy tourists would be easy prey. Today they were in Bath and their target was the wealthy tourists, milling around the Abbey busy taking photographs. These tourists were easy pickings for the pick pockets. The tourists were completely focused on trying to get the best possible photographs of the Abbey that they could, whilst totally ignoring their valuables.

Skelton pretended to be chatting on his phone whilst carefully watching the dipper. He saw the dipper approach a rotund, well-dressed middle-aged man, who looked to be an American. The tourist was completely concentrating on getting a photograph of his wife and did not feel the hand slide into his hip pocket and remove his wallet containing cash and credit cards. The dipper slowly walked away to where the banker was standing smoking a cigarette. The wallet was passed to the banker and the dipper looked for his next victim.

Skelton radioed the control room and reported the fact that there was a gang of pick pockets operating around the Abbey. He described the two members of the gang that he had spotted. He asked for the CCTV controllers to look out for more young eastern European males. He said that they were most probably working in the more expensive shopping streets in the city. He ordered that all plain clothes officers should go immediately into the city centre and liaise with the control room for sightings. He ordered Lowik to join him outside Crisp Cowley, the up-market estate agents in York Street and for the custody van to park up outside the Ale House and wait. No officers in uniform were to set foot in the city centre until the entire gang of pick pockets had been identified.

A few minutes later, Skelton was joined by Lowik. As Lowik approached him, Skelton stuck out his hand as if he was welcoming a friend. Lowik played along with the little charade. "Right Peter, we are going to have to nab those thieving bastards together". He indicated the dipper and banker to Lowik. "I will get behind the banker and you grab the dipper as soon as you can. When you make your move, I will be on top of the banker. Be careful, these guys don't like getting caught and invariably run if they can or fight dirty. So, we take them out hard and fast. Understand?" "Sure, I got it. You get behind the banker now, I'm on the dipper."

Skelton pretended to say goodbye to Lowik and started to walk towards the tourist information shop, which was immediately behind the banker, who was lighting up a fresh cigarette. The banker was closely following the dipper who was just manoeuvring into position, behind a Japanese lady whose handbag was hanging over her right shoulder. She was oblivious to the hand carefully opening the bag and the dipper was oblivious to Lowik. As Lowik got behind the dipper, he drew his right fist back and hit the dipper's right kidney. The dipper fell to his knees gasping at the punch that Lowik had so beautifully delivered.

Meanwhile the banker sensed that Lowik spelt trouble and was just about to shout a warning, but Skelton cut the man off, as he slammed his right hand over the banker's throat and pulled him to the ground. The banker was strong and began fighting back so Skelton hit him hard on the throat again and followed that up with an almighty punch to the banker's solar plexus. Struggle over. Skelton cuffed the banker's wrists behind his back.

Skelton looked up to find Lowik leading the dipper towards him, in cuffs. "Well done Peter, that's two of them off the streets. It should only be a matter of time before we catch the rest of them." He had only finished getting the words out, when on the radio, he heard that two more were in custody. "Right let's get these two around to the Ale House, the custody van should be waiting there. We can hand these over to uniform and then pop into the Ale House for a celebratory Fosters and some grub." Lowik burst into a wild grin, "That sounds like a plan to me sir." Skelton would have to pay by card as he no longer had time to go to the bank!

Chapter Thirty-One

Back at the station, Skelton was going through the various reports from the scientific team. At 3.15pm Bill Alexander knocked on his door and entered. Skelton looked up and saw a tired looking Alexander slowly sit down opposite him. "Bill, I've tried phoning you a few times, but it kept going to voice mail. Why is that?"

Alexander took a handkerchief from his pocket and wiped his forehead and gave a noisy sigh. "Oh, I know, I'm sorry sir but I've been running around like a blue arse fly all day and I think I must have put the phone down and left it somewhere." Skelton gave a frown and said "I hope it turns up, those phones are expensive you know? I also tried your personal mobile, but I couldn't reach you on that either." Alexander gave his head an embarrassing shake. "Sorry the battery is dead, I forgot to put it on charge last night."

Skelton stood up and said, "Never mind about that Bill, how did you get on at the mortuary?" Alexander put his hands behind his head and took a deep breath. "Well at first, I thought we were going to get nowhere. As I explained to you the other day, everybody was short staffed when it came to the post-mortem and strictly speaking, we should have waited for the chief pathologist to do it once he had recovered from the flu. But with Christmas coming up, we wanted the wee girl to be processed and returned to her family for burial. However, the DCI persuaded the Coroner to let young Dr Thomson do the autopsy as he was convinced it was an accidental drowning. If he had thought it was a suspicious death and possibly homicide, then of course we would have to have got a Home Office Pathologist to do the autopsy." Skelton sat back down having absorbed this information. "Go on Bill."

Alexander leaned forward, taking his hands from behind his head. "Well, I saw Dr Thomson this morning and I explained to him about your concerns that Marion's death might have been murder and not accidental drowning. The good doctor was naturally horrified and was determined to be as helpful as possible. I explained to him that we needed to know, if there had also been a drug or drugs in her system which could have rendered her unconscious, leading to her being raped. The poor guy virtually turned grey when I put this to him and he agreed that with hindsight, he should have sent a blood and urine sample to the lab for toxicology testing."

Skelton wanted Alexander to get to the punch-line but he had got to know him well enough, to let him explain matters in his own way and Skelton nodded his head and asked, "Did he keep any blood back?"

Alexander sat back in the chair. "Well Dr Thomson said he had been a trifle nervous about doing the autopsy on his own, even though the Coroner had sanctioned it. But for his own peace of mind, not only did he save some blood, but he also kept back some urine as well as all the swabs taken from the anus and vagina."

Skelton got out of his chair and came around the desk so that he was standing above his DS, "Right Bill don't keep me in suspense any fucking longer. Can the lab undertake toxicology tests now even though the samples are about six months old?" Alexander gave himself a small encouraging cough, putting his right hand over his mouth, whilst doing so. Looking at Skelton and looking smug at the same time, "Yes, they can but it will take about six weeks for the results to come through." Skelton leaned down and patted Alexander's forehead. "Well done Bill, now we are cooking with gas!" The men exchanged high fives.

Skelton went to see Williams and reported on the arrests of the pick pockets. They had managed to detain all eight of the gang and retrieve thousands of pounds in cash and other currencies, plus dozens of credit cards. Williams was pleased with the result. Skelton then told him that it was most unlikely that there would be a need to exhume Marion's body, owing to the pathologist having retained the blood and urine samples. Williams was delighted with the news. Both men agreed that they would withhold these facts from the press and media for the time being.

At 4pm the conference room was full of his detectives and Skelton stood up to address them. "Right boys and girls, we have had a few developments today which I need to share with you. Firstly, I am treating the case of Marion Busby who you may recall was found dead in the river last Christmas as suspicious" There was much exchanging of glances between the detectives at this news. Skelton went on. "I don't believe that we properly investigated her death at the time and I am not seeking to blame anyone for this. There were major operational issues at the time, which simply prevented us from having her blood and urine checked for drugs. At the time of the post-mortem, the pathologist had confirmed that the girl was three times over the driving limit for alcohol and in the absence of any injuries to her body, it was concluded that she had simply been intoxicated which caused her to fall into the river and drown. However, the pathologist confirmed that she had engaged in rough sexual intercourse before she died and for that reason, I have ordered toxicology reports for drugs just in case she had been drugged and then raped." The detectives once again exchanged glances.

Skelton peered at his notes and looked around his teammates and said. "Now, I've been giving a lot of thought to the fact that we have absolutely no forensics on Edwards. In my view, he cleared his flat of every shred of evidence and somehow moved Linda's body. I suspect he dumped the body in the river but it's more likely that she was still alive at this point. Edwards wants us to think that she was intoxicated and simply fell into the river and drowned. Just as he appeared to convince us that the same fate befell poor Marion. If Linda was put into the river, then her body should appear any day soon. So far as I can be sure, he also removed the bed sheets and perhaps towels which had covered the bed. Those he has removed either to another flat, lockup or garage that we have yet to find.

Edwards has been clever, but the one thing which raised my curiosity from the outset was that he claims not to own either an iPhone, computer or any such device that would enable him to have been in communication with Linda. I can tell you now, that he was sacked from his job as a chemistry teacher, for viewing porn on his school laptop. I think that at this other flat, lockup or garage that he most probably rents, he keeps a phone or laptop or whatever and goes there whenever he feels the urge. I want a volunteer to check with the council to see if it has a record of our man Edwards renting such a property." Janet Griffin raised her hand and said, "I can do that sir." Skelton looked across to Griffin, smiled and said, "Thank you Janet."

Skelton shuffled up his notes and announced, "That's all folks, briefing adjourned."

Chapter Thirty- Two

It was Tuesday morning, eight days after Linda had last been seen alive. Skelton spent some time answering emails and reading the latest crime reports. It was just before 11am and he and Alexander were sitting down to square sausage sandwiches and tea. It was another lovely May morning outside. Skelton had decided that he and Alexander would have lunch in a different pub today, as the Ale House had been getting busy with tourists at lunch time. This made it difficult to get a seat and be served quickly and Skelton did not possess a great deal of spare time. He was just pondering which hostelry they would visit for lunch when the door bust open and Dave Lake rushed in. "A girl's body has just been found in the river at Twerton. A man walking his dog found it half an hour ago, but he didn't have a phone on him, so he had to wait until he got home to phone us." Skelton and Alexander rose from their chairs. Now that they had a body, a proper investigation could now be launched, and Skelton was going to play it by the book!

Alexander was driving, and Skelton was in the front passenger seat and it only took ten minutes to reach the spot where the body had been discovered. Skelton noticed that there were already several marked police cars on site and blue police tape had been put up, restricting access to the site. There were also two crime scene investigation vans parked up. Alexander parked the car and both men got out. As they walked closer to the site, Skelton could see two police divers in the water, clearly waiting for instructions. As they approached the police tape, Skelton recognised inspector Graham Symonds. He would oversee the crime scene and would register the names of everyone who entered or left the crime cordon. The forensic guys were already suited and booted, in their plastic protective suits. Every individual no matter what their role was in visiting the crime scene, would wear similar protective clothing, to prevent any contamination of evidence.

Skelton approached Inspector Symonds and said, "Good morning Graham, and who found the body?" Symonds looked up from his clip board and saw Skelton and Alexander. "Morning Dan morning Bill. The gentleman sitting in the back of that patrol car there." Pointing to the car immediately behind him. "He's a Mr Murray, a retired school caretaker. Had been out walking his dog this morning. As he got to about here, the dog started barking. On looking down the riverbank, he saw what he thought was a dead body. He went home and called us and when the officers arrived on the scene, they confirmed his suspicions. From what I can see of it, the body is bloated, and so must have been in the river for some time. My guess is that it's the body of the missing girl."

Skelton dispatched Alexander to get Mr Murray's details as they would want a witness statement from him later. Meanwhile Skelton was updated that the undertakers were on their way as well as the Coroner, Mike Jones and the Home Office Pathologist, Dr Rob Challis. As Skelton was getting into his protective suit, he noticed a technician carefully photographing the scene. Two other forensic officers had climbed down the riverbank sifting for evidence. They would not remove the body from the water until both the coroner and the pathologist had seen the body in situ.

The coroner arrived minutes before Dr Challis and they both approached Skelton and Inspector Symonds. Skelton introduced himself as he had not yet had the privilege of working with either man before. This was Skelton's case and he would play it strictly by the book. Skelton began, "Well gentlemen, as you know we have been searching for a missing girl for a week now. I suspect that this body may well be that of Linda Carson. I am treating her disappearance as suspicious and if that is her body, then her death will also be treated as suspicious. For that reason, we will follow established protocol for recovering the body and this site is for now officially a crime scene. We need to ensure that whatever forensic evidence there is, remains on the body."

The Coroner Mike Jones, a former rugby player of some ability, spoke in response to Skelton's update. "Very well inspector, you have my permission to retrieve the body and Dr Challis will make his preliminary examination on scene. The body can then be removed to the mortuary where the forensics team can do their job and when that has been completed Dr Challis will conduct the autopsy."

The police divers carefully hauled the body on to a stretcher and this was carried up the riverbank and placed inside a blue tent that had been erected. The body was fully clothed and considerably bloated, because of decomposition. The body had no shoes on its feet, most probably as a result of the strong current. More photographs were taken. When it was deemed appropriate, Dr Challis knelt for a closer examination. He held a portable dictaphone in his left hand into which he dictated his initial findings. When he was finished, he returned to where Skelton and the coroner were standing, at the entrance to the tent.

Dr Challis cleared his throat and began to speak. "Well, it's the body of a young woman possibly late teens early twenties. The body has been in the water for about a week. There are no signs of obvious trauma except for some slight bruising around the nose and mouth which could have happened on her entering the water. There is evidence of petechia (tiny haemorrhages which occur either as a result of drowning or strangulation) around the eyes but no marks or bruising to the throat to indicate strangulation. I would say that in all probability, death was due to drowning. I will know precisely at the PM. Now forensics have a lot to do with bagging up the body for removal to the mortuary and once there, they will have to tape the clothes for hairs etc., and once that's done, they will tape the body as well. Best to give them plenty of time for that, so I will schedule the autopsy for five o'clock this afternoon, if you gentlemen want to attend?"

The coroner spoke first, "Sorry but I have a social engagement this evening which I can't put off but I'm sure that Chief Inspector Skelton will wish to attend." Skelton looked at both men and said, "Yes, me and Bill Alexander will both be there."

Chapter Thirty-Three

Developments occurred quickly following the discovery of the body. The police family support officers had been informed of the discovery immediately. Linda's parents were staying in a local hotel and were being supported by these dedicated officers who tried their best to comfort them and give them every possible assistance. Once they had broken the news that a young woman's body had been recovered, all their hopes would be dashed, and they were going to have to identify the body. Given the fact that the body had been in the water for over a week and had started to decompose, identification could wait until after the post-mortem, when the morticians had had a chance to improve its appearance. The parents would only be permitted to view the face in a private chapel at the mortuary. Linda's DNA had already been obtained and strictly speaking the body did not have to be formerly identified, but parents tended to need comfort in ensuring that it was indeed their child that they had to lay to rest.

Ross Turnbull was busy rounding up CCTV footage from the businesses on Widcombe Parade. He had even got some footage from the external CCTV on the Travel Lodge Hotel, which was about four hundred meters along the waterfront from the pedestrian bridge linking Poultney Road with the train station.

Janet Griffin had checked with the council to see if Edwards was renting any council property such as a flat, garage or lockup. The council had no records of Edwards renting any such property.

It was reported on the lunch time news that a body had been recovered from the river, but the police had refused to say that it was that of the missing girl until formal identification had taken place. Police family support officers were with the missing girl's family. Few people doubted that it was the body of the missing university student.

Skelton and Alexander were at the mortuary along with the coroner's officer Romney Cox and all three were struggling to get on their surgical gowns and into their boots. Once ready, they entered the dissecting room where Dr Challis was already suitably attired and was sharpening his post-mortem knife. A mortuary technician was busy arranging instruments and tubes into which the good doctor would place various samples of blood, urine and tissue from the body.

Dr Challis turned to face the gathered audience and said, "Well gentlemen I will begin. But as the body is what's known as a "bloater" owing to it having begun to decompose, there will be an obnoxious smell when I make the first incision. If you feel sick or faint, please walk away immediately as I do not want the body contaminated with puke!" Alexander grimaced but Skelton did not see it behind Alexander's face mask.

On conclusion of the post-mortem, Dr Challis invited the group into his office for his initial conclusions. Skelton and Alexander were seated but Romney Cox had to stand owing to there being only two chairs available for guests.

Dr Challis looked up from his notes and said, "Well gentlemen, this is my initial assessment of the post-mortem. The body is that of a Caucasian girl aged approximately between 18 and 25 years. She was well nourished and there was no evidence of disease or major trauma. There was some slight swelling around the nose and mouth consistent with a fall into the water. Petechia was present around the eyes extending towards the forehead. This I would have expected to see in a case of drowning. I have excluded as a cause of death strangulation which also leaves petechia on the face and eyes but there is no evidence of any force being applied to the throat or neck"

"There was some slight bruising to both upper arms which would be consistent with a sexual partner holding her during intercourse. She had prior to death, consumed alcohol and she was two and half times over the drink driving limit. She had had vigorous sexual intercourse shortly before she died and there is swelling around the vagina. I have taken swabs of the vagina and there is clearly blood present. There does not appear to be any residual semen, which indicates the use of a condom. I believe she was a virgin which is interesting when we consider the fact that she had also had anal sex. Again, whilst blood was present, there was no evidence of semen. That, in my experience, is very unusual for a girl to consent to on her first date. It would imply, that she may have been incapacitated by way of drugs. If the sex was not co-consensual but she was unconscious, it would explain the lack of further bruising."

"Death was as a result of drowning there is no question about that. However, I am very concerned that the girl may have been drugged and rendered unconscious. She could then easily have been raped, her clothes replaced, and her unconscious body carefully removed from wherever the rape took place. The girl is quite petite, and a strong man would have had no difficulty in gently pushing her into the water. I have scraped her fingernails and there is no evidence of her having scratched her assailant. Nor are there any signs that she made any attempt to grab hold of any vegetation when she entered the water. A drowning person, if conscious, will literally fight for their life and will attempt to grab hold of anything which might allow them to exit the water. I think that this is a suspicious death and if the toxicology results confirm the presence of a drug or drugs, then in my opinion she was most certainly murdered."

Skelton had been making detailed notes. "Dr Challis, I have been reviewing the post-mortem report of another girl's body that was recovered from the same location in the river as Linda. This was back in December last year. That body was not tested for drugs but the blood and urine samples that were retained were sent off for analysis yesterday. She had also undergone both vaginal and anal sex and she too had been a virgin. I am now linking these deaths as being connected and both will be treated as murder unless the toxicology results prove otherwise." Dr Challis thought for a moment. "Yes, I remember that case. I had come down with that god awful flu and the mortuary was at bursting point with all the additional deaths due to it. And it was getting close to Christmas. Mike Jones called me at home to ask if he should wait until I was recovered and undertake the PM. He told me that the police were certain that it was purely accidental and bore all the hall marks of an intoxicated student falling into the river. I told Mike that given all the circumstances, I had no objection for the PM to be conducted by a junior pathologist provided both he and the police were happy with that. The PM was conducted by Dr Thomson, who reported no evidence of any foul play and that the girl had been intoxicated. His opinion was that death was caused by drowning and in the absence of any injury, accidental."

Skelton finished writing his notes and said, "Dr Challis, we may have been wrong to assume that that was indeed an accidental drowning. That girl had also been a virgin until shortly before she died. She too had experienced rough sexual intercourse both front and back. Although Dr

Thomson had extracted samples of both her blood and urine, but unfortunately these were never sent off for the toxicology analysis. As a result of the similarities between the two deaths, I am now treating Marion Busby's death as suspicious and the coroner agreed that we should have those retained blood and urine samples, sent off for testing for any evidence of drugs."

As Skelton and Alexander were getting up to leave, Bob Richards knocked on the door and entered. "Gentlemen, sorry to interrupt but I have the initial report on our tapings from the body and clothing. No evidence of blood or other bodily fluids. The only fibres and hairs belong to the girl which is extraordinary." It was Dr Challis who was first to interrupt. "Your right, that is extraordinary! That girl had rough sex possibly numerous times and yet her sexual partner, if I can call him that, left absolutely no trace of DNA on her body or clothing. Now, I could understand the absence of any contamination by the perpetrator on her clothing, given that it had been in the river for a week. But the absence of any DNA on her body would suggest to me, that the perpetrator had gone to a great deal of trouble to ensure he had totally removed all traces of his DNA. This further suggests, to me anyway, that he has a significant understanding of crime scenes or at least a good understanding of DNA."

It was Skelton who spoke next. "Dr Challis, I think we are all agreed that we have one if not two murders on our hands. The murderer is clearly quite clever and has managed to remove any trace of his DNA on both victims. How he achieved that remains to be discovered. The only suspect that we have so far managed to identify, happens to have been a school teacher who was head of science at a prestigious school in Brighton. If I was a gambling man, and I am, my money is on him!"

Chapter Thirty-Four

It was October, the previous year and a Saturday morning. It was a bright morning but cold with a strong east wind blowing, making it feel even colder. It was shortly after ten and Edwards had called into the Widcombe Pharmacy to collect his monthly prescription. He was on statins and other medications to control the high blood pressure from which he suffered. As he emerged from the pharmacy, he had a choice of either turning left which would lead him down towards the pedestrian bridge over the river and through the railway station. Or he could turn right and walk down Poultney Road and eventually take a left onto North Parade. Both routes were probably equal distant to his flat. He decided to turn right and cross the road. As he slowly walked, he checked out the various commercial premises. There was the Rams Head pub, not yet open for the day. A takeaway hamburger shop where he could see an employee busy cleaning down the serving counter. Next door was the Bath Lock and Key Company. Then there was a florist where he stopped at to admire the flowers on display. The owner was coming out of the door with a huge bunch of flowers and was busy placing them in the back of her van. As he walked on, he noticed on his left a church with a small car park and there was a lane which he had no idea would lead to. Having nothing better to do, he turned left onto the lane and a few seconds later, he was standing in a small council car park. It had about a dozen spaces and there was a ticket machine above which was a large sign, "Pay & Display".

Standing in the car park, Edwards got his bearings and discovered that he was at the rear of the commercial premises that he had just walked past on Widcombe Parade. This was a very sheltered spot which was protected from sight by traffic using Poultney Road by way of a row of garages or lockups. These were immediately behind the pub and the Bath Lock and Key Company. Once you entered the car park from Poultney Road and pulled up behind the row of garages and workshops, you were virtually invisible. The only people who could see you would be the residents in the flats over-looking the car park or the tenants of the commercial premises below the flats. Edwards immediately thought to himself, "What a fantastic place to have a workshop. I could come and go as I please. Hardly anyone would ever see me."

As he stood surveying the garages and the rear exits to the commercial premises on Widcombe Parade, a blue Ford Focus entered the car park but then turned right and pulled up next to the end garage. A man in his forties got out of the driver's door. He was about 5"8 slim build and had a neatly trimmed beard and a bald head. Edwards did not know whether the man had lost his hair or had shaved it. Either way it was of no interest to him. The man closed the driver's door and walked to the garage door and took out a key from his pocket and put it in the lock and unlocked the door. He swung the door up and leaned in and switched on a light. The inside of the garage lit up and the man walked to the boot of his car and opened it. He then went inside the garage and picked up two large black refuse sacks and heaved them into the boot. He repeated the exercise, lifting two more bags of rubbish into the boot. He then picked up a couple of old tyres and they also went into the boot which was now full. He closed the boot and opened a rear door. He went back into the garage bringing out two more black bags.

Edwards was very curious and a little excited. He slowly walked over towards the Ford Focus just as the man was coming out with a large cardboard box which he was carefully placing into the open door. The man placed the box on the seat and turned around to see Edwards standing by the rear of the car. Edwards gave him a friendly smile and said, "Good morning, having a bit of a clear out then?" The man had seen Edwards as he had driven into the car park and just assumed he was waiting to meet someone. "Good morning, yes, I am having a clear out. The garage belongs to my father, and he's had to go into a care home. Unfortunately, he has dementia and would not sell his flat whilst he still could. So now, I'm going to rent out his flat until such time as he passes away. He has left it to me in his Will, but the council will probably get the lot depending on how long he lives for to set off the cost of his care. Bloody ridiculous, dad worked all his life to buy that flat and put some money away. Now that he can't look after himself, the council says it can't afford to care for him, so they get first claim on whatever assets he has. Pisses me off big time."

Edwards nodded his head as the man spoke, sharing the man's anger at the system. It was so unfair. "Oh, I'm really sorry to hear that. So, what's happening to your dad's flat now?" The man rested his arm on the roof of the car and sighed. "I've let the flat to a banker who just wants it as a base. He travels abroad a lot which means he will hardly use the flat much, which suits me because he won't hassle me when things like a light bulb needs changing. You know?" Edwards smiled, "Yes, I've heard that being a landlord can be a bit testing at times. So, are you clearing out the garage for the tenant?"

The man pulled out a cigarette packet from his jacket and offered the pack to Edwards who politely declined. The man lit the cigarette with a lighter and gave a little cough. "No, actually the guy does not have a car and says he has no use for the garage. So I'm going to rent it out. Garages are hard to come by in the centre of Bath, so I won't have any problem finding a tenant, that's for sure." Edwards laughed out loud. "Actually, I think you just found your ideal tenant. I don't have a car either but I'm looking for a garage to store some stuff and to use it as a workshop." The two men discussed the rent and Edwards agreed to pay six month's rent in advance in cash. He certainly did not want to leave a paper trail for the police to find. Nothing would pass through his bank account that would alert the police to the possibility that he was renting a workshop!

Chapter Thirty-Five

Skelton gave the dogs a big cuddle before leaving the house and setting off for his daily walk into the city. It was a cloudy morning, but the forecast was for it to brighten up later with some sunshine in the afternoon. As he strode down the hill, past the

Devonshire Arms on his left, Skelton was thinking about the most likely site on the river, to drop a body. He concluded that the most obvious site would be somewhere around Widcombe and so he decided that once he had answered his emails and emptied his in-tray, he and Alexander would take a walk out to Widcombe.

Once he had finished with his emails, Skelton made a start on his in-tray. The gang of pickpockets would be appearing before Bath Magistrates Court this morning. It turned out they were all Romanian's and four of them had been using fake passports. All of them had previous convictions both in England and in Romania for theft and violence. There were two international arrest warrants out for two of the men using fake passports. All in all, this had been a very worthwhile exercise and most probably, all would be remanded in custody to appear later at Bristol Crown Court, where the Judge had much more sentencing authority.

Also, in his in-tray, was a summary of the door-to-door enquiries that uniform had conducted on garages and lock ups in the Widecombe area. It summarised the fact that there was a total of 12 garages in the immediate area close to the river. Enquiries had revealed that the garages were owned by the occupants of various flats on Widecombe Parade. Officers had been able to confirm that 11 out of the 12 garages were in use almost daily and were used for parking cars and storage. The 12th garage was reported as being empty as the owner was suffering from dementia and had been admitted to a care home for the elderly. It was further reported that his son, had sold his father's car and had emptied the garage. The officer compiling the report, had noted that a neighbour, a Mr. Martin Wilson, had been most cooperative and had been able to identify the owners of all the garages. Mr Wilson had, it was noted, been a resident of Widcombe Parade for thirty-two years. In other words, Skelton guessed that Mr Wilson was a busybody, who kept close tabs on everyone and everything. Such neighbours could be worth their weight in gold to the police.

Skelton was disappointed that the door-to-door enquiries had not revealed a potential hiding place for Edwards to contact potential victims on the internet. One of those garages would have been ideal but if he was not using a garage there, he had to have a place somewhere else. He needed to follow up with Janet Griffin as soon as she got in. As he was lifting the next report demanding his attention, Skelton heard a knock on the door and looking up, he saw Detective Inspector Patrick

Rees enter. "Patrick, good morning and what can I do for you today?" Skelton rose to greet his friend and held out his hand. The men shook hands warmly and Rees sat down in the chair opposite Skelton. "Morning Dan, how are you settling into your new job"? Skelton stretched out both his arms in front of him before pulling them back and resting them on the desk in front of him. "To be honest Patrick, I could have done without this fucking mystery of the missing girl. It's absolutely bazar that she gets off the bus and vanishes into thin air only to wash up a week later in the river.

Although officially, the cause of death is drowning, I'm convinced that she was drugged and then raped. Following that, the rapist carefully put her clothes back on whilst being extremely careful not to leave his DNA on her. Then somehow, he manages to transport her whilst she is still unconscious, to the river where he simply pushes her into the river where she drowns."

Rees stood up and walked towards the window but stopped and turned halfway. "Dan, I hear that you are linking this girl's death with that of another girl who drowned in the river last Christmas?" Skelton looked at his friend for a second and realised that Rees was looking a trifle anxious. "Yes, Patrick that's correct. The girl last

Christmas was called Marion Busby and the investigation was conducted by my predecessor DCI Smith. At the post-mortem, which incidentally was conducted by a junior pathologist, there were no obvious signs of trauma and the cause of death was given as accidental drowning. The girl had been drinking as a blood test confirmed. However, they never tested her blood for drugs which I think was a mistake. So, we have managed to retrieve some blood and urine that was taken at the PM and that has been sent off for toxicology analysis."

Rees walked back and sat down on the chair and fixed his eyes on Skelton. "Dan, there is no easy way for me to say this, but I think it's best you hear it from me first. DCI Smith was very much liked and respected not just here in Bath but throughout the entire force. There are already whispers going around that you are trying to damage his reputation and make a name for yourself." Skelton looked totally shocked. He stood up and walked around the desk and looked down at his friend.

"Patrick, that is absolute shite and you know that. Why on earth would I want to besmirch the reputation of a man who I never even met? All I am trying to do is to seek out the truth and discover what happened, to these young girls. If they were murdered, as I suspect they were, then we need to accomplish two things. First, find the murderer and try and prevent him from striking again. And secondly, give the families and friends of these girls, the closure that they deserve. That's all I'm trying to achieve Patrick, nothing else and I'm certainly not looking for any glory."

Rees stood up and placed his hands upon Skelton's shoulders. "Dan, I know exactly what it is that you are trying to achieve, and I wish you nothing but the best of luck with your endeavours. All I am trying to do, is to warn you that some of your predecessor's friends and colleagues do not like what you are about. He was in the masons you know, and those guys always look after their own. Just be careful Dan, that's all I am saying because if they can find anything which they can use against you, they will. You can be sure of that!"

Skelton thought for a second as he contemplated the warning that Rees had delivered. Skelton realised that his friend had gone to considerable trouble to drive over from Bristol to deliver the message in the spirit of friendship and was only doing his best to ensure that Skelton was aware that not all his colleagues were necessary friends. "Thanks Patrick, I appreciate the trouble you have taken this morning to keep me appraised of the big picture. To be honest, I never gave it a thought that what I was doing would upset anyone other than Bill Alexander who also worked on that case. But I told Bill from the outset that I was not, in anyway, criticising him or his DCI particularly considering the circumstances' they found themselves in. I guess that message was never picked up by those who should know better."

Chapter Thirty-Six

After Rees had gone, Janet Griffin had popped in to up-date Skelton on her enquiries with the council to determine whether Edwards was registered as renting any type of property in Bath. The simple answer was no, he was not registered with the council except for council tax purposes and as an employee.

At 11.45am Bill Alexander wondered into Skelton's office. He had been down to the Magistrate's

Court for the appearance of the pick pockets. "Just back from the court sir, they all got remanded in custody which seemed to piss them off good and proper." Skelton smiled, "That's the first bit of good news I've heard this morning Bill. Well done. Now whilst you have been ruining the pick pockets morning, I've been having a bit of a think. I want us to take a walk down to the river by Widcombe and see if we can find a likely place that Edwards might have used for pushing the girls into the water." Alexander stretched his arms and said, "How come you have to walk everywhere? I mean, I have a perfectly good car sitting outside which could easily and quickly convey us to Widcombe in minutes." Skelton stood up. "Bill if I had been in a car yesterday, I would not have been able to drive down York Street and consequently, I would never have spotted those pick pockets. Besides, as I have said before, you need a lot more exercise and for my part, I have been far too relaxed about your food consumption. As of today, sunshine, you are on a diet of salad and soda water." Alexander let out a soft growl and followed Skelton out of the door.

On exiting the police station, they turned left and began walking towards the train station. The train station and indeed the whole of the Great Western railway had been built by Isambard

Kingdom Brunel. In fact, the Royal Hotel which is situated opposite the station has various function rooms named in honour of that brilliant engineer who was responsible for opening the west-country to trade with the rest of England and onwards to North America. At the hotel, they crossed the road and walked past the row of taxis waiting for passengers coming off the trains. They walked under the railway arch past the rear entrance to the station and the car park to their left. They then crossed the narrow pedestrian bridge where a homeless man was selling the "Big Issue". On moving back to Bath, Skelton was dismayed to discover the number of homeless people on the streets of Bath. Many had mental health problems. The largest proportion seemed to be alcoholics or drug addicts. Throughout the city centre, you could find these people sitting in doorways drinking cheap wine or very strong cider and most were usually unconscious by mid-afternoon. The police had a difficult job in being seen to be even handed with these people but at times, owing to their aggressive behaviour, they had no choice but to arrest them and lock them up. This was only a short-term solution to a very difficult and tragic problem. There was no easy answer to dealing with people with such complicated social issues.

Once they had crossed the bridge, they turned left neither man saying a word, they were both focused on how Edwards could have made such a journey. Both men were pondering how could it be possible to move a body all the way from Edward's flat to the river without a vehicle of some description? He could not have carried a body that far without being noticed, that was for sure. He did not possess a vehicle and had no access to one. This to Skelton was the greatest mystery of all. He had been unable to sleep properly, trying to imagine how Edwards could possibly have moved the bodies. Time and time again, Skelton had simply hit a brick wall. Whatever the answer was, it was so far eluding him, no matter how hard he tried to solve the problem.

They walked on for about 150 meters until they found the track which leads down to the river. They slowly followed the track which steeply sloped downwards and stopped at what appeared to be a landing stage used by boats. Both men surveyed the ground carefully. Alexander broke the silence. "Well, if you ask me, this would be the perfect place to drop a body into the river. As the track slopes down, you can't easily be seen from the main road." They were now standing below the pedestrian bridge which they had crossed just minutes earlier. From here, they were also hidden from anyone crossing the bridge. Skelton thought for a minute as he carefully recorded the scene in detail in his mind. "You are right Bill. This is the perfect spot. We don't have a fucking clue as to how Edwards got the girls down here. But once here, it would have been easy for him to just push them into the river." Skelton looked into the river and noted how fast the current was running. "Once he had pushed them in unconscious, they would have drowned very quickly. Remember what the pathologist said, a conscious person falling into water literally fights for their life. They will grasp at anything which might keep them afloat until help arrives. But these girls must have been unconscious when they went into the river otherwise, they would have attempted to have grabbed hold of anything to keep them afloat and alive.

They both stared into the river watching the various bits of flotsam being carried along in the strong current. Branches from trees, carrier bags, empty plastic bottles and so much more. "Right Bill, I think we are both agreed that this is where the girls went in. Neither girl's handbags have been found. It's my guess that Edwards probably chucked them into the river just here unless he saved them as trophies. Get the divers to conduct a detailed search of the river starting from here and working downwards. See if they can locate the girl's handbags. Mind you, I doubt if they will tell us anything given how skilful Edwards is when it comes to DNA and the fact that they have been in the river. But if he left the phones in the handbags, we might be able to somehow link him to them. Mind you, I'm not holding my breath on that score. So far, he has destroyed every piece of evidence linking him to these girls. We need a bit of luck Bill, that's for sure."

The two detectives re-traced their steps up the narrow track on to the foot path on Poultney Road. They stopped at the pedestrian crossing and Skelton pushed the button that would stop the traffic and allow them to cross the road safely. Once they had crossed over to Widcombe Parade, Skelton turned to Alexander and said, "Let's take a walk down there, Bill where that little council carpark is situated. If I had just dumped someone in the river and had some stuff that might implicate me in the dastardly deed, I'd want to get rid of it as quickly as possible. There are several garages down there that would be ideal for the job. Let's go look and see what we can discover." Alexander took his hands out of his pockets and adjusted his jacket and said, "I agree Dan, but uniform have been down here doing door-to-door enquiries and every garage is vouched for, except one which is empty." Skelton was adjusting his tie and was considering Alexander's statement. "Yes, I know that Bill, I read the report, but it won't hurt for us to go down and check for ourselves."

It was a tricky walk down to the council carpark as there was no footpath for them to walk on. So, they had to walk single file on the main road with traffic approaching them from behind. Neither man liked the idea of the fact that some driver might just be paying more attention to their mobile phone than to the road and might run into them without any warning. They were both mightily relieved to get off the main road and into the relative safety of the carpark

Both officers stood at the entrance/exit to the carpark quietly surveying the layout of the carpark and the adjacent garages. Skelton counted just seven cars parked in the carpark which did not really surprise him as this carpark is so badly signposted that few Bathonian's knows that it exists. He then cast his eyes on the rear entrances to the commercial premises situated on Widcombe Parade. The largest entrance was that of the Ram, a pub that Skelton had never been in before. He quickly took the decision that he and Alexander would now pay it a visit and see what food it had to offer. Just as he was about to mention lunch to Alexander, he heard a car approaching from behind. On turning around, he saw it was a black Toyota and it was being driven by an elderly gentleman who gave them a wave as he drove past and pulled up short of one of the garages. They watched as the man got out of the car. Skelton estimated him to be in his mid-seventies. He was wearing a navy-blue blazer, grey flannel trousers, a white shirt and tie. From a distance, Skelton could not make out if the tie was regimental or not. The man had a slight limp but apart from that he seemed rather sprightly and he appeared to have an air of determination about himself. He unlocked the garage door and pulled it upwards until it was fully open. He then got back into the car and drove it inside the garage. Skelton looked at Alexander, "let's go introduce ourselves Bill."

The man was pulling down the garage door as the officers approached him. It was now just after 12.30pm as Skelton approached him with his warrant card at the ready. "Good afternoon sir, I'm Detective Chief Inspector Skelton and this here is Detective Sergeant Alexander of Avon and Somerset police. The man had turned to face them, and he was carefully checking the officer's warrant cards. The man smiled softly and said,

"There's been lots of police coming down here all week asking all sorts of questions, but they never said what they were looking for. I don't know how they expect our help if they won't tell us what it is, they are after." Skelton pondered this news for a second. "Sorry sir, can I ask you for your name please?" The man was putting his car keys in his blazer and buttoning it up. "Oh, I'm Martin Wilson and I live up there", pointing to a flat on Widcombe Parade. "I've lived here for thirty-two years and there's nothing goes on around here that I don't know about." Skelton recognised the man's name from the door-to-door enquiries report. Skelton could tell immediately that Wilson was a busybody who clearly kept a very close eye on his neighbours, not to mention their personal business.

"Mr Wilson, I know that you have already spoken with one of my officers in uniform and you were very helpful indeed." Skelton noticed the smug look appearing on Wilson's face. I'm sorry if my officer did not tell you the nature of his enquiries but at the time, we were just speculating a little, that's all. However, as you no doubt know, we recovered the body of a young girl from the river the other day and we think she may have entered the river just across the road from here." Wilson was absorbing this news with what appeared to

Skelton, with some relish. No doubt this news was brightening up what was for Wilson, just another routine day. It was obvious to Skelton, that this gentleman seldom got to speak with a senior police officer. Skelton had no doubt that Wilson would do his utmost to be fully cooperative.

"You don't think she was murdered, do you?" blurted Wilson. "Mr Wilson, we are treating the girl's death as suspicious that's all. What we are trying to do is create all different sorts of scenarios which might have occurred. Now let's just suppose for a minute, that someone did harm the girl and pushed her into the river. Let's also suppose he had taken some of her belongings and wanted to hide them. Now it seems to us, that a good place to hide such things would be in these garages." Skelton was closely watching Wilson and he could see that the penny had suddenly dropped.

"Oh, right, I've got you now. You think the killer is using one of these garages here. Is that right?" Mr Wilson, as I said a moment ago. We are just checking out a few scenarios of what could have happened. So please don't go telling your friends that we are looking for a killer as all we are doing is making some enquiries, that's all."

"Don't worry inspector, your secret is safe with me. But to be honest with you, I think you are barking up the wrong tree." Skelton gave the man a quizzical look and said, "Why do you say that Mr Wilson?" "As I told you earlier, I've lived here thirty-two years with the wife. We know everything that goes on here in the Parade and some of it would make you blush. As for these garages, everyone of them is owned by the owners of the flats up there." Wilson was pointing to Widcombe Parade. All the owners have lived here for at least ten years and some of them more than twenty years. As you would expect, they are all retired and are getting on a bit. Some of them have been widowed and live on their own but I make a point of going around every day checking on them to make sure that everything is as it should be."

Wilson was now pointing at the garages. "These garages inspector, are in use almost every day. My neighbours are all still quite independent and they like to go shopping. So nearly every day, they get into their cars and drive down to Morrison's on the London Road. It's an easy drive and there is plenty of parking. I help in any way I can, particularly when it comes to servicing their cars. I've a mate who runs a little garage just off the Lower Bristol Road and I take their cars there to be fixed and serviced or even for an MOT. So I'm regularly in and out of all these garages inspector and believe me, I haven't seen anything unusual stored in any of them."

Both Skelton and Alexander could sense that Wilson was clearly a very good neighbour if just perhaps a bit nosey but there was no mistaking the fact, that whatever was going on around Widcombe Parade, Wilson knew all about it.

"Right, that just leaves one garage which I haven't yet mentioned. That's that end one on the right there." Wilson was again pointing. "That garage is owned by Ben Black But sadly he has dementia. It was all a bit sudden really. I went to see him in his flat one day. He lived alone you see, his wife died about eight years back. I'd noticed he was getting a bit forgetful but this day, it was like the lights were on, but nobody was home. Anyway, to cut a long story short, his son got him into a care home. His son Philip is a nice guy and I gave him a hand to clear out the flat and the garage. Do you know, we filled two bloody skips with rubbish not to mention about a dozen trips down to the dump."

Alexander asked, "So what happened to the flat. "Well Philip did not have the power to sell it, so he rented it out. The man who rents it is an American and he does a lot of travelling around Europe. He's a banker and basically, he uses the flat as a base. I sometimes see him here at weekends. He's not got a car. I said to Philip that he ought to rent the garage to someone else, but he said he would leave it be in case the American left and he had to re-let the flat." Skelton placed his right hand on his mouth for a second and then said, "So as far as you are concerned, eleven of these garages are in daily use and that one over there is empty. Is that correct?" Mr Wilson considered the question and replied, "Yes, I'm certain about that inspector. I'm down here every day and I regularly see all eleven garages in use, but nothing has gone in or out of Ben's garage since the day that me and Phil cleared it out. If I had the key to it, I would show it to you but it's up in my flat. Do you want me to go and get it?" Skelton could see that Mr Wilson was sure of his facts and he did not want to insult his feelings by asking him to get the key. "No, that will not be necessary Mr Wilson, I'm sure that you are correct in what you have told us. Thank you very much for all your help. We really do appreciate it."

Chapter Thirty-Seven

Having thanked Mr Wilson for his most informative report on the comings and goings of those resident in Widcombe Parade, Skelton led Alexander through the carpark onto Widcombe Parade. It was almost 1pm when Skelton opened the door of the Ram and entered. As always, when he entered a strange pub, Skelton's eyes focused on the bar to see what beers were on sale. "Oh, look Bill, bingo. They sell Fosters in here." Skelton ordered a pint for himself and a pint of soda water and lime for Alexander. From the menu, Skelton chose the steak pie and chips and he ordered a salad for Alexander. This would not have been Alexander's own choice especially when he saw Skelton tucking into his steak pie.

"What have you got on this afternoon Bill?" Alexander thought for a second and said, "Actually, I need to go over to Bristol when I'm finished here. I've got a trial coming up in a couple of weeks and the CPS lawyer wants to go over my Witness Statement with me." Skelton pondered this for a minute. "Right whilst you are over in Bristol, I will get Lowik to take me out to that

BMW dealership at Peasedown St John. A case of his involving multiple thefts has a theme in common. All the victims get their cars serviced there, so I am betting on the fact that someone at the garage has been making spare house keys when the owner drops the car off, to be serviced."

As they walked back to the station, Skelton turned to Alexander and placed his right hand on his shoulder. "It's time we spoke to the parents of both the girls. I understand that Linda's parents are staying in Bath now. Get on to the liaison officers when we get back and fix up an appointment for tomorrow, preferably in the morning. I don't mind if we have the meeting at the station or at their hotel, whichever they feel the most comfortable with. We need to go and see Marion's parents who I seem to recall live in Swansea. Ask the liaison officers to make an appointment as soon as possible and we will need them to be there with us. Just tell them that we have been reviewing the investigation into her disappearance and want to up-date them on it." They were just walking into the carpark and Alexander stopped and said, "Neither meeting is going to be easy Dan but the one with Marion's parents is going to be awful. For the last six months they have been under the belief that their daughter went out for the evening, drank a little too much and fell into the river and drowned. Totally accidental and nothing suspicious. Now we are going to turn up and tell them, that we might have cocked up the investigation and in fact your daughter might have been drugged and raped and that her death was not an accident. How do you think that's going to make me feel?"

Skelton placed his hands on his head and stared at Alexander and gave him the most pitying of looks. "Bill, how could I have been so bloody stupid and insensitive? You are in no way to blame for how the original investigation was handled, as I have already said before. What was so crass of me was to even consider taking you along to meet Marion's parents. I will go and see them with the two liaison officers. I will make it clear that I am a new DCI that's investigating another drowning recently and I have noticed similarities between both cases. That should hopefully avoid them asking too many awkward questions." Alexander looked relieved. "Thanks Dan I'd rather not be there, it's going to really upset them, that's for sure."

Chapter Thirty-Eight

Lowik was driving the unmarked police car and Skelton was sitting in the passenger seat going through the list of names and addresses that Lowik had given him. Next to the names he had shown the model of BMW, registration number and the date when the victim had reported the disappearance of cash or valuables. There were eight names on the list and total losses amounted to several thousands of pounds. Lowik was wearing sunglasses, something which Skelton had noted Lowik seemed to invariably favour. Not surprising for a guy brought up in Australia. Lowik was wearing a light grey suit, white shirt and a pale blue tie. Skelton had on a dark pinstripe suit, blue shirt and dark blue tie. As always, he had made a perfect Windsor knot and the tie looked perfect. In his breast pocket a crisp white handkerchief gave him the appearance of a smart banker or businessman. His black shoes had been highly polished that morning. Skelton's father had installed in him at an early age, the need to polish shoes every time they were worn.

Lowik drove into the large carpark of the BMW dealership at Peasedown St John, which is about six miles from the centre of Bath. The building was new, and the show room was huge. The detectives got out of the car and headed for the reception desk, Skelton was leading the way whilst Lowik savoured the delights of the dozens of brand-new cars awaiting an owner. A tall blonde girl of about twenty-five was stood behind the desk and she was completely absorbed with her mobile phone. Skelton guessed she was more interested in arranging tonight's shag than serving him and Lowik. Skelton detested being ignored by someone more interested in their mobile phone. He had lost count of the number of people he had walked into because they were staring at their phone rather than what was in front of them.

"Excuse me, do you actually work here, or do you just come in to use your phone?" barked Skelton. The girl was totally shocked by the rudeness of this man and was just about to mouth a sarcastic reply when she noticed him holding out the Avon and Somerset Constabulary warrant card. Now she was confused and slightly scared. "Oh, sorry about that, I was just answering an urgent text. How can I help you sir?" I'm Detective Chief Inspector Skelton and this here is my colleague Detective Constable Lowik. We would like a word with whoever is in charge please." The girl nodded her head, "Well that's the manager Andy Young. I will go and let him know that you are here. Can I get you a drink, tea or coffee or bottled water?" "No, we are fine thanks. We will just take a seat and wait for the manager."

Skelton saw the man coming down the stairs from a suite of offices. The man was in his early fifties, his hair or at least what was left of it was grey and the guy was carrying far too much weight. Skelton reckoned that he was probably a type two diabetic, a heavy smoker and drinker. The man was a heart attack just waiting to happen. The exercise of walking down the staircase had caused an outbreak of profuse sweating across the man's forehead and he was busy wiping it away with a handkerchief as he approached. "Hello there, I'm Andy Young and I'm the manager here. How can I help you gentlemen?" Skelton and Lowik stood up and Skelton made the introductions. "We have a delicate matter that we need to discuss with you Andy. Is there somewhere private where we can go?" Young pointed to the stairs and said, "Yes of course my office is up there." Skelton thought he heard Young softly moan as he contemplated another assault on the stairs. Skelton imagined that it probably felt like climbing Everest to Young.

The three men were seated around Young's large desk. The walls were covered in photographs of BMW's and merchandise. "Andy, we are investigating the disappearance of money and valuables from the houses of customers that use this garage both to buy their cars and have them serviced." Young looked totally shocked. But said

255

nothing. The thefts occurred weeks ago but we only recently discovered the connection between the thefts and this garage recently. I have here a list of the names, addresses and registration plate numbers of those customers and I need you to tell us, if any one individual was involved with all eight vehicles." Skelton handed over the list and Young carefully read it.

"Yes, I recognise all these names here. I personally sold some of them their cars. To be honest I can't imagine how this garage, or my staff could be in any way involved. I think it must just be a coincidence as my staff are first class and we have a very low turnover of personnel." "Andy, I doubt it very much that this is a coincidence, I think that a member of staff has had access to the house keys of these owners and used them to gain access to their houses whilst they were out at work or shopping. Can you check and see who the mechanics were that worked on these cars when they came into be serviced?"

Young had the list and was busy on the computer entering the vehicle registration numbers. He had a pen in his hand and every so often he wrote something down on the list. Neither Skelton nor Lowik could see what was being written. Finally, Young entered the last registration number onto the computer and scrolled through the various details. Young was sweating even more profusely now, and his white shirt was clinging to his body. He was staring at the screen in what Skelton considered to be disbelief, if he was reading Young's body language correctly. Young pulled a hand down his face and then wrote something else on the list. At last he looked up from the screen and looked Skelton directly in the face. Their eyes met, and Skelton guessed correctly what Young was about to say. "I don't believe this, but the same mechanic was assigned to service all eight vehicles. His name is Gerry Malone and he is a first class, mechanic. He has been here for about four years and we have never had a single complaint about him. I honestly can't believe that Gerry is in any way involved in these thefts' inspector. You see, from time to time, especially with new staff, we purposely leave valuables in vehicles to check that the staff don't steal. To my knowledge, Gerry would not even take the odd pound coin from some owner's parking change which they invariably leave in their car."

Skelton leaned across the desk. "Andy given that Gerry has been responsible for servicing all eight vehicles, we need to speak to him. Is he here now?" Young stood up and rested his hands on the desk. "Well here's a funny thing. He came to work on Monday and he seemed fine, but he never turned up yesterday and he's not come in today. I tried phoning him yesterday but just got his answer phone. I've left loads of messages, but he has not called back. His mate, Joe Tucker, went around to his house last night to find out what was going on and to make sure he was alright. But Joe said that when he went to the house, the curtains were drawn, and nobody seemed at home."

Skelton was worried by this news of Malone's disappearance from work. "Is Joe about now?" "Yes, he is, let me go and get him. Are you finished with me?" Skelton stood up as did Lowik. "Yes Andy, we are finished with you and thank you for all your help. I'd appreciate it if you kept this confidential." Young nodded his head and once more set off down the stairs, his huge arse wobbled with each stride.

Joe Tucker came up the stairs rubbing his hands in a cloth. Tucker was about twenty-five and clearly worked out in the gym. He was about 6" tall and had an athletic body. His head was shaved, and both arms were tattooed. He was wearing a BMW overall with the sleeves rolled up. Tucker introduced himself and was clearly a little agitated. Skelton tried to put him at ease.

"Joe, I understand that Gerry has not shown up for work these last two days and that you went around to his house last night. Is that right?" Tucker took a seat and put the rag in his overall pocket. "Yes, its bazar really. Gerry and me, are good mates, we've known each other since school. He didn't turn up for work yesterday and never called in. Now that's odd. I texted him yesterday morning but got nothing back from him. So, I phoned but just got his answer phone. By the afternoon I was getting worried, so I texted his girlfriend. But she did not reply either. But she is a nurse and sometimes she won't reply. Anyway, after work, I drove over to their house. They live in Oldfield Park. Gerry's father died about five years ago and left him enough money for a deposit to buy the house. I got there just before seven o'clock last night. Melanie's car was parked outside but I could not see Gerry's but that's not unusual as parking down there is a nightmare. I eventually managed to get parked and went up to the house. All the curtains were drawn and there were no lights on that I could see. I rang the bell, knocked on the door and even called through the letter box. I don't think they were home. So, I thought maybe they have gone away somewhere in Gerry's car. I know that Melanie's mum has been in hospital recently and according to Gerry she's in a bad way.

 Skelton thought carefully for a minute deciding on what his next move would be. "What's Gerry's girlfriend called?" "It's Melanie Hind and she works as a nurse in A&E at the RUH." Skelton and Lowik made a note. "Tell me Joe, did Gerry have any financial worries that you know about?" Tucker closed and opened his eyes and was becoming even more nervous. "It's all right Joe, whatever you say to us, is in total confidence. We will not mention it to Gerry, you have my word." Tucker rubbed both hands over his face and sighed.

"As I said, me and Gerry are best mates. We used to go out every weekend together, play pool, go clubbing, pull the birds and generally have a great time. The wages here are good so we always had plenty left over to enjoy ourselves. Then about a year ago, maybe longer, he met Melanie and after only a few weeks she moved in. Initially, Gerry seemed happy but after a few months, I could tell that something was not right. As I said, Gerry bought this house, it's only a two bedroom terraced down in Oldfield Park. It needed modernising and Gerry was content to do the work himself at the weekends and I volunteered to lend a hand. But that was not good enough for Melanie. She wanted everything done yesterday, using builders, and she did not give Gerry any choice. Before he knew it, she had ordered a new fitted kitchen and fitted bedrooms. The whole house was decorated from top to bottom plus new fitted carpets. It cost a fortune. Gerry had to take out loans and they both maxed out on their credit cards."

"It seems that Melanie is a shopaholic. She is forever buying new things that she could easily do without, like new handbags and clothes. Anyway, it got to such a point that Gerry couldn't afford to come out for a drink. Every penny he earns, goes to pay the mortgage, the loans and credit cards. I don't know how he manages to pay the usual bills like the council tax, electricity and water. For the last couple of months, Gerry has not been the fun-loving guy that I used to know, that's for sure."

Skelton wrote down the address of the house. He thanked Joe for all his help and with Lowik in tow, they went down the stairs and outside to the unmarked car. As they settled in their seats, Skelton took out his phone and called Janet Griffin who answered almost immediately. "Yes sir, what can I do for you?" "Janet, I need you to get onto the RUH right now and find out if a nurse called

Melanie Hind was due in work yesterday and today. See if she turned up and phone me straight back." "Yes sir, I'm on it now." "I don't like how this is panning out Peter. If Gerry was struggling to pay the bills, as Joe said, then it looks like he has taken to stealing from his customers. What's worrying me though, is his sudden disappearance. I think if something had happened to the girlfriend's mother, he would have at least phoned in to say so. You have the address Peter, let's go now."

A few minutes later, Skelton's phone rang. He took it from his shirt pocket and looked at the screen. It was Griffin calling back. "Yes Janet, what have you got?" "Melanie Hind was supposed to be on day shift yesterday and today but never showed up. There has been no word from her and the hospital has tried to contact her, but they had no luck." "Shit, shit, shit! Sorry Janet but that is not good news. Get yourself and two uniformed officers down to 164 Newfield Drive now and wait for us to get there. Tell uniform to bring the spare key with them." There was a pause on the other end of the line. "Janet, did you get that?" "Sorry sir but where will we find the spare key?" Skelton closed his eyes and put his left hand on his head to compose himself. He realised that Griffin was unfamiliar with the terminology he had just used.

"Janet, when I said bring the spare key that actually means bring the battering ram for opening doors. Do you understand?" "Oh, sorry sir, I never heard it called that before! We will be there in about ten minutes."

Lowik drove slowly along Newfield Drive checking the numbers then he saw the marked police car just ahead, parked on the right. There was a space to park just a few hundred meters further on, and he pulled in. They both got out the car and closed the doors. Lowik locked it up and they headed towards the marked police car. Two male officers got out the front and the driver opened the rear door to let Janet Griffin out. Meanwhile the officer in the front passenger seat was opening the boot and extracting the "spare key" All five officers stood in front of the police car.

"Peter and I have been investigating a number of thefts and we suspect that a young garage mechanic called Gerry Malone is responsible. We have just been to the garage where he works, and it transpires that he did not show up for work yesterday or today. He has a girlfriend who lives with him called Melanie Hind. She is a nurse at the RUH. Janet has checked with the hospital, and she too failed to turn up for work yesterday and again today. We need to get inside the house and determine what has happened to them. But I have to say I am getting bad vibes about this. If we must break the door down, Lowik and I will go in on our own. The rest of you remain outside. Understood?" The officers confirmed that all was understood. The driver was called Ben Knight. Skelton looked at him and said, "Ben you get around the back now, just in case." Knight took off and made his way around the back of the building.

Skelton rang the bell and hammered on the door. "It's the police. Open the door please." Skelton could see that all the curtains were closed. He peered through the letter box, but the hallway was in darkness. He tried the door handle, but the door was locked. Constable Robbie Taylor had the "spare key" ready. Skelton pushed Lowik back and moved himself away from the doorstep. "Right Rob, do your stuff." Taylor got himself into position and slowly swung the "spare key" backwards then he heaved it forwards. There was a shattering sound of wood crumbling, but the door did not open. It took three more swings for the door to finally give way.

Skelton went in first and felt for the light switch which he quickly found and at last they could see clearly. On the floor was a pile of mail which Skelton bent down and scooped up. He quickly scanned the envelopes and he concluded that they were nearly all bills. There was a door on the right which Skelton opened and after finding the light switch, turned it on. This was the kitchen and it was magnificently fitted-out with brand-new appliances. Skelton thought it must have cost a fortune. There was to his left, a breakfast bar on which sat a pile of bills. Skelton placed the un-opened mail next to them. Everything seemed as it should be in the kitchen, so they left it as it was and went back into the hallway. There was a door opposite and so Skelton turned the handle and entered. Once again, he found the light switch and turned the lights on. This was the sitting room or lounge. On looking around the room, Skelton noted the brand-new carpet, the enormous TV and entertainment centre. The room had been very tastefully furnished and redecorated. There was no one in here either. "Let's take a look upstairs Peter." Skelton led the way. They climbed the stairs and Skelton could see three doors, all of which were closed. He reckoned the one in front was the master bedroom and the one to the right was the guest bedroom. The door to the left was the family bathroom.

Skelton opened the door to the master bedroom and switched on the light. The room had been in total darkness as the blinds were pulled down. His eyes scanned the bed. He immediately saw the blood stains on the headboard and up the newly painted wall. He could tell that someone was lying under the duvet on the right hand side of the bed. Slowly he walked around the bed and noticed the claw hammer lying on the floor. It was covered in blood as was the bedside cabinet and the box of tissues. Skelton pulled a pair of latex gloves from his pocket and quickly pulled them on. He took out his phone and turned on the camera and took some shots. He moved along the bed and slowly and carefully he pulled back the duvet. A woman's naked body lay in the bed. The back of her head was caved in from the repeated blows from the claw hammer. Skelton gently lifted the woman's right arm which he found to be both cold and supple. Rigor mortis had already passed off, so she had been dead for at least thirty-six hours.

Lowik was closely watching Skelton from the foot of the bed. Skelton took a few more shots with the camera and then he replaced the duvet, once again covering the victim's head. "Well, I guess we just found Melanie. Let's go and look for Gerry." Skelton squeezed past Lowik and opened the door of the guest bedroom. He turned on the light and found everything as it should be. The bed was made-up, the room had been newly redecorated, and a new carpet covered the floor. Skelton said, "He's not in here. He must be in the bathroom.

Skelton turned the handle and opened the door. He reached out his hand and felt the light cord switch, which he gently pulled. The smell of death hit him. There was no other smell quite like it. To his right was a bathtub and straight ahead was a sink and above it a large cabinet containing two sliding mirrors. To his left was a shower, the door of which hung open. Malone was hanging by a rope which had been fashioned into a noose and was tied to the door frame. Skelton edged closer and looked closely at the rope which was blue in colour. It was a nylon tow rope probably from the boot of Malone's car. Skelton lifted Malone's left arm. It too was cold and supple meaning that he also had been dead at least thirty-six hours. Skelton took a few more photographs. "Come on Peter. We are done here. I will call it in as a murder and suicide, there are no suspicious circumstances here. The poor bastard got himself into a pile of debt and that's what started him thieving."

Lowik had not moved. "Jesus Christ sir, I never thought when I started this investigation that it would end like this. What a fucking waste of two lives just because Melanie could not control her spending." Skelton put his arms around Lowik. "Are you okay Peter?" Lowik gripped Skelton's arms and said, "Yes, I'm fine just a bit gutted that's all." They went down the stairs together and went out into the street where the other officers were waiting. Skelton filled them in on what they had found and then called it in. Within a few minutes the place would be swarming with the CSI team, the pathologist and the coroner. Suddenly, Skelton had a thought. "Hang on a minute Peter, there's something I need to check. Skelton climbed the stairs again and entered the bathroom. He put on a fresh pair of latex gloves and slid the mirrored panel of the cabinet above the sink. He looked inside but realised it was the wrong side. He closed it and opened the other side which contained Malone's aftershaves. There were only four bottles, all of which he recognised, but it was the dumpy white bottle which he had not seen in over twenty years that held his interest. It was called "Old Spice" and his father used to put it on every Saturday night when he took Skelton's mother out dancing. It had a peculiar smell he remembered, and he gently picked the bottle up and unscrewed the top and lifted it to his nose. The smell and the memories of his father getting ready to go out on a Saturday night came flooding back. He put the top back on the bottle and removed an evidence bag from his inside jacket pocket.

On walking back outside, he saw various police vehicles arriving. Inspector Graham Symonds had arrived to take charge of the crime scene. Skelton walked over to where Symonds was standing. "Afternoon Graham, we meet once again." Symonds gave him a smile. "We better stop meeting like this Dan, people will begin to talk." Skelton laughed as did Symonds. "It's a straightforward domestic Graham. Boyfriend kills the girlfriend and then tops himself. Absolutely nothing suspicious. Could you please log this bottle of "Old Spice" as having been removed by me from the bathroom cabinet?" Symonds stared at the evidence bag containing the bottle of after shave. "What's this Dan, have you got a date tonight and trying to impress with the aftershave?" They both laughed, and Skelton nodded to Lowik that it was time to leave.

It was just after six when they got back to the station and as they approached the officer's entrance, Superintendent Williams was just coming out. "Dan, there you are. What's this murder and suicide all about? I am going to have to make a statement to the media." Skelton looked at Williams and said, "I would just keep it

269

simple sir. Next of kin need to be informed. We can give more details after formal identification has taken place and when Dr Challis has done the PM's." This satisfied Williams, who was last seen heading towards his car.

Back in his office, Skelton checked his phone directory and found the number he was looking for. He called the number and after a few rings it was answered. "It's Dan Skelton here from Avon and Somerset police. Are you at home by any chance?" Hello Dan, yes we are both at home now, we just got in." Skelton had called the gay couple who had reported the strange smell of aftershave. "Would you mind if Peter and I stopped by in about fifteen minutes? I have something to show you and I think we have discovered who it was who stole the money." "That's brilliant, yes fifteen minutes is fine.

Once again, Lowik drove and Skelton was seated on the passenger seat holding the evidence bag containing the bottle of "Old Spice". Lowik found a parking space and both detectives got out of the car. Lowik locked the car and began following Skelton towards the door. As they were approaching the door, Brown was pulling it open. "Dan, Peter good to see you, come on in. Could you guys use an ice-cold beer?" "We could bloody

murder an ice-cold beer" was the immediate reply
from Lowik. "Yes, please" echoed Skelton, "Peter
and I have had quite an eventful day and as soon
as I get home, Ken will be on gin and tonic duty."

Tom Brown pulled out two bottles of Heineken
from the fridge and after removing the tops,
poured them into two tall glasses. The kitchen
door opened, and David Lloyd walked in. "Hi guys,
nice to see you again. Have you had a good day?"
Skelton and Lowik both laughed, and Skelton said,
"Well to be honest we have had better days but at
least we think we have solved the mystery of your
money that strangely disappeared." Brown was
taking a drink of beer from his glass and when he
had finished said, "Well that's great news. How did
you manage to solve the case Dan?" Skelton
drained his glass and Brown immediately opened
the fridge door and pulled out two more beers and
began opening them.

Skelton picked up the evidence bag which he had
carefully placed on the breakfast bar of the
kitchen and held it in his hands. "Now you guys
told us that you had detected an unusual smell of
aftershave in your bedroom when you had noticed
that the money had gone missing. Is that right?" It

was Lloyd who spoke. "Yes, that is correct. It was a kind of old- fashioned aftershave that I think either my dad or my grandfather used to wear. It's not something that either of us would use, that's for sure." "I have in this bag, a bottle of aftershave that I removed earlier today, from the house of our suspect. I would like you both to smell it and tell me if you think it's the same as you can remember from the day of the robbery." Skelton carefully opened the evidence bag and pulled out the bottle. His hand was covering the bottle, so no one could see the name. He unscrewed the lid and placed it on the breakfast bar and then walked over first to Brown and put the bottle under his nose. Brown took a sniff and said "That's it, I will never forget that smell. It's unique.

From across the kitchen Lloyd called out, "I can smell it from here, he is right, there is no question about it. That is the same aftershave that we could smell in our bedroom that day. What's it called Dan?" Skelton sat the bottle down on the breakfast bar and replaced the top. "It's called "Old Spice" and it sort of stood out from the other aftershaves that our suspect keeps. The others were much more modern but like you guys, I remember my father splashing this on, before taking my mother out on a Saturday night."

Chapter Thirty-Nine

The next morning, Skelton was in the kitchen fully dressed in a fresh pinstripe suit, the trousers newly pressed and his shirt ironed to perfection. He was enjoying a mug of tea whilst polishing his shoes. The dogs were lying on their beds, all three munching on a Boneo which Skelton had just given them. Ken was getting ready to take them out for their morning walk. Ken opened the kitchen door and entered. "What are we having for dinner tonight Dan?" Ken adored food and Skelton was a first class cook. Ken always needed to know what was for dinner. It seemed to Skelton that this was vital information to allow Ken to function properly throughout the day. Skelton enjoyed cooking and never saw it as a chore that needed doing. It gave him tremendous pleasure to cook for his partner and any guests that joined them for a meal. Skelton had already settled on what was for dinner whilst having a shower. "I will get some lamb chops for tonight, new potatoes and green beans and cabbage." "Oh great, I love lamb chops. Is there anything I need to do?" Skelton thought for a second and said, "No I will text you when I am on my way home, so you just concentrate on fixing me a G & T." "That sounds like a plan to me. Come on boys, let's go for a walk." The dogs got off their beds and started wagging their tails enthusiastically. Dan and Ken kissed goodbye and Skelton held the door open whilst the dogs ran outside into the garden.

Skelton set off walking into Bath. The morning was distinctly chilly, and Skelton walked at a brisk pace to warm himself up. It was forecast to get warmer, later in the morning. He was thinking about what he needed to do that day and realised that he would need to spend a fair amount of time writing up his report into yesterday's murder and suicide. He wondered if Alexander had been able to arrange a meeting with Linda's parents for this morning. He needed to contact the police liaison officers that had attended to Marion's family last Christmas. That would involve a drive down to Swansea but that was only about an hour or so from Bath.

When Skelton arrived at the station, he went to his office and switched on his computer and took off his jacket and put it on a coat hanger which he hung on a filing cabinet. He had just sat down when Alexander knocked on the door and entered. "Morning Dan. I see that you and young Lowik had a busy day yesterday. How come when I go out with you, we never come across a murder and suicide?" Skelton looked up from his computer screen and gave Alexander a half smile and said, "I believe you attended a possible murder with me on Monday. I thought that might be enough for you in a week and besides, you went swanning off to Bristol yesterday, so I had to take Peter with me. You don't expect me to drive myself, do you?" "I, sometimes wonder if you can drive Dan. I've never seen you behind the wheel since you joined us." Skelton leaned back in his chair and smiled at Alexander. "Just doing my bit for the environment Bill. If I can walk, I will, which means that you get the same exercise as me."

Alexander sat down for a minute. "I've made an appointment for us to see Linda's parents at 11 o'clock this morning. They said they are quite happy to meet us here. I've booked a nice meeting room for us. I spoke to Mr Carson on the phone and he seems to be bearing up quite well, in all the circumstances." "I'm not sure how he and Mrs Carson are going to react when we tell them that their daughter was possibly drugged, raped and then allowed to die in the river. Dealing with a tragic accident is one thing Bill. Being told that your daughter may have been murdered is a whole different matter."

"I need to go and see Marion's parents as soon as possible Bill. They need to hear the news from me before some reporter picks up that the two cases might be connected." Alexander leaned across the desk. "I spoke with Terry Nugent yesterday. He was one of the police liaison officers assigned to the case. The other was Ann Ritchie, but she is on maternity leave now. Terry said he would give them a call yesterday and was going to send you an email with some suggested dates." "Hang on a second Bill, let me check these emails now." Skelton scrolled down the dozens of emails awaiting his attention and found one from Terry Nugent. He quickly read it and replied. "That's great Bill, Terry and I will drive down to Swansea tomorrow morning. We are meeting Marion's parents at 10.30am. All being well, I should be back in Bath in time for lunch. And DS Alexander, I think lunch is on you tomorrow." Alexander stood up and was heading for the door when he turned around and said, "I will have to consult my calendar on that one sir. You know I'm a busy detective sir." "Bill as tomorrow is Friday, you can have a proper pint, not soda water and lime." "Do you know what sir, I've just remembered my calendar is completely free tomorrow. See you at one o'clock sharp." Both men smiled, and Alexander gave a half-hearted salute and left.

Skelton and Alexander took the stairs down to the reception desk and on looking around the waiting room, they saw several people waiting to be seen. There was only one middle-aged couple both dressed in black. Skelton vaguely recognised the smartly dressed woman sitting with them but could not remember her name. She was a police liaison officer and was providing as much comfort to the bereaved couple as was possible. Skelton approached them. "Mr and Mrs Carson?" Skelton stretched out his hand. "I am Detective Chief Inspector Dan Skelton, and this here is Detective Sergeant Bill Alexander." The handshakes were completed all round. The police liaison officer introduced herself to Skelton as Helen Rodgers, but Alexander needed no introduction as he had known Rodgers for years. "I am so terribly sorry for your loss and I hope Helen here has been looking after you well?" Mr Carson spoke. "Yes, Helen and Terry have been ever so helpful, and we can't thank them enough. We are going back home this afternoon, but Helen and Terry have said they will keep in touch and help organise getting Linda's body back for the funeral."

Skelton led the way to the meeting room and on entering could see that tea, coffee and biscuits had been laid on. Alexander and Rodgers poured the drinks and Skelton declined as he had had his tea and bacon roll just prior to the meeting. Skelton knew that when it came to conveying news, good or bad, you had to be direct. "As you know, we recovered Linda's body from the river on Monday. Bill and I attended the post-mortem and the Home Office Pathologist confirmed that she had died from drowning." The Carson's both nodded their heads, indicating that they already knew this. "The Pathologist also stated that Linda had consumed alcohol before she died, and that she had had sex shortly before she died." This new piece of information caused Mrs Carson to pull a handkerchief from her handbag and to quietly cry into it. Mr Carson caressed his wife's hand but did not speak.

"I have to say that we are treating Linda's death as suspicious for two reasons. Firstly, after she got off the bus outside Lambrettas, no one ever saw her alive again. Secondly, and forgive me for being so direct, there is a strong possibility that Linda may have been drugged and raped." Mr Carson stood up and put his head in his hands. "Oh my god. Are you suggesting that our daughter was murdered inspector?" "Please Mr Carson, sit down. I think your wife needs you. Rodgers calmly intervened and took charge of trying to console the couple. After a few minutes, Skelton judged that he could proceed. "Yes, I'm afraid to say that Linda may have been drugged and then raped. Then whilst she was still unconscious, we think that she was taken to the river where her attacker placed her in the water which caused her to drown. The pathologist has taken blood and urine samples, and these have been sent to the lab for toxicology testing. It will take two to three weeks for the results to be known. If Linda does test positive for drugs, then we will treat her death as murder."

This latest information caused more tears from Mrs Carson and Rodgers once again provided fantastic support. When Skelton judged that it was safe to continue, he informed the Carson's that he was linking Linda's death to Marion's death. Mr Carson was outraged. "Are you telling us, that a girl died in similar circumstances to Linda, but you never treated her death as suspicious? Is that what you are saying, or have I got this all wrong, inspector?"

Skelton had known that this was going to be a tough meeting and he needed to make sure that the Carson's could trust the police. "Mr Carson, last Christmas when this other girl's body was discovered, there were no suspicious circumstances surrounding her disappearance. Unlike Linda's disappearance which I have already said is highly suspicious. This other girl was called Marion and it appeared that she had been out drinking and had fallen into the river. The pathologist confirmed that she had been intoxicated and that her death appeared to have been a tragic accident. Consequently, and because it was fast approaching Christmas day, and everyone concerned was keen to return the body for burial, he did not test for drugs. Since Linda's body was recovered I have reviewed the investigation into Marion's death. I have asked the pathologist to send off for toxicology testing blood and urine samples that had been retained however, because Marion died almost six months ago, it will take about six weeks for the results to come through. We should have Linda's results in about two to three weeks and only then will we know for certain, whether or not she was drugged."

Once Skelton had carefully explained the situation to Mr and Mrs Carson, they understood the complexities of the investigation that the police had to undertake in order to discover what had really happened to both girls. There was nothing that Mr and Mrs Carson could do in Bath and so when the meeting concluded, they left the police station with Rodgers giving support to Mrs Carson. Alexander and Skelton saw them out of the building. "Bill, I need some fresh air and I also need to pop into Marks and Spencer and pick up something for dinner tonight." "That's fine Dan, and by the way, I thought you handled that meeting brilliantly." "Thanks Bill, I just hope that my meeting with Marion's parents goes as well, tomorrow morning."

Chapter Forty

Skelton walked out of the station and crossed the road. M & S was just around the next corner and about two hundred meters on the right. As he walked towards the supermarket, he passed two police constables on patrol and they exchanged pleasantries for a few minutes. On entering the supermarket, he picked up a basket and headed to the vegetable isle where he selected a bag of new potatoes, a cabbage and some green beans. Next, he headed to the meat isle and eventually he found some thinly cut fresh Welsh lamb chops. The pack contained six chops, so he and Ken would have three each.

Skelton then decided to have a quick browse along the meat isle and his eyes homed in on some sausages which he had never seen on sale in the south of England although he had tried finding them for years. He had even googled them to see if any supermarket in the south stocked them. They did not. Skelton carefully picked up the pack and read the label. "Lorne sausages Made in Scotland." Lorne sausages are also known as square sausages because they are square shaped. Skelton had been brought up on these delicious sausages when he lived in Scotland. On every visit back to Scotland to visit his family, he would always buy as much as he could carry as well as some traditional steak pies. When it came to square sausages and steak pies, Skelton reckoned that the Scots made the best!

He placed the pack of four Lorne sausages in his basket and walked to the checkout. Once back in his office, he put the shopping in his fridge except for the sausages. These he put on his desk, turned upside down, so that it was impossible to tell what the pack contained. He then walked into the CID room where Alexander was just hanging up his phone. In a formal voice Skelton said, "DS Alexander my office now." Skelton turned around and walked back to his office. Alexander stood up and scratched his head wondering what on earth he had done wrong. The DCI had never spoken to him like that before and he could not think of anything he had done or not done to land him in hot water with the boss.

Alexander walked in and Skelton was already sitting at his desk and his facial expression was one of anger. Alexander closed the door. "Sir, you wanted to see me?" Skelton pointed to the chair, indicating that Alexander was expected to sit. "DS Alexander, why have you been hiding this evidence from me?" Skelton was pointing to the square package sitting on his desk. Alexander looked closely at it but did not have a clue as to what it contained. "Sir, I have no idea what you are talking about. I have never seen that thing in my life, so I haven't a clue what it is." Skelton looked at Alexander sternly and asked, "How long have you been stationed in Bath and how long have you been a detective?" "Well, I have been stationed in Bath for just over five years sir and I was made a detective eleven years ago becoming a detective sergeant when I moved to Bath."

Skelton sat back in his chair. "So, you've been a bloody detective here in Bath for five years and yet as a fellow Scot, you did not have the courtesy to tell me about these?" Alexander wondered what on earth the DCI was going on about and what was in the package. Skelton picked up the package and turned it over and threw it in front of Alexander. Alexander looked at it and stared, his eyes wide open with disbelief. "Where the hell did you get those from?" Skelton was now beginning to enjoy himself as he looked at his hapless friend. "Bill, I just bought those in M & S. That's only the second time I've been in there since I moved back to live in Bath. But I know for a fact that you are in and out of that place nearly every day. So why did you not tell me I could get square sausages in there?" "Dan, I have never seen them for sale in there. It must be a new line for them. But how come you just brought back the one packet, where is mine?" Skelton stood up and walked around towards Alexander who was getting out of his chair. "I wanted to check the quality Bill, so I thought we would have two sausage sandwiches for lunch. I need to go out and get some fruity brown sauce and a Danish loaf of bread. Meet me in the kitchen at one o'clock." They exchanged high fives and Skelton put the sausages in the fridge and went out to buy the bread and brown sauce.

At one o'clock Skelton walked into the kitchen. It was staffed by two ladies who turned out bacon rolls, full English breakfasts plus various pies, sausage rolls and Cornish Pasties. Margaret was the older lady and in charge. She was about fifty-five and her hair had gone grey. She was quite stocky probably as a result of tasting too many meals that she cooked. Her side-kick was called Janice, who was in her early twenties. She had a very plain face and certainly did not attract much attention from the male police officers. In one hand, Skelton had a box of chocolates and in the other was a plastic bag containing the sausages, a bottle of corn oil, a loaf of fresh bread, a tub of margarine and a bottle of fruity sauce.

Margaret and Janice were busy chatting to each other but stopped when they saw Skelton. "Good afternoon ladies and how are you both today?" Margaret smiled and said, "Hello Mr Skelton, we don't usually see you in here at lunchtime. Don't you usually go to the pub?" Skelton was smiling and using his utmost charm said, "Well yes, Bill and I like to take a stroll at lunchtime and have lunch in a pub. But today, I need a big favour from you ladies and may I offer you this box of chocolates as a token of my appreciation for all your help." Skelton handed the box of chocolates over to Margaret who took them and showed the box to Janice, who seemed very pleased with the gift.

"What is it you want Mr Skelton?" enquired Margaret. "I need the use of a frying pan for about ten minutes that's all. You see I have managed to obtain some square sausages which you can only usually get in Scotland. With Bill and I being Scots, this will be a little treat for us." "Yes, of course help yourself Mr Skelton."

Skelton fried the sausages and prepared the bread by spreading the margarine thinly over it. Alexander was watching his every move. "Do you know something Dan? I have never ever eaten a square sausage sandwich in my life. I always fry them with bacon, mushrooms, eggs and a bit of haggis. I never thought of putting them in a sandwich." Bill, I used to be like you but a good few years ago, I was not particularly hungry, so I decided to try one in a sandwich. Since then, it's the only way I eat them." Skelton made the tea and put two and a half spoonful's of sugar in his mug and none in Alexanders and some fat free milk.

Skelton carefully lifted out the sausages and put one on each slice of bread. Next, he put a little salt and white pepper on the sausages and then added some brown fruity sauce which he carefully spread over the sausages. He cut the bread in half and finished off making the sandwiches. He placed two on a plate for Alexander and another two on a plate for himself. Both men were now salivating heavily. They picked up the plates and mugs of tea and headed to Skelton's office. They quickly sat down, and Skelton was the first to bite into a sandwich. Alexander was only a second behind as he bit into his. Both men made soft moaning noises as they ate their meal in complete silence, washing it down with tea. When they had finished Alexander stood up. "I tell you now Dan, I have never ever enjoyed a square sausage so much in my life. You are right, the only way to eat them is the way you just showed me. I think from now on, we will pass on the bacon rolls in the morning and have the square sausages instead." Skelton let out a contented burp. "We need to keep a supply in my fridge. I would not dare leave them in the kitchen. Did you see the number of folks watching what we were up to, in the kitchen? Not a word to anyone where we get those sausages Bill, otherwise they might sell out. Come on Bill, let's go stretch our legs and walk some of those calories off." It was two very contented detectives who strolled out in the afternoon sunshine.

Chapter Forty-One

The drive the next morning to Swansea was unremarkable and Skelton and Terry Nugent discussed who would say what to Mr and Mrs Busby. Nugent had been to the house once before, shortly before the funeral, to finalise some paperwork. It was a pretty grim council estate where Mr and Mrs Busby lived. There were rusting cars parked in front gardens some of which were sat on bricks, the wheels having been removed. Nugent recognised Mr Busby's car; an old Volvo parked outside the semi-detached house. They got out of the car and Skelton noticed that the garden was neat and tidy, and the door and windows had recently been painted. The garden gate had been given a fresh coat of wood preserve. The garden was small with a little lawn and a few rose bushes were covered in bloom. A single magnolia tree had pride of place in the middle of the lawn.

Nugent rang the doorbell and waited. The door was opened by Mr Busby, who was wearing a suit, probably as a mark of respect to the police officers who had come to visit. Mr Busby was in his mid-forties, but he looked much older, no doubt brought on by the loss of his daughter, thought Skelton. Mr Busby shook hands warmly with Terry Nugent, who then introduced Skelton. They went into the house and Mr Busby led them into the sitting room. The room contained many photographs of a once smiling Marion, sadly no longer a part of their lives. Mrs Busby was standing in front of one of two armchairs which occupied either side of a fireplace containing a gas fire. A three-piece suite was pushed against the wall opposite the fireplace. It was a small room with a couple of small tables and a large TV which left little room for any more furniture.

Nugent gave Mrs Busby a peck on the cheek and introduced her to Skelton. Mr Busby asked about their journey down and offered them tea and coffee. Nugent chose coffee whilst Skelton went for the tea. Skelton could not drink coffee due to having irritable bowel syndrome. (I.B.S.) For some reason coffee and tomatoes would trigger an almost immediate attack, causing Skelton to run to the bathroom.

Nugent began by explaining that Skelton had recently taken over from Detective Chief Inspector Smith who had led the investigation into Marion's death. He explained that DCI Smith had been seriously ill at the time but had not realised how ill he was. The Busby's were shocked to hear that he had subsequently died and were clearly a little upset. Mr Busby sat in one armchair and his wife occupied the other whilst Nugent and Skelton sat on the sofa. Mrs Busby was wearing a black dress with a string of pearls around her neck. She, like her husband looked a lot older than in the photographs on display in happier times hugging her daughter. The poor woman had probably aged by ten years.

Skelton cleared his throat. "You may have seen on television or read in the newspapers, that another girl recently went missing after a night out in Bath and that we recovered her body earlier this week from the river." Mr Busby nodded his head and said, "Yes, we watched it on the news, it brought back terrible memories for us Mr Skelton. We know exactly what her poor parents must be going through, and we would not wish that on anyone."

"Yes, I can understand that and what I am about to say may come as a shock to you." Both Mr and Mrs looked slightly confused and apprehensive. As you know, at the time Marion went missing, there was nothing suspicious about her disappearance and the pathologist confirmed that she had died from drowning. The fact that she had alcohol in her system, led us and the pathologist to conclude that it was a tragic accident and we did everything we could to return Marion's remains to you for burial. Mr Busby spoke, "Yes, we were very grateful for all that you did for us, especially Terry here who was brilliant. So, what's the purpose of your visit today?"

Well, the circumstances of the dead girl that we are now investigating are different from Marion's. You see Linda Carson was meant to be meeting someone called Tommy. She took a bus into Bath one night and after she got off the bus, she was never seen again until her body was found. Despite appeals for Tommy to come forward his identity remains a mystery. At Linda's post-mortem, the pathologist confirmed that she was intoxicated and that her death was due to drowning. The pathologist also told us that Linda had had sexual intercourse before she died. The pathologist has taken blood and urine samples, and these have gone off to be tested for drugs. Because of the unusual circumstances of Linda's disappearance, I must suspect the worst. We are concerned that Linda may have been drugged and raped and then she was put in the river whilst still alive and she drowned."

Mr and Mrs Busby exchanged anxious looks. Mr Busby asked, "But what has this got to do with Marion inspector?" Skelton gave a slightly nervous cough and said, "The thing is at Marion's post-mortem, the pathologist noted that she too had recently had sexual intercourse just before she drowned. Mrs Busby burst into tears and Mr Busby looked like he had just been poleaxed. Skelton waited until they had both regained their composure and Nugent handed Mrs Busby a bunch of paper handkerchiefs from a supply that he always kept in his pocket.

"The pathologist believed that Marion had drowned owing to being intoxicated but he did not have her blood and urine tested for drugs. In view of the unusual disappearance of Linda, I am now treating Marion's death as being suspicious. The pathologist had retained her blood and urine samples, and these have gone off to the lab to be analysed. However, due to them being nearly six months old, it will take about six weeks before we get the results. Once we get those, we will know for sure whether Marion's death was accidental or deliberate. Terry will keep you posted once we get the results. I'm sorry for having to break this news to you but I felt I had to come down and see you face to face and tell you exactly what is going on. I did not want you to find out from a reporter or on the TV."

Skelton and Nugent thanked the clearly distraught couple for the refreshments and their time and told them to contact them if they had any further questions. They said their goodbyes and left them to continue to grieve and no doubt despair in their own surroundings and without prying eyes.

Chapter Forty-Two

It was Friday morning, just four days after Linda's body had been recovered from the river. Skelton had gone into the CID room at a little after 10 having spent some time answering emails and giving Superintendent Williams, an up-date on various matters, including the meetings with the parents of the dead girls. He was sitting alongside Detective Constable Ross Turnbull who had been conducting a full review of all the CCTV images from the night that Linda had disappeared. They were once again reviewing the CCTV footage taken from the bus that Linda had boarded at the university and had alighted at Lambrettas. Turnbull was replaying the tape for the third time. As the bus approaches the bus stop, it is obvious that there is no one on the street but impossible to tell if anyone was hiding in a doorway. At about one hundred meters from the bus stop, Skelton notices a metal object of some description that appears to be resting against some iron railings. "Stop it their Ross." Turnbull stopped the tape, but it had gone past the point that Skelton had been staring at. "Go back a fraction." Turnbull slowly played the tape back. "There stop."

Both detectives stared intensely at the screen. "That's the entrance to Edward's flat. There seems to be something against the railings but it's impossible to tell from this angle, exactly what it is." Turnbull was playing the tape back and forth to see if they could get a better view. "I don't know what it is sir. It might actually be nothing more than a shadow from the bus." Skelton thought for a minute. "Well, when we searched the flat the following day there was certainly nothing against the railings then, that's for sure. You might be right Ross, it could just be a shadow from the bus or maybe someone, probably a student has padlocked a bicycle to the railings whilst they went into Lambrettas for a pint. Tell you what Ross, see if one of our experts in IT can enhance the image. It might be nothing but then again it could be significant."

The next thing on Skelton's to do list, was to get the latest news on Linda's phone and the phone that had texted her. Janet Griffin had taken charge of the phone investigation and so Skelton left Turnbull and went and sat down with Griffin. "Right Janet, tell me all you can about the phones." Well sir, there is nothing interesting to report. You recall that Linda sent a text on her phone to someone just after she had boarded the bus at the Uni?" "Yes, I do Janet, and have we been able to trace who the text was sent to?" Griffin shook her head. "No sir, Linda's mobile phone provider have been as helpful as they possibly can be, but the problem is that whilst they can tell what number the text from Linda went to, the phone is a burner, so it's not registered to anyone. It's the phone favoured by criminals, particularly drug dealers, as you know. All that we do know is that the user of that phone was situated somewhere in the area of North Parade Gardens when the text was sent. That would put him somewhere in the vicinity of Lambrettas and in all probability this was the guy called Tommy that she was supposed to be meeting.

"What we also know is that after Linda got off the bus, her telephone was switched off just a few minutes later. It has never been switched on since and it has not been found. So far as the other phone is concerned, the one she texted, the phone company has confirmed that it too has never been used again since it was turned off somewhere in the vicinity of North Parade Gardens."

Skelton was deep in thought. "Damn, we have got sod all to go on. When I interviewed Edwards in his flat, the only phone he had was an old Nokia which can't connect to the internet and you cannot send or receive texts on it. His flat has been completely searched and he does not have any other mobile phone, or iPad. Despite that, I'm convinced it was him that met Linda, raped her and somehow managed to move her to the river, where he simply pushed her in to die." Griffin was silent for a minute. "Sir, do you not think that maybe we are barking up the wrong tree here? I mean, we haven't got a shred of evidence linking Edwards forensically despite Bob Richards and his team taking the flat to pieces and so far we have no forensics from Linda's body either. The only thing we have is a coincidence that Edwards happens to live where he does. And, as I understand it, he vehemently denies having anything to do with her disappearance and his lawyer is complaining about harassment." Skelton stood up. "I know that Janet, but my gut instinct is telling me it's Edwards and until someone comes up with a better suspect, I will continue to go after Edwards."

Skelton next went and sat down with Alexander. "Bill, Edwards told me that he had been married but had got divorced and there were no kids. See if you can trace the former Mrs Edwards and find out what she is doing these days and where she is living. When you have done that, you and I will take a drive out and have a little chat with her." Alexander made a note. "Are we by any chance going to be having square sausages for our elevenses?" Skelton stood up and looked at his watch. "Follow me Bill, I took a couple into the kitchen before I came in here with strict instructions on how they were to be cooked. I said we would pick them up at 11am which is in exactly four minutes time." Alexander leapt out of his chair and followed Skelton towards the kitchen. Both men were wringing their hands in anticipation of devouring the sausage sandwiches!

It was just after mid-day when Alexander popped in to tell Skelton about what he had discovered concerning Mrs Edwards. He was standing in front of Skelton's desk with a sheet of paper. "Well Mrs Edwards is alive and well. She is fifty-one and has remarried. She is now Mary Jones and she is living in Brighton. She is a traffic warden as is her husband. They have no children. I made a call to Brighton police, I have a mate there called Charlie Stokes and I had a chat with him. Apparently, Mrs Jones is a very likeable lady. Very friendly and well regarded. She finishes work today at 4pm, so we could easily drive down and interview her at

Brighton nick as she operates out of there."
Skelton checked his calendar, he had nothing
pressing this afternoon. "Yes Bill, go ahead and fix
it up. We can have that lunch that you owe me
and then you can drive us down to Brighton. The
only trouble is that the traffic will be murder when
we are driving back especially with it being a
Friday." Alexander grimaced. "Looks like I've
drawn the fucking short straw again. First, I have
to buy you lunch and then drive you all the way to
Brighton." Skelton smiled, "Well I am keeping you
stocked up on the square sausages Bill, so I think
that makes us even." Alexander did not bother to
answer.

Alexander parked the car in the visitor's carpark at
Brighton police station. It was a few minutes
before four and Charlie Stokes had arranged the
meeting which was to be conducted in a small
meeting room. Skelton led the way into the
reception area and both he and Alexander showed
their warrant cards to the civilian employee on
reception. A few minutes later, Charlie Stokes
appeared. He was wearing a sergeant's uniform
out of which his belly was struggling to remain
inside. He was at least six feet tall and Skelton
reckoned that he must have played rugby in his
younger days. Alexander made the introductions
and Stokes took them to the interview room

where Mrs Jones was sitting waiting for them. After the introductions were over, Stokes left them to get on.

Skelton and Alexander were seated at one side of the desk whilst Mrs Jones sat opposite. She had kept her good looks and looked slightly younger than her years. She was still in her traffic warden's uniform, but she had removed her personal radio. Alexander had his notebook out and he waited for Skelton to start. "Mrs Jones thank you so much for taking the time to see us today at such short notice. We very much appreciate your cooperation and anything you tell us will be treated with the strictest confidence." Mrs Jones looked slightly nervous. "What is it you want to know inspector?"

Skelton tapped his hands on the desk. "Mrs Jones we are investigating the deaths of two young university students, both girls, who drowned in the river Avon in Bath. We suspect that your former husband might somehow be involved with those deaths." Mrs Jones put her hands on her face. "Good God, that's terrible! Are you saying that he killed them inspector?" "Mrs Jones, I need you to treat everything that I say in confidence. Our enquiry is at a very early and delicate stage and we don't want either the press or your former husband to hear anything about it, as it could seriously hamper the investigation. Do you understand that Mrs Jones?" Mrs Jones took her hands off her face and gave a slight cough. "Yes of course inspector, this is just between the three of us."

"Thank you, Mrs. Jones. I am going to have to ask you some very personal questions so please try not to be too shocked." Alexander wondered what that meant but said nothing. "Mrs Jones was your husband in any way violent towards you either before you got married or afterwards?" "No, he never ever hurt me inspector, but we did have our arguments. You know the usual domestic stuff, money and housekeeping. He was a stickler for being tidy. He was always telling me off for leaving things lying around the house. Not doing the washing up properly or not ironing his shirts correctly. Eventually I got sick of it and I guess he got fed up with me. The marriage just sort of broke down and he decided to leave. It was all very amicable inspector. I got the house and he got a clean break. We never had kids so there was no problem there either."

"Mrs Jones, did your husband have any pornography in the house?" Mrs Jones looked slightly embarrassed. "Well, yes he did actually but I don't think he knew that I had discovered it. He

303

kept it in his brief case which he took to work. He was a Science teacher you know and a very good one at that." "Can you tell us about his pornography collection?" "Oh gosh well I only saw it the once. It was only a few magazines. They were all young girls, maybe late teens, and they were having sex with older men. It quite disgusted me, and I don't think we ever had sex again after that. I mean we were barely talking at the time and that really finished it for me."

"Mrs. Jones I am really sorry to ask you about your sex life, but it could be very important. Alexander was now becoming distinctly uncomfortable, but he knew that Skelton would never ask such personal questions unless he thought that they were essential. "Okay inspector, ask away." "Would you say that you had a normal sex life or did your husband make any unusual requests or demands Mrs Jones?" "No not really inspector except for the anal thing." Alexander blushed but continued writing. Skelton held his gaze and said, "What do you mean by that Mrs Jones?"

Mrs Jones took out a handkerchief and blew her nose quietly and replaced it in her handbag. "Well, we had not been very long married and one night when we were about to have sex, he told me to turn around. I said what for? And he said he wanted to give it to me up the bum. I was a bit nervous, but he put some lube on me and on himself and we did it. It was a bit weird the first time, but he seemed to like the anal sex better than the usual way. That basically became his favourite position and well I got to enjoy it too. I mean we were both young and we had no plans to have kids, so doing it that way I was never going to get pregnant was I?"

With the interview over, the officers said farewell to Charlie Stokes and made their way to the car. Once inside with their seatbelts fastened, Alexander turned and asked, "What was that all about Dan? You know, asking about anal sex, that's awfully private don't you think?"

Skelton turned and looked Alexander full in the face. "Bill, I had to ask those questions for a very good reason. The post-mortem on both Marion and Linda revealed that they had both had undergone vigorous if not forceful intercourse before they died. Both had been virgins up until that point but coincidentally both had had anal sex. Dr Challis reported to us that it was very unusual for a virgin to consent to anal sex on a first date so to speak. The inference being that Linda was most likely drugged and so could not avoid consenting to anal sex. Now we know that

Edwards seems to prefer anal sex to vaginal, which for me makes him even more of a candidate for being the rapist and murderer. We have also learned that his pornography collection consisted of older guys having sex with young girls. So that's another connection. However, until we get the tests back from the lab, we cannot make a move.

Chapter Forty-Three

Edwards had returned to his flat after having finished work and picked up some shopping from Sainsbury's. It was Friday evening and lots of people were going out for drinks and meals. As usual, the city was bustling with tourists. The council was considering a tourist tax of £1 to be levied against tourists staying in hotels and guest houses. Almost six million tourists visit the city, so the revenue would be very useful. Edwards checked his mail which consisted of an electricity bill and nothing else. He switched on the electric oven and let it warm up whilst he sat down and watched the news on the TV. It was almost six thirty so the local news for the south-west would be on soon. He was keen to see how the status of the police investigation was faring. Surprisingly, it did not get a mention. The last time it was on the news was when a senior police officer gave a statement saying that the body had been formally identified and that the cause of death was drowning. Edwards gave a contended smile and thought to himself. "Looks like I got away with this one as well!"

He stood up and took the shepherd's pie out of the box and placed it in the oven. It would be ready in twenty-five minutes. He would microwave some peas to go with the pie. He took a shower and put on clean clothes. It was a warm evening, so he wore a t-shirt and a pair of jeans and pulled on a pair of white trainers. He sat down to his meal and poured himself a glass of white wine from the fridge. When he had finished eating, he did the washing up and put away the dishes. Now it was time to visit the garage, something he had not done since dumping the latest girl in the river. He was already getting stiff at the thought of making a date with another victim." Bring it on", he was saying to himself.

He left the flat and turned left but instead of turning left again on to Manvers Street, he crossed over to Bog Island. He did not feel comfortable walking past the police station, a copper might see him and follow. So, he walked past the Ale House which was packed with drinkers starting the weekend. He took a left on to York Street and walked casually towards the bus station. He crossed the road at the pedestrian crossing and walked past the bus station entrance. He skirted past the station and on to Lower Bristol Road which took him on to Pulteney Road. This would lead him to Widcombe Parade. This was the route he had taken with the refuse cart, that contained both his victims. He casually strolled along the pavement thinking all the while about who he might get to chat with on the dating website which had so far provided him with both victims.

As he approached the pedestrian bridge which linked Pulteney Road with the train station and under which he had disposed of both the girls, he slowed slightly and checked if anyone was crossing the bridge. There was just one person on the bridge, an old man who was walking towards the station. He stopped on the bridge and slid his hand under the first metal support. He was searching for the key to the garage. He had attached it to a magnet and it was impossible to see from either the bridge or from the narrow pathway below the bridge. It was the perfect hiding place and he had felt a sense of relief when the police had searched both himself and his flat and had found no keys which might have raised suspicion. After just a few seconds, he found the key and pulled it away from the metal support and placed it in his pocket.

He then crossed the road at the pedestrian crossing and made his way along Widcombe Parade. When he came to the church hall, he turned left and made his way into the small council carpark. Here he paused for a moment, checking that no one was about. Satisfied that no one was there to see him, he walked to the rented garage and pulled the key from his trouser pocket. He slid the key into the lock and unlocked the door, removing the key and returning the key to his pocket. He quickly pulled the door up and went inside, closing the door behind him. He was in total darkness and it took him a few seconds to find the light switch. He turned on the switch and the two fluorescent light tubes sprung into life.

He checked around the garage and was satisfied to find that everything was exactly as he had left it after his last visit, when he had just tipped Linda into the Avon. He smiled and congratulated himself on his ingenuity. He was particularly pleased at having dumbfounded the two Scottish detectives who had arrested him but had to let him go as there was not a shred of forensic evidence to link him to Linda's disappearance. What made him feel even better, was the incompetence of the police last Christmas, when they concluded that Marion's death was accidental drowning owing to her being intoxicated. Had they taken the trouble to analyse her blood, they would have found that she would have been rendered unconscious owing to the amount of the drug he had given to her. Edwards had watched the news, and had read both the national newspapers, the local "Bath Chronicle" and the police had so far not connected the two deaths. Sheer incompetence but he was not for complaining. He wondered how many more could he get away with before those idiots Skelton and Alexander woke up to what was really happening?

He switched on the laptop and waited for it to boot up. When it had gone through all the start-up motions, he noticed that he was not connected to the WIFI. He checked which free WIFI's were available and discovered that the Ram, the pub just fifty meters away, was showing as being locked. It had been over two weeks since he last used it and he guessed that they may have changed the user code and password. He cursed to himself and got out of the chair but left the laptop running. He switched off the lights and opened the door, checking to ensure that no one was outside. Satisfied that all was clear, he stepped out and quickly closed the door and locked it. He made his way back up the lane leading to Widcombe Parade and turned right and walked on until he came to the entrance to the Ram. There were a few customers standing outside having a smoke and he brushed past them and entered the pub.

He was surprised to find that it was not yet busy despite it being eight-thirty and guessed that people were still out enjoying dinner before getting down to some serious drinking. The barman was a young man in his early twenties. He had the physique of a rugby player and clearly spent a great deal of time in the gym. The barman watched him as he approached the bar and gave him a welcoming smile. "Hello, what I get you?" Edwards checked the beer taps and noted the "Thatcher's Gold" cider. This was a local Somerset cider and very popular in the west-country. "I will have a pint of Thatcher's please" The barman pulled a pint glass from the shelf below the bar and began pouring. "Is your WIFI working?" asked Edwards. "Yes, it is but we change the user code and password every day. We think half the folks in Widcombe were using it for free, so the boss fixed it so that if anyone wants to use it, they at least have to come in and buy a drink before they get the daily password and user code." Edwards shook his head and said, "That's terrible, it's amazing what liberties some people will take just to get something for free. It would never have crossed my mind to stoop so low" he lied.

The barman put the pint on the bar and Edwards handed him a ten-pound note and said, "Take one for yourself." The barman smiled and said "thanks, I will have the same as you." He rang the till and took out some coins. He then pulled out a piece of paper from a coffee mug and handed the change and the slip of paper to Edwards. "That's today's user code and password. It's valid until midnight then it automatically defaults to a new setting. We print off the new codes every morning and keep them behind the bar." Edwards thanked the barman and took his pint and placed the piece of paper in his pocket. Edwards thought to himself and decided that he would have to come in here every time he wanted to use the WIFI on his laptop in the garage. It was no great hardship and besides he liked the odd pint or two of Thatcher's.

He quickly downed the cider and said goodbye to the barman and left the pub. He took the same route back to the garage and once again he checked to make sure that no one was around. It was all clear, so he opened the garage door and closed it behind him. Finding the light switch, he turned on the lights and sat down at his laptop. He typed in the user code and password and seconds later he was connected to the Ram's WIFI. He accessed the website that had provided both Marion and Linda and discovered three messages were waiting for him. He got quite excited and quickly checked his inbox. The three messages were from girls who had accessed his false profile and photograph. He was a little disappointed that the three girls were in their late twenties, far too old for him. It was teenagers that he was after. Slim, petite and preferably virgin. Oh, how he liked to break them in and feel them bleed. It was always a hard decision whether to fuck them first up the ass or vagina. So far, he had gone the vagina route first then anal next, but he did not really care, he loved doing both especially with the girl unable to resist him. He was hard again just thinking about it.

He had been on the website for nearly an hour before he got lucky. According to the girl's profile, she was eighteen years old and studying visual editing, whatever that was. She looked perfect. She had long blond hair, a freckled face and was on the petite side. According to the profile, she was born in Belfast, the eldest of three children and was in her first year of her course at Bath Spa University. He thought for a second and wondered how many more could he take from that university

314

before they got suspicious. Her name was Patsy.
Edwards guessed that her father was called
Patrick.

He had modified his own profile but kept the same
fake photographs that he had downloaded from a
gay men's website. He was no longer Tommy the
delivery driver but Charlie a motorcycle courier. If
the police were looking at websites for Tommy the
van driver, they would be disappointed. He sent
Patsy a message and waited anxiously for a few
minutes until she replied. Within minutes Charlie
and Patsy were chatting away like long lost
friends. Time flew by, and it was almost midnight
when Edwards realised that he would soon lose
his WIFI connection. He explained to Patsy that he
needed to be up early in the morning for work and
had to go to bed. He promised to see her on the
website tomorrow evening and she said she could
not wait to chat again.

Edwards disconnected the WIFI and closed the
laptop. He switched off the lights, opened the
door quietly and looked out. The whole area was
deserted. Perfect. He closed the door and locked it
and headed back to the pedestrian bridge where
he secreted the door key and took the same route
home.

Chapter Forty-Four

It was early Saturday morning and Skelton took the boys out for their morning walk. It was a lovely fresh morning and the boys were running around eagerly smelling every new scent and looking out to see if any of their playmates, were out at this time of the morning. It was only six-forty-five and Skelton was delighted not to encounter anyone on the walk as he loved the solitary benefit of it just being him and his three boys enjoying the hour-long walk. Once back at the house he gave the boys a chew stick each and switched on the kettle and took out a mug and popped in a teabag. Radio two was on which was his favourite channel but there were a few presenters' that he could not stand and whenever they came on, he would switch to Classic FM.

His partner Ken had unusually had to work today as most weekends he was free. Having made his tea, he took out a KitKat and happily munched on it he washed it down with the delicious tea. He had a shower, shaved and got dressed. He put on a perfectly ironed long sleeve shirt and a pair of light grey trousers. He then took out a double-breasted navy-blue blazer. Skelton had long been a fan of Prince Charles mostly because of the man's excellent dress sense. Prince Charles invariably wore double-breasted suits and jackets as did Skelton. Skelton possessed at least a dozen double-breasted suits and numerous jackets and blazers. There was hardly a day that passed without someone complimenting him on how well he was dressed. Unusually, he did not wear a tie this morning. Once he had sprayed his hair in place and dabbed on some aftershave, he gave the dogs a cuddle and they quite happily went back to sleep.

Skelton had the day off and he had been pondering what to do. Whilst in the shower, he had the idea of taking the train to Weston-Super-Mare, a seaside town which he had not visited in years. He planned to leave his iPad at home and buy both the Times and the Telegraph. He liked the latter for its coverage of horse racing. He would take the train from Bath Spa to the seaside and find a pub to sit and read the papers. After that, he would select some horses to bet on and find a bookmaker to place the bets with. Then he would find a traditional fish and chip shop where he would sit down to fish and chips and white buttered bread and a mug of tea. It was years since he last did this and by the time he had walked to the train station, he was in a fine mood.

He bought the train tickets and noted that his train would be arriving in eight minutes. He quickly made his way upstairs to the platform and went into the coffee shop which sold newspapers. He bought the Times and Telegraph and walked out on to the platform where he was amazed to find Peter Lowik and Luke Meehan dressed in civvies. "Good morning Peter and good morning Luke. What are you lads up to?" Lowik and Meehan were surprised to see the DCI standing on the platform. "Well, it's all his fault" began Lowik. I was chatting to Luke yesterday morning and I told him that my wife had given me the day off as she had some girl- friends coming around to do girlie things. I mentioned that I felt like a day out at the seaside and Luke said he would take me to Weston-Super-Mare, which is a place I've never been to." Meehan was smiling as Lowik told the DCI of their plan. Skelton chuckled to himself and said. "Well boys that is a coincidence, because that's where I am headed. I haven't been there since my uni days and I fancy a few beers and some fish and chips. You are welcome to join me if you don't think I will cramp your style. Lowik glanced at Meehan and exchanged smiles and nods. "Please be our guest Dan, it will be great to have a beer or four with you!"

They got off the train at Weston which is universally known in the west-country as, Weston-Super-mud owing to the large mud flats on the beach. It was just a few minutes after 11am so the pubs would be open. As they were exiting the station, Lowik said, "Dan, Luke and I need a haircut so why don't we find you a pub where you can read your papers whilst we go to the barbers?" "Sounds like a plan to me. I haven't been here in years so let's take a walk, stake out a pub and find you guys a barber shop. I will man the pub and when you guys are finished with the barber, come and join me. After about ten minutes they found a big pub called Sass and Skelton opened the door and peered in. He checked the beer pumps and was delighted to see that they sold Fosters. "This looks perfect guys, you go and get your haircuts and join me when you are finished."

Skelton walked to the bar and had a look around. He was the only customer and the pub was huge. In fact, it had two doors, one beside the bar and another at the far end of the pub. He could hear noises coming from down in the cellar and presumed that the barman was down there. "Hello anyone down there?" A muffled voice called back. "Coming up." A few seconds later, a handsome young guy of about twenty emerged from the cellar carrying a crate of cider bottles. He was quite short with a ponytail and had an earring in each ear. "Sorry about that, I am on my own this morning and just stocking up. What can I get you?" Skelton smiled and said, "I will have a pint of Fosters, please."

The barman started pouring and asked" Are you just visiting or are you a local." "Oh, I am just here for a day trip then it's back to Bath." The barman smiled and said, "I love Bath, but I can't afford to live there." Skelton handed the barman a twenty-pound note and said, "Take one for yourself." "Thank you very much. I will put in a pint of Thatcher's and have it with my lunch." Skelton took a mouthful of beer and made his way to a table at the far end of the bar. The pub could easily seat two hundred but Skelton was the only customer. He took a seat with his back to the wall so that he could see anyone coming into the pub. He placed his pint on the table and found the Sports Section of the Telegraph and began reading.

Suddenly, the door nearest to him burst open and in walked two guys dressed as hell's angels. The first one in was aged about thirty and he was quite a stocky guy with a beer belly and a fat backside. His head was shaved, and he sported a large earring in his left ear. He was wearing blue jeans held up by a thick leather belt. He wore a black t-shirt and a leather waistcoat. His arms were covered in tattoos and he also had one on his forehead. He was a mean looking guy and from the grey pallor of his skin, Skelton reckoned the guy had just recently left prison.

His mate, who was closing the door behind himself, was a little younger maybe twenty-five and a bit taller, probably about 5" 10. He also had a shaven head and a goatee beard which needed a trim. He was dressed similarly to his mate the only difference being that his t-shirt was white. They both reeked of tobacco smoke and needed a good wash. Skelton ignored them and continued studying the horse racing. There were three race meetings that day, which were of interest to him. They were at Sandown Park, Lingfield Park and Newcastle. This was the height of the flat season with Royal Ascot just a couple of weeks away. Skelton tended to follow three trainers during the flat season, but he did not restrict his choice to them alone. His favourite trainer, John Gosden, whom he admired not only for his training skills, but the man was an out and out gentlemen with beautiful manners which Skelton greatly admired. He failed to understand why Gosden, had not been knighted for his services to horse racing. Next came William Haggis whose father-in-law was perhaps the greatest flat racing jockey of his generation, the mighty Lester Piggott. His nickname was the long fellow because he was rather tall for a jockey. Skelton's other star trainer was Andrew Balding the brother of Clare Balding the broadcaster and journalist.

Skelton glanced up at the bar and saw that the two guys were being served their drinks and were chatting with the barman. Skelton turned his attention back to the racing. Gosden had a horse running in the two-thirty at Sandown. Its jockey was the famous Frankie Dettori who Skelton was greatly fond of, not just for his considerable talent as a horseman, but also because of his infectious humour.

Despite the pub being empty apart from Skelton and the two hells angels, and there was lots of seating throughout the bar, the two men decided to sit at the table closest to Skelton. As they got closer, Skelton could smell the cheap tobacco smoke that clung to their clothes. Skelton doubted that either man had washed that morning and was rather put out that they had decided to sit next to him when there were so many other places where they could have sat. Both men were silent, which suited Skelton, as he was absorbed with studying the form of the eight runners in the two-thirty.

That was until the first peanut hit him in the face. Skelton looked up to see the older guy holding a bag of peanuts. He and his mate were grinning.

"Look guys, I am just sitting here reading my paper. I'm not looking for any trouble and I would appreciate it if you would stop throwing peanuts at me. Understand?" The guy with the peanuts looked at his mate and said, "Hear that, the bastard is Scottish as well." The younger guy shook his head. "It's bad enough for a stranger to come into our pub but being Scottish that makes the offence much worse." Skelton had been hoping for a peaceful day but these guys were clearly looking for trouble. Skelton would have no trouble in taking the men down, he had no doubts about his ability to fight. The thing that concerned him was that he was wearing a £600 blazer and a shirt that he had only worn once. There could be a lot of blood, not Skelton's blood but blood would ruin his jacket and shirt and he wanted to avoid that.

"I don't know what it is I have done to upset you guys, but I am warning you now. Just back off, you have had your fun with the peanuts. Just sit there and enjoy your cider and I will sit here and read my paper until I have finished my pint. Then, when I have done that, I am leaving to have some fish and chips." The two hells angels looked at one

324

another. The older one said, "Let's teach him some manners Dick. It's been a while since I kicked the shit out of a jock."

Skelton groaned silently and stood up and stepped back from the table. The two hells angels also stood up. The one called Dick was putting his hand inside his waistcoat pocket. He pulled out a knuckle duster and slipped it on his right hand. Meanwhile his mate pulled out a heavy lead cosh. "I am going to allow you guys to leave the pub whilst you still can. Unless you go now, I guarantee that both of you will leave here on stretchers and you will spend a fair amount of time in the hospital." This provoked a wave of laughter as if Skelton had just told a great joke.

"Do you know what Dick? This joker has got some balls. Well, at least he has for the moment anyway. I think we should cut them off and stick them down his throat." The two men continued to laugh and did not hear Lowik and Meehan as they quickly approached them from behind. They had entered the pub through the door beside the bar and had witnessed the exchange of words and realised that Skelton was about to get into a fight.

"Right guys, final warning, leave now whilst you still can otherwise you will get the worst fucking kicking you have ever had in your lives." Dick went

325

to make his move but Lowik punched him in the right kidney and the guy dropped to his knees. The older guy was moving towards Skelton when Meehan grabbed him by the shoulder and swung him around. Skelton watched Meehan as he pummelled the guy's face. The guy fell backwards on to the floor as Meehan's uppercut from his left fist knocked him out cold.

Lowik was not finished with Dick. He proceeded to batter his fists into the guy's face. Skelton saw teeth flying as well as blood. Dick tried to cover his face and was now lying on the floor doing his utmost to protect himself. Skelton said, "That's enough." Lowik stopped and stood up straight. "Right guys well done but please stand by the door and look away. I don't want you to witness this. Lowik and Meehan did as they were told. Skelton drained his pint and walked over to where the older guy was lying. He was just regaining consciousness and Skelton surveyed the damage. The jaw was broken, as was the nose and he had lost several teeth. The jaw would probably need surgery, so the guy would be on fluids for about six weeks. Skelton kicked him hard in the ribs. The guy screamed and grasped his ribs trying to protect them from further damage. Skelton swung his right foot and hit the guy squarely in the nuts. The guy screamed again and began pleading for mercy.

Skelton turned to Dick who was kneeling on the floor with his hands over his head. He kicked him as hard as he could in the ribs and the guy screamed and fell on to his back. "Please don't hit me again mister. We are sorry we were just kidding. Honest we were not going to hit you." Skelton ignored the man and instead kicked him right in the balls. The guy could barely scream and began to sob. Both men had had enough.

Skelton walked over to where Lowik and Meehan were standing. "Right boys, let's go find the CCTV recording, we don't want to leave that." They walked towards the bar. The barman was still down in the cellar and had missed the entire fight. To the left of the bar was a small office. Meehan approached the door and turned the handle and the door opened. He held it open whilst Lowik and Skelton entered. Bingo, this was where the CCTV was recording. They looked at the cameras and there on the bar floor lay the two men. Lowik ejected the film and handed it to Skelton. They left the office and closed the door. The three officers left the bar and went outside. They were casually walking along the side of the pub when Lowik said, "Where are your papers Dan?" Skelton stopped. "Bugger, I left them in the pub. Just a minute, wait for me here." Skelton re-entered the pub just as the barman was coming up the stairs from the cellar. Skelton walked past the casualties who were still sprawled on the floor groaning. When he got to the table, he withdrew a white handkerchief from his pocket and carefully wiped the pint glass that he had used of any fingerprints and DNA. He picked up the newspapers and wiped the table. All evidence gone.

As he walked towards the bar, he said to the barman, "I think you should call an ambulance for those two hells angels. I don't think the cider has agreed with them." The barman looked slightly perplexed and lifted the bar counter and walked towards where he had seen the men sit down. He saw the two badly injured men lying on the floor. As far as the barman was concerned the only people who had been in the pub that morning were the two hells angels and the smartly dressed stranger. But the stranger was unmarked, his clothes were intact and there was no sign of any blood on him. The two lying on the floor were covered in blood and had lost some teeth. The barman shook his head in disbelief and could not wait to see the recording of the fight on the CCTV. The barman would dine out on this story for weeks, that was for sure!

Chapter Forty-Five

It was Monday morning and Skelton had to take an umbrella to work with him as it was raining heavily when he left the house. The weather forecast on the BBC said that the rain would clear by late morning, but it would remain mainly cloudy. He was glad that he had mown the lawn the previous day. The garden was just over an acre in size and was on a very steep slope which made it too dangerous for a sit-on mower. Instead, he had to use a powerful petrol mower. This was great exercise and Skelton loved to admire the freshly mown lawn when the task was completed. The dogs were always kept inside when the mower was being operated but once the grass was all cut, they loved to run around marking their ground.

Skelton found Alexander sitting at his desk reading his emails. "Good morning Bill, can I have a quiet word with you in my office please?" "Good morning Dan. Yes of course give me two minutes, I'm just finishing this email." A few minutes later Alexander was sitting across from Skelton, enjoying a mug of tea that Skelton had made for him.

"Bill, have you got any friends in the CID in Weston-Super-Mare by any chance?" Alexander put down his mug and smiled. "Yes, I do actually. A guy called Phil Gallagher, he's one of us. He started his career in the old Strathclyde Police. Then he met his future wife who was a nurse in Bristol and he ended up coming down here. Before I moved to Bath, I was stationed at Weston. Phil was the DS and a great guy. Not known for sticking to the rules if you get my meaning." Skelton sat back in his chair and cupped both hands behind his head.

"Bill, I need a big favour from you and your friend Gallagher. You see, I got into a spot of trouble with a couple of hell's angels on Saturday morning in a pub in Weston. We had a bit of a punch-up and

these two thugs got quite badly injured."
Alexander's jaw dropped at this news, but he said
nothing. "Nobody witnessed the fight, as the pub
was empty, and the barman was down in the
cellar. I wiped my beer glass of fingerprints and
DNA and borrowed the CCTV film. Those guys
would have needed hospital treatment which
means that the police would have been called.
Obviously, I don't want a major investigation into
this in case it comes back to me."

Alexander was digesting this information from his
boss, with some admiration. "What was the fight
about?" Skelton removed his hands from behind
his head and rested them on his desk. I was just
reading my paper when these two guys walked in
and started throwing peanuts at me. One of them
looked like he had just got out of prison. When I
asked them to stop, they recognised my Scottish
accent and said I was going to get a good hiding.
One took out a knuckle duster and the other had a
cosh which left me no option but to fight dirty. As
far as I could tell, they both had broken jaws and
ribs and won't be enjoying sex for a few weeks
either."

Alexander stood up. "Bloody hell that's
impressive! Leave it with me. I will have a discreet
word with Phil Gallagher and get back to you."

It was close to lunch time when Alexander walked into Skelton's office and closed the door and sat down. Skelton closed down his screen and gave Alexander his full attention. "Any luck with your mate Gallagher, Bill?" "Remind me never to pick a fight with you Dan! Do you know how much damage you did to those scum bags?" Skelton folded his arms across his chest. "Well, they looked a bit of a mess I must admit but they were breathing fine and both were conscious when I left them."

Alexander had a bunch of papers in his hand and he was now looking at them. "The older of the two is Eddie Grant, who I happen to know. I arrested him a couple of times a while back. He has form, as long as your arm. He was just released from jail ten days ago for a serious assault. He needed surgery for a broken jaw and nose. He lost five teeth and has six broken ribs. He has acute bruising around his groin consistent with having been kicked.

His playmate is called Richard or Dick Love. He too needed surgery for a broken jaw and he lost three teeth. You broke five of his ribs and he too has very painful private parts. The barman called an ambulance and the paramedics alerted the police. Uniform attended, and they called in the CIS

(C.I.S.) who examined the table and glass that you used. No fingerprints and no DNA. The barman said he checked the CCTV as he was keen to see these two scum bags getting this beating, but the disc is missing. Uniform handed the case over to CID this morning and Phil Gallagher got assigned to it. He had just got back from interviewing the barman when I called him. The barman told him that there were only three people in the pub when it happened. The two hell's angels and a very smartly dressed Scottish gentleman. Phil was hugely impressed that one man could have given those guys such a kicking. Now that he knows that it was a fellow Scot that administered the beating, he has closed the file owing to a lack of evidence. However, Dan, you owe me and Phil Gallagher a night out and a curry."

Skelton stood up and looked at his watch. It was going on one o'clock. "Thank you, Bill I am grateful to you and Phil for sorting that out. Consider it a done deal, a curry and a piss-up on me. Just sort out a night and let's do it. Come on, I need some lunch."

Skelton would never mention to anyone, the role that Lowik and Meehan had played in the fight. That would be their little secret.

Chapter Forty-Six

Whilst Skelton and his two companions had been on their trip to Weston-Super-Mare, Edwards had been at work. He did not usually work Saturdays, but a glitch in the computer system, had caused some serious delays, and he wanted to make up for the lost time. When he finished, he went home and showered and changed. He usually had his evening meal at the flat but this evening he had decided to visit the Ram and have dinner there. He took the same route to Widcombe which avoided walking past the police station. He entered the pub and noticed that it was a different barman behind the bar. He ordered a pint of Thatcher's and fish and chips. He got a piece of paper from the barman with the user code and password and sat down at a vacant table.

There were about a dozen people in the pub and no one was paying him any attention. He had bought the "Bath Chronicle" from the newsagent next door to the pub and he sat and began reading it whilst he waited for his meal to arrive. The paper reported that Linda Carson's death was due to drowning and that she had consumed alcohol. It went on to say that the police were awaiting the results of toxicology tests. This news caused Edwards some agitation. The tests would come back positive for the drug which he had given her in the glass of wine unless it had completely vanished owing to her having been in the river for a week. He sighed and then smiled to himself. Even if they were able to detect the drug, there was nothing to forensically link him with her. The police would obviously be suspicious and would probably mount a murder enquiry but so far as he was concerned, the police had no way of proving that it was he who administered the drug. He had been ultra-careful to remove any trace of his DNA on the body and clothing. The police had found no trace of the girl's DNA on him or in his flat, so as far as he was concerned, he had little if anything to worry about! And besides, they had not one single sighting of the girl after she had got off the bus. The cops had still not worked out how he had arranged the vanishing trick!

His fish and chips arrived along with mushy peas and he tucked into them. He decided to have another pint as he had put a little too much salt on his meal which made him thirsty. When he finished the second pint, he left and walked around to the garage. He glanced all over the carpark but there was nobody about.

He made his way over to the foot bridge where he kept the garage key. He found the key and slipped it into his pocket and walked back to the garage. A car had just driven into the carpark. It was a green

Volvo and he waited until the driver got out. The driver locked the door and walked away. Edwards opened the garage door and went inside and closed it behind him.

Having logged into the dating website, he was delighted to find a message had been received from Patsy. He opened it up and read it. Hi Charlie, I hope you had a good day at work. I am going to be online tonight if you would like to chat? Looking forward to hearing from you.

Patsy xxx'

Edwards opened the chat room and scrolled down until he found Patsy's profile. He clicked on it and began typing. 'Hi Patsy, thanks for your message. Work was ok. Just had some dinner and a couple of pints. How was your day?'

'Charlie' and Patsy were soon chatting as they had done the previous evening. Edwards had no doubt that Patsy really wanted to meet "Charlie". Edwards did not want to rush things as he understood the police would be keeping a close eye on him. He wanted to make sure that when he did make a move on Patsy that once again, he would leave no clues for the police to follow. He got Patsy to give him her mobile phone number and he gave her "Charlie's number. He explained to her that where he was currently located, he had no signal but promised to text her in the morning. They finished chatting at 11.30pm with 'Charlie' confirming his promise to send her a text in the morning. Edwards was not going to re-activate the phone that he had used, to lure Linda, He was too clever to leave such a valuable lead for the police to follow! He had already bought another disposable phone and sim card, without having to give any ID. So, neither the phone company nor the police would know who the owner was. He was to all intents and purposes, "invisible" again. He did not want to activate the new phone at Widcombe, as this would be a significant clue for the police. No, in the morning he would head out of Bath and activate the phone somewhere, that would leave the police puzzled. And more importantly, the less the police knew about Widcombe the better!

Chapter Forty-seven

Edwards got up on Sunday morning at nine. He had not slept terribly well as the anticipation of meeting Patsy and what he was going to do to her, had kept him awake. But sheer exhaustion overtook him and at seven o'clock he fell into a deep sleep. When we awoke at nine, he threw back the bed covers and got out of bed. He switched on the radio and heard Frank Sinatra singing fly me to the moon. He then emptied the kettle and replenished it with some fresh water. He switched the kettle on and went to the bathroom. When he returned the kettle was just boiling. He made some coffee and put a slice of bread in the electric toaster and waited for his toast. He buttered the toast and sat down at the kitchen table and began plotting where he would send Patsy a text. He had brought the new phone home last night and would use it to contact Patsy this morning. He could not risk talking to her, as his voice would not sound right for a young man of "Charlie's" age!

After showering and shaving, Edwards had completed his plan for the day. He would leave his usual mobile phone in the flat. There was no way that he would take it with him as the police would be able to use it to establish where he had been. He would take the new phone with him which the police did not know he had bought. He would not switch it on until he had arrived at his destination. Once there he would send Patsy a message and she would feel close to him by having his phone number. She would be working today in a pub called the Cat and Fiddle. University had just finished for the summer, but she had decided to stay on in Bath for a few more weeks as the pub had offered her the work and free accommodation. She planned to go home to Ireland, in three weeks-time. She would spend the summer with her family and return to Bath in September, to continue her studies at the University.

Edwards picked up the new phone and placed it inside his jacket pocket. He was wearing jeans, a clean shirt and as it was an overcast day, he had put on a jersey and a sports jacket. He was aware that in Bath, he would be picked up on CCTV if he went into the city centre. However, he knew that there were certain "blind" spots. He should know, as he had studied where the CCTV cameras were situated. Where he lived on North Parade was a perfect example. The police had tried their best to find him and Linda on CCTV but had failed. He would take advantage of this once again. He left the flat and crossed the road and turned right on North Parade and walked for about fifty meters. On the bridge over the river Avon, a stairwell leads down to the river and Edwards made his way down the stairs. He was heading towards Pulteney Weir where the pleasure boats operated, providing regular boat trips along the river. The route that he took had no CCTV cameras, so the police would be unable to verify his movements.

A cold breeze was blowing off the river and Edwards shivered as he made his way towards the jetty. A small queue had formed waiting to board the boat that was travelling to Bath Hampton, a couple of miles down-river. He could get off the boat at Bath Hampton and he could either go for a walk or have a drink in the pub on the riverbank. Given the cold breeze that was blowing, he decided that he would opt for the pub where not only would he have a drink but would have lunch as well. He could send his text message to Patsy and wait for her reply in the comfort and warmth of the pub. He knew that when he switched the phone on, it would alert the phone signal provider that he had activated the phone. But neither the phone company nor the police would have any idea who the phone belonged to.

The passengers in front of him began boarding the boat which was called the Lady Florence. Edwards boarded the boat and paid the fare. He then took a seat and waited for the remaining passengers to board. After about ten minutes, the boat began moving and Edwards settled down for the commentary to begin, the skipper pointing out various features as they cruised down the Avon. Despite the chill, Edwards was enjoying the trip which was his first on the Avon. He stared into the water, recalling how he had sent two girls to their death in it but not before he had enjoyed the most fantastic sex he had ever known! He began relishing what he would do to Patsy when he met her and how she too would end up another victim of the Avon. He could hardly contain his excitement!

As the boat tied up at Bath Hampton, Edwards took out the phone and switched it on. After a few minutes he had a signal. He then took out the piece of paper that contained Patsy's phone number. He entered her details in the "contacts" section and then typed her a message. "Hi Patsy, I really enjoyed chatting with you again last night online. I'd really love to meet you and maybe we can start going out together? I forgot to ask if you have a car?

Lots of love

Charlie"

Edwards sent the message. He got off the boat and walked up the riverbank to the George, pub which is very close to the boat moorings. The phone bleeped indicating a message had arrived. Edwards stared at the phone. There was a message from Patsy. His hand began to tremble as he opened the message. 'Hi Charlie, yes I loved chatting with you as well. Yes, I have a car. Happy to pick you up any time you like!

Patsy Xxx'

Edwards could hardly control himself. The thought of Patsy having a car was a real bonus! He knew that he could no longer use the flat to meet his next victim as that would be too risky and he was pretty sure that the police were watching him. Edwards smiled to himself as he made his plan to lure Patsy to drive her car over to the Widcombe garage. Fucking her in the garage would not be as comfortable as in his own bed, but he could put up with that! He went into the pub which was already quite busy. It was obviously very popular for Sunday lunch. He looked at the menu and decided that he would have roast beef, washed down with a few pints of Thatcher's cider. He sat down with his pint and waited for his lunch to arrive. He sent Patsy another message. 'Hi Patsy, that would be fantastic! How about one night this week after you finish work? Do you know the Travel Lodge at Widcombe? I'm free every night next week.

Charlie Xxxxx'

A few seconds later, Patsy replied. 'Yes, I know the Travel Lodge. I can meet you there on Thursday night at 11.30pm. xxxx'

Edwards read the message and his heart started racing. His hands were shaking as he texted the message back. 'That's perfect Patsy. What type of car do you have and what colour is it?' He sent the message and a few minutes later came the response. 'I have a black ford fiesta' Edwards read the message. Edwards sent her a final message for the day. 'Excellent. Have a great day and I can't wait to see you on Thursday xxx'

Edwards switched the phone off and slipped it into his jacket pocket. He would not switch it on again until he was in a place of his own choosing.

Chapter Forty-Eight

It was Monday morning and Skelton was reading
the crime reports from the previous night when

Janet Griffin knocked on his door and entered his office. Skelton could tell by the look on her face that she was not bringing good news. "Good morning Janet, have a chair." Skelton pointed to the chair opposite his desk and Griffin sat down. "What have you got for me." Griffin sighed and looked earnestly at the papers she had in her hands. "It's not good news sir. We have checked on his movements from when he was arrested up until yesterday, which was Sunday. The locations all point to him just going about his working life. He switches his phone on at about the same time every morning before leaving for work. We can then see that he goes to the council depot. Each day at about 1pm, he travels about 500 meters probably for his lunch. Then he just goes straight home in the evening after work. On Sunday morning, he switched his phone on just after nine and it stayed in the same location throughout the day." Skelton asked, "And where was that Janet?" "His flat sir, he stayed in the whole day." Griffin stood up and walked towards the window and then turned and faced Skelton.

"We have checked to see if he rents or even owns a property in Bath other than his flat. There is no trace of any such property. We haven't a shred of evidence that Edwards has in anyway acted suspiciously or has committed any crime."

346

Skelton ran his hand through his hair and then banged it down hard on the desk. "Shit, shit, shit! He is either being very clever or we have the wrong man." Skelton stood up and paced the room. "If I wanted to convince the police that I was at home, I would leave my phone there, knowing full well that if they checked with the phone company, it would show that my phone never left the house. Let's face it, no one goes out without their phone. I think Edwards knows that we would be monitoring his phone and if he left it at home it gives him the perfect alibi. I reckon that he leaves his phone at home whenever he goes out except when he is working."

Griffin was studying Skelton's face and watched him closely as he sat down. He had closed his eyes, clearly deep in thought and she remained silent, so as not to disturb his thought process. "I am totally convinced that he has a place that we have so far not found, where he keeps a laptop, or iPad. I think he has been visiting this location in the evenings after work and by leaving his phone at home he thinks he has fooled us into believing that he stays at home. He is a cunning bastard for when we searched him and his flat, we found no keys that would indicate that he had access to other premises. We also searched his locker at work and again no suspicious keys. We need to start surveillance on him as I think he has contacted another girl and it's only a matter of time before he strikes again."

Skelton's desk phone rang, and he picked it up on the second ring. "DCI Skelton, can I help?"

The voice on the other end of the phone said, "Good Morning Dan It's Chief Superintendent Sawyers here. Can you pop up to my office now and see me?" Skelton stood up as he said, "Yes sir I am on my way now." Chief Superintendent Sawyers had welcomed Skelton to the station on his first day but the very next day he had left on annual leave which had left Superintendent Williams in charge. Skelton guessed that Sawyers wanted an up-date on what he had been up to, whilst he had been away. "Sorry Janet but the chief wants to see me now. I will catch you later." Skelton put his suit jacket on and made his way to Sawyer's office. Sawyer's secretary had a desk close to her boss's door and she saw Skelton approach. As Skelton got closer, she smiled and said, "You can go straight in sir, he's waiting for you." Skelton returned the smile and said, "Thank You Christine."

Skelton knocked on the door and heard "Come in". He opened the door and closed it behind him. Sawyers was sitting at his desk. He looked remarkably sun tanned no doubt heightened by the crisp white shirt that he was wearing. His uniform jacket was hanging on the coat stand to the left of his desk. Sawyer's steel rimmed glasses rested on his nose. His white hair had been recently trimmed and he looked the picture of health. Sawyers was a true copper's copper. He had over thirty-year's experience in the police and had seen it all and done it all. He would back his officers to the hilt, but woe betide a bent or dishonest officer. Skelton knew that if Sawyers discovered what he had done in Weston-Super-Mare with the two hell's angels, he would probably find it highly amusing! On the other hand, if an officer took a bribe or brought the force into disrepute, that officer was finished.

"Ah Dan, come in and take a seat. Would you like tea or coffee?" Skelton sat down. He glanced at his watch and it was 10.30am. He would be having his eleven o'clock sausage sandwich in half an hour. "No thank you sir, I'm fine thanks. You look very tanned and well sir"

Sawyers gave him a broad smile. "You can't beat some Florida sunshine and a week or two on a boat to give you a great tan, that's for sure." Skelton smiled and said, "I can see that sir." "Well Dan, I've had Superintendent Williams in this morning, giving me an up-date on what has been happening whilst I was away. You seem to have been busy! A domestic murder and suicide. A gang of pick pockets in custody and you have linked the two girl students that drowned in the river as possible murders despite not even having the results of the toxicology tests. You could be skating on thin ice here Dan. Plus the fact that by suggesting that the first girl who drowned was not accidental leaves the force and your predecessor, DCI Smith, open to severe criticism by the press and media. I understand that you even went and visited the parents of the first girl to drown, to say that she may have been murdered. Why the hell did you do that Skelton?"

Skelton shifted his weight on the chair. He had guessed correctly that Sawyers would be naturally protective of his force's reputation and that of the late DCI Smith. It would be up to Sawyers to explain the whole sad story to the Chief Constable and Skelton needed to convince Sawyers that what he had done was the right course of action to take.

"Sir, whilst we don't yet have the results of the toxicology tests on either girl, I feel certain that Linda Carson was somehow abducted before she ended up dead in the river. The post-mortem confirmed that she had been a virgin, but on the night she disappeared, she had endured vigorous sexual intercourse both front and back. The boy she was supposed to have been meeting has never been traced and despite viewing every CCTV recording in the area around where she got off the bus in North Parade, neither she nor the boy can be seen. I think that when she got off the bus, she was lured into a flat next to the bus stop owned by a man called Norman Edwards. He somehow administered a rape drug which rendered her unconscious. He then raped her and removed every trace of her DNA from the flat. He then somehow transported her to the river whilst she was still alive. All he had to do then, was to push her into the river where she drowned. This would look accidental as she suffered no other injuries to indicate foul play. And that's exactly what we concluded when Marion Busby was fished out of the river. I am not suggesting that DCI Smith was in anyway negligent. He was ill at the time and it was Christmas. There was a flu epidemic and the mortuary staff were under incredible pressure to process bodies as quickly as possible for funerals. He wanted Marion's body repatriated to her family. If you ask me, it was just a set of highly unusual and rare circumstances which resulted in

Marion's blood and urine not being screened for drugs sir."

Sawyers sat back in his chair and he carefully scrutinised Skelton's face and body language for any sign of weakness. There was none. Sawyers had made discreet enquiries into Skelton before deciding that he was the man to head his CID team. As one officer in the metropolitan police had put it, "Our loss is your gain." Sawyers wanted to hear it all straight from Skelton. The man was dealing with an exceptionally complicated enquiry. He had to decide whether to back him or hang him out to dry. It was an easy decision to make. "Okay, I've heard it from the horse's mouth and I fully understand the actions you have taken. I don't know if you are right or wrong Dan, about these girl's deaths being linked. What I do know, is that you are following your gut instinct, which I will always respect in a detective. You have my full backing. Let me know the minute you get the toxicology results."

"Yes of course sir, they should be through any day now, on Linda Carson. It will be some time yet before Marion's results come through." Sawyers rested both his arms on the desk and looked Skelton in the eye. "But how the fuck did he move the body, or should I say, the bodies from the flat?

According to Superintendent Williams, you guys have reviewed all the CCTV in the vicinity of the bus stop and yet neither the girl nor Edwards appears in any of them. If it was not for the fact that the girl's body turned up in the river, I would have said that her body was hidden in the flat. So, what is your theory on how your only suspect managed to evade all the CCTV cameras?" Skelton leaned back in his chair and clasped his hands on the back of his head for a few seconds and then brought them to rest on the desk. "Sir, I've been pondering that very question since day one. We must have missed something, or we have failed to see something. The clue must be with the CCTV footage, but it's been reviewed several times and my guys can't see anything out of the ordinary. We have interviewed every driver of all the vehicles that passed the bus stop that night and eliminated them from our enquiries. I'm sorry to say that I've got a suspect who I am sure is our man, but he is extremely clever and forensically very adapt. He has so far not put a foot wrong and he thinks he has got away with two murders. My concern now is that he might strike again and if he does then I will have failed in my duty to stop him. I know that the financial budget is critical sir, but can we really afford to let Edwards walk free and risk the life of another innocent girl?"

Sawyers stood up and walked to the window and looked out. It was raining. He was holding his chin when he turned around and faced Skelton. Right Dan, two things. First, stop thinking of seeing things on CCTV that are out of the ordinary. This bastard Edwards has hood winked us into looking for him or the girl. Have you considered that he might have an accomplice? And secondly, fuck the budget! You are authorised to put him under surveillance right away. Get them to put a microphone in his flat so that we can listen to what he gets up to when he's at home."

Skelton was delighted and relieved that Sawyers had decided to give him his total support. He was warming to this man. He felt that it could become the same close professional relationship that he had enjoyed with his old boss, Alan Warwick. "Understood sir. I don't think that Edwards has an accomplice, he is very much a loner. But I do agree with you, there must be something in the CCTV footage that we have dismissed as irrelevant when in fact it holds the key to unlocking this mystery. I'm going to have the CCTV looked at again but this time with a fresh pair of eyes. I was going to ask for permission for the surveillance once the toxicology tests were in later this week, but I am more than happy to start it right away sir."

Skelton stood up and Sawyers moved towards him with his hand out stretched. As they shook hands, Sawyers said, "We can't bring those poor girls back, but we can give their families justice and some closure. But for god's sake do whatever you can to stop him killing another one."

Chapter Forty-Nine

The detectives were in the incident room awaiting Skelton's arrival, to brief them on Chief Superintendent Sawyers' decision. It was at noon precisely when Skelton opened the door and entered. He went straight to the lectern and raised his right hand for silence. "Ladies and gentlemen, I had a meeting this morning with Chief Superintendent Sawyers regarding our progress or should I say the lack of it, in this case. We are both agreed that the key to solving the mystery of how Linda ended up in the river is in the CCTV footage. There is something in that footage that we have missed, and the clue to that, is we are seeing something we have dismissed as irrelevant, as it's not in any way unusual. In other words, we can't see the wood for the trees. I am therefore ordering that the entire CCTV footage that we have in our possession be looked at again. I am not in any way being critical of the officers that have already reviewed the footage, but the chances of us not spotting what we have already missed is too great to ignore. I therefore want this review of the CCTV footage to be conducted by officers who have not previously viewed the footage.

"I am concerned about the timing of Linda's disappearance and at what time she ended up in the river. So far, we have assumed that Edwards somehow met her as she got off the bus just after 22 hundred hours. He took her to his flat where he drugged her right away and raped her. As far as I am aware, we concluded he would have removed Linda and all forensic evidence, by no later than 4am the next morning."

Skelton cleared his throat, "I think we were wrong to restrict the time of her removal until just 4am. So, when the fresh review of the CCTV footage is undertaken, I want the time frame extended until 7am. We all assumed that Edwards would want to remove Linda from the flat under the cover of darkness but I'm beginning to think that this may not be the case."

The detectives exchanged glances and a few words were exchanged. Skelton raised his hand for silence. "We will have the results of the toxicology analysis for Linda any day now, so we will be certain whether or not this is murder. Marion's results will not be known for some time yet. In the meantime, Chief Superintendent Sawyers has authorised surveillance on Edwards. We will also place a hidden microphone in his flat. I suspect that he has tried to fool us by leaving his phone at home, causing us to believe that he never goes out at night or at the weekend."

Skelton cast his eyes around the room and continued. "With regards to the surveillance, we know for a fact that he goes to work at the same time every morning and returns at about the same time every night. So, we don't need to watch him during the day, unless we think he's up to something. So, we will concentrate on what he gets up to after work and at the weekend. I've arranged for the surveillance team to take up position in an upstairs bedroom of the Ale House. There is only one door that Edwards can enter and exit his flat and that's on North Parade. The Ale House offers excellent visibility, of Edwards front door, so it should be relatively easy to keep a close eye on him. Any questions? Ross Turnbull raised his hand. "Yes Ross?" Turnbull stood up. "Sir could we not mount the surveillance from the bar of the Ale House?" There was a roar of laughter. "Yes, I had thought of that Ross. And just to put everyone's mind at rest, Bill Alexander and I will be at the bar to provide back-up!" There was more laughter as the team began making their way out of the briefing room.

Chapter Fifty

Skelton glanced at his watch, it was 12.45pm and he was getting hungry. His good friend Patrick Rees had called earlier to get an up-date on the investigations, but Skelton sensed that it was just a supportive call, to wish him well. Rees was another lover of Fosters lager, and during the call, had asked Skelton which pubs he had been using, now that he was back in Bath. Skelton ran through the list and Rees had asked why Skelton was not using the Poultney Arms. Although it sold Carling lager and not Fosters both men also enjoyed the former. But what persuaded Skelton the most to try it, apart from the fact that it apparently did good food, was that the owners had two black labs. Skelton was a sucker for black labs and if he could get the opportunity to pet one at lunchtime, it would make his day. The pub was, he guessed, about a fifteen-minute walk from the police station. He smiled to himself when he thought of Alexanders' impression of a 30-minute walk, today!

On que, Alexander knocked on the door and walked in. "God I'm starving sir, I missed my elevenses this morning and only had an egg roll before I left the house this morning. Skelton stood up and gave his friend a smile." Good news, and bad news Bill." "Bad news first please." Skelton was putting his jacket on as he said, "Bad news is that the pub that we are going to today entails a thirty-minute walk in total." Alexander let out an exasperated sigh, "Bloody hell Dan, I'm going to be a shadow of my former self! So, what's the good news?" Skelton was securing the buttons on his double-breasted suit, "The good news is that we are going to the Poultney Arms, which I am led to believe does good food and they have two black labs. And even better than that Bill, I put £40 on a horse yesterday and it duly obliged at odds of 8/1 giving me a tidy profit of £320. So, lunch is on me Bill." The detectives exchanged high fives and headed out the door.

They came out of the police station and turned right. They were heading in the direction of Poultney Bridge but first had to cross over North Parade. There was a pedestrian crossing at the junction, and Skelton pushed the button and waited for the green man. Turning his head to the right, he saw a large white van approaching, the driver of which, was talking excitedly into his mobile phone. Skelton hated people who constantly chatted or used some sort of App whilst walking, but he would invariably give an offender using their phone whilst driving, a ticket on the spot. This would result in a £200 fine for a first offence and six penalty points on their licence.

The van driver stopped at the red light. Skelton saw that he was of Middle Eastern appearance, in his mid-forties and heavily built. He had a long flowing beard and was still yelling down the phone. "Bill, I'm going to ticket this guy", pointing at the driver of the van. "Do a licence plate check whilst I get him out the van." Skelton stepped off the kerb and reached inside his pocket for his warrant card. Alexander got on the radio to do the licence plate check.

Skelton appeared at the driver's window with his warrant card in his left hand, but the driver did not seem to notice his approach. Skelton suddenly realised from the man's blood shot eyes that he was clearly on drugs, and his gut instinct told him that something was seriously wrong. Skelton got on his radio and called for immediate back-up. He was taking no chances. He asked for a firearms unit to be dispatched immediately. The driver's window was halfway down and Skelton could hear the driver was speaking in Arabic. Skelton was getting worried. He pulled the door handle and the door opened. Somehow, the driver had been oblivious to his approach. Now he turned to face Skelton just as Skelton had grabbed the ignition key and turned off the engine and pocketed the keys. Meanwhile, Alexander had discovered that the licence plates belonged to a ford Mondeo and not this van, into which he was now peering into the passenger door window. Owing to the size of the driver, Skelton could not see past his large protruding belly as to what was on the passenger seat, but Alexander could! Alexander desperately tried opening the door, but it was locked. "Dan, he's got knives. Watch yourself."

Skelton's mind raced. He had turned off the engine, so the van was no longer a weapon unless it was full of explosives. He couldn't see what was in the back of the van, so that was an unknown risk. The driver suddenly put his right hand on the passenger seat just as Alexander was frantically trying to smash the passenger window with his baton. Skelton realised that his life was in danger. He was dealing with a drug fuelled extremist who was exceedingly well-built and with whatever drugs he had taken, was pumping masses of adrenalin. He was going to be incredibly difficult to subdue. It was at times like these that Skelton wished he had a gun. The sound of sirens gave him some hope but unless an armed response unit arrived very shortly, he and Alexander as well as innocent bystanders were in mortal danger.

Skelton grabbed the man's right arm with all his might, but it only slowed the driver and Skelton could at last see the ferocious meat cleaver that the driver, was hell bent in killing Skelton with. Skelton heard the passenger window smash; Alexander had swung his baton like a man possessed. Although Skelton was strong, he knew that he was no match for this much larger drug induced terrorist. The sheer strength of the man scared Skelton. If he had a gun, Skelton could easily stand back from the danger, pull his gun and shoot the guy in the head, which would most probably prevent him from detonating any explosives. But he and Alexander, only had a pair of batons and handcuffs between them!

The driver was bringing the meat cleaver round without much difficulty. Skelton was a mere inconvenience and very shortly the hacking would begin. Skelton roared to Alexander for help but there was no reply. "Bill for fuck's sake give me a hand." There was no answer, save for the sound of sirens that were getting closer. The meat cleaver was just inches away from Skelton's neck and his strength was sapping. Any time now he would lose the struggle but if he had to sacrifice his own life, to save others, so be it. By the time the driver had butchered him, the firearms unit would have arrived, and they would at least avenge his own death.

Skelton was on the point of exhaustion. His last thoughts before he knew that he had lost this fight were, "Where the fuck is Alexander?" Suddenly the noise in his ears, he thought must be the sound of the blood gurgling from his jugular vein although he had not felt the cut. Realising that he was dying, and that the cavalry had failed to arrive, which was not in his script, he heard screaming and then another sound that mystified him. It was the sound of metal colliding with what sounded like a pumpkin. Then came the unmistakeable Scottish accent of Bill Alexander. "Take that you bastard" And then another metallic bash on pumpkin. Skelton opened his eyes as he realised that the driver was no longer trying to cut his head off. In fact, the guy's arm had gone limp. Skelton put his hand on his neck, he was covered in blood, but alive.

Skelton looked up but had to wipe the blood from his eyes. Standing above him was Alexander panting for breath. "You alright Dan?" Skelton was totally confused. Slowly he got off his knees and stood up. Alexander held out his hand to steady him. Skelton looked at the driver and almost wretched. His face was beaten to a pulp and his eyes looked as if they had been sprayed with acid. Wedged between the driver's chest and steering wheel was a CO_2 fire extinguisher. It had contained liquid CO_2 and Alexander had sprayed it at point blank range into the eyes of the driver, which, at a temperature of -90o had instantly frozen his eyeballs, blinding him and causing unbelievable pain. The quick-witted Alexander had "borrowed" it from the vegetarian restaurant directly opposite to where the van had stopped. Having blinded the driver, he then used the fire extinguisher as a battering ram, so to speak. The

driver was unquestionably dead, and it slowly
dawned on Skelton that all the blood on his face
and clothes had come from the terrorist. There
was no question that Alexander had just saved his
life.

Chapter Fifty -One

The morning after the terrorist attack, Skelton was
in the shower, reflecting on how close he had
been to losing his life. Had it not been for the
quick-witted actions of Bill Alexander in getting
the fire extinguisher and blinding the driver with
its freezing contents before battering him to death
with it, Skelton would not be having this shower
this morning. Unfortunately, his suit, shirt and tie
were ruined from the blood from his attacker. A

small price to pay compared to his life! His right arm was painful and stiff from the wrestling contest with the van driver.

Skelton got dressed and went downstairs to the kitchen. The dogs leapt from their beds to greet him and he rewarded them with a Boneo each. He switched on the TV and the news was on. The terrorist attack in Bath was the headliner. Chief Superintendent Mike Sawyers would be giving a news conference at 10am. Meanwhile, the Home Secretary was being interviewed. The terrorist, he revealed, had criminal convictions for drug offences but was unknown to the intelligence agencies. It was believed that he had been acting on his own and no explosives or guns had been found either in the van or at his home. The Home Secretary said that we must all take comfort in the actions of Detective Chief Inspector Daniel Skelton and Detective Sergeant William Alexander, who had bravely fought with the armed van driver despite not being armed themselves. He went on to say that their heroic actions in killing the driver had prevented a major act of terrorism and had undoubtedly saved the lives of many.

Skelton scowled at the screen and he called out, "What about the bloody hours Bill and I spent being interviewed by the independent complaints commissioners! Instead of giving us a pat on the back for doing a good job in killing the fucker, they wanted to see if they could prosecute us!" Skelton sighed He knew that there was always an independent enquiry when a member of the public was killed, but it was difficult not to take it personally. It would all blow over soon and he could get back to dealing with the investigations into Linda and Marion.

Skelton opened the drinks cabinet before leaving for work. At the back of the cabinet, he found a bottle of Mcallan's Malt Whisky. This was his favourite whisky. He put the bottle in his briefcase, gave the boys a cuddle and set off for work.

Approaching the police station, he could see the TV vans in the car park. Yesterday's attempted terrorists attack was the top story in the news. They had lost interest in the Linda Carson case for the moment, but that would soon change.

Skelton opened the entrance door with his fob and began climbing the stairs to his office. Coming down the stairs was Superintendent Williams. "Good morning Dan and how are you feeling today?" Skelton stopped climbing the stairs as he came level with Williams. "Good morning sir. I'm a bit stiff and tired but apart from that I'm fine. "Williams smiled. "Well that's hardly surprising after what you went through yesterday. You and Bill both deserve a medal for your bravery. There is no doubt that you guys saved a lot of people's lives that's for sure." Skelton looked Williams straight in the eyes and asked, "Can you tell that to the IPC investigators sir? The way they treated Bill and I yesterday, you would have thought that we had no right to do our duty!" Williams placed his hand on Skelton's right shoulder and said, "Sorry about that Dan, but you know that it's standard practise whenever we kill someone. But I can assure you that both you guys are totally in the clear. This has been addressed at the most senior levels in the government and with the Chief Constable. You and Bill are to be commended for your actions and the IPC blokes will be gone today. You and Bill will need to finish writing your statements and once that's done, you can continue with your usual duties. Skelton smiled and said, "Thank you sir. The first thing that I'm going to do is let Bill know and give him a big hug for saving my life!"

Skelton opened his office door and was surprised to see several greeting cards and bottles of booze from well-wishers. He put his briefcase on the floor and began opening the greeting cards. He heard a knock on the door just before it opened and in walked Alexander.

"Good morning Bill and how are you feeling today?" Alexander focused on the bottles and cards on his boss's desk. "Well, I'm okay but a bit stiff and my head hurts like hell." Skelton screwed up his face in alarm. "Did he hit you on the head Bill?" Alexander put his hands on his head and said, "No, but that bloody bottle of whisky that I drank last night certainly did!" Skelton roared with delight. He bent down and picked up his briefcase and sat it on his desk. He opened it up and removed the bottle of McCallan. "Right Bill you have my permission to come in tomorrow with another sore head!" Skelton gave the bottle to Alexander who took it and admired the label. "That's my favourite whisky Dan but I don't get to drink it often owing to the price of it." Thanks Dan, I will keep this for a special occasion. But I'm afraid I can only accept this on one condition?" Skelton gave him a quizzical look and said. "Oh, and what's that Bill?" Alexander placed the bottle on the desk. Alexander stood looking at his boss and then spoke. "You share it with me my friend." The tears started rolling down Alexander's cheeks which started Skelton off. Yesterday's experience had cemented this friendship and they were now as close as brothers. They hugged each other for several minutes before Skelton could find his voice. When he did so he said, "It will be an honour and a privilege my friend!"

Chapter Fifty-Two

It was just after three, that afternoon and Skelton was sitting at his desk, which had been cleared of the greeting cards and booze. Skelton and Alexander had agreed that Skelton would take the three gifted bottles of gin whilst Alexander would take the four bottles of whisky. The remaining bottles of assorted vodka, rum and brandy would be divided up amongst CID.

Skelton's phone rang. He looked at the caller display and saw that it was the lab calling. He picked up the handset. "Skelton here." He heard a man's voice on the line. "Mr Skelton, it's Dr Crispford here from the lab. Skelton had never met Dr Crispford but had spoken to him several times on the phone. He was not one for making small talk, he always got to the point straight away. This was fine with Skelton. "We now have the results of the toxicology tests that we conducted on the blood and urine taken from the body of Linda Carson at the PM." Skelton's muscles tightened as he said, "Go on please Dr Crispford."

"Well as you know, we knew at the post-mortem that the girl was intoxicated with alcohol when she died. However, we needed to establish if she had taken or been given any drugs before she died. The tests that we undertake to establish what, if any, drugs she may have taken are very complicated. We had to determine not only what drugs were in her system, but we also had to calculate the dosage of the drugs. This would allow us to assess whether or not they would have rendered her unconscious." Skelton was sweating in anticipation of what Dr Crispford would say next.

"I will not bother you with the full chemical name of the drug that we have established was in the girl's body when she died but it's probably best known to you as Rohypnol. This is a widely available rape drug that anyone can buy on the internet, as I'm sure you know." Skelton took out his handkerchief and dabbed his brow. "Yes, Dr Crispford I am familiar with it. Can you tell how much she was given?" Dr Crispford cleared his throat and continued. Again, I'm not going to get all technical with you, but I will email you my report shortly which gives you all the facts and figures. I think what you want to know Mr Skelton was whether or not the drug would have rendered her unconscious?" Skelton spoke into the phone.

"Yes doctor, that is really what I need to know."
The tension was unbearable. "Well, I can say this
with total conviction Mr Skelton. That young girl
had enough of that drug in her system to have
made her comatose very soon after she had taken
it. In all probability, her murderer had slipped it
into a glass of wine. We now therefore know that
she was raped and after that, she was taken to the
River Avon and was put into the water. Given the
amount of drug in her body, she would have still
been unconscious and would have had no chance
of saving herself. One last thing, Mr Skelton. We
estimate that the drug had been in her system for
about six to seven hours before she died."

When he finished the call with Dr Crispford, he
rang Terry Nugent, the police liaison officer
assigned to Linda's family. It was important that
Nugent should personally visit Mr and Mrs Carson
and inform them that her death was now being
treated as murder. The last thing that Skelton
wanted was for them to hear it on the news or
from some newspaper reporter knocking on their
front door. Skelton stood up from his desk and put
his jacket on. Then he headed for Chief
Superintendent Sawyers' office. Luckily,
Superintendent Williams was just coming out of
Sawyer's office when he saw Skelton approaching.
"You look like you are on a mission Dan!" Skelton

374

stopped just in front of Williams and said, "I'm glad you're here sir. I need to brief you and the governor on the toxicology results on Linda Carson." Without saying a word, Williams knocked on the door and opened it and stuck his head in. "Skelton is here sir, he wants a word with both of us." Sawyers was standing by his desk shuffling some papers. "Yes, by all means come in." Williams held the door open for Skelton and closed it after him. "So, Dan what have you got for us? Sorry, excuse my manners, take a seat please, both of you." The three officers sat down.

Skelton cleared his throat and began speaking. "I have just had Dr Crispford from the lab on the phone." Both Sawyers and Williams were watching Skelton intently. "Dr Crispford is certain that Linda Carson was given enough of the rape drug called Rohypnol, to have rendered her unconscious almost immediately after she was given it. Furthermore, given the dosage that she ingested, she would still have been unconscious when she went into the river. Gentlemen, she was murdered and the only suspect that I have is Norman Edwards. I anticipate that when the lab has completed its analysis of Marion Busby's blood and urine, it will confirm that she too was murdered."

Sawyers let out a sigh and said "Bloody hell Dan, what are you going to do with Edwards? Are you going to arrest him again?" Skelton placed both hands on the desk in front of him and glanced at Williams before facing back at Sawyers. "Well sir, at the moment, we haven't got a shred of evidence against him. The only thing that links him to Linda Carson is the fact that he just happens to live next door to where she was last seen alive. Forensics went through his flat with a fine-tooth comb and they could find no trace of Linda having ever been in there. They checked all of Edwards' clothing for any evidence of Linda's DNA but again drew a blank. Then when we recovered her body, yet again there was nothing on her body or clothing to connect Edwards. My hunch is that Edwards now feels convinced that he knows that he managed to destroy or at least hide any DNA of his and that of Linda and indeed Marion. I think he knows that we are watching him and being as clever as he is, will realise that he can't use the flat again for the next murder. But, make no mistake about it, he is becoming like a typical serial killer. Having got away with at least two murders so far, he thinks that he is invincible and its only a question of time before he strikes again. We have, as you suggested sir, placed a microphone in his flat and when he comes home from work, we are watching him. This is now a waiting game. Our biggest problem now is finding his lair. At some point, he will have to go there to contact his next victim. I am convinced that the key to solving these murders is finding his lair. That will give us the forensic evidence that will allow us to put him away for the rest of his life!"

Sawyers stood up and grabbed his uniform jacket from the coat stand. "Right, I need to give another press conference in time for the six o'clock news I don't think that I am going to be very popular with the Bath Tourist Board! First, yesterday's terrorist attack and now confirmation that this young student was murdered. I won't make any announcement on the Marion Busby case until we are sure that we know what we are dealing with." Sawyers looked at Skelton and asked, "Has her family been informed?" Skelton stood up, "Yes sir, as soon as Dr Crispford called, I got on to Terry Nugent. He's headed out to see the parents. They will have been informed before the press conference."

After his meeting with Sawyers and Williams, Skelton stopped off at the CID office and signalled for Alexander to join him in his office. When Alexander had closed the door, Skelton said, "It's as we thought Bill, the lab has just confirmed that

Linda Carson had been drugged and given the dosage involved, would still have been unconscious on going into the water." Alexander slowly sat down and began pondering this new piece of information. "Where does that leave us with Edwards sir?" Skelton sat down and put his arms behind his neck and grimaced at the pain from his right arm after yesterday's wrestling match with the van driver. "Well Bill, I have just been explaining that to the big chiefs upstairs. We have no grounds to arrest him again as we still have no evidence whatsoever against him. It's my guess he will strike again soon but he knows that he can't use his flat again as that would be far too risky. We have got to keep him under close surveillance and discover where it is, he is operating from. If we find his lair, in all probability we will find a laptop or some other device on which he accesses the internet and selects his victims. And I bet we will find all the forensic evidence we need to nail the bastard for life!"

Chapter Fifty-Three

The next morning, Skelton was brushing his shoes in the kitchen. The dogs were happily chewing on a Boneo each. The news was on the TV and as Skelton slipped his tea, the familiar figure of Chief Superintendent Sawyers appeared. It was a repeat of the previous night's press conference, when he confirmed the identity of the terrorist and stated that the man had been acting alone and that there was no evidence that any more attacks were likely to happen. He sought to reassure those people living and visiting Bath, should carry on as normal, but to be alert and report any suspicious activity to the police. Sawyers went on to say, that extra uniformed patrols would be operating in the city along with armed support units.

Sawyers then turned his attention to the Linda Carson case. "I have to inform you, that this afternoon, we received the results of the toxicology tests on the blood and urine samples of Linda Carson, The Bath Spa University student whose body was recovered from the River Avon approximately two weeks ago. The results of those tests, I can now reveal, are that Linda was drugged and then raped before being put in the river whilst she was still unconscious. Consequently, we are now treating her death as a murder enquiry. Detective Chief Inspector Dan Skelton is leading the enquiry and he is actively pursuing a definite line of enquiry."

Edwards had been finishing off his corn flakes and he was watching the same news broadcast as Skelton. When Sawyers announced that they were treating the girl's death as murder, he dropped the spoon on the table and began to tremble slightly. When he thought that he had got away with killing the first girl, he assumed that they would treat the second girl's death as just another tragic drowning. Suddenly he began thinking. What if they re-open the enquiry into the first girl's death. The police assumed that she had just got drunk and fell into the river. As far as he knew, they had not checked for drugs, but he knew it was still possible to do so even after six months or so. Would they have kept blood and urine samples from the post-mortem? If not, they surely would not go and exhume the body. That would be too embarrassing for the police.

Edwards stood up and took the breakfast dishes to the sink and washed them. He left them on the draining board to dry. He yawned and thought again about Linda Carson's death which was now being treated as murder. The police had arrested him but had to let him go because there was no evidence whatsoever against him. He would just have to make sure it remained like that and he would be sure not to alert them by doing anything stupid. The police would probably put him under surveillance but that was fine, he could easily cope with that. There was another way out of the flat and he was damned sure that the police did not know of its existence!

He took his phone from the charger, switched it on and slipped it into his trouser pocket. He put on his work jacket, picked up the remote control and turned the TV off. The room was silent except for the sound of the traffic outside. Then Edwards made his first mistake. As he placed the TV control on the table, he said something out loud which he would bitterly regret. "But the bastards have got fuck all on me!" The concealed microphone that Sawyers had ordered to be placed in Edwards' flat, picked up every word and was recorded. Now Skelton had something positive to work on.

Skelton was just about to leave his house and walk to his office, when his phone rang. He took it out of his shirt pocket and checked the caller ID. It was Tim Ashton, one of the members of the surveillance team. He assumed that Ashton was just calling to report that Edwards had just left for work. "Good morning Tim, is that Edwards off to work then?" Skelton listened. "Morning sir, yes he has just left for work. But there is something that you should know sir." Skelton's heart missed a beat. "Really, what's that Tim?" Ashton coughed and continued, "Well, he was listening to the news on TV and he heard the big chief announce that we are treating the girl's death as murder. He then switched the TV off sir." Skelton was struggling to understand the relevance of this information. "And?" urged Skelton. "Well sir, the microphone picked him up saying, "But the bastards have got fuck all on me" that was it, sir" Skelton closed his eyes and smiled. "Thank you, Tim you have just made my day!"

Skelton had called the team into the incident room for a ten o'clock briefing. He gave them the news that Edwards had been caught out by the hidden microphone and Skelton was positive that they had the right man. He went on to explain that prior to Edwards having been put under surveillance, it was highly likely that he had been leaving his flat in the evenings without his phone and in all probability, he had obtained another phone which undoubtedly was a "burner". He went on to say, "Now you might be asking, why I

382

don't arrest Edwards again just to see if he has another phone? Well, there are two reasons as to why I am not going to arrest him, just yet. Firstly, he has always been one step ahead of us and I doubt very much if we would find that new phone on him or at his flat. Secondly, even if we did find that phone, it would only enable us to identify other potential victims who of course we would warn off. However, it would not help us to nail Edwards for the murder of Linda and the likely murder of Marion."

Skelton clutched the lectern with both hands and went on to say, "We should finish today, re-evaluating the CCTV footage from the night that Linda went missing. It's taken us a bit longer to carry out the review, owing to my instruction to extend the time frame until 7am the next morning"

Skelton leaned on the lectern and closely surveyed his team of detectives. They were all staring at him with their fullest attention. "As you know, there are many similarities in the circumstances in which both Marion and Linda disappeared. They both left the campus just after 10pm at night and were due to meet a male thereafter. They both took the bus from the campus into the city and we have the CCTV footage from the bus that verifies that Linda got off the bus at Lambrettas. Unfortunately, we never obtained the CCTV footage from the bus that Marion took, and we were never able to obtain any evidence of where she went after getting off the bus. We had no witness sightings of her at all. I am convinced that she got off at Lambrettas and was met by Edwards. Having successfully lured Marion into his flat, he drugged her and raped her repeatedly. He then somehow removed her from the flat and transported her to the river, where he simply pushed her into the water and she drowned. It looked to us like a tragic accident owing to her being drunk. The pathologist agreed, and we closed the case."

Taking his hands off the lectern, he began speaking again, this time using his index finger to emphasise the next points. "Having successfully fooled us into thinking that Marion's death was an accident, he repeated the same tactics with Linda. This time however, we got lucky in that we immediately formed the view when she was reported missing, that it was a possible abduction. We therefore reviewed all the CCTV footage from every camera in the vicinity of Lambrettas and as of now, there is not one single sighting of her. It should also be noted, that both girls were not dissimilar in looks, age and physique and it's my guess that his next intended victim will be similar in appearance also. I don't think Edwards will risk meeting his next victim as she gets off the bus. I suspect that Edwards will have assumed that we are watching him particularly as we arrested him and have now confirmed that we are treating her death as murder. For that reason, Edwards will not risk adopting the same technique with his next victim."

Skelton paused for a moment deep in thought. He tapped his mouth with his right hand and then said, "We can't take any chances with what Edwards will do next. As of now, I want him followed everywhere. That means that this afternoon, when he finishes work, I want him tailed to make sure that he goes home and does not slip off to his lair, wherever that might be. If he goes shopping, I want to know what he buys. When he does go home, we need to be on the alert to him leaving his flat. The only way that he can contact his next victim, is by him getting access to the internet. I am certain that he does this from a garage or room that he is renting but which so far, we have failed to discover. If we can discover where it is, then we will be able to prevent him from killing another poor girl and we will have the evidence to lock him up for life!"

After having briefed his detectives, Skelton went to the loo and he met Constable Dave Lake coming out. "Hi Dave, I haven't seen you for a few days. Have you been off?" Lake smiled and said, "Yes, I had Monday and Tuesday off sir. The wife had several jobs for me which couldn't possibly be put off any longer. As they all related to the kitchen, I knew full well that if I didn't do them when ordered, then food would no longer be provided!" Both men laughed. "Oh, by the way sir, that bloke Edwards that you are interested in?" Skelton wondered what Lake knew about him. Lake was the eyes and ears of the station and his intelligence reports were usually highly accurate. "Yes Dave, what about him?" "I saw him on Sunday in the George at Bath Hampton." Lake now had Skelton's full attention. "Christ, what time was this at and did he have anyone with him?" Lake put his right hand on his lips, deep in thought. After a few seconds he removed his hand from his mouth and said, "Well the wife and I got there at about 1pm for lunch, and he was sitting on his own tucking into the roast beef. It looked like he was drinking cider. When he finished his meal, he got up and left." Janet Griffin had told Skelton on Monday morning that Edwards' phone had never left the flat, which had caused her to wrongly

386

conclude that Edwards had stayed at home all day!

"Dave, when Edwards was eating his lunch, was he using a laptop or iPad?" Lake thought again for a moment and the suspense was killing Skelton, but he needed to let Lake complete his thought process. "No, he certainly didn't have a laptop or an iPad, I'm sure of that but he definitely had a phone. He didn't speak on the phone, but he was busy texting and he was getting messages. I heard his phone bleep several times." Skelton processed this information and realised immediately that this was bad news. Lake could tell from Skelton's body language that something was wrong. "Sir, is there something wrong?" Skelton placed his right hand on Lake's shoulder and said, "Yes Dave, I think that Edwards has been arranging a meet with his next victim!"

Having finished in the toilet, Skelton headed to the room where the CCTV footage was being reviewed. There were four detectives sitting at desks closely looking at the screens in front of them. As Skelton entered the room, he called out, "Don't worry about me chaps, I've just come to see how you are getting on." The four detectives briefly looked at him then went straight back to their allotted task. Skelton decided to sit down next to DC Chris Spurrey, a keen young officer and the sort of guy that you would want on your side in a fight. He was about 6" 4 and physically well-built. Although Skelton doubted if even Spurrey could have over-powered the drug fuelled terrorist in the van!

Skelton looked at the screen that Spurrey was analysing and what he could see was footage from the police station's own cameras. The date and time were being displayed at the top of the screen and Skelton noted that the time was 04.31. A police car was just entering the station car park. Having parked the car, the officer could be seen getting out of the driver's door and he was clutching what appeared to be a large cup of coffee. Skelton did not recognise the officer, it was possible that he worked out of a different station and had just come into Bath for a break.

At 04.51 an electric powered dust cart came into view. The operator was wearing a high visibility vest and had a baseball cap covering his head. His progress was slow but steady. Twice he stopped and with a long pole he scooped up some discarded rubbish and placed it in the black bag mounted on the rear of the cart. There was nothing unusual about the man, so far as Skelton could tell. He could not see the man's face partially as a result of the baseball cap and the angle of the camera. At 04.53 the operator stopped the cart in front of the public entrance to the police station and picked up a discarded empty beer bottle and placed it in the black bag. Skelton thought to himself that these four detectives must be bored out of their minds. Skelton had personally viewed hundreds of hours of CCTV footage and it was generally boring but occasionally thrilling.

Skelton spent a few minutes with each officer, carefully reviewing the footage but he soon concluded that he was of no help here and quietly left the room. He went back to his office and sat down at his desk and logged on to his computer. It was 5.30pm and he was feeling tired from the countless tasks that he had performed that day. There was a knock on the door and Alexander walked in. "I don't know about you Dan, but I could do with a drink!" Alexander eased himself into a chair and watched Skelton lean back in his chair and clasp his hands behind his neck. "Bill, I could murder a beer so why don't we stroll over to The Pulteney Arms now and I promise not to try and ticket anyone driving a white van! Alexander laughed. "Actually Dan, I don't have to drive this evening as the wife brought me in this morning. She had to drive to Reading this morning, on business and she just phoned to say that she will pick me up around 7.30, so that gives us nearly two hours. Skelton quickly logged off his computer and stood up. "Let me call Ken, he can go and collect a Chinese takeaway. Can you drop me off at my house?" Alexander stood up and said "No problem Dan, lets head over to the Poultney Arms and meet these black labs that you told me about."

Chapter Fifty-Four

The detectives left the station, turned right and walked towards North Parade and the junction where Skelton had confronted the van driver. There was nothing to mark the fatal struggle between the driver, Skelton and Alexander just two days earlier. Not even flowers for the dead man, which was an indication of how well he was loved! As they waited to cross the road, Skelton glanced at Alexander who responded by raising his eyes towards the sky. Neither man would forget that desperate struggle for a long time to come. As they walked along Poultney Bridge, both men stopped to admire Poultney Weir, where literally thousands of gallons of water flowed every day. The bridge and weir were major tourist attractions and it was always difficult to manoeuvre past the hordes of tourists taking photographs. At the end of Bridge Street, they turned right into Great Poultney Street, one of the grandest streets in Bath. The majestic Georgian buildings looked superb and it was easy to imagine how the street must have looked in the days when gentlemen and ladies dressed in their finery, paraded along on the pavements, as horses and carriages sedately passed by.

The street was very wide, adding to its majestic charm. They had a choice of walking towards the end of Great Poultney Street, or to take a short cut through some back streets and a small, picturesque park. Skelton took the latter route. Both men had said little as they made their way towards the pub, both were lost in thought.

The pub door was open as it was a warm evening, and Skelton noticed quite a sizeable number of smokers sitting outside, enjoying their drinks as well as their fags. Skelton smiled to himself, as he usually did when he used the word "fags" which he knew was an American slang word for gays. But in Scotland, where he grew up, it was more commonly used as slang for cigarettes. Skelton used to laugh when his eldest brother used to say that he was just going outside for a fag, when he already had one standing next to him!

Skelton stepped inside and saw about a dozen people, some standing at the bar and others sitting at tables. Skelton's eyes were immediately drawn towards the barman. He was a hunk of a boy and guessed that he was maybe eighteen or nineteen. Well over six feet tall and strikingly handsome. It was obvious that he spent a lot of time in the gym. He clearly had the physique and looks to be able to make serious money as a model. Skelton would have to thank his friend Patrick Rees for suggesting that he should try out this pub. What more could he wish for than a pub that had two black labs and the most-handsomest barman in Bath!

A guy at the bar was ordering a pint of Guinness and he heard him call the barman by his name which was Angus. Skelton decided that he would lose no time in getting to know Angus. He much preferred the company of younger people as he liked to understand their perspective on life. "What are you having Bill?" Alexander was busy looking to see what beers and lagers were available. "I think I will have a pint of Carling, please Dan." Angus had finished serving the man his Guinness and now he turned towards Skelton and gave him a beautiful smile which caused Skelton's heart to miss a beat. Skelton gave Angus a huge smile revealing his near perfect teeth. "Hi what can I get you please?" asked Angus. "Hello Angus, my name is Dan, and this is my colleague Bill." Skelton leaned across the bar with his hand out and firmly shook hands with Angus and Alexander did likewise. "Can we have two pints of Carling, please Angus and whatever you want for yourself." Angus gave his new customers another big smile and said, "I will have a Guinness please Dan."

As Angus was pouring the drinks, Skelton said, "A friend recommended this place to me as he knows that I adore black Labradors." (He didn't think it would have been appropriate, to add, "and young muscled hunks!) Angus, gave Skelton another friendly smile and said, "Oh, yes the owners have got two black labs but only one is here today and he's called Hugo." This response caused Skelton to conclude that Angus was not part of the family and most likely a student at the university. "Do you allow dogs in the bar Angus?" Angus was handing over the two pints of Carling. "Yes of course Dan, some days we have more dogs in here than customers!" That settled it for Skelton, the next free Saturday or Sunday he would bring Ken and the boys down to the pub. They would have to come by car though. Coming into town was all downhill and consequently going home was very much uphill!

Skelton looked around the bar, and to his right was a passageway that led to a series of alcoves of different sizes. Lifting his glass in time with Alexander, the men clinked glasses, "Cheers!" Skelton touched Alexander on the elbow and said, "Lets go find a seat Bill, I've got something to tell you." Skelton led them through the passageway and at the end of it found a room with a few tables and chairs but there were no other customers. This was perfect for the two detectives to chat without being overheard. As usual, Skelton sat so that he could see if anyone entered the room and Alexander sat opposite him.

"Bill, I bumped into Dave Lake today as he was coming out of the loo. He gave me some very interesting information about our man Edwards." Alexander sat to attention waiting with curious anticipation as to what Lake had discovered. "What's that Dan?" Skelton took a sip of his Carling and gently placed the glass on the beer mat on the table. "Well as you know, we have been monitoring Edwards' phone, and regular as clockwork, he leaves his flat in the morning and goes to work and returns at about the same time, every evening. He does not appear to go out in the evening, as his phone is always showing as being at the flat." Alexander cut in. "Yes, but he could be going out but leaves his phone at home to fool us into thinking that he never goes out!" Skelton smiled and sipped his lager. "Precisely Bill, there's every chance that he's been slipping out at night, and going to his lair, and contacting his next intended victim. Now last Sunday, according to the phone company, his phone never left the flat and Janet Griffin reported this to me on Monday morning. I told her, that if I wanted the police to think that I was at home, that is where I would leave my phone. After all, who leaves their phone at home intentionally? Phones have become not just a fashion accessory but a vital and essential part of our lives." Both men took a drink from their glass and Alexander said, "Exactly, but how can we prove that he has been leaving the house?" Skelton smiled and said, "Go and get us two more pints Bill and I will tell you the answer to that!" Both men drained their glasses and Alexander went off to the bar to get refills.

Sitting comfortably with their fresh Carlings, Skelton continued. "Dave Lake took his wife out last Sunday for lunch at the George pub in Bath

Hampton. Whilst he was there, he spotted our man tucking into some roast beef. He was alone, and he had no laptop or iPad. But he did have a phone on which he was sending messages and worryingly for us, he got messages back!" Alexander asked, "Did Dave happen to see what sort of phone he was using?" Skelton lifted his glass and said, "Dave thinks it was Nokia, which as you and I know is most likely to be a burner!" Alexander banged the table with his right hand and said, "Shit!"

Both men took a deep drink from their glasses and carefully put them back on the table. "I reckon Bill, that Edwards has already established contact with his next intended victim. He must have done that in the evening or at night whilst we thought he was either watching TV or was tucked up in bed. But the sly bugger must have been slipping out of his flat and going to a flat or a garage or a workshop where he must have access to the internet. There, he's got on to a dating website like Tinder, where he has a profile of a much younger man and no doubt, a photograph of some young hunk, who's picture he has borrowed. Now Bob Laws and his team have been scouring Tinder and other dating websites for our boy called "Tommy" and they did find two possible matches. They were able to obtain the identities of these two possible suspects, but both turned out to be genuine young men, just looking for a shag, and both have cast-iron alibis for the night that Linda was murdered."

Alexander took a deep slug of Carling and Skelton checked the levels of their drinks. He would need to pay Angus another visit soon but that was no hardship! Alexander put down his near-empty glass and said, "I bet you, our Tommy or should I say Edwards, deleted his profile soon after he killed Linda." Skelton drained his glass. "You can bet on that for sure. Bob's team have looked at hundreds of profiles of young guys in the Bath area, but anyone of them, could be Edwards and we can't go arresting every young lad hoping for a shag, can we?" Skelton stood up and picked up both their glasses. "Time for refreshers!"

Skelton brought the drinks back to the table and sat down. "Cheers Bill" The two detectives sipped their drinks and Skelton resumed. "Edwards' made his first mistake today by talking into our hidden microphone, which confirmed that he is defiantly our man. Now that Dave Lake saw him using a phone on Sunday, suggests to me that he he has probably already arranged to meet a girl, sometime soon. Incidentally, Janet Griffin checked to see if it could be the same phone that he used to contact Linda. But the phone company says that phone has never been reactivated. I think that he has gone to Bath Hampton with the new phone and has activated it there, rather than at his flat or more importantly, at his lair. He did that in case we caught him with the new phone which would have given us a clue as to where his lair is situated. I'm still convinced that it is somewhere in Widcombe as it's convenient to where we think that both victims went into the river. Our door-to-door enquiries in and around Widcombe Parade drew a blank so far as giving us a possible location where he might be operating from. I think that he has been incredibly lucky which means that we have been incredibly unlucky!

The detectives both lifted their glasses and drank in silence. After a few seconds, Alexander said, "Well if he does make a move now, at least we have him under surveillance and the hidden mic might yield up some more clues." Skelton leaned back in his chair, hands clasped behind his neck. "Yes Bill, we have men watching the flat and we have the hidden mic. But suppose he manages to leave the flat un-seen or we spot him, but he loses the tail?" Alexander placed his hand on his chin and thought for a few seconds. "Well, we have CCTV cameras across the city Dan, and as we know what Edwards looks like, we are bound to find him before he can do anyone any harm."

Skelton drained his glass once more. "Bill, we know what Edwards looks like, and on the night that he killed Linda, we have hours and hours of CCTV footage, but despite that, there is not one single sighting of him. He's a cunning devious bastard Bill, and if he was able to kill Linda, move her whilst unconscious without a car, to the river, without one single sighting, then what's to say he can't avoid us again! We've got to watch him like a hawk, because if he does manage to kill another victim, then you and I will both be destroyed by both the press and social media!"

They were just finishing their drinks when they heard a dog bark from somewhere upstairs. Suddenly a large black Labrador bounded down the stairs followed by a young man. The dog did a quick tour of the bar before coming to check-out Skelton and Alexander. Skelton grabbed the dog by its collar and began to gently stroke its forehead. He put his hand in his pocket and found a few dog treats and took them out. He now had the dog's full attention. He held a treat in the palm of his hand and the dog gently took it. The young man appeared and said, "Hugo what are you doing in here?" Skelton said, "Oh don't worry, I'm just making friends with Hugo. I have three of these at home and you best be careful as I might end up having four!"

Chapter Fifty-Five

The Alexanders dropped Skelton off at his house at 7.45pm. Skelton opened the front door and was immediately greeted by a woof from his beloved Brenty-Boy. All three dogs had been lying on their beds in the kitchen where Ken was fixing Skelton a gin and tonic. After a stressful day, Skelton liked nothing better than to come home to one of Ken's famous G&T's. On many occasions, when they were having a lunch or dinner party, many of the guests would elect to stick with the gin and tonic rather than go on to drinking wine. This meant that they had always had to keep two litre bottles of gin in the freezer and a good stock of limes.

"There you go, one freshly made G&T" Skelton picked it up and took a sip, perfect as usual! The dogs had crowded around him and were wagging their tails waiting for a cuddle. Skelton bent down and gave them each an individual hug before they all took part in a group hug. He stood up and went to the dog treat drawer and took out three biscuits and gave them one each which they all took gently. They then scurried off to their beds to eat them.

Ken had been out to collect the Chinese takeaway. Beef and green pepper with black bean sauce. They would share an egg fried rice and banana fritters and syrup was for dessert. Skelton said, "I will just go up and get changed and then we can have dinner." Skelton picked up his drink and went upstairs to change and freshen up before returning downstairs to eat dinner in the sitting room and watch TV. After dinner, they rinsed their plates and placed them in the dishwasher. Skelton made his partner a spritzer (white wine and soda water) and then he took a can of Fosters from the fridge and poured it into a pint glass, and went through to the sitting room, where the dogs were strategically placed around his and Ken's chairs. These were expensive electric reclining chairs, similar to what you would expect to find in business class, on an aircraft. They could recline into flat beds but both Skelton and Ken refrained from choosing that option, as it invariably led them to fall fast asleep. "So, did you have a good day Dan?" Ken asked. Before he could answer, Josh had nuzzled up to him for a cuddle which Skelton duly provided. The other dogs were content to lie where they were, their bellies full of the meal that Ken had given them two hours earlier.

"Well, it wasn't as exciting as Monday, thank god, but we are gaining some good intelligence on our suspect. But I'm worried that he's going to strike again soon, and knowing how devious he is, I wouldn't be surprised if he gives my surveillance guys the slip, which will really put a spanner in the works!" Ken looked over to Skelton and sipped his drink. "But you have got a good team and there's plenty of CCTV cameras around the city. If he does manage to evade your guys, CCTV is bound to spot him." Skelton smiled, picked up his Fosters and took a drink. Putting it back down, he said, "Do you know, I had this same conversation with Bill in the pub. Like you, he's sure that if Edwards does make a move, CCTV will pick him up, but it never picked him up when he killed that last girl."

"Well, I'm sure that you will solve it Dan, you always do, you are a bloody good detective!"

Skelton laughed. "I might be a good detective Ken, but you need luck in this game, something that we have been rather short of in this case. Oh, talking of luck, let me just check the result of the 3.05 at Doncaster today." Skelton stood up and went to his iPad which was charging in the kitchen. He clicked on the App and scrolled down the racing results. His horse was called "Happy Days". He clicked on the result of the 3.05 and happy days had won by half a length at 9/1 beating the odds-on favourite. His £40 bet had just made him a profit of £360 and added to his stake money, he had £400 to collect from the bookie! Skelton went back into the sitting room and announced the result to Ken and they did high fives. Skelton just hoped that there were more happy days ahead!

Ken went through to the kitchen to recharge their drinks and Archie followed him in order to get a drink of water. Ken was busy attending to the drinks whilst Archie drank happily, from his water bowl. Having satisfied his thirst, he wandered back into the sitting room and stuck his head on Skelton's lap, knowing full well that he was in for a cuddle! Ken returned with the drinks and sat down as Skelton was busy channel hopping trying to find something decent to watch on the TV. "Oh, tomorrow night, I'm taking a client out to dinner Dan, so can you sort something out for your dinner?" As Skelton always did the cooking or made the arrangements for takeaways, this was not a problem. "Yes of course, I might go for a curry or get another Chinese takeaway. What about the boys? Will you have time to feed them and take them out for a walk before you leave?" Ken picked up his glass and took a drink and said, "Yes don't worry about the boys, I will feed them at about five o'clock and take them out, so you don't need to rush back." Skelton was relieved at this, as it meant that he had freedom to choose when and where he would eat. "Who are you taking out to dinner?" Ken ran a small business called Arbortech Tree Technology, which specialised in providing various types of equipment that encouraged trees to grow as well as protecting them from being damaged. The products included strimmer guards to prevent trees from being damaged or killed by strimmers. Tens of thousands of trees are damaged or killed in the UK each year by strimmers which are used to trim grass and weeds around trees but if the operator gets too close to the tree, damage will most certainly occur. In addition to this, Ken developed products to make sure that trees received the correct amount of water and various devices to protect trees from motor vehicles as well as from vandals.

Prior to the financial crisis in 2007 most of Ken's clients had been local authorities who have a duty to look after trees. Unfortunately, following the economic crash, local authorities ran out of money and tree planting and protection are no longer on the agenda for receiving funds. Luckily, the emergence of charities that realise the importance of planting and protecting trees have been a welcome boost for tree preservation. One such charity, Trees for Cities, donate generously to ensure that cities continue to plant trees and give them the best help that they can, to ensure that young trees are looked after so that they become mature, and help the environment to fight carbon emissions.

"I'm actually taking out the Tree Officer for Bath. I think that as we live in this beautiful city, we should try and convince the council to plant and protect its trees. But as you know, the council keeps announcing more cuts to its budget and I doubt if trees or other environmental issues are at the top of the agenda. Except, of course, the congestion charge, to deter motorists from driving into the city. This will no doubt raise millions of pounds in income for the council and might reduce pollution caused by vehicle exhaust fumes. But do you think Bath will be any different from any other city that operates a congestion charge? The money raised is supposed to benefit the environment and prevent thousands of deaths every year from lung and heart disease. But where does the money raised, go to? Well, as far as I know, it certainly does not go into planting new trees, that's for sure! If it did, the air quality in these cities would be far better as the trees are natural filters of bad air."

Skelton had listened intently to his partner's view on the local authority and could only agree with him. "So where are you taking the Tree Officer to dinner?" Ken took a sip from his glass. "I'm not sure Dan. I'm meeting him in Lambrettas at 7pm but they don't do food as you know. So, we will just have a drink and decide where to go from there. I should be home by about 10."

Chapter Fifty-Six

The alarm went off the next morning at 6am and Skelton switched it off and got out of bed. The second his foot touched the floor Brenty-Boy barked to let him know that he knew he was awake. Skelton put on his bath robe and went downstairs to be greeted by all three dogs. He opened the kitchen door to the garden and let them out to do their business. He emptied the kettle and filled it enough for two mugs of tea. He took out two mugs and placed a tea bag in each. He then took down a saucer and placed two digestive biscuits on it for Ken. When the kettle boiled, he poured the water into the cups and then carefully used a teaspoon to gently stir the tea bag and when he gauged that the tea was at its correct strength, he removed the tea bag. He added two and half teaspoons of sugar to his own mug and then added milk to both.

Skelton then opened the door for the dogs to come in from the garden. He took out three biscuits and gave them one each. He then took Ken's tea and biscuits upstairs and came back down to drink his own tea whilst he polished his shoes. He switched on the TV to listen to the news whilst he was polishing his shoes. Once this task was complete, he went back upstairs to have his shower. Dan and Ken's bedroom was huge. When they bought the house, there were four bedrooms. But they decided to knock two of the bedrooms into one large bedroom which contained two large picture windows which on one side gave them a view of the garden, and on the other side a view of the golf course. They could have built an en-suite bath into the room but decided to preserve the space. The bedroom had been fitted-out with built-in wardrobes and had matching bedside cabinets. Next to Skelton's cabinet stood a trouser press in which his trousers were now being pressed.

Skelton walked into the bathroom. The shower was enclosed within the bathtub. He turned on the tap and waited whilst the water got hot. Satisfied that the water was at the correct temperature, he took off his bath robe and climbed into the shower. Skelton loved taking a shower not just for its refreshing qualities but for some reason he always was able think much more clearly as the hot water covered his body. Whilst he was applying the shampoo to his hair, he began to think again about why none of the CCTV footage had given them a clue as to how Edwards had been able to evade being seen. Slowly, he began remembering the footage that he had viewed the day before on Chris Spurrey's screen. He rinsed the shampoo from his hair and then applied some conditioner and continued to play the CCTV footage over and over in his mind.

What was it that Mike Sawyers had said about the CCTV footage? Something about not looking for anything unusual! Skelton began rinsing the hair conditioner from his hair and continued to focus on what he had seen on the CCTV footage. There was the council street cleaner with his electric dust cart, casually picking up rubbish outside the police station at 04.51 in the morning. Nothing odd about that! Suddenly the shower began working its magic. Skelton thought for a second, and said to himself, "Wait a minute, that's bloody early to be cleaning the street!" He let the hot water pour over him. "Hang on, that bloody cart could easily conceal a body and Edwards works for

409

the damned council." Suddenly the penny had dropped, and Skelton had at last worked out how Edwards had managed not only to have moved Linda Carson from his flat but how he had also managed to avoid being detected on the CCTV.

Skelton turned off the shower, took a towel from the towel heater and quickly dried himself off. He brushed his hair and shaved. His mind was racing ahead with what he would have to do that day. Number one on his list to do list, was to go visit the council depot and check with the foreman, Mr Smith as to whether or not Edwards would have had access to that electric dust cart. He brushed his teeth and went into the bedroom and was barely able to contain his excitement. Ken was just about to get out of bed and take the dogs out for their morning walk. "I've worked out how the bastard did it Ken!" Ken was slightly groggy and was unsure what Dan meant by that comment. "Sorry, you have worked out who has done what?" Skelton was getting into his underpants and was hastily trying to get dressed. "This guy Edwards who I think has killed those two girls. I looked at some CCTV footage taken early in the morning outside the police station. There is a guy with an electric dust cart and I'm bloody sure that it must be Edwards. It was the dust cart that he used to move the unconscious girls around in and take them down to the river where he simply pushed them into the water and they drowned." Ken got out of bed. "That's a pretty ingenious way to avoid detection. No wonder it took you so long to work out how he did it. Are you off to arrest him now?"

Skelton was finishing getting dressed. "No, I can't arrest him yet. We still don't have the forensic evidence that will convict him. I desperately need to find out, where it is that he contacts his victims. I'm certain that wherever that place is, it will contain all the evidence that we need to arrest and convict him. The problem is, he has been so clever and devious, that when he came to remove the girls, he almost completely fooled us. I mean who would pay the slightest bit of attention to a street cleaner wearing a high visibility vest picking up rubbish early in the morning? One thing's for sure, wherever he has his lair, you can bet that we have probably completely over-looked it!"

Ken was sitting on the bed putting on his socks and had been carefully listening to what his partner had been saying. "Dan, you say that this guy Edwards has been very clever. So, if he is that clever, do you not think that he will have destroyed or got rid of any evidence that would convict him? I mean its been nearly three weeks since you found that girl's body in the river, that is plenty of time for her killer to have got rid of any evidence!" Skelton was putting on his suit jacket and was considering what Ken had just said. "Yes, I can see your point and it is very logical, but in my experience, killers don't necessarily follow the same logic that you or I would adopt. For some reason, a killer likes to retain a trophy of their kill. Perhaps like a game hunter that has shot a deer and keeps the head and antlers as a trophy to show friends that he had the skill and ingenuity to be able to stalk and kill his prey. The same applies to killers of human beings. It's not that they want to show off their trophy to others, that would probably get them arrested. No, they need to keep some keep-sake of the killing which they can touch and feel. Very often, if the killing was sexually motivated, such as in this case, then the killer will be sexually aroused by stroking whatever keep-sake he has retained. So, I am just praying that this is Edwards' Achille's heal, and that he has kept something from the killings in which case, he goes to jail for life. On the other hand, if he has dumped all the evidence, then I am up the creek without a bloody paddle!"

Chapter Fifty-Seven

As Skelton left the house that Thursday morning, for his walk into the city, he was experiencing mixed emotions. He was very relieved that he had identified Edwards as the street cleaner using the dust cart. Although the CCTV footage from the camera at the police station had not given a clear image of his face, Skelton was convinced that it could only be Edwards. However, he still had work to do on that score and he needed to see Chris Spurrey as soon as he got to the station. He also needed to visit Mr Smith again, the council foreman, to make sure that Edwards would have access to the dust cart. These were the positive thoughts in Skelton's mind and should have caused him to feel happy. However, Skelton was convinced that Edwards had already made a date to meet his next victim. What he didn't know was that it was to be at 11.30pm that very night! Skelton needed to make sure that Edwards was followed everywhere and if he did meet with his next victim, he would have men in place to make sure that the girl came to no harm.

Skelton called Andy Walker. Walker was the officer on watch this morning in the Ale House along with Tony Smith. The phone was answered at the second ring. "Good morning sir, how are you this morning?", asked Walker. "I am good thanks Andy. Has Edwards left for work yet?" Walker cleared his throat. "No, he has not left yet sir. He seems to be watching the news like he does every morning. I reckon he will be off in a few minutes from now sir." Skelton thought for a second. "Okay Andy, I am getting very concerned that he is going to strike again soon but this time it will not take place at his flat. As of now, I want him under surveillance twenty-four hours a day. So, when he leaves for work this morning, follow him. Make sure that he goes to work and keep his workplace under observation today. If he leaves, follow him. I also want him tailed when he finishes work. So, make sure that he goes home and more importantly, if he goes out this evening, we go with him. Understand?" Walker stood up. "Yes sir, he is actually just coming out the door now, I will be right behind him in two minutes." Skelton relaxed slightly. He had given the order that should keep Edwards' next victim safe and well. What could possibly go wrong?

Skelton went into his office and took off his jacket and hung it up. Normally he would make himself a mug of tea but this morning he had too much to do. He went straight into the CID room where Alexander was chatting to Ross Turnbull. On seeing his boss, Alexander broke off his conversation and said, "Good morning sir and how are you today?" Skelton was busy scanning the room to see which officers were present. It was hard to miss Chris Spurrey who was just walking in with a mug of coffee and two bacon rolls. Skelton called out, "Chris my office now. Bill you come as well" Alexander turned to Turnbull and said, "The boss is in a hurry this morning. I wonder what's up?" Turnbull shook his shoulders and said, "I would not keep him waiting Bill, he looks bloody determined this morning!"

Skelton was sitting at his desk when Alexander and Spurrey came through the door. The latter had left his coffee and rolls behind, suspecting that this was not a social matter. "Right, sit down lads, I have something very interesting to tell you." The two officers were looking intently at Skelton, obviously trying to work out the reason for the urgent summons to the bosses' office. "Yesterday, I sat down briefly with Chris here, and his colleagues who were reviewing all of the CCTV footage from the night that Linda went missing. I saw something on Chris's screen, which at the time I did not think was relevant. Obviously, neither Chris, nor any of his colleagues, thought that it was relevant either!" Spurrey raised his eyebrows trying to remember what was on his screen when Skelton had joined him yesterday. But, having spent so much time reviewing the footage, his mind was blank.

"Chris, do you remember watching the street cleaner in the high visibility vest with the dust cart as he cleaned the street in front of the police station?" Spurrey thought for a second. "Yes sir, I remember him now and I saw him several times after that on other cameras." Skelton stood up and walked towards the window and looked out. It was quite a dull morning, but the clouds seemed to be clearing. "And tell me Chris, was there anything remarkable about this street cleaner?" Spurrey put his forefinger on his mouth and thought for a few seconds before saying, "No nothing remarkable about him at all sir. If I remember correctly, he passed the cop shop at about 4.45am and then I picked him up on the camera at the Royal Hotel about five minutes later. He then crossed the road and went past the train station and the last time I saw him, he was passing the entrance to the bus station."

Skelton absorbed this information and then asked, "Did you see him again after that or in which direction he was headed?" Spurrey again thought hard to remember. "No sir, I don't recall seeing him after the bus station, but it looked like he was heading towards the Lower Bristol Road." Alexander was following the conversation intently but had yet to understand the significance of what was being said. Skelton returned to his desk and sat back down on his chair. He put his arms on the desk and asked, "And if our street cleaner went on to the Lower Bristol Road and turned left, where would that take him?" It was Alexander who spoke first. "That would lead on to Poultney Road sir." Skelton banged his right hand on the table and said, "Yes Bill that's right and that leads towards Widcombe and to where you and I both think that the killer had pushed the girls into the river." Skelton stood up and pressed both his hands on the desk. "Bill that was not a street cleaner that was fucking Edwards!"

Alexander was sitting with his head in his hands trying desperately to compute what Skelton had just said but was having difficulty in doing so. Skelton could see that both men had still not registered the significance of what he had just said, so he set about explaining it to them. "Right Edwards works for the council but in an administrative capacity. We know that he does not have a car and that the council don't supply him with any form of transport. Linda gets off the bus and vanishes, never to be seen again, until we fish her body out of the river. Now we have always suspected that somehow Edwards persuaded her to come into his flat where he drugged her and raped her."

Skelton leaned back in his chair and Alexander and Spurrey were both giving him, their total attention. "Now we have been scratching our arse trying to work out how the hell he managed to transport both Marion and Linda to the river. Well, our prime suspect, works for the council and would have been able to borrow an electric dust cart for the night. He could have left it outside his flat, used it to take the girls to the river and returned it to the depot early the next morning. Nobody at the council would have suspected a thing. More importantly, we have him on CCTV, but we dismissed him as being an early morning street cleaner and might have continued to do so but for my early shower this morning, when the penny finally dropped!"

Spurrey stood up and said, "Bloody hell sir, he had us completely fooled. He was dressed in a high visibility vest but instead of making him appear conspicuous, it had the opposite effect and it made him inconspicuous! Not one of us had any suspicion that the street cleaner was anything other than that. With the baseball cap on and his head bowed, he was to all intents and purpose, invisible!"

Skelton stood up, "Wait here a second, I need Ross Turnbull. Skelton went through to the CID room

418

and found Turnbull busy sending someone a text. "Ross remember we viewed the CCTV from the bus and watched the girls getting off at Lambrettas. And as the bus approached the bus stop, we got a glimpse of the doorway to Edwards' flat?" "Yes sir, you asked me to get the technicians to try and blow the image up. I forgot to get back to you, but the results were not helpful. I've got it over here." Skelton followed Turnbull to a desk that had piles of photographs on it. Turnbull sorted through a pile and said, "Yes here it is." He carefully placed the photograph on top of the pile and both men stared at it. "You see here sir, this looks like mesh wire we think. So, it's not helpful, I'm afraid". Skelton gripped Turnbull by the shoulder and looked him in the eye. "I will tell you what that is Ross, it's a bloody dust cart, the one that Edwards used to move those two girls with!" Turnbull had a look of shock on his face and the only word that he could manage to say was, "Blimey!"

Skelton went back to his office where he found Alexander staring out the window and Spurrey playing with his phone. Spurrey put his phone in his pocket and Alexander sat down. "Right, we now have a photograph taken from Linda's bus which shows what appears to me to be the dust cart. Bill, you and I are heading off to see Mr Smith at the council depot. Phone him now and tell him to meet us in the yard in fifteen minutes and tell him not to mention our visit to Edwards. Chris, I want you to review the footage of every camera that shows the street cleaner. Now that we know that its Edwards, look more closely and see if you can get a face shot. You probably did not pay one hundred percent attention when you last reviewed it, because like me you assumed it was a street cleaner and not Edwards."

Chapter Fifty-Eight

Edwards left his flat that Thursday morning feeling very excited. Tonight, he was meeting Patsy and already he could feel the erection in his underpants. As he crossed the road at Bog Island, he did not notice the detective that had just started following him. He went into the news agents and bought the Daily Telegraph and a packet of wine gums. As he emerged from the news agents, he paid no attention to the man at the ATM talking on his phone. Edwards was making his way to work on this rather dull morning and he was wishing that it 11.30pm at night, because that was when Charlie's dad would be meeting Patsy. He had it all planned out and provided he played his cards right, she would be victim number three. The only difference was that he was going strangle this one when he was having sex with her. He had seen a video of a guy having sex with a young girl and when he saw her being killed, he climaxed like he had never done before. Once he had killed her, he would put her in the back of her own car and drive to a quiet spot in the country where he would set the car on fire. The police would never link the case to the girls that ended up in the river dead. That bastard Skelton would not have a clue that Patsy was victim number three.

Edwards stopped at the pedestrian crossing and pushed the button and waited. He glanced to his right and noticed that the man that he had seen at the ATM was close by. The man suddenly stopped and dug into his jacket pocket and pulled out his phone and began speaking into it, like he was answering a call. Edwards began thinking that it was rather odd that this guy was taking the same route as himself. Suddenly Edwards wondered if in fact he was being followed by an under-cover police officer. If he was being followed, then he needed to make sure, as he would have to implement plan B. When the green man indicated that it was safe to cross the road, Edwards started to walk and decided that he would call into the bakery and buy himself a cake. He went into the bakery and he was pleased to see that several people were waiting to be served, so it would be several minutes before he would emerge again from the shop. If the man was still there, then it would confirm Edwards' suspicion. Having paid for his cake he stepped out onto the street and glanced left and right. Bingo, the man was talking into his phone pretending that he was in fact looking at the houses for sale in the estate agents' window.

Edwards was delighted that he had spotted his tail. He felt slightly sorry for the guy or woman that had the responsibility to tail him tonight. When it was time to go out tonight, he would not be leaving by the front door. To all intents and purposes, Edwards would be staying at home watching TV like he usually did. If the police didn't see him leave the flat, then he would have the perfect alibi. The police would have to conclude that when they found the cremated remains of Patsy, Edwards could not have killed her, as he was at home watching TV!

As Edwards was about to enter the council yard, he glanced behind and saw the under-cover police officer. This time he had stopped to look in the window of the shop selling electric appliances. Edwards had no doubt that when he went out at lunch time to buy a sandwich, he would be followed, as he would when he was heading home after finishing work. He could easily live with that. However, when he left the flat to meet Patsy tonight, he would not be using the front door. The police clearly wanted to follow him and discover where it was that he was contacting his victims, and where it was that he kept evidence that would incriminate him in the murders. But he was not going to play ball with them. No, he would have some fun at the Widcombe garage tonight whilst the cops were busy keeping watch on his flat in the mistaken belief that he was safely inside watching TV.

Alexander had called the foreman Mr Smith and told him that he and Skelton were coming to see him and to meet them in the yard. On no account was he to tell Edwards about the meeting. Alexander drove into the yard and he saw Smith coming out of the large building where they parked and maintained the vans and lorries. Alexander parked the car and Skelton got out the front passenger door. "Good morning Mr Smith, thank you for seeing us at such short notice." Skelton held out his hand and Smith shook it. "That's alright Inspector, I am always happy to help the police in any way I can. Alexander was locking the car.

"Mr Smith, you told us that Edwards has no access to any motor vehicles. Is that correct?" Smith took off his white hard hat and began playing with it in his hands. "Yes, that's right Inspector, he never gets to drive any of our vehicles. As I told you before, he oversees the admin, so there is no reason for him to have a vehicle." Skelton pulled out three photographs taken of the street cleaner taken at 4.51am on the morning after Linda disappeared. "Mr Smith you have men that use electric dust carts, is that right? Yes, we have two electric dust carts, one is operated by Colin and the other is operated by Paul." Skelton was noting this down. "Tell me Mr Smith, could Edwards operate a dust cart if he wanted to?" Smith thought for a second and gave a small chuckle. "Oh, I suppose anyone could operate one. I mean they are dead easy to use. You just press a button to go forward or back and they are very easy to steer."

Skelton pulled the three photographs from his pocket and placed them on the bonnet of the car. "Mr Smith, these are photographs taken by CCTV cameras at the police station at 4.51 on the morning after Linda Carson went missing. Can you look at them please?" Smith looked closely at the photographs and ran has hand across his jaw. "Wait a minute, these are not right. That's not Colin and that's not Paul either, and they don't start work until 7.30. I don't know who it is, that's operating that dust cart, but I can tell you this, he had no authority from me to borrow it." Skelton looked closely at Smith and asked, "How can you be so sure that the man in the photographs is not Colin or Paul?" Smith chuckled to himself before saying, "That's easy Inspector. You see Colin is six feet three and Paul is five feet two. The man in these pictures is about medium height I would say. Although the guy is wearing a baseball cap and you can't see his face, he certainly has the same build as Norman Edwards."

The detectives got back into the car and Alexander drove out the gate. He saw Walker standing at the bus stop and gave him a wave. Walker would be relieved shortly, so that Edwards would not get suspicious that he was being followed. Well, that was the theory anyway, but the police had no idea that Edwards had already clocked Walker earlier. Skelton was hoping that Edwards would lead them to his lair sometime soon. But he was unaware that Edwards had spotted the tail following him and would make sure that when he left the flat, the police would never see him.

Chapter Fifty-Nine

Back at the police station, Skelton reported to Chief Superintendent Sawyers on the progress of the investigation. They now knew how Edwards had transported the unconscious girls from his flat to the river, using the dust cart which he had borrowed from the council depot. With Edwards now under twenty-four-hour surveillance, it was just a question of time before he led them to his lair. Skelton however, did express his concern that he feared Edwards had already arranged a meeting with his next victim. But Sawyers had assured him that with Edwards being followed wherever he went, they would be able to prevent any harm befalling the next intended victim. Whilst Skelton knew that his men were very capable, he was still perturbed at how Edwards had so discreetly carried out these two murders. What if Edwards had another trick up his sleeve? Skelton just wished for a bit of luck and they would have Edwards in the bag.

Skelton had called for a mid-day briefing so that he could brief the team on the latest developments. He showed the team photographs of Edwards and the dust cart which had been taken by the camera on the police station. Everyone expressed their admiration at such a novel way in which to transport a body. More needed to be done to try and get a face picture of Edwards using the dust cart. Chris Spurrey was working on this but so far Edwards had kept his head down. The surveillance team were in place ready to follow Edwards should he leave the flat. He concluded the briefing by saying, "It is only a question of time before Edwards strikes again and we need to be ready for him. I am certain that he will not use the dust cart trick again. In my opinion he is going to lure his next victim to the premises that we know he must be operating from but which we have been unable to discover. DS Alexander and I are going to have another crack at finding these premises this afternoon. We believe that both Marion and Linda entered the water around Widcombe. Despite extensive searches of the river around that area by the underwater search team, we have found no trace of their handbags or other personal effects."

Skelton checked his notes and continued. "Last Sunday Edwards was spotted in the George pub at Bath Hampton, using a mobile phone. We believe that he left his phone at home to make us think that he had not left the flat. He has therefore obtained a new phone which we think is also a burner. We also think that the reason he travelled to Bath Hampton was to activate the new phone there. The reason for doing this was to ensure that if we caught him with the new phone, it would have caused us to think that his lair was in Bath

Hampton and not in Widcombe. This is a very cunning man and I suspect that he could turn very nasty when cornered. He has a conviction for GBH so we know that he can be violent. He has also murdered at least one innocent girl, most likely two. So, if we do apprehend him, I want you to be very careful. I'm quite sure that he would be happy to kill a police officer just as he would a young girl. So be safe out there and good luck."

After the briefing, Skelton walked over to Alexander. "Bill its only just gone 12.15 but I had no breakfast this morning and I missed out on our usual sausage sandwich today. Let's have an early lunch in the Ale House." Alexander put his arm on Skelton's shoulder. "Lead on Dan, I'm pretty hungry myself. The detectives made their way downstairs and out the door into the early afternoon sunshine. Unusually, Skelton took them by the direct route to the pub rather than the normal detour. "Christ, you must be hungry Dan. This is the first time we have ever walked in a straight line to the pub for lunch. My feet are usually killing me, by the time you have taken me on a five-mile detour!" Skelton smiled and gave his friend a playful punch on the arm. "Well Bill, we have a lot to do today, so I decided to give you a little treat." As they walked, Skelton was trying to decide what he would have for lunch and after a little thought, plumped for the fish and chips.

As it was earlier than usual, there was only one customer in the pub, an old man reading his newspaper. He had a pint of John Smiths' in front of him and he seemed content enough looking at the race card, in his paper. Skelton glanced over and saw that the racing was at Newmarket. He wouldn't have a bet himself today as he did not have enough time. Paul came downstairs and made his way behind the bar. "Good afternoon Dan and Bill, what can I get you today?" Skelton smiled at Paul and said, "Good afternoon Paul. We are a bit earlier today, but I missed breakfast this morning, so I thought we would come in early and hopefully avoid the lunch time rush. It's a pint of Fosters for me and the fish and Chips." Alexander thought for a second and said, "Make that two of each please Paul." As Paul started pulling the pints, he looked up and said, "Oh I need to tell you something. As of tomorrow, the Fosters is going, and we are replacing it and all our other draft beers. I have got a terrific deal with another brewery, so everything is changing. But don't worry, I will be keeping cans of Fosters in the fridge for you."

Skelton felt that he had just been punched in the stomach, at the news that Paul was getting rid of the draft Fosters. What about looking after your loyal customers, he wondered? "Paul, I can drink cans of Fosters at home. I come in here to drink pints of draft lager, which I can't do at home. So, I'll tell you now, if the draft Fosters goes so do I!" It was time for Alexander to join in. "That's not a very nice way to treat your regulars Paul. You have half a dozen regulars that come in here every day and they all drink draft beer. I think that you are making a terrible mistake and may live to regret it." Paul seemed a little bit crest fallen. He clearly had not factored into the decision-making process, the impact that denying his regulars their favourite tipple would have. "Well, I'm sorry but the decision has been made and it can't be reversed now. As I say, you are welcome to come in and have cans of Fosters, there will always be some in the fridge."

Skelton and Alexander said very little during lunch. Skelton had made up his mind that he would no longer be using the Ale House. The problem for Skelton was that there were so few pubs in Bath that sold Fosters. The ones that did, either did not serve food at lunchtime or did not open during the day. Skelton was seriously pissed off. He loved going for a walk at lunchtime as it cleared his head and got Alexander some useful exercise. The last thing that he wanted to do was to have to drive to a pub. Not that he would be doing the driving. That was Alexander's job! It was beginning to look like the Poultney Arms was going to become their new local by default. Although it did not sell Fosters, he would be happy to drink Carling. It was bad news for Alexander, as it was a thirty-minute round trip, provided they did not meet any terrorists!

"When we have finished lunch Bill, let's take a walk over to Widcombe. There is something over there that we have missed, just like we missed the street cleaner for so long. I think we need to go and see that busy- body that claims to know about everything that goes on in Widcombe. Let's see if he has a spare key to that flat that is supposedly let to an American banker. What if that American is really Edwards?" A startled expression appeared upon Alexander's face. "Christ Dan, I never thought of that. It makes an awful lot of sense when you think about it. And if our man has arranged to meet another victim, that would be the perfect place to take her. And it's just across from the river, so he would not have far to travel to dump her. That would make it three, meaning he would have progressed into being a serial killer!" Alexander took a sip of his drink and asked,

"I suppose we are going to be walking to Widcombe?" Skelton gave him a big smile. "Yes Bill, I knew that you would be bitterly disappointed at not having our usual lunchtime walk, so after lunch, we will take a stroll over to Widcombe and see if we can discover Edwards' lair. And another Fosters for me and do have one yourself, seeing as you are buying!"

The detectives left the Ale House and headed back to the police station. It was 1.45pm when they entered the CID room. There were only two detectives at their desks, Peter Lowik and Chris Spurrey. Lowik was deep in conversation on the phone, whilst Spurrey was tucking into a sandwich which he was washing down with a large carton of coke. Skelton left Lowik to finish his call and approached Spurrey's desk. He was just shoving the last piece of the sandwich into his mouth. Skelton looked at the mess of wrapping paper on the desk and concluded that Spurrey had probably eaten more lunch than himself. "Chris, have you had any luck in getting a face pic of Edwards and that dust cart?" Spurrey was busy cleaning away the rubbish left over from his lunch. Finally, he dumped the empty coke carton in the bin. "Sir, that guy has either been incredibly lucky or he knew precisely what he was doing. I have checked every frame from that film and in every shot, his face is hidden either by the baseball cap or by the angel of his head. I have carefully checked for any distinguishing marks on what parts of his face we can see, but there is nothing there." Skelton thought as much. "Okay, Chris, let's forget about his face and concentrate on what he was wearing. Have a closer look at the HV vest that he was wearing and see if there are any badges or rips or anything like that, which we might be able to identify. Also look to see if he was wearing a tie or shirt that we might be able to pick-out from his wardrobe. Check his trousers and shoes and see if there is anything there that is unusual."

Lowik had now joined Skelton and Spurrey and had caught most of the conversation. "You know something, I don't think that this guy is lucky at all. I think that he is extremely sensitive to leaving us any forensic clues whatsoever. He was, after all, a science master with a degree in chemistry, so he is no mug, that's for sure." Skelton had been listening carefully to what Lowik had been saying. Of course, what he had said was nothing new but it did cause Skelton to speculate. "Yes, being a school master would have given him a great deal of school holidays. He clearly loves books as can be seen by the bookcase full of them in his flat. I think that Edwards has studied forensics in a clinical manner and probably has as much knowledge of the subject as any of us here. Do you guys want to hazard a guess where he might have gained this knowledge?" "Books!" Both Spurrey and Lowik said it in tandem. Skelton smiled at them and said, "Peter, I want you to go to Brighton and visit every library there. Take a mug shot of Edwards with you and see if the library staff recognise his face. If they do, find out what sort of books he was reading and perhaps borrowing. It would be nice if we could show a jury that our suspect had been studying forensics with a view to confounding the police!"

Chapter Sixty

Alexander had phoned Martin Wilson, the nosey busybody that lived in Widcombe Parade, as soon as he and Skelton had got back from lunch. They had arranged to meet in the council car park near the garages. Skelton was on a mission today. Whilst he had no reason to doubt anything that Wilson had told him, he wanted to check-out the possibility that Edwards was either using the flat that belonged to Ben Black who was now in a nursing home or the garage which he owned. According to Wilson, the flat was being rented by an American banker and the garage was lying empty. Today Skelton wanted to see inside both the flat and the garage and hopefully they would finally find some forensic evidence to put Edwards away for the rest of his life.

As the two detectives walked into the car park, they could see Wilson standing by a car chatting to someone on the phone. When he saw the detectives, he finished the call and slipped the phone into his jacket pocket. He was, as ever, smartly dressed in a shirt and tie, black trousers and sports jacket. "Hello Mr Wilson, it's very good of you to spare us your time again, and we very much appreciate it, "said Skelton, as he held out his hand. "You are always very welcome Inspector" and they shook hands. Alexander held out his hand and said, "Good to see you Mr Wilson, are you keeping well?" Wilson shook Alexander's hand and said, "Yes thanks, I'm pretty good for my age except for this blasted hip. I'm on the waiting list to have a hip replacement but I reckon that the crematorium will have me before I get the bloody hip done!" They all laughed at Wilson's little joke.

"Now then Mr Wilson, as you know we are investigating the murder of Linda Carson and the possible murder of Marion Busby and we think we know who is responsible for their deaths. The only problem is that we have no forensic evidence whatsoever, which is far from helpful when you are trying to convince a jury that he is guilty. Now, as before, Mr Wilson everything that we tell you must be kept in total confidence, as this man is highly intelligent and if he discovers that we are sniffing around, he may very well destroy any evidence which might put him behind bars." Wilson had listened in grave silence to what Skelton had been saying and said, "Don't worry Mr Skelton, I will not tell another soul about your investigation not even the wife. In fact, especially not the wife!" The three men all smiled at Wilson's little joke and it helped ease the tension.

Skelton glanced around to make sure that no one was in earshot and asked, "Mr Wilson, have you ever met this American banker that is renting Ben Black's flat?" Wilson put his hands in his pockets and cocked his head to the left. "Well, I haven't actually spoken to him, but I have seen him a few times getting in and out of taxis." Interesting, thought Skelton. "So how do you know who he is?" Wilson gave a little knowing smile. "That's easy Inspector. I was standing by Ben's garage there with his son Philip one afternoon last November. We had been cleaning out the garage, you see. When a taxi pulled in and Philip said' this is the guy that's going to be renting the flat'. I was a bit pushed for time, as I had to go and pick up the wife from her hospital appointment. So, I just clocked his face and got in the car and drove off to collect the wife."

Skelton gave Alexander a curious look and said, "What did this guy look like that was in the taxi?" Wilson paused in thought for a second or two and said," He was in his fifties I would say, fairly well-built and looked the clever sort. Of course, as he was sitting in the taxi, I couldn't tell you his height, but from the few times that I have seen him, I'd say he's average height maybe 5"8 or 5"10." Skelton was carefully noting this description and realised, quite excitedly, that this matched Edward's description. This was something not lost on Alexander either. "Mr Wilson, do you know the man's name?" asked Alexander. "Yes, let me think now, it's Robert McEnroe and I think he is from New York. I hardly ever see him except when he is getting in and out of taxis."

Skelton and Alexander excused themselves from Wilson for a moment and walked over to the "empty" garage. "Bill, there is just a chance that Edwards is in fact the tenant using an American name and accent. Let's see if Mr Wilson has a key to the flat, otherwise we are going to need a search warrant." The two detectives strolled over to where they had left Wilson. "Mr Wilson do you by any chance have a key to the flat?" asked Skelton. A smug smile appeared on Wilson's face. "Yes, indeed I do, and I also have one for the garage."

The officers wanted to rush up to the flat but owing to Wilson's dodgy hip, they had to restrict their speed somewhat. Wilson went first into his own flat and retrieved the keys before they could move on to the suspect's flat. As they came to a red door, Wilson pointed and said, "This is the one" and he moved to insert the key in the lock. "Just a moment Mr Wilson, this is a job for the police. Can you please stand here outside and make sure that no one comes in?" Skelton could see the disappointment on the man's face as he grudgingly handed over the keys. Both Skelton and Alexander took out latex gloves from their jackets and slipped them on. Skelton turned the key and pushed down on the handle and they went in.

"It's the police, is there anyone at home?" shouted Skelton but there was no reply. It was a modest two bedroom flat with a sitting room and bathroom. Alexander had lifted the mail off the door mat and turned the lights on. He looked at the bundle of letters. Disappointingly, they were all addressed to Robert McEnroe! They quickly went around the various rooms and discovered no electronic communication devices. They found some banking manuals for the bank where the tenant probably worked but there was no evidence of any drugs. This flat was indeed being rented by an American banker and not Edwards.

They tried to hide their disappointment and Alexander said. "Come on Dan there is always the garage, you have always favoured a garage or workshop from day one." Skelton held his friend by the shoulder and said, "It has to be the garage Bill. I know that Edwards has been ahead of us for most of this enquiry, but the noose is tightening on him now. We know he used a dust cart to move the bodies and we suspect that he put the girls in the water just across the road from here. We are watching his every move and we will be ready for him. Come on, let's go see what evidence he has left us to lock him up for the rest of his life."

Once again, the detectives wanted to rush down and see what treasures awaited them in that garage, but they felt sorry for Wilson who had given them so much of his time and had been ever so helpful. So, at what seemed like a snail's pace they gradually reached the garage. For evidential reasons, Skelton wanted Wilson to formally identify the end garage as being owned by Ben Black. When they eventually reached it, Skelton said, "Mr Wilson can you please point to the garage that belongs to your former neighbour Ben Black?" Wilson adopted a formal attitude and pointed to the end garage and said, "Yes Inspector that is Ben Black's garage there."

Skelton's heart was pounding, and he was feeling weak at the knees. He had thanked Wilson for his cooperation and asked him to return to his own flat whilst he and Alexander searched the garage. The officers had taken off the latex gloves that they had worn in the flat and given them to Wilson to dispose of. They had put on fresh gloves and Skelton held the keys in his right hand. The tension was indescribable, and both men were heavily perspiring, the sweat running down their foreheads.

"Bill, I can't do this! I want you to take the key and open the door. We will not go inside the garage as I don't want us to contaminate it in any way. We will have to get Bob Richards and his team down here, whilst we go and arrest Edwards. So just open the door and switch on the light and let's see how clever the bastard is now!"

Alexander had to use both his hands to insert the key in the lock as they were shaking so hard. He gently turned the key in the lock one hundred and eighty degrees. Slowly he began turning the handle and he could hear the bars in the door exiting the wall that secured the door in place. Ever so gently he raised the door and a small amount of daylight crept in. He leaned inside and felt for the light switch and after a few seconds he switched it on. The garage exploded in light and the only words that Alexander could say were, "Holy Fuck, look at this!"

Skelton marched forward, his eyes straining to see what it was that Alexander had discovered. Skelton's jaw dropped in total disbelief at what they had found. "Fuck, fuck, Fuck, I am going to kill that bastard! I swear it Bill even if I have to use my bare hands.

Chapter Sixty-One

On the Monday morning, the day that Skelton and Alexander had confronted the van driver and neutralised him, Edwards was getting ready to go to work. He was not yet under surveillance, but he knew that it was only a question of time before he would be. He was sure that the police had calculated that he was operating out of

Widcombe, but they had so far failed to identify his precise location. He knew full well that if they did find the garage, there was so much forensic evidence in there which could put him away for life. He therefore needed to remove that evidence as soon as possible, which would really piss the police off big time!

The foreman at the council, and with whom he shared an office, was not coming in to work today as he was attending a friend's funeral. That would give him time to slip out of the office for as long as he needed to clear out the garage. Having got dressed for work and picked up his phone, he was ready to go. But before leaving, he opened the door of the cupboard where he stored various bits and pieces and took out a large suitcase. It had wheels and so was easy to move, even when fully packed. He left the flat carrying the suitcase until he was outside on the pavement, where he put it down and pushed it easily in front of him. He was by no means in any way out of place. Bath had so many visitors staying in hotels and guest houses, that the pavements were full of people going to and from the train and bus stations. Edwards at the time did not realise how lucky he had been in choosing this day to make his move, as from tomorrow his flat would be under watch by the police.

When he got to the council depot, he opened the door to his office with his fob and went in. He took the suitcase and placed it under Smith's desk where it would be hidden from view, should anyone come into the office. Edwards busied himself with the usual Monday morning tasks, which mainly involved dealing with answerphone messages from the public, complaining about litter problems, that had occurred over the weekend. At 12.30 he had dealt with everything that needed his attention and now he was free to go off and clear the garage. He pulled out the suitcase from under Smith's desk and went outside. The yard was clear, which suited him, and he made his way towards Widcombe. First, he went to the pedestrian bridge, which crossed the river and linked Widcombe to the rear entrance of the train station. He stood on the bridge pretending to admire the view, and deftly retrieved the key to the garage. He placed the key in his pocket and made his way to the garage. As he entered the car park, he scanned the area for people but there was no one about. He took out the key and quickly unlocked the door and went inside. He felt for the light switch and turned on the lights.

He opened-up the large suitcase, which had two compartments, and which could contain an amazing volume of clothes and holiday essentials.

He set about carefully packing up the neatly folded bed sheets and plastic covers, which he had used to prevent any forensic evidence being left either on his bed or elsewhere in the flat. He then packed away the two tins of used condoms as well as the fresh box of condoms. He took the box of pills with which he had spiked the girl's drinks and packed them carefully away. He opened the fridge door which contained about half a bottle of white wine. It had a screw lid, so it would not leak when he placed it inside the suitcase. He switched the fridge off, in order to give the appearance that the garage had not been in use for some time. He would leave the fridge, the chair and the fire extinguisher. They might come in handy at some point in the future.

All that was left now was the cardboard that he had used to cover the girls with, which not only hid them from view, but also acted as a buffer to prevent them from getting bruised. He slid the cardboard out from below the work bench and opened the garage door. He looked out and scanned the car park but again there was no one around. He quickly picked up the cardboard and carried it over to the large bins outside the rear entrance of the Ram. The Ram paid for the council to come and takeaway for re-cycling, its glass bottles, plastic and cardboard. Edwards knew that

447

at around 6pm today, those bins would be emptied.

Edwards went back inside the garage and closed the door. He then took the bag of rags which he had taken out of the suitcase, when he arrived, and began carefully cleaning every surface in the garage. He would not leave a single fingerprint, not even on the inside of the fridge. When the police did find the garage, it would be completely empty save for the fridge, the chair and the CO_2 fire extinguisher, and there would be no evidence to suggest that he had ever been there. More importantly for Edwards, however, was that there would be no forensic evidence linking him to the girls. This would be a major blow to the police and he almost felt sorry for Skelton and Alexander.

After locking the garage, he took out a handkerchief and wiped the handle and replaced it in his trouser pocket. He pulled the suitcase behind him and the wheels made his task easy. He crossed the road to the pedestrian bridge where he once again, hid the key. It was just going on 3pm when he got back to the council depot. We walked across the yard and opened the door to his office and he lifted the suitcase through the door. He then made his way to the stationery cupboard. The room was large, and it contained everything from envelopes to toilet paper. The shelves were stacked with every conceivable item needed for running an office. He made his way towards the back of the cupboard and found a space on the bottom shelf. He placed the suitcase on the shelf and then took several boxes of printing paper and placed them on the case. It was now virtually concealed, and it was unlikely that anyone would spot it. Overseeing administration, it was only Edwards who used this room.

Chapter Sixty-Two

Skelton was sitting at his desk. He and Alexander had returned from Widcombe a couple of hours earlier, following the fruitless search of the flat and garage. Skelton felt totally drained and all he wanted to do was to go home and have a refreshing gin and tonic. But that was not going to happen. Ken was taking a client out to dinner but would feed and walk the dogs beforehand. There was therefore not much point in going home just yet, and besides, he needed to have dinner. He was pondering whether to get a Chinese takeaway or go to the pub. A knock on his door made him look up to see Alexander standing in the doorway.

"What are you up to Dan?" Skelton leaned back in his chair and watched his friend as he slowly walked in and sat down. "I don't know about you Bill, but I am severely pissed off! Edwards must be laughing his head off at us. Not only has he so far got away with raping and killing two young girls, but he has also managed to get rid of all the forensic evidence as well. It's time we had some luck Bill otherwise he is going to knock another one off and if that happens, sunshine, then you and me, are for the bloody chop!" Alexander put his hands on his head and leaned back in the chair which creaked under the strain. "Well Dan, we now have him under twenty-four-hour watch, and we have a microphone in the flat. If he makes a move now, we will be right onto him, that's for sure." Skelton stood up and walked around the desk and sat on the end of it and stared at Alexander. "Bill, this guy is one of the most intelligent criminals that I have ever come across. He is so forensically aware that he has not left us a single piece of evidence which in anyway links him to the crimes. Then, when we think that we have at last found his lair, we go and search it, but the garage is empty. I had a good look around it and decided not to bother having it forensically examined. It was as clean as a whistle, no doubt courtesy of Edwards. There was another knock on the door. It was Peter Lowik. "Yes Peter, what can we do for you?" asked Skelton. Lowik walked over and stood in front of Skelton's desk and stood next to where Alexander was seated. Alexander invited him to take a seat, which he did. "I just got back from Brighton, where I have been checking-up on Edwards' reading interests." Skelton sat back in his chair and said, "What did you discover Peter?" Lowik cleared his throat. "Well, there are two public libraries as well as the university library and

I went and visited all three. Our friend Edwards was well known to all three librarians, for the number of books which he read. He apparently was keen on crime novels but more interestingly, he seems to have read every textbook on forensic medicine and toxicology, which the libraries possess. Hence the fact, that he hasn't left us a bloody clue!"

The detectives were sitting quietly thinking when Skelton's phone rang. He took it out of his shirt pocket and looked at the screen. It was Richard Pierce, one of the surveillance team. "Yes Richard, what is it?" Pierce had been working under-cover for years and Skelton was glad that he was on duty this evening. "Just letting you know sir, that the subject has just returned home from work. I picked him up as he left work and he went straight home. He has just put on the news and if my guess is right, he will shortly take a shower." Skelton had expected that Edwards would follow his usual routine. "Okay Richard, I understand that, but I want you and the rest of the team to be on the alert. This guy is very smart, and he may just be playing us along, hoping that we will relax our guard. If he sets foot out of that flat, I want him followed and I want to be told straightaway. Do you understand?" Pierce gave a nervous cough and said, "Don't worry sir, we know what we are

452

doing. He won't give us the slip, you can depend on that." Skelton stood up and said, "He had better not Richard, otherwise you will be joining Bill Alexander and me for the big chop!"

Skelton put the phone back in his shirt pocket. "Come on Bill lets grab some fresh air and I will buy you dinner. We both need a drink and some cheering up." Alexander stood up and said okay but let me just phone the wife to say that I am having dinner out. That will please her, as she is going around to her sisters tonight and that will save her needing to cook for me. Lowik got up and headed for the CID room.

When they got outside the police station, Skelton had an idea. He remembered that the Oak on Poultney Road served food in the evenings and just as importantly served Fosters. "Bill lets take a walk down to the Oak, it's not far from the station and when we are done there, we can walk back, and you can drop me off at the house on your way home." Alexander gave this a little thought. "Well, I only had two pints at lunchtime and that was about six hours ago. So, I should be good for another one now, and still be under the limit for driving"

As they walked along to the junction at North Parade they turned right and passed Lambrettas, where Ken was meeting his client for a drink. They walked on past it in silence until they reached Edwards' flat. They both stared at it as they walked past, each wondering what the cunning bastard was up to. As they walked on Alexander asked, "So, why are you not having dinner at home tonight?" Skelton was having to skirt past a tourist taking a selfie. "Ken is taking a client out to dinner this evening and I don't like eating alone. For some reason, I never have much of an appetite when I am on my own. And anyway, after our visit to Widcombe this afternoon, I think we both need cheering up." Alexander put his arm on Skelton's shoulders and said, "Well, the fact that you are buying me dinner has cheered me up already!" They both laughed and continued walking. It was just as well that they were oblivious to the fact that Edwards was due to meet Patsy in just a few hours' time. Otherwise, they would not now be contemplating a relaxing meal.

Skelton held the door open for Alexander and they walked inside the Oak. There were about a dozen customers sitting around, some eating and the others just drinking. The young girl behind the bar was probably a student and she was more concerned with studying her phone, than she was in serving Skelton. "Excuse me love, do you work here, or do you just come in to use your phone?"

The girl immediately looked up from her phone, her face bright red. She was not used to being told off and she did not like Skelton's attitude. "Sorry, I just needed to check something. What can I get you?" Skelton noted that she was hardly the politest barperson that he had come across. There was no sir or please. The girl had just blown her chances of a tip. "Two pints of Fosters please." The girl began pouring the drinks, but she was not engaging Skelton in any conversation.

Alexander grabbed a couple of menus' and he handed one to Skelton. The men began studying the menu when Skelton noticed the sirloin steak. It was his favourite type of steak with a nice piece of fat running along one side of it. "Well Bill, I am going to have the sirloin steak. What about you?" Alexander took Skelton's menu and placed it along with his own, onto the bar. "No contest Dan, make that two sirloin steaks please, both cooked medium please." The girl wrote down the order and asked, "Where will you be sitting?" Skelton cast his eyes around the pub and indicated a seat by the window. As Skelton had been to the bookies earlier, to pick up the £360 winnings plus his £40 stake money, he paid for the meal and drinks in cash.

Meanwhile, in Lambrettas, Ken was having a drink with the Tree Officer. The guy was good company, and they were now on to their third pint. "Where do you fancy having dinner Jack?" Jack thought about the question for a second or two and said. "I'm not really into spicy foods Ken, so that kind of rules out Thai and Indian. To be honest, I am really a meat and two vegetable kind of guy. So, pub grub usually suits me best." Ken was thinking about which pub he should take him to, when he remembered Dan had said that he had been to the Ram in Widcombe recently and that the food had been good. It was only a ten-minute walk from Lambrettas. "Right a pub it is Jack, when we have finished these off, we can take a walk up to Widcombe and have dinner there.

Skelton and Alexander had devoured their steaks and both men seemed a bit more relaxed. There had been no call from Richard Pierce to say that Edwards had left the flat. Skelton had to trust Pierce after all, he and Joe Squires were both watching the flat from the Ale House and the hidden mic would alert them to anything unusual happening inside the flat. Nevertheless, Skelton felt compelled to phone him just to put his mind at rest. Pierce answered the call on the third ring. "Pierce here sir, how can I help you?" Skelton spoke quietly into the phone. "Hi Richard, anything happening?" Pierce felt a bit put out by the call, but he hid the irritation from his voice. "Nothing to report sir. After he got home, he had a shower and put on the TV. He cooked himself some dinner and then he seemed to have been cleaning the flat. He had the vacuum cleaner on about an hour ago. I think he is now just sitting down watching the TV." Skelton finished the call. "Well Bill, Edwards seems to be at home watching TV, so I think that we may as well finish here and walk back to the nick and then go home. Can you drop me off at the house?" Alexander was getting to his feet. "I really enjoyed that meal Dan. Thank you very much." Skelton stood up and said, "Don't thank me Bill, it's the bookie that you should be thanking!"

Chapter Sixty-Three

Edwards had indeed had a shower and cooked some dinner and then cleaned the house. He wanted to make sure that whoever was watching him, would be convinced that he was behaving normally. For all he knew, the police might have taken over one of his neighbour's flats and might be listening. The television being switched on, would give the impression that he was having a night in. But Edwards had plans for tonight, and in about three hours' time, he would have young Patsy at his mercy. Not that he would show her any mercy of course! Edwards checked his watch, it was just going on eight-thirty. It was time to go.

He stood up and went to the cupboard and took out a sports jacket and put it on.

He walked to the bathroom, unaware that Pierce could hear his footsteps on the hidden mic. He opened the door and closed it behind him, which Pierce could also hear. He slowly opened the window which was at the rear of the building away from the main road, where his door to the street was located. There was a drop of about ten feet to the back garden which in an emergency, such as a fire, he could use as a means of escape. From the back garden there was no exit unless you had a key to the basement flat. Edwards did not have a key, something which had troubled him since the day he moved in. He decided that he needed a method of getting in and out of the flat without being seen. If the police were ever to keep watch on the flat, they would conclude that his only way into and out of the flat was by the front door. Edwards had given this problem, much thought, and had hatched an ingenious plan.

Shortly after moving into the flat, he had bought an adjustable metal ladder which he had secured underneath the bathroom window. The windowsill hid the ladders from view and anyone using the bathroom would be unaware of their existence. Getting access to the ladders was tricky, but he

459

had practised doing so. Edwards leaned out the window and felt beneath the windowsill for the brackets which held the ladders in place. Slowly, he pulled the ladders away from the bracket until he had a firm grip of them, he pulled the ladders inside and adjusted them to the correct height to make his escape. Slowly and quietly, he let the ladders down until they were secure to the ground. Next, he climbed onto the windowsill and manoeuvred himself onto the ladders and climbed down into the garden.

Once on the ground, he pulled the ladders away from the bathroom window and took them over to the boundary wall. He placed the ladders against the wall and climbed up. He sat on the top of the wall and lowered the ladders over the other side. He then climbed down into the neighbouring garden. He lowered the ladders and collapsed them into their storage size and left them at the bottom of the wall. He walked across the courtyard to the gate and lifted the latch. He was free. Now all he had to do, was to evade the CCTV cameras. As he had spent many months studying their location, this would not be difficult. Bath had scores of back alleyways and lanes. Provided he kept mostly to them, the police or the civilian camera operatives would have little chance of spotting him.

Twenty minutes later, he was at the council depot. It was empty at this time of night, but the CCTV would record him entering and leaving the site. That was not a problem, as part of his duties was to look after the CCTV system. In the morning, he would delete the recording and the police would have no record of his nocturnal activity. He made his way to the stationary cupboard and retrieved his suitcase, which contained all that he needed for his fun time with Patsy.

Pulling the suitcase behind him, he took a somewhat unusual route to Widcombe but one which avoided the CCTV cameras monitoring the city. At Widcombe Parade, he turned into the car park where the garage was located, which Skelton and Alexander had searched hours earlier. He crossed over the main road and headed for the pedestrian bridge over the river. Once on the bridge, which was empty of people, he located the key to the garage and put it in his jacket pocket.

He returned to the garage and took out the key and turned the lock. Quietly he lifted the door open and went inside pulling the suitcase behind him. He closed the door and switched on the light. He began unpacking the suitcase, firstly removing the little bag of chocolates which he carefully placed on the workbench. These were no ordinary chocolates. He had painstakingly hollowed a small amount of the fillings from the chocolates and inserted them with pills, which had neither taste nor odour. Once Patsy had swallowed one or two of these little gems, she would be his for the taking. He hadn't decided how many times he would rape her before strangling her. Just the thought of her was making him go hard and he hadn't even touched the Viagra yet!

He removed the blankets from the suitcase and spread them on the floor. He wanted it to be as comfortable as he could make it. He slid a packet of condoms underneath the blanket, where they would be handy to use. Satisfied with his handywork, he picked up the bag of chocolates and switched off the light. He carefully opened the door and stepped outside. He looked around but there was no one about. He closed the door, locked it and put the key in his pocket. He checked his watch, it was ten minutes to ten. He began walking round to Widcombe Parade and headed for the Ram. When he got to the door, he found half a dozen men sitting outside enjoying their fags and beer. He went inside and found it to be quite busy but managed to ease himself to the bar. He recognised the young barman, but he could not remember his name.

The barman spotted him and said, "Hello, what can I get you?" Edwards pointed to the tap marked Thatcher's. I will have a pint of this please and take one for yourself." The barman said, "That's very kind of you. I will have one of them as well. It's been busy tonight, so I will enjoy that when we close." Edwards was never really one to make small talk but he was excited at what lay ahead tonight, which made him feel very happy. "What time do you close tonight?" The barman looked up at the clock and said, "Well the kitchen will be shutting in a few minutes time at ten and we close the bar at midnight." Edwards gave the barman a twenty pound note and waited for his change. The barman rang the till and took out the change and closed the till. He then took one of the pieces of paper containing today's WIFI username and codeword and handed both the change and the paper to Edwards. "There you go, that's your change and today's code for the WIFI." Edwards laughed and said, "It's okay, I don't need the code today but thanks anyway." He handed back the paper and the barman gave him a puzzled look but said nothing.

Although the bar was busy, there was one table free, so he headed towards it carrying his pint and the bag of chocolates. He carefully placed both on the table and sat down. At the table opposite him, two men in suits were clearly enjoying themselves. Probably work colleagues having a drink after work. One guy had taken out his phone and had switched on the camera. He was taking a picture of his mate. Now he was looking at the picture and he heard him say. "That did not come out very well. I was too close. Hang on a minute, let me stand up." The guy got up and stood back from the table and began focusing on his mate. The camera flashed, and the man viewed the picture. Evidently satisfied, the guy sat down and was handing his mate the phone, so that he could see it for himself.

Edwards sat in silence, preparing to send a reply to Patsy as soon as she had texted him. The two work colleagues were getting up from the table and it looked like they were headed for home. He downed the remains of his pint and went to the bar to get another. He would not have to leave the bar until about 11pm. He just wanted to go back to the garage and make a final inspection before he walked down to the Co-operative Funeral Home where Charlie's "father" was to meet Patsy!

Chapter Sixty-Four

Alexander dropped Skelton off at his house. Skelton climbed the stairs to his front door and he heard Brenty-Boy giving a friendly woof as he inserted the key in the lock. He closed the door and opened the kitchen door where all three black labs were waiting to greet him, tails wagging furiously. Skelton switched on the lights and got down on his knees and gave them each a cuddle. They then had a group hug which resulted in Skelton needing to wash his face. He opened the rear kitchen door and let the boys out into the garden. He checked the mail, just an electricity bill and a phone bill. He went upstairs and took off his suit and put the trousers in the trouser press and switched it on. He went through to the bathroom and washed his hands and face.

Having got changed into some casual trousers he pulled on a jumper as it was getting chilly. He closed both sets of curtains in the bedroom, and went downstairs and let the dogs back in. He took a can of Fosters from the fridge and poured it into a glass. He and the dogs went through to the sitting room and Skelton closed the curtains and switched on the TV. The boys were lying by his feet and he would rub their heads with his feet regularly. He was relaxing, knowing that Edwards was at home being watched by Pierce and his colleagues. He was hoping that Ken would be home soon, so that he could have his night cap and go to bed. Even though he had a good dinner, Skelton would invariably have cheese and toast with Branson Pickle and white pepper. This little supper was the perfect snack to go with his G & T and he always looked forward to it as the evening wore on.

Ken's taxi was sitting outside the Ram as he and Jack left the pub. Jack had refused a lift as he could easily get a bus home. Ken got in the taxi, and he gave the driver his address. Ken had to endure the moans and groans of the taxi driver who clearly felt that life was not being good to him. He was glad to get out of the taxi and get into the house. As soon as he opened the front door, the boys came charging through to greet him, as if he had been away a month and not just a few hours. He walked into the sitting room to find Dan watching

TV. "Hi, how was your night out with the tree man?" Ken smiled and said, "It was actually very enjoyable. The guy is good fun and he can certainly knock the beers back. We must have had about seven pints tonight. Ken did not usually drink pints, preferring instead white wine and soda. But on a lad's night out he would happily drink lager, particularly if it was Fosters. Dan stood up to go through to the kitchen for another beer.

"Where did you go to for dinner Ken?" Ken was taking his jacket off and was about to head upstairs and change out of his suit. "Actually, we tried the Ram tonight and I must say it was rather good. I had some lovely fish and chips and Jack had steak pie." Skelton gave a yawn. "I spent a bloody awful afternoon at Widcombe today, so I am glad at least one of us had a good time." Ken put his arm on Dan's shoulders. "What were you doing there?" "Bill and I were trying to find Edwards' lair but we think the garage that we located today, was it but he has cleared it out. So, I still have nothing on the bastard!" Dan opened the fridge door and said, "Do you want a drink?" Ken was holding his phone in his hand looking at the screen. "Yes, I will stick to beer, I think. I must send this pic to Jack tomorrow, I took it in the Ram." Dan was pouring Ken's drink and said, "Lets have a look." Ken handed Dan the phone and he looked at the smiling face of Jack. Then he froze. He could feel the blood draining from his face. "When was this taken?" Ken thought for a second and said, "Just before we left the pub. Why?" Skelton handed back the phone and with his right index finger pointed to the man sitting behind Jack. That is Edwards and he is supposed to be at home watching TV. Can you email me that picture now? I just hope I am not too late!"

Chapter Sixty-Five

Skelton ran upstairs to put on a pair of shoes and to collect his warrant card and handcuffs. He was sitting on the edge of the bed with his phone in his hand. He clicked on "Richard Pierce" from the recent calls log and hit the call button. It was answered on the second ring. "Evening sir, have you no bed to go to?" Skelton ignored the remark and said, "Where is Edwards?" Pierce replied rather sarcastically, "He's sitting at home watching TV like he has been doing all night." Skelton could not contain the anger from his voice. "Well how the fuck am I looking at his ugly face on a picture taken about half an hour ago in the Ram. Tell me that?" Pierce jumped up from his chair and said, "We have been keeping close watch on him all night sir. It's possible that our line of sight might have been obstructed by a bus or lorry. He could have left the flat and he may have turned left into Manvers Street and we would not have seen him."

Skelton considered this and said. "We will leave the post-mortem on how he did that for tomorrow. Get your arse across to the flat now and call me straight back.

Next, he dialled the number for Inspector Graham Symonds, who was duty inspector this evening. Symonds answered on the fourth ring. "Yes Dan, have you already heard the news then?" Skelton was slightly confused. "What news Graham?" Skelton could hear that there was a lot of background noise and it sounded like Symonds was in the operations' room. "I was just about to call you. There has been a murder at Kings Mead Square. A young lad has been stabbed and we have one guy in custody, but his two accomplices got away. I've got every available officer down there now and we are searching CCTV for the two that got away. Will you be coming down to take charge Dan?"

Skelton got up from the bed, his mind was racing. Skelton was calling Symonds to order him to get every officer out searching for Edwards. Now with a bloody murder scene to contend with, he couldn't divert officers from that. "Graham listen to me. Edwards managed to slip out of his flat without being seen tonight. Luckily, he was photographed in the Ram about half an hour ago.

Can you tell your folks to look out for him and get his picture over to the CCTV operators? We need to find him in case he has another victim lined up for tonight. If he does, then we will have another murder victim on our hands!"

Symonds was barking an order at someone. "Bloody hell Dan we have our hands full tonight. Leave it with me and I will see what I can do." Skelton was grabbing a jacket from the wardrobe. "Thanks Graham. I will call Bill and he can take charge at Kings Meade Square until I can get there."

Skelton was putting on his jacket when Pierce rang. "Sir he is not in the flat and I don't think he could have got out the back way. He must have slipped past us. I am sorry sir." Skelton was heading downstairs. "Right Richard, get yourself over to the river at Widcombe. That is where we think he has been dropping his victims into the water. Stay there until I get there."

Skelton next called a taxi to take him to the Ram as he was over the legal limit to drive. He then called Alexander and gave him the news. Alexander would leave immediately for Kings Mead Square and hold the fort until Skelton could get there.

Chapter Sixty-Six

It was at 10.55pm that Edwards received the text from Patsy confirming that she would be at the Travel Lodge at 11.30pm. Edwards sent her a text back. "Hi Patsy, sorry I am running a bit late. I have just spoken to my dad and he will meet you and take you to the Travel Lodge until I can get there. He lives beside the Co-operative Funeral home about half a mile past the TL. He will be outside the home waiting for you. Will be there as quick as I can.

Charlie XXX"

A few minutes later Patsy replied. "OK I will sit with your dad until you arrive. XXX"

Edwards smiled and thought to himself. This is so easy! He put his hand in his jacket pocket and took out the Viagra tablet and slipped it into his mouth and washed it down with the remains of his pint. He picked up the empty glass and took it to the bar and said good night to the barman. It was exactly 11pm when he walked out the door and headed to the garage. He quickly opened the garage door and went inside. He switched on the light and he carefully checked that everything was where he wanted it to be. Satisfied, he switched off the light and let himself out. In less than an hour he would be shagging young Patsy. He started walking to the funeral home where he would pretend to be Charlie's dad. He was carrying the bag of chocolates which would incapacitate his latest victim and by the end of the night, he would officially be a serial killer. That's if that idiot Skelton could link the latest murder to the two girls from the river!

It was 11.10pm when Skelton got out of the taxi and walked into the Ram. There were only two guys playing darts and the barman. There was no sign of Edwards. He cursed quietly to himself. The barman was looking at something on his phone and looked up when he heard Skelton approach the bar. "Good evening sir, and what can I get you?" Skelton pulled both his warrant card and his phone. He flashed his warrant card and said. "Hi there, I am Chief Inspector Skelton. Have you been on duty all evening?" The man placed his hands on the bar and said, "Yes I started my shift at 6pm and I finish at 12." Skelton rested his left arm on the bar in which he held his phone. "I would like you to look at a picture that was taken in here tonight around 9.45 and tell me what you know about the man in the background. The barman looked intently at the phone and saw a smiling Jack and in the background he recognised the face. He pointed his finger at Edwards' face and said, "Oh yes, I recognise him alright. He was in earlier and had two pints of Thatcher's and he bought me one. He comes in every now and again, but I wouldn't call him a regular. I don't know his name and he never really says much. Sometimes he has a meal but its usually just one or two pints. To be honest with you, I think he just comes into get the code for the WIFI."

Skelton had listened very carefully to what the barman had been saying. "Sorry, what is your name, I may have to get a statement from you later?" The barman looked slightly nervous about having to make a statement but that was not unusual. I am Tom Mansfield, but I only work here part-time." Skelton smiled and said, "Do you have a contact number please? Skelton wrote down the number and asked, "Why do you think he came in here to use the WIFI Tom?" The barman gave a small chuckle. "I didn't actually say that he came in here to use the WIFI. He would just come in and get the code. I never ever saw him with a laptop, and iPad or even a phone. Well apart from tonight, I saw him texting someone on a phone."

Skelton's heart sank. The fact that he had been in here earlier, using a phone meant that he had left his own phone at home. He must be using a new burner phone, most probably the one that Dave Lake saw him use in the George pub in Bath Hampton. There was no doubt in Skelton's mind that Edwards' had lined up victim number three for tonight.

"Tom, tell me when did this guy leave the pub tonight?" The barman thought for a second and said, "Well you only missed him by about five or ten minutes." Skelton thanked young Tom for his help and quickly walked to the door. He glanced at his watch and it was 11.20pm. He left the pub and headed towards the garage that he and Alexander had searched earlier that afternoon. He approached it, as quietly as he could, listening intently for any noise emanating from inside the garage. He stopped at the door, and listened for several seconds, but it was all very quiet. He put his hand on the door handle and tried turning it, but it was locked, and he had given back the key. Satisfied that Edwards was not in the garage, he left and headed for the spot across the road where he reckoned Edwards had dropped his two victims in the water and where Pierce should be standing guard. As he got close to the water, a ray of torch light hit him the face. "It's me sir, Richard Pierce."

Skelton shielded his eyes and cried out. "Turn that bloody light off, I can't see a thing."

Pierce turned off the torch and stood nervously waiting for Skelton to give him a severe dressing-down for allowing Edwards to evade him. "Right Richard, tell me what you found at the flat?" Pierce was rather relieved at the question. It was not what he was expecting. "Well sir, I got no answer when I rang his bell, but I did manage to get a neighbour to open the main door to the flats. The lock on Edwards' flat is only a Yale and so I used a credit card to open the lock. It never fails. I went in and everything seemed normal. I checked to see if he had perhaps slipped out the bathroom window, but it was closed. I think he must have just slipped past us at some point when our vision was obstructed. Skelton stared at him and said, "If I discover that your vision was obscured because you were knocking back pints in the bar, then god help you!"

"No sir, we have not been in the bar tonight and feel free to check the CCTV, that will prove it." Skelton had had enough. Having a row with Pierce was not going to help find out where Edwards was. "Right, you stay here. If he has managed to trap another girl, the chances are that he will bring

476

her down here. I am going back to the Ram to check the CCTV."

Skelton made his way up to the main road and then crossed over into the car park. He checked the garage again, but it was still locked and peering through the slit between the door and wall, it was obvious that there was no light on. Well he hadn't brought his victim here. Where else could he have taken her? He knew that Edwards would do his utmost to avoid CCTV so wherever he was going to take her, it was unlikely to have CCTV. Skelton was now getting desperately worried. It seemed certain that once again, this evil creature was going to get away with yet another murder. He spoke to himself. "Shit, bloody shit!"

Edwards was standing near the funeral home carefully watching for the black Ford driven by Patsy. He checked his watch. It was 11.35pm and he was getting worried that she had decided not to come, when suddenly he saw a car travelling slowly, approach. It was the right colour and make and it was being driven by a young girl. He gave her a big wave and smiled. The girl waved back and stopped the car. Edwards leaned down and opened the door. "Hello are you Patsy?" The girl was looking nervous which was hardly surprising given that her date was with a twenty-two-year-old, and not his father! "Yes, I am Patsy" she said in her Irish accent. "Is there something wrong with Charlie? We were supposed to be meeting at the Travel Lodge." Edwards gave her a warm reassuring smile and said, "No Charlie is absolutely fine. He is just running late that's all. He should be here in about fifteen minutes. He was concerned that you might think that he had stood you up that's all. So, he asked me to meet you just reassure you that everything is fine. Is it okay if I get in?" He was putting on his perfect gentleman act and it was working a treat. "Yes, of course, I will drive us back to the Travel Lodge."

When Edwards had fastened his seat belt, he opened the bag of chocolates and said, "Here Patsy have one of these, they are my wife's favourites. Oh, and by the way my name is John." Patsy looked down at the bag of chocolates and nervously, she put her hand in the bag and took one out. She undid the wrapper and popped it into her mouth. It tasted delicious. Shall I just turn around here John?" Edwards thought for a second and said, "well we have plenty of time. If I were you, I would drive straight on. There is a big roundabout about half a mile down there. You can turn there." Patsy was sucking on her chocolate, totally unaware of the danger it was putting her in.

"Yes, that's fine, its probably safer anyway as I am not very good at doing three-point turns." They both laughed, and this seemed to settle Patsy's nerves. She put the car into gear and they moved off.

She had to stop at the traffic lights at the magistrate's court, where she swallowed the remains of the chocolate. She had not eaten since lunchtime and so the drug would begin to work very quickly. When the lights changed, she drove on and a few minutes later they were at the roundabout. She slowly drove round and headed back the way they had just come. "So, you haven't actually met Charlie then, is that right?" Patsy was beginning to feel warm and so she rolled down her window to let in the cool air. "No, we haven't met before. This is our first date and I'm a bit nervous to be honest." Edwards gently tapped her on the shoulder and said, "Don't worry Patsy, Charlie is a good boy. My wife and I adore him, and you can be sure that he will treat you like the young lady that you are." Patsy smiled. Edwards couldn't tell whether it was what he had said that was making her relax or what was in the chocolate!"

They were now approaching the Travel Lodge. "Don't park at the Travel Lodge Patsy, they charge for parking. There is a small council car park just along on the left. It's free after six o'clock so we can park there and walk back to the Travel Lodge. Patsy was yawning and could not be bothered to argue, so she drove past and followed Edwards' directions. She drove into the council car park as instructed and turned off the engine and pulled on the hand brake. She could barely keep her eyes open. "You just have a seat there, Patsy. I will go and keep a look out for Charlie." Patsy made no reply, she had fallen asleep.

Chapter Sixty-seven

It was 11.40pm when Skelton walked through the door of the Ram. He found Tom behind the bar drying some glasses, but the two darts players had left. "Are you back again Inspector?" Skelton gave Tom the best smile he could manage in the circumstances. "Tom, would you mind if I quickly review the CCTV for tonight? It might give me a clue as to where that guy was headed. We need to find him otherwise a young girl could end up dead tonight." Tom looked shocked. "Do you think that guy could kill someone?" Skelton put both hands on the bar and said, "Yes, I certainly do, and I think he killed the two students that drowned in the river. We think he was using a garage near here to contact them, hence why he was coming in here to get the WIFI code. But he has moved out of the garage and I desperately need to find out where he has gone." Tom was clearly horrified and said, "The CCTV is in the office. Come this way please."

Edwards opened the garage door but did not switch the light on. A man walking his dog suddenly appeared but he totally disregarded Edwards and soon disappeared, from view. Edwards walked back to the car where Patsy was slumped unconscious on the driver's seat. He opened her door and bent inside feeling for the buckle of her seat belt. He found it and released it. He gently lifted her out of the car and he closed the door with his foot. He carried her into the garage and laid her gently down on the blanket and closed the door. He switched on the light and walked over to where she lay. It was only in this better light that he could see how beautiful she looked. He was fully sexually aroused now and could not wait for the fun to begin.

Skelton was reviewing the CCTV and he carefully studied Edwards' movements from the moment he walked into the bar until he left. He saw him using his phone to text but could not identify the make of phone. He had entered the pub alone, and he had left alone. Skelton was sure that he had left to meet his next victim but where precisely that was, he had no idea. Having thanked Tom, the barman for his cooperation he left. Skelton stood outside the pub for a few moments, considering his options. He decided that his only option was to join Pierce by the riverbank. Whilst he would be unable to prevent the victim from being raped, he could save her life. He began walking to the car park and almost walked past the parked Ford.

Skelton stopped walking and looked at the three cars sitting in the car park. He was sure that the Ford had not been there when he had passed here only minutes earlier. Curious, he walked over to the car and was intrigued to see that the driver's window was down. He looked inside and was surprised to see the key in the ignition. He opened the door and got in. The driver was obviously a lot shorter than Skelton as he was cramped for space. He put his hand down under the seat and he felt something soft. He grabbed it and pulled it up onto his lap. It was a handbag. Skelton thought it remarkably strange that someone would leave a window down with the key in the ignition and their handbag. His heart started racing as he opened the handbag. Inside was a phone, a purse and other bits and pieces. He opened the purse and inside were some credit cards and a driver's licence. He pulled out the licence and took out his phone and activated the torch. There was a picture of the driver, a pretty nineteen-year-old named Patricia Fagan. The girl looked petite and not dis-similar to Marion and Linda. Skelton leapt out of the car and started running. He was praying to God that he was not too late!

Edwards was sitting on the chair untying his shoelaces when he heard the garage door open. He was startled by the noise and it had been totally unexpected. He recognised the face as soon as Skelton entered the garage. "Good evening Inspector, have you come to join in the fun?" Skelton stopped in his tracks and began to survey the scene in front of him. Edwards was sitting in a chair undoing his shoelaces. He still had on his shirt and trousers, but his jacket lay on the bench. The naked body of Patricia Fagan was lying on a blanket and he could hear her gently snoring. Thank God she was still alive, and it looked that by the state of Edwards only partial undress, he had not harmed her yet. Although you could hardly say that drugging a young girl was not harmful!

"Right Edwards get on your feet, I am arresting you on suspicion of rape and murder and for drugging Patricia Fagan." Edwards stood up and initially, Skelton was under the impression that he was being compliant. On that score, he was very much wrong. "If you think you are going to stop me having my way with young Patsy here, you are very much mistaken. Edwards' hand went under his jacket, which was lying on the bench, and he pulled out a knife which was sheathed in a leather holder. He undid the clip and the blade of the knife was very clear to see in the bright lights. Skelton recognised it as a boning knife. It had a very thin blade with an exceptionally sharp blade and point. He had once attended a post-mortem examination of a young man who had received a single stab wound to the heart, with the same type of knife. The pathologist had invited him to view the wound. Externally, the wound looked very superficial but when the pathologist had opened-up the dead man's chest, the extent of the damage and bleeding were catastrophic. Skelton suddenly realised that for the second time this week, he was in mortal danger.

"Hold on Edwards, you are in enough trouble as it is. Put the knife down and we can go to the station and sort this out." Edwards laughed and said, "Look here Skelton, I have nothing to lose here. If I get arrested, then I will get sent to prison for life with no prospects of getting parole. Killing you is not going to get me any extra time, but it does let me finish on a high, as I get to shag her all night long!" For the second time that week, Skelton wished he had a gun. It would give him nothing but pleasure by putting a bullet through one of Edwards' kneecaps. He didn't want him dead that was for sure. No, he could rot in prison for years, with the bonus, of a very painful knee.

The adrenalin was beginning to kick in. Flee or fight? The former was not an option, as there was an unconscious girl about to be raped and murdered. Skelton had to fight but that knife was a very serious threat. Edwards only needed to cut his throat or stab him in the chest and Skelton was a dead man. Skelton needed a weapon. There was the chair, but Edwards had that covered. He glanced down to his right and saw a large suitcase. Now he could use that as a makeshift shield, but he still ran the risk of being stabbed in the melee, which was about to happen. No, he needed something better than that. Something that would make Edwards drop that bloody lethal blade.

Suddenly his eyes locked on it, and he mentally, thanked God and Bill Alexander!

Edwards was coming towards him slowly but steadily. Skelton moved as fast as he could. The fire extinguisher was immediately to his right and mounted on the wall. He grabbed it and it came away from the bracket easily, as it was supposed to do. Skelton pulled away the safety switch and fired it up. The freezing gas shot out at an incredible speed and he directed it straight into Edwards' face. Edwards screamed as the gas blinded him and he could barely breathe as the gas entered his lungs. He collapsed in a heap, dropping the knife as he tried to use his hands to shield his eyes and lungs from the gas. Skelton threw the fire extinguisher out the door. He walked forward and picked up the knife and placed it on the bench. It would be safe there, as the gas had blinded Edwards. Skelton looked at him cowering on the floor. Well, he might be going to prison for life, but he certainly wouldn't be seeing his days out!

Epilogue

Skelton was sitting at his desk, carefully reviewing the file on the two murders of the girls and the drugging of Patricia Fagan. The lab had confirmed that Marion had also been drugged, and so her death was re-classified as murder. The file would be sent to the Crown Prosecution Service, and they would confirm what offences Edwards was to be tried for in court. After being discharged from the hospital, Edwards was remanded in custody.

The doctors had confirmed that he would never see again.

Alexander had turned over the Kingsmead Square murder, to Skelton. The other two suspects had been arrested and all three had been charged with murder.

Skelton and Alexander had both been commended by the Chief Constable for their bravery in tackling the terrorist. After the ceremony, both men had retreated to Skelton's office where they had drunk the bottle of McCallan's' Scotch Whisky, plus a case of Fosters!

It was almost six o'clock and Skelton felt tired. He was looking forward to going home and cooking dinner. Suddenly the door burst open. It was Alexander. "Dan, a body has just been found in Alexander Park. It sounds like murder!

Acknowledgements

I am immensely grateful to my wonderful editor Claire Selishta for her patience and guidance in editing this my first novel and crime thriller.

I hope that the characters of Dan Skelton and Bill Alexander will continue to give the readers an enjoyable, roller coaster ride in the next book called Rogue.

I am also very grateful to my family and friends who have encouraged me to start writing detective thrillers, and I have to say that I have enjoyed the challenge enormously.

Lastly I have to thank my partner and best friend Ken Davies for all the support and encouragement which he has given me.

About The Author

Dan Rafferty was born in a small town some 10 miles east of Glasgow.

The youngest of four boys he initially worked in law before moving to London where he enjoyed a highly successful career in finance.

For the past 20 years he has practised as an Independent Expert Witness in the High Court of Justice.

He retired to become an author of crime novels and lives with his partner of 41 years, and their three black Labradors on the southern slopes of the beautiful Georgian city of Bath.

Coming soon...

Rogue

Here is a taster of the next book in the series, Rogue.

Chapter One

Detective Chief Inspector Dan Skelton was sitting at his desk on a Friday afternoon in June. It was almost 6pm and he was feeling tired after a particularly busy week in which he was almost killed twice. On the first occasion, his colleague and friend, Detective Sergeant Bill Alexander had saved his life by killing a terrorist for which Skelton would always be grateful. On the second occasion, Skelton had managed to blind his attacker with a CO_2 fire extinguisher. His attacker had raped and murdered two teenage girls and was about to rape and kill a third victim before Skelton intervened.

Skelton had grown up in Scotland in a small town fifteen miles east of Glasgow. A highly intelligent kid, he did well at school and had the ability to make friends easily. He had always shown an interest in the law and especially in how the police were able to solve a crime. On leaving school, he went to Bath Spa university and studied criminology and three years later, he graduated with a 2.1 degree. He then joined the Metropolitan Police in London as a graduate recruit and, after ten years in the force, had risen to the rank of Detective Chief Inspector. Although perfectly happy with his lot in the Met, he yearned to be back in Bath, where he had studied and which was a city that he adored.

He was just closing-down his laptop when there was a knock on his door and in stepped Bill Alexander. "A body has just been found in Alexandra Park. It looks like murder sir." Skelton put his face on the desk and capped his hands behind his head. He remained in that position for several seconds as Alexander stood in the doorway, waiting for instructions. Slowly, Skelton raised his head and leaned back in his chair, his hands still cupped behind his head and neck. "Bill, I was just coming to get you. I thought we would pop over to the Poultney Arms for a few beers before heading home. If this is a murder, we can forget that drink and that will be the weekend screwed up as well!"

"I'm sorry Dan, I was just putting my jacket on before coming to get you, when the call came in. A young lad walking his dog discovered the body of a man in Alexandra Park, a few minutes ago. Uniform are on their way as is the CSI team, led by Bob Richards". Skelton stood up and stretched his arms. "Alright Bill, let's take your car, with a bit of luck we might be able to have a glass or two later."

Bath Police station is situated on Manvers Street, right in the heart of this beautiful Georgian city, which dates back to Roman times. It is only a few minutes from both the train and the bus stations and the magnificent Bath Abbey. Bath is a world heritage city which attracts some six million visitors a year. In addition to all the visitors, there are two universities. Bath and Bath Spa which brings in a combined 23,000 students. Consequently, the police are kept pretty busy, although serious crimes such as rape and murder, are hardly an every day occurrence.

As usual, DS Alexander was driving, and Skelton was sitting in the front passenger seat. Skelton rarely drove. He would rather walk, which was always a bone of contention with Alexander, who until Skelton's arrival in Bath, only three months previously, would have been content to have driven everywhere. Walking had never scored highly on Alexander's to-do list, but Skelton had changed that. Skelton seemed obsessed in making sure that Alexander got as much exercise in the job as was possible. Alexander had to concede that in the three months since Skelton's arrival, he had lost two kilos in weight, something which Mrs Alexander had noticed and approved of!

Alexander was a fellow Scotsman, who in his youth had grown up in Glasgow, in a tough neighbourhood. Alexander realised that if he was not careful, he could easily end up in jail, just like some of his friends. After an apprenticeship as a tool maker, he joined Strathclyde Police, eventually becoming a detective constable based in Maryhill. This was a very tough division and Alexander had had to learn how to fight dirty just to survive. He met his wife Laura when she had been seconded by the Ministry of Defence (Naval Construction) to work in Glasgow for twelve months. However, she had been born in Bath and had lived there all her life. She had no intention of living in Glasgow. Bill and Laura had visited Bath shortly after they had met and Alexander decided that he would have to move to Bath. This was a decision that he would never regret having made.

They were driving up towards Bear Flat, an area of Bath renowned for its artists and poets. Indeed, three of the roads leading off from Bear Flats are known as the poets. These are called Wordsworth, Shakespeare and Milton.

Alexander turned left into Shakespeare Drive and accelerated up the steep hill which led to the entrance of Alexandra Park. This park provided stunning views across the whole of Georgian Bath, due to its elevated position over-looking the city. A "Road Closed" sign had been erected at the park entrance and a uniformed police officer was standing guard. Skelton recognised the young constable; it was Luke Meehan. Alexander pulled up. Skelton lowered the window, "Are you manning the fort Luke?" Meehan smiled at Skelton and said, "Yes sir. Inspector Symonds said I was to charge every driver £10 for entry." Skelton laughed. "I tell you what Luke, I will give it to him personally, but I don't think he will appreciate me shoving it up his arse!" Meehan giggled as he moved the sign post from the entrance. "Yes sir, I think you best give him the tenner yourself otherwise I might end up directing traffic for the rest of my career!"

Skelton recalled the first few days at Bath Police Station. It had come as something of a shock to his colleagues and the men and women under his command, when he had informed them that he was gay and lived with his partner Ken. Skelton certainly did not look gay and was not in any way effeminate, a trait that Skelton disapproved of. Perhaps the only clue to his sexuality was the way in which he dressed. All his suits were bespoke and were of the finest quality as were all the clothes he wore. Hardly a day went by, when he was not complimented on how well he was dressed. Whether on duty or off duty, he invariably looked more like a rich businessman or banker, rather than a police officer.

Alexander slowly drove into the park and turned left. It was a single lane orbital track, which meant it was one-way traffic. There were several parked cars in the laybys but the owners would not be allowed to leave until every car had been thoroughly searched. In the distance Skelton could see flashing blue lights and as they got closer, he saw four marked police cars and an ambulance, as well as two CSI vans. Inspector Graham Symonds was standing by a large bush with a clip board in his hands. He would oversee the crime scene and would record the names of every officer or civilian that entered or left. He would also keep an inventory of every item that was removed from the scene as potential evidence. Skelton liked Symonds. He was a man who could keep a cool head in even the most trying circumstances.

Skelton got out of the car just as Dr Challis was pulling up in his Land Rover Discovery behind him. Dr Challis was the Home Office pathologist that Avon and Somerset Constabulary consulted on suspicious deaths. Skelton approached Symonds and said, "Can you book Bill and I in as well as Dr Challis please? Oh, and young Luke Meehan said I had to give you £10 entrance fee." Symonds smiled and looked at Skelton quizzically. "I think we will waive the £10 charge as I doubt it won't be worth the pain knowing where you would stick it sir!" Skelton laughed. "Fair enough Graham, you are getting to know me too well."

Skelton and Alexander went and joined Dr. Challis who was getting into paper overalls to prevent contamination of the crime scene. Skelton asked Symonds, "What have you got for us Graham?" Symonds looked at his clip board and said, "A young lad, called Trevor Thomas was walking his dog at approximately 17.45 when the dog ran into this bush behind me. It started barking and despite it being a trained gun dog, it refused to come back despite Trevor blowing his whistle and calling its name. Trevor walked into the bush to find his dog barking at a man who was lying on the ground. He could see that the man was covered in blood and was not moving. He put the dog on its lead and called 999 for an ambulance and the control room alerted us. We were on the scene first and it was obvious to the officers that the man was dead. His throat has been cut but we haven't turned the body over, so there might be other injuries that we can't see. When the paramedics arrived, he confirmed the man deceased at 17.54 and estimated that he had died probably within the last hour. The injuries do not appear to have been self-inflicted and indeed, no weapon was found with the body."

Skelton absorbed the information that Symonds had provided. "Where is young Trevor now Graham?" Symonds was speaking into his radio and when he had finished, he said, "He called his dad and he and his wife came over straight away. They are waiting in their vehicle which is that green Range Rover parked just over there. Skelton looked over his shoulder and saw a man in the driver's seat. He guessed that Mrs Thomas was in the back of the vehicle with young Trevor and the dog. "Send someone over to let them know that I will be over to speak to them shortly. I better take a look at the scene so that I know exactly what we are dealing with here." Alexander handed him a pair of paper overalls which included a head cover. He quickly pulled them over his shoes and pulled the zip up. "Right let's go see what awaits us."

Skelton was followed closely by Dr Challis and Alexander. Bob Richards, the head of forensic investigations, was standing near the body holding up a white plastic bag into which he was peering. On seeing Skelton approaching, he lowered the bag and said, "Good evening sir. This looks like a sex meeting gone horribly wrong, if you ask me." Skelton lowered his face mask. "What makes you think that Bob?" Richards walked over to where Skelton and the others were standing and held open the plastic bag so that they could see what it contained. Richards said, "I suspect that the victim brought this with him. All it contains is a beach towel, a tube of lube and some condoms. I've searched the body and there is nothing in his pockets. No phone, no ID, no credit cards, no wallet and no keys. It's my guess that the victim had arranged to meet someone here. I don't know if it was a robbery gone wrong or if he was lured here by the killer. Whatever it was, the guy was not expecting trouble that's for sure.

Skelton thought for a moment and said, "I think you are probably right Bob but it's too early to say for definite. It's possibly a robbery that has gone wrong given that the killer took all the victim's belongings. On the other hand, the killer may have wanted to remove the guy's phone to prevent us from making any connection between the killer and the victim." Alexander coughed and asked, "But why would the killer take all the victim's possessions but leave the plastic bag?" Skelton rubbed his nose and said, "Well it could be one of two things. Maybe he was disturbed possibly by the boy's dog and ran off or perhaps he was deliberately leaving us a clue." It was Dr Challis who spoke next. "But why would he leave a clue like that? It seems to me that he's done his best to make it difficult to identify the victim." Skelton shrugged his shoulders and said, "Who Knows?"

Skelton took a deep breath and looked at Richards. "What's your view on the forensics so far Bob?" Richards placed the plastic bag gently on the ground. "Well, we are of course conducting a fingertip search around the locus and when we remove the body, we will examine the site in minute detail. But interestingly on looking closely at what footprints we have discovered so far; I can be pretty sure that the victim definitely made some as we can easily match them to those distinct trainers he is wearing. The other footprints have made no distinctive marks which could suggest that the killer had covered his shoes suggesting that he is very much forensically aware."

Skelton touched Dr Challis on the elbow and said, "Would you take a look at the body doctor and let us have your initial thoughts?" Dr. Challis carried his bag over to the body and carefully put it down. Skelton and Alexander watched and saw that there was a great deal of blood on the ground next to the victim's head. The victim's trousers and underpants were down around his ankles. He was lying on his stomach so it was not easy to get a clear view of the man's face but Skelton reckoned he was in his mid-fifties. "Come on Bill let's wait outside for the doctor to finish. Bob, let me have a summary of your findings in the morning. We will have a team talk at nine, but if you find anything significant, call me straight away. As soon as the doctor is finished, take the victim's fingerprints and see if we can identify him from those. It's too early for anyone to have reported him missing. If the guy lived on his own that's going to mean that it will take even longer for someone to realise that he's gone missing."

Skelton and Alexander had removed the forensic overalls and had been busy making arrangements for the rest of the murder squad to be called in. Officers had been detailed to conduct house-to-house enquiries. Others were busy interviewing potential witnesses who had been in the park. Cars were being searched before being allowed to leave the park. All CCTV cameras in and around the park were to be checked in the hope that they would pick up both the victim and his killer. DC Ross Turnbull was heading back to the police station to make a plea on social media for any information that could identify the victim and his killer.

Eventually Dr Challis emerged from the bushes and started taking off his forensic overalls. As he did so, he addressed the two detectives. "Well gentlemen, the victim was in his mid-fifties I would say. It looks like a commando style killing. He was stabbed in the heart from behind and his attacker was a good deal taller than the victim. I would say that the killer grabbed the victim by the jaw and covered his mouth using his left hand and brought the knife downwards over the victim's right shoulder and stabbed him with significant force to the heart. He then pulled out the knife which would have caused a lot of blood to spurt from the wound and that would have undoubtedly sprayed onto the hand and arm of the attacker. He then slit the victim's throat causing even more spillage. The knife was definitely about seven inches long and had a serrated edge to it. He almost decapitated the poor fellow. There are no defensive wounds on his hands which would indicate complete surprise. There are no

502

indications of any sexual activity having taken place. It's my hunch, that the victim had been expecting to engage in a homosexual encounter, hence the beach towel and the condoms. I think he had willingly dropped his trousers and underwear and was expecting that the killer was simply putting on a condom before engaging in sex. The absence of any defensive wounds confirms my conclusion. The killer would have been heavily bloodstained, so I would not be at all surprised if he changed his clothes before leaving the bushes. After all, as I understand it, the park was fairly busy and the site of a bloodstained man would have caused alarm and would almost certainly have been reported to the police."

Skelton gave the command that the body be released to Bob Richards' team who would carefully tape it for hairs, fibres and any possible DNA evidence before being taken away to the mortuary.

Skelton made a note of Dr Challis's initial findings. He had not yet made up his mind if it was a robbery gone wrong or premeditated murder. However, his instincts were telling him that the victim had been lured there and the absence of defensive wounds suggested that the killer had surprised his victim giving him no opportunity to defend himself. No witnesses had so far reported any screams or shouting, which again pointed to the victim having been taken completely by surprise. It was agreed that Dr Challis would conduct the autopsy at 9am on Monday morning.

Skelton headed off in the direction of the green Range Rover and he could see the man at the wheel was talking on his phone. The man saw Skelton approaching and ended his call, opened the door and got out. He was aged about forty, tall and good looking. He was wearing a blue Polo long sleeved shirt and white Chino slacks and an expensive looking pair of brown brogue shoes. This was clearly a wealthy individual. "Are you Mr Thomas"? Skelton asked politely. The man was closing the Range Rover door and was looking at Skelton intently. "Yes, I am David Thomas and I'm Trevor's father, the boy who found the man's body". "Mr Thomas, I am Detective Chief Inspector Dan Skelton of Avon and Somerset police" Skelton held out his hand and the men shook hands. "Mr Thomas this must have been a terrible experience for young Trevor. How is he? Do you think he needs some counselling to help him cope?" Mr Thomas folded his arms across his chest and looked Skelton up and down. "No inspector, that will not be necessary. My wife there in the back sitting with Trevor is actually a doctor. She is a GP here in Bath and if Trevor needs any help my wife will be right there for him. But Trevor is a very resilient lad and I don't think this will give him any nightmares or whatever. I took him deer stalking when he was just ten years old and he killed a stag with his first shot. When the game keeper slit the stag's throat to drain the blood, Trevor was right by his side. He also comes game shooting with me, so he's seen plenty of dead things inspector." Skelton shook his head slightly and put his right hand on his jaw and said, "Even so Mr Thomas, this was the body of a man who we believe was murdered and had his throat cut. You will have to keep a close eye on him just in case he bottles it up." Thomas lowered his hands and smiled. "Thank you, inspector. My wife and I will certainly be keeping a close watch on him. I take it you want to have a word with him"? Skelton rested his hand on the bonnet of the Range Rover and said, "Yes if I could have a few minutes with Trevor I would very much appreciate that. You and Dr Thomas are entitled to be present if you so wish. But Trevor is not a suspect and is not in any trouble Mr Thomas." Thomas stared closely into Skelton's eyes, smiled and said. "I well know the law Inspector. You see I am a lawyer, but I don't practice criminal law. I specialise in commercial conveyancing and contract law. Let's ask Trevor what he wants to do"

Thomas opened the rear door of the Range Rover and said "Amanda darling, this is Chief Inspector Dan Skelton. He would like to have a word with Trevor about what he found earlier." Dr Thomas slid out of her seat and got out. Skelton reckoned she too was around forty and about 5"10 tall. She was wearing a pretty summer dress and her hair was tied in a bun. Despite the seriousness of the situation, she was immensely calm and very self-assured. She held out her right hand and said in a very cultured voice, "Inspector Skelton I'm sorry that we have had to meet in such tragic circumstances. Dr Amanda Thomas at your service." Skelton took the doctor's proffered hand and shook it warmly. "Dr Thomas it's an honour to meet you and I am sorry that we have had to detain you here, but I would just like a little chat with Trevor whilst it's still fresh in his mind. I won't take a formal statement this evening, but I will have to do that in the next day or two." Skelton heard the other rear door of the Range Rover closing shut and a second or two later young Trevor emerged around the bonnet. As he approached, Skelton guessed him to be about maybe fifteen years old. He had the good looks of his parents and was at least an inch taller than

Skelton's "5 10. His skin was well tanned and his long blond hair would probably be due for a trim when the school holidays finished. His father smiled at him and said, "Trevor come and meet Inspector Skelton. He needs to have a word about what you saw earlier." Trevor approached Skelton in a confident manner, his intense blue eyes emanating both intelligence and warmth. Skelton stood forward thrusting out his right hand and giving Trevor a very warm smile. "Hi Trevor, I'm Dan Skleton. Sorry to meet you under these circumstances and I am very grateful for what you did back there." Trevor gripped Skelton's hand very firmly but warmly and said. "It's a pleasure to meet you Mr Skelton. How can I help?"

The boy was incredibly mature for his age. He seemed more like a twenty- year-old. The boy was muscular and clearly attended the gym regularly and no doubt had a few hobbies. Skelton guessed that he probably played rugby, a game which was close to his heart, unlike football, which held no appeal for him whatsoever. "Trevor, I need to spend a few minutes with you going over what you saw earlier. We can do it with your mum and dad present or we can go for a walk on our own if you would prefer that. Whatever you are most comfortable with suits me fine." Trevor smiled and said, "Is it okay if we take the dog for a walk? His last walk kind of got cut short. Skelton, who absolutely adored dogs suddenly remembered that Inspector Symonds had mentioned that the boy had a gun dog. Skelton had three black Labradors which were all gun dogs and which Skelton had trained himself to the highest possible level. Skelton noticed the whistle hanging on a lanyard around the boy's neck. "Yes of course you can bring the dog. What's its name? The boy was already walking purposefully to the rear of the Range Rover. "He's called Johnny and he's nearly two years old." The boy opened the tailgate door and out jumped a black Labrador tail wagging in greeting. The dog came running around to say hello to Dr and Mr Thomas and then went over to Skelton to sniff him out. The dog immediately scented Skelton's dogs on his clothes and Skelton wasted no time in getting down and gave the dog several hugs. The dog sensed that Skelton was a new friend and wagged his tail furiously.

Skelton was beaming with pleasure to see this young family enjoying the dog as part of the family, just as Skelton and his partner Ken regarded their dogs as their family. Skelton stood up from patting the dog and laughed. "Well this is a pleasure for me. I have three black labs which I trained myself as gun dogs." Mr Thomas was smiling at this news. "Really? Where do you shoot

Mr Skelton?" Skelton rested against the wing of the Range Rover. "Please just call me Dan. I have shot all over the country but my favourite shoots are in Devon where you can almost guarantee some seriously high pheasants." Mr Thomas held out his hand and said, "Dan it's a pleasure to meet you and please call me David and my wife is Amanda." The adults shook hands again, instantly recognising that a new friendship had just been created. Trevor had put Johnny on the sit command and the dog was happily sitting at his master's right hand side slightly behind his right foot, waiting patiently for his next command.

Despite having found a dead body, Trevor seemed far from concerned about what he had seen, but Skelton needed to gently coax the boy to try and remember as much detail as possible. In a way, the murder scene itself was almost irrelevant so far as Trevor was concerned. Skelton's forensic team would go over that with a fine-tooth comb and Dr Challis had already told him how the man had been killed. What Skelton needed to tease from Trevor, was what he had heard and saw before his dog had discovered the body.

Skelton had suggested that he and Trevor and of course Johnny, the Labrador, should head off in the opposite direction from the murder scene.

Trevor asked his mum and dad to wait in the Range Rover. The parents immediately gave their consent and so Skelton led the way.

Alexandra Park is quite large and very popular with families and dog walkers. It regularly hosts concerts and is a big attraction on Guy Fawkes night when a huge fireworks display takes place. It has a tennis court and an outdoor lawn bowls green with six rinks. The park is always busy unless the weather is bad. Today was Friday and the weather had been hot and sunny so the park would have been fairly busy. There are many trees in the park as well as substantial bushes which both dogs and young children love to explore.

"So, tell me Trevor, how old are you and what school do you go to?" Trevor was watching Johnny as he carefully worked the bushes just ahead of him. "I hope he doesn't find another body in that bloody bush!" Skelton had to laugh. This was a young man not a boy and his parents had done a wonderful job in bringing him up. "Well Trevor, I have three black labs and they have never yet found a man's body, so you with just Johnny are highly unlikely to ever find another one but if you do, be sure to let me be the first to know!" They both laughed. "So, are you going to tell me your age and school?" Trevor gave a lop-sided grin.

Actually, it's my birthday next Friday, I will be sixteen. We are having a party at the house. You can come if you like and bring the dogs. We've got plenty of room." Skelton smiled and said "Thank you Trevor that's very kind but can we just concentrate at the moment on my questions." Trevor stopped walking and looked at Skelton. "Sorry Dan. I guess I'm not concentrating as well as I should be. It's just that the last thing I expected to find today was a dead body." Skelton immediately put his arm around Trevor's neck. "Hey, are you okay buddy? If you want, we can go back and sit with your mum and dad?" Trevor looked Skelton in the eyes and said, "No its okay. I will dine out on this for years to come. And to answer your question, I attend Beechen Cliff school."

Skelton had guessed the answer. Beechen Cliff was an outstanding school with a high percentage of its pupils going on to university to study medicine, engineering, law and other such notable professions. Skelton had noted down Trevor's date of birth, address and mobile phone number, as well as that of his parents.

Trevor said that he had entered the park at around 5pm having walked the dog from home when he had left at close to 4.45pm. He had not seen anything unusual nor had heard any shouting or screaming. He was certain that he had not seen the deceased until Johnny had refused to leave the bush which was most unusual and had caused him to enter the bush and discover the body.

"So, you don't remember seeing the dead man, before you found him in the bushes?" Did you see anyone going into the bushes our coming out?" Trevor thought for several seconds and said, "Well no, I never saw anyone going into the bushes or coming out, but I did see a guy out jogging. I had sat down on the grass and was playing with Johnny, so I was not really paying much attention. But I remember looking up and I saw a young guy jogging towards us, but he sort of changed direction and carried on down towards the exit" Skelton noted this down. Which exit was he headed for?" I can't remember what the Avenue is called but it's the one near the bowling green." This was the entrance which Skelton and Alexander had used when they arrived earlier, and is the only vehicular entrance/exit to the park.

"Can you describe the man to me, his age and build and what he was wearing?" Trevor put his whistle in his mouth and gave two sharp calls. Johnny, who had gone on a bit ahead, immediately came running back and Trevor called him to heel.

The dog instinctively ran to Trevor's right side and walked behind him. Skelton admired their companionship and had never been so content in conducting a murder enquiry. "Let's see, I would say the guy was in his early twenties but he was wearing a hoody so I didn't see much of his face but I don't think he had a beard. He was tall that's for sure probably about 6" 4 and well-built. The guy must work out a lot judging by his body and probably plays rugby. One thing I did notice before he sort of changed direction, was that he seemed a bit out of breath. Maybe he had been out jogging too long and was a bit tired. And he had a backpack on his back."

Skelton had noted all this down. "Tell me what he was wearing Trevor?" "He was wearing a black top with a hood on it and black bottoms. He was in white trainers, but I don't know which make. There are so many now and they didn't look like they were that expensive or new."

Skelton and Trevor walked back to the Range Rover with Johnny dutifully following behind. Dr and Mr Thomas got out as they arrived. "Well Trevor has been a great help to me. You should be very proud of him. There is a good chance that he saw the killer and has given me an excellent description of the man. He is bound to show up on CCTV and when he does, we will circulate his image on social media and hopefully, we will have his name in no time. I will need to take a formal statement from Trevor in a day or two depending on how busy we are with this enquiry. But I will phone and make an appointment in advance." They said their goodbyes and Skelton radioed that the green Range Rover was free to go.

Chapter Two

Alexander drove Skelton back to the police station and parked up. The detectives made their way to the CID office and there were about a dozen officers busy either on the phone or on their computers. Ross Turnbull had just put down the phone when he saw Skelton and Alexander enter the room. "Sir we got the jogger on CCTV. The bowling club apparently have him jogging towards the club and the Cooperative store on the corner of Shakespeare Avenue, and have him coming towards them from the direction of the park. The film is on its way right now, so it should be here in a few minutes." Skelton began taking off his suit jacket. "That's great news Ross, well done. Hopefully we will have this guy identified pronto and we can go and arrest him. With a bit of luck, we will have some good forensics that can nail the bastard. Talking of which, any sign of Bob Richards?" Turnbull answered. "He's gone to the mortuary with the body, so you won't see him for ages. He did however send us the victim's fingerprints and Peter Lowik is working on them now. Hopefully we will get a match any time now and we can discover who the poor guy was. Some poor woman is probably sitting at home now wondering where the blazes he is." Skelton was holding his jacket over his shoulder. "Right, I will be in my office. As soon as Peter gets the results on the prints send him in. And as soon as the CCTV evidence arrives, I want to see it."

Skelton was on the phone to his partner Ken explaining what was happening and that it was unlikely that he would be home until the early hours of the morning. He was just putting down the phone when there was a knock on the door and Alexander led in Turnbull and Lowik. "What news men?" Lowik was an Australian and had been working for Avon and Somerset for over two years. Skelton liked and admired Lowik for his dedication and professionalism. He also had a great sense of humour which was a major asset when the pressure was on. Lowik sat on one of the two chairs opposite Skelton. "Sir I ran the prints through our system, the MOD, Interpol and every other system available to us. Nothing! This guy has never been fingerprinted in any country that we have access to. He is a John Doe at the moment. Our only chance now is if someone recognises him from his photograph from the CCTV. But the problem at the moment is that we have so far not been able to recognise him from any of the CCTV recordings but we are still working on that. If we can't find him on the CCTV footage, then we might have to release a photograph of his face taken at the mortuary."

Skelton stood up and walked across the room to the window. It was black outside and it was now 10.15pm. "Well, that's a shame about the prints. It would have been helpful to have got a positive ID on the poor bugger. I don't really want to put out a face picture of him lying dead in the mortuary unless we really have to. I want you guys to go over the CCTV footage again and see if you can get an image of the victim. Make it a priority." Skelton started towards the door, "Right let's go take a look at what we've got."

DC Janet Griffin, another rising star in the police, was staring intently at the screen in front of her. Skelton got down on his knees so that he could get a good view. "Right sir, we have two lots of footage taken this afternoon at about an hour before and an hour after the body was found. More work needs to be done, to it to determine when both the victim and the killer, entered the park. At the moment we have not been able to find the victim on the film." Skelton cleared his throat and said, "Yes, so I understand. I have given instructions that the film is to be reviewed again just in case we missed him first time around. He may have been wearing a jacket over the shirt that we found him in. So as soon as we have looked at the jogger, get back to trying to find the victim."

The officers were standing at Griffin's desk, staring at the computer screen. The CCTV film was currently frozen. "Run the film please Janet." The detectives watched intently as the images appeared on the screen. Suddenly a man dressed in black and wearing a hoody as described by young Trevor, appeared on the screen. "Bingo we've got him. You can't ID him with the hoody up but get it on social media and someone will put a name to the face." Peter Lowik was breathing heavily. "Oh, fuck sir. He's one of us." Skelton was looking incredulous. "What's that supposed to mean?" "That is Police Constable Fergus Walsh sir. I would know him anywhere. We were at the police training academy together. He lives here in Bath and works out of Bristol. He cannot possibly be the murderer sir. He is as clean as a whistle. He must have just happened to be jogging in the park at the time of the murder."

Skelton got off his knees, stood up and stretched his arms. Seconds ago, he thought he had identified the prime suspect, only for Peter Lowik to tell him that the guy was a police officer. Of course, it was perfectly possible that he was the killer, but Lowik reckoned that the guy was one hundred percent trustworthy and just happened to be in the wrong place at the right time.

"Right Peter I am re-assigning objectives here. Janet, I want you to find the victim on the CCTV footage and as soon as you do, get it on to social media straight away." Griffin nodded her head and said, "Right sir I am on it now." Skelton leaned on Griffin's desk and said "Peter you know this guy Fergus Walsh so you will be working with Bill and me on this. We are going to have to interview him right away. Given that he was in the park earlier, he could not have been working but of course he could be on night shift later. If he is not at work then he is either out socialising or at home. Let's go into my office and I want you to call him and we need to record the call just in case he is the killer. Remember Peter that just because he is a cop that does not automatically mean that he is innocent." Lowik looked slightly embarrassed and said, "Yes, I know that sir but I met him on my first day at the academy. He and I are good friends. It's just that I can't put Fergus down as a killer."

Skelton was watching Lowik's face closely. "Peter, we are both police officers and we must be professional at all times. I know that this guy is your friend, but we have to treat him for the moment as a suspect. It will probably turn out that he just happened to have gone out for a run this afternoon. Unfortunately, it just happens to have been at the time when a guy gets killed. Our young witness describes very clearly that he saw a guy dressed in black, wearing a hoody and running away from very close to where he found the body. He also says that when the guy saw him, he slightly changed direction. Another interesting observation that he made was that the jogger was slightly out of breath. Now that could easily be explained that he had been running for some time, or it could have been caused by the fact that the guy had just plunged a knife into a man's heart and cut his throat almost decapitating him into the bargain."

Printed in Great Britain
by Amazon

41884989R00288